CHELSEA LEACH

Downforce

This book is for my nephew Jamie. Never sleep on your dreams, Kiddo. You can do anything in life if you have the strength and will to succeed.

Acknowledgments

Many, many thanks to…

…my mom, Christie, who has done more for me than I could ever express with words. She has always encouraged me to push the limits of my own capabilities and believed in me when I didn't always believe in myself.

…my dad, Matt, who not only gave me his love of motorsports, but has always supported my independent nature and drive for success wherever life takes me.

…my brother, Kyle and sister-in-law, Riley, who never let me sleep on my own ambitions and always push me to take the next step.

…my maternal grandparents, Rex and Donna, whose love of Disney gave me such a passion for fairy tales and happy endings that I decided to create a few of my own.

…my paternal grandparents, Jim and Jodi, who, more than anything else, instilled in me the value of a hard day's work.

…my editor and dear friend, Lacey Braziel. Your expertise, organizational skills, and endless support are the only reason

Downforce ever saw the light of day.

…my fabulous cover designer, Kim Bailey. The cover of this book is absolutely gorgeous, and more than I ever could have imagined.

…my proofreader, Andrea Hutchison, for agreeing to take on this project with such short notice. I appreciate you!

…my professional references, Alexa Martin RN and Laura Culp Elliot PT, DPT, PPSC, for making Alaina and Grayson's story as realistic as possible.

…my wonderful readers. Without you, I could not do what I love to do. Thank you for loving these characters and this world as much as I do!

1

A Matter of Opinion

Do you ever look at your life and wonder how on earth you got where you are now? Because as I stood in the mass of people crowded into the Indianapolis Bridal Expo, I was wondering the same thing myself. Women, of all shapes and sizes, were crowded around different booths, volleying questions at the nearest vendor and reading through brochures. The occasional groom or father of the bride passed by, avoiding eye contact with as many people as possible for fear an errant merchant would press him for his bank account information. Several bright-eyed brides flitted from table to table, gushing over dress designs and venues. I sighed and looked over at my business partner Jessica, who, sensing my gaze, glanced up from her spreadsheet and smiled.

"We got three new bookings today, so not a complete loss," she offered with a shrug.

"What are the dates?" I asked, observing the crowd absently.

"Ummm…looks like we've got two for October and one for December."

I felt some relief. At least I would have different color palettes to play with. I caught the eye of one very lost-looking blonde as she ducked and weaved around her more enthusiastic counterparts and gave her a small smile. She looked over her shoulder apprehensively at a woman that could only be her mother and made her way toward me.

"It's a little overwhelming, isn't it?" I asked, opting for a casual greeting.

She smiled. "A little. I had no idea what I was getting myself into." Her eyes drifted to the banner heralding our company name, Decadent Designs. "So, what are you guys selling?" she asked, curious, as she fingered through the displayed binder.

"Well, it's not a product. We're more of a 'what can we do for you' company."

I'd caught her attention. Her speculative green eyes held hesitant interest. "So, you're wedding planners?" she asked, once again glancing over her shoulder to where her companion was now chatting up the photographer in the stall next to us.

I gave her a wider grin. "Not exactly. You pick colors, flowers, fabrics, and a venue, and we take care of the decorating: place settings, centerpieces, you name it."

Her eyes widened a little bit. "But I would have to pick designs and stuff?"

I shrugged. "Not necessarily. I like to design, so if you have a space in mind, but aren't sure what to do with it, we could walk through your ceremony space, and I could get back to you with some ideas."

A stunned smile was starting to form on her lips. *Bingo.*

"My mom wants to plan the whole thing, but I don't know…I just don't have the time. And the whole idea of worrying about place settings and seating charts…" She stretched her neck to one side and then the other like she was stressed out just thinking about it.

I picked up a business card from the front of the table. "I'll tell you what, I'll give you my card. My name's Alaina. If you have any questions at all, give me a shout. What date are you thinking about?" I asked.

"We were hoping for a spring wedding. Probably April of next year…"

"Perfect! Our calendar is pretty open for next spring, so if you decide you want to book, give us a call at the office and we'll go from there."

"Awesome! Thanks!" she exclaimed and continued down the bustling corridor.

I glanced at Jess who met my gaze for a second before turning back to the computer with a smile and a shake of the head. "I think you could sell a cow a hamburger…"

I snickered. "You have to know your audience," I insisted, turning to rest against our booth table.

"She literally just walked over here. You had never met that girl in your life! How on earth could you know what she wanted to hear?"

I waved her off. "You're just jealous."

"Not at all," my best friend claimed, miffed. "I am perfectly happy working behind the scenes." She continued typing away on her computer. "How long until she calls, you think?"

I shrugged, gazing after the girl. "I'd give it a couple hours."

The whole reason we started this business was for women who wanted the perfect wedding but had no idea where to start. This bride-to-be was clearly in that category. I knew she was interested. Only time would tell *how* interested.

The overbearing noise of the crowd slowly filtered out as the Expo's occupants called it a day. I was in the middle of packing up a box of supplies when I heard a throat clear behind me.

I whirled around, caught off guard to see my guest from earlier poised in front of the booth, our brochure worn with fold marks in her hands, and her mother close behind.

"How was the rest of the Expo?" I asked, glancing around to see if Jess was headed back from the car.

The girl gave a hard laugh. "Overwhelming. I..." she glanced at her mom, who squeezed her daughter's shoulder lovingly. "I'd really love it if you guys would come on board."

I smiled. "We'd love to! Do you want to set up a time where you can come to the shop and go over the particulars?" I asked, searching for the planner. I'd seen Jess with it earlier and found it wedged under her laptop. Flipping it open, I was surprised to find it pretty full. "How about next Thursday at 10:00 a.m.?"

"Sounds fantastic!" The girl exclaimed with a flip of her blonde hair.

"What's your name?" I asked, not taking my eyes off the planner.

"Laurel. Laurel Hastings," she replied, her timid tone taking on more confidence by the second.

"Okay, Laurel, I have you down for 10:00 a.m. next Thursday, and the address for the shop is located on the business card I gave you. Do you still have it?" I asked.

She held it up and smiled. "Thanks so much, Alaina! I'll see you Thursday."

I waved after her with a smile and chuckled to myself as she walked out of sight. I would love to know what went down between her and her mother before she came back to our booth. It seemed like she had been nervous to put her foot down. Oh well, she was finding her sea legs well enough. I turned introspective as I continued packing up. I knew what it was like trying to find those legs, especially when the seas were rough. For someone who had always pictured herself as a professional photographer, I was pretty far off the marked path, lost in an ocean of silk flowers and taffeta.

Jess returned to the table, now empty-handed, and huffed. "Hurry, I'm double parked." I stacked a box on top of the one she had just picked up and gathered the remainder of our materials before making a hasty exit.

As we pulled out of the Indiana State Fairgrounds and onto 38th Street, I exhaled in relief. "Well, that's over for another year," I said, rubbing my eyes and yawning. "I can't believe we only have four bookings to show for it." A slight dejection showed in my voice.

"Well, that's two more bookings than we got out of it last year, and you're forgetting about the three bookings we got yesterday. Besides, we have follow-up appointments for six other bridal parties!"

I nodded. "Yeah, that's something." It wasn't an instantaneous result, but it was something I could work toward.

"You're out of the office tomorrow, right?" Jess asked as she checked over her shoulder before merging onto the traffic-riddled interstate.

"Opening day at the track! So yes, I am out of the office," I allowed, giddy excitement barely contained in my voice.

"Ugh," she sounded in the back of her throat. "You're

ridiculous. I don't understand what's so great about watching cars go around in circles all day."

I rolled my eyes. "How many times have we had this conversation?"

"How long have we known each other? Twenty-some-odd years? So, *at least* twenty times…and I don't understand it any more now than I did the first time." She laughed.

"It's like me asking why you like to go out to bars and hook up with guys. It's just something you do, and I've stopped trying to understand," I said, hinting she should do the same and shut up.

"You know, you could probably benefit from spending a little more time out with friends and a little less time doing whatever it is you do up there. That camera isn't going to get you laid."

I could feel my cheeks heating up. "And I'd say that's none of your business."

"But it is! Girl, I just want you to be happy! I hate seeing you spend so much time alone. I can tell you from experience there is nothing quite like—"

"Jess—"

"No, listen, my friend Anika is friends with this guy—I think they went to law school together." She shook her head, getting back on track. "Anyway, he's single, and he's a lawyer, and he is *super* cute. He's twenty-eight and—"

"And what's wrong with him?" I asked, staring out the window. It seemed to me there was probably a reason this guy was still single.

"Why does every guy have a problem?" she barked.

"Jess." I looked over at her and held up a finger for each point. "He's single. He's cute. He's a lawyer." I shook my head. "Either he's a workaholic or a player. Neither one of those sounds attractive."

She ran her tongue over her teeth, making her lips protrude. I could see the muscles of her jaw tighten as she tried to come up with a valid argument. "You're going to have to come off your high horse at some point," she finally murmured. "I get it's a defense mechanism and all, but you can't spend the rest of your life worrying about getting hurt."

I stared out the passenger window watching my surroundings fly by. "I'm not afraid of getting hurt," I muttered, my hackles rising.

"Right, you're just waiting for the perfect guy to come along? You think it's going to be a one-and-done type of thing? That you're just going to stumble into each other and fall madly in love, the end, case closed?"

My heart rate was rising. She was half an inch away from falling into a dino-sized pile of shit. I took a deep breath, trying to get my temper under control. "I think lowering my standards to your typical bar troll isn't going to help me find a serious boyfriend."

"A serious boyfriend?" she scoffed. "And where do you think you're going to find one of those? In the storeroom at the shop or under your bed? You're twenty-four years old, Alaina! It's not about finding something serious right now. It's about living your life. That's all I want for you."

"Well, maybe that's not what I want for myself, Jess. Have you ever thought about that? It's fine if you want to spend your Friday nights going home with random guys, but that's not who I have ever been or ever will be!" I shouted. I didn't lose my temper often, but the bear could only be poked so much before it mauled somebody.

Her mouth popped open and she promptly closed it, putting her eyes back on the road, allowing me to enjoy the rest of the ride back home in peace.

2

Back Home Again

The sun beat down, burning all remnants of coolness from the crisp spring air. I tilted my head upward to relish the feel of the early afternoon rays as they caressed my face. With a deep breath, I resumed the trek toward my destination, the soft crunch of gravel vibrating up through the soles of my shoes. Suddenly, the mechanical roar of a high-powered engine filled the air at decibels akin to a fighter jet passing overhead at an extremely low altitude. My heart leaped at the sound and goosebumps rippled across my skin, the tiny hairs on my arms standing on end. The towering grandstands of the Indianapolis Motor Speedway loomed in the distance, gleaming in the afternoon sun. Spectators made their way across the walkways on the outer rim of the structure: a massive stadium built to house three hundred thousand spectators.

I thought of my dad as I continued my steady pace. It was because of him I had such a deep love of IndyCar racing. When I was young, we came to the track for qualifying every May, and the memories of my first Indianapolis 500 were still vivid in my mind, despite the fact it had been fifteen years ago. I flashed my credentials at the yellow-shirted gate attendant and walked over the threshold into my favorite place on earth. The air around me buzzed with the reverberation of a dozen screaming engines, made even more deafening by the echo off the four-story metal bleachers. Yes, it was loud, but man, did I love that sound. I inhaled deeply, allowing the sweet chemical odor of ethanol to waft through my nostrils and settle in my sinuses. I was home.

I trotted through a large gap between two sections of seating and stood by the track as several cars sped by me once again, their bright liveries dancing across the smooth racing surface like the play of light through a prism. My hair whipped around my face, the air violently displaced as more cars blew past me. After a few more moments of revelry, I made my way up the stairs to the top level of the stands and settled in. I pulled my camera out of my bag carefully and clicked my lens into place, gently wiping the polarizer on my cotton T-shirt. It was easy to lose myself in the click of the shutter, zooming in and zooming out, trying different angles and shutter speeds.

Only when the air fell silent and I looked up from my viewfinder did I realize it was almost the end of the practice session. I sighed and carefully disassembled my camera, packing everything away. Growing up in Indiana had given me an appreciation for the Indy 500 and IndyCar, but it wasn't my heritage that kept me coming back for more. It was the intangible, the X factor, the idea one person could beat the odds and come out on top. Whether through talent, intellect, luck, or sheer force of will, there was always the chance *this time* the result would be different. It's the same allure most sports hold for their fans, but add in the high stakes environment of a car whipping around a track at over two hundred miles an hour within inches of the car next to them and, well…need I say more?

In the United States, the high-banked oval racing of NASCAR's stock cars may have more notoriety, but on a global scale, the elite athletes of open-wheel racing series like IndyCar and Formula One take center stage. Endeavoring to operate a motor vehicle for upward of five hundred miles without power steering, braking, or acceleration, IndyCar drivers must rely on their own physical strength and stamina to make it to the finish line. So, while most people use their personal cars as a mental reference to the world of motorsports, in reality, IndyCars have very little in common with your average Toyota Corolla.

Looking out over the expansive infield, I felt peaceful. My life was more than one could hope for: great friends, great family, great job, but I never felt more complete than when I was at the Speedway. Standing on the terrace outside Turn One, I could see everything—well, almost everything. The track was too vast for complete visibility. The race teams along pit road were towing their cars back to the garage area for the night, and a small wave of sadness washed over me. Day one was nearly finished.

Against the protest of my chilled arms, I decided to walk in the opposite direction of my car, following a gravitational pull toward the infield. The Paddock was unique to Indy alone: four long, parallel, concrete buildings with several large garage doors down their lengths. *This is where the magic happens.* I remembered my first time in Gasoline Alley, getting closer than I ever dreamed to such marvelous feats of engineering. As a little girl, I didn't wonder about the concept of racing. I was more concerned with which car had the prettiest color scheme. But as I matured, I began to have educated questions. What propelled these cars? What was the science behind it all? And most importantly, how did they not take flight at such high rates of speed? That was when my dad explained to me that the structure of the wings and winglets on the cars redirected air to keep them grounded as they sped around at two hundred miles per hour; it was a magical thing called downforce.

I paced up and down the aisles, getting the lay of the land. Each team had a portion of the garage area reserved for the month, so I was curious to see where everyone was placed this year. The sound of cued-up engines, pneumatic wheel guns, and clinking tools resonated through the garage, a natural complement to the smell of oil, tire rubber, and exhaust. I loved everything about this place. It was a euphoric assault on the senses I only got to enjoy for one month out of the year.

The sensation of a hand clamping down aggressively on my upper arm snapped me out of my reverie. I would have been offended had I not caught sight of the fully-loaded tire cart barreling straight toward me. The strong hand yanked, making me skip two feet backward as the cart screeched by. The driver of the cart gestured manically and tried to brake, but slowing down any faster would have sent forty-pound projectiles flying across the Paddock in all directions. Flushed with embarrassment, I looked over at my rescuer. "Sorry, I…" My flustered voice cut off as I took in the young man behind me. He was medium height, maybe five-foot-ten, with sparkling brown eyes and dark hair. *Holy shit…*I gulped, trying to regain control of my tongue. I felt nauseous.

"You okay?" he asked in a mildly concerned baritone voice—one I recognized well.

I shifted my feet and swallowed again. "Um…yeah." I looked over my shoulder to one of the garages, where I caught a couple of team members staring before awkwardly busying themselves again. My heart thundered in my chest, and I felt the color coming back to my face with a vengeance. "Sorry, I was just…lost in thought…" I choked, looking down at my feet.

"I could tell." He smirked, subtly teasing me.

My face, already flushed a delicate pink, flamed to a bright red in embarrassment. *Oh my God, I am a total idiot.* "I just…this place…" *Complete sentences, Alaina,* I scolded. "I get sentimental every time I come here. It's…special to me." The wind carried my voice off, but his eyes stayed locked on me.

His playful smirk softened to a gentle smile. "I suppose I get that."

"Hey, when you're done flirting with the pretty lady, Tom wants your opinion on the setup for tomorrow!" one of the aforementioned crew members yelled from across the aisle.

He looked back toward them. "Yeah, coming!" His voice was both self-conscious and annoyed. Turning back to me, he gave another heart-stopping grin, and I couldn't help but smile in return. "I've gotta go. Try not to get run over. People like to speed around here." With a wink, he skipped back toward the garage.

I chuckled, even as my heart stuttered. He had that effect on people. "I'll keep that in mind."

He turned back around halfway to his destination. "I didn't

catch your name."

"Alaina," I said with a shy curl of my lips.

He nodded his head as if committing it to memory. "I'm Grayson," he offered before disappearing through the open door in front of him.

Yes, I knew who he was—the biggest talent to come out of the IndyCar ladder system since its inception. The headlines practically wrote themselves: *Grayson Miles: Racing Sensation.* Everyone wanted to be his friend, but no one wanted to see him in their side mirror with five laps to go. He was a force of nature in more ways than one: charismatic, intelligent, and a world-class competitor, not to mention easy on the eyes. I turned and walked back toward the main gate, thinking I'd had enough excitement for one day. My hands were shaking and my knees felt weak, but I couldn't help the silly grin that crept over my face.

* * *

The whole way home, I replayed the incident over and over again, and the more I replayed it, the more I felt like an absolute and total moron. How could I have been so oblivious I had almost been run over by a tire cart? With any luck, I wouldn't see him for the rest of the month, and I could forget the whole thing ever happened. *That could happen, right?* I had been around the track long enough to know you usually didn't see the same driver twice unless you were looking for them, and God knows I wouldn't be seeking him out after that fiasco.

I pulled into my apartment complex and grabbed my bag from the back seat, ready to go inside, sit down with a nice glass of sauvignon blanc, and go through the day's pictures. My Golden Retriever, Copper, met me at the door, ecstatic for me to be home after a long day away. "Hi, boy!" I greeted, kneeling down to rub his ears. Copper's thick tail alternated thumping against my leg and the kitchen cabinet as I reached up to grab his leash from the peg next to the coat rack. He jumped off all four feet like his legs were spring-loaded as he waited for me to open the door. While Copper dragged me along our usual route, down the sidewalk and across Plum Street to the nearby dog park, I pulled out my phone.

Sweet, patient, kind, and sometimes brutally honest, my mother was one of the few people in my life I knew I could count on to give me her unadulterated opinion—even if that opinion wasn't what I wanted to hear. She would tell me if I'd made a fool of myself or if I was being dramatic. Not that it would change my mind on the situation, but it would probably take a load off my frazzled wits. After living under my mother's roof all my life, I had finally moved out three months ago, but we still talked. To be honest, my day felt incomplete without our nightly therapy sessions.

"Hey, Sweetie," she greeted me warmly on the third ring.

"Hi, Mama. How was your day?" I asked, as I reached the gate to the dog park and raised the latch. Copper sat impatiently at my feet, twitching with the anticipation of freedom from his bondage.

"Oh, not bad, just another day in paradise. I think I finally have enough money saved to fix the kitchen floor!"

"You should take a trip. Have some fun! The kitchen floor can wait," I argued with a chuckle.

"Some things are more important than leisure, unfortunately," she replied with a longing sigh. "How was opening day?" I could hear the clank of dishes over the phone and pictured her loading them into the dishwasher as she spoke.

I rolled my eyes and sighed. "Oh, pretty typical opening day: chilly weather, lots of single file, and me making a fool of myself."

"Oh no, please tell me you didn't make another trip to the infield care center. They're going to start charging you an annual fee!"

"Almost. I'd have probably been flat on my back in the hospital if someone hadn't pulled me out of the way of a fully-loaded tire cart."

"Alaina." She sighed. "What am I going to do with you?"

"Oh, that's not even the best part…" I unclipped Copper's leash and tossed his tennis ball before parking myself on our usual bench. "The guy that pulled me out of the way? Yeah…it was Grayson Miles."

There was a beat of stunned silence as my mother struggled toward comprehension. "Grayson Miles?" The incredulity in her voice somehow managed to make me feel even worse.

"Oh yeah…I was mortified." My stomach vaulted at the thought of it. Copper trotted back, his ball now caked with drool and dirt which had combined into a slimy paste. I grimaced and tossed it with as little contact as possible.

"So, what happened? Did he pull you out of the way and that was that, or…" she asked, curious, despite my humiliation.

"Well, I think I said something about me daydreaming…and then he was like 'you think' or something…I panicked, and to be honest, I think I blacked out."

My mom sighed, fighting to keep the laughter out of her voice for the sake of my pride. "Alaina…"

I moaned, momentarily forgetting my dirty fingers as I flung my head into my hands. "My life is over…my one chance to impress *Grayson Miles*, and I blew it. Big time."

"Don't sell yourself short. I'm sure you made an impression," she said with an uncontrollable giggle.

Impression, indeed. "Ha. Ha. Yeah, I'm sure he'll be using me as a conversation piece at every sponsor party from here to eternity." *This is a disaster.*

She sighed. "I'm sure you're making it out to be worse than it was. You probably won't see him for the rest of the month, and then if by some chance you see him after that, he probably won't remember! I'm sure you aren't the first person it's happened to."

"Oh yeah, that makes everything better."

"It should! It'll be like it never happened. Promise," she consoled.

I let out a deep breath, not entirely convinced.

"I love you," she murmured softly.

"Love you too, Mama." I sighed and sat up from my slouched position as the line went dead. Copper made his way back over to me and buried his head in my lap, begging me to massage the soft spot behind his ears, which I happily obliged. "What am I gonna do with myself, Copper?"

He let out a contented huff, and I smiled. "Alright, you wanna play fetch for a little while?" He raised his big head off my lap and wagged his tail, blissfully unaware of my humiliation. *Must be nice to be so clueless.*

3

Half-Truths and Falsities

I kept feeling his fingers on my upper arm: firm, but gentle. Did I imagine the way they grazed down toward my elbow, leaving a trail of tingles as they went? Was I crazy for thinking his molten brown eyes sparkled when he smiled at me? My heart fluttered anxiously.

"Alaina!" Jessica yelled from across the room.

I jumped out of my mind's eye, hackles raised like a frightened tomcat. "Geez, what?" I asked. I'd been lost in thought, reliving the…situation with Grayson. I couldn't make up my mind whether it had been the most horrific nightmare or the most glorious daydream of my life. It had been a week since my run-in with him, and every day I went to the track, I had purposefully avoided his garage area. The last thing I needed right now was "Dumb Ass: The Sequel."

"I've been trying to get your attention for five minutes."

I felt my cheeks warm as I dialed back the attitude and drew my thoughts away from my reverie. "Sorry. Lost in thought. What's up?"

"Well, it looks like you ordered three hundred red chargers

for the MacGregor wedding…"

"Yeah…so?" I asked, getting up to go over to her desk.

"The MacGregors wanted one hundred fifty silver chargers with dusty rose napkins on June fourteenth. The Chungs wanted three hundred red chargers with the gold trim china on August thirtieth."

My eyes went wide, and I stopped mid-stride. "Oh, crap!"

"Mmhmm…" she agreed, pivoting her computer screen to display Exhibit A.

I whimpered, "Alexis is going to hate me. I've already screwed up two orders this month."

"I'll call and see if I can get everything straightened out, but for the sanity of everyone involved, how about you leave the ordering to me from now on?"

I rolled my eyes. "Fine. As long as you stay away from my floral arrangements."

Jess shrugged. "Sounds good to me."

I walked into the back room of our little shop and studied the assortment of silk flowers sprayed all over the craft table. "So, do we have a plan for these yet, or are we hoping they'll arrange themselves?" I asked, hands on my hips, trying to envision a final product out of the chaos.

Footsteps came closer. "Well, I like the idea of peonies with Queen Anne's lace and roses." Jess commented as she came to stand next to me.

"Hmmm…" I thought as I paced around the table. I picked out a beautiful faux marble vase and began plucking flowers out of the heap. "How about the peonies…" I glanced up at my bestie for approval. "…gladiolas, and a little bit of myrtle?" I snipped as I went, arranging the height of the flowers for a cascade arrangement.

"This is why you're the creative director. Leave product orders and all things number-related to me." She laughed. "Seriously though, that looks great. I'm sure she will be thrilled." Jess and I had been best friends since kindergarten, and after graduating from college, we had decided to pool our collective efforts and open our own business. She'd always had more of a head for figures which is why a business management degree made sense for her. I, on the other hand, was a creative soul, so event planning was on the docket for me. In a nutshell, we were perfect for each other and for our business.

I sighed and began on the second arrangement. "I hope so. This is our biggest wedding all season, so I'm hoping to get some good word-of-mouth to her fancy friends."

"Don't stress about it. Our other weddings might not be big, but we have events every other weekend from here through July. It will be fine."

"I guess," I muttered. We were just now getting our small business off the ground, and if we couldn't deliver on our promise to create the perfect day, we could kiss our spotless reputation goodbye. "Is the salon ready for our nine o'clock?" I asked her over my shoulder, sensing she'd gone back to her desk.

"Should be! I laid out some of our cloth samples and put the catalogs on the coffee table."

"Champagne in to chill?"

"Yep!"

"You're the best!"

Our shop was the first of its kind in the Indianapolis area, and the whole thing focused on convenience and elegance. Going to college for our respective degrees, Jess and I had contacts in all sorts of markets from wedding planning, to catering, to photography, but we noticed there was a wide-open market for decoration and event prep. So, last year, we had decided to pioneer and bring in brides who were looking for a more hands-off approach to their big day. Wedding planning is stressful when you have no idea where to start, so we took things into our own hands. With the colors, patterns, and settings they gave us, we designed the aesthetic of their wedding by providing everything from place settings to centerpieces to bouquets. We wanted to be the one-stop shop for all things bridal.

This wedding I was putting centerpieces together for now was our biggest client yet. The celebration was going to have upward of three hundred guests and a bridal party of sixteen. This couple had connections and I needed to keep us in their good graces. Unfortunately, that meant I had a little over an hour to prepare three different centerpieces and place setting arrangements for her approval. Luckily, she was going for an elegant vibe so the assemblage was fairly simple.

With fifteen minutes to spare, I placed a lotus folded napkin in the middle of my third place setting, straightened a salad fork that was slightly off-kilter, and admired my handy work. *Man, I love my job!* I walked over to the full-length mirror and tucked my long brown hair behind my ear, smoothed out my eye makeup, and took a deep breath. The bell on the front door rang and I smiled at my reflection. "Okay. She's just a girl, and you are her fairy godmother. Let's make some magic!"

With a smile plastered on my face, I walked in to greet our guests. "Emma! How are you?" I asked with a big smile on my face, leaning in to kiss her on both cheeks.

"I'm good, I'm good. How are things going?" she asked, looking around.

"Very good. I think I have some options you're really going to love!" Gesturing toward the parlor, I noticed she'd brought a guest.

"Is this the groom?" I asked, only ever having met her and her mother. He had his back to us, studying some of the floral arrangements in the window display as we chatted. At the sound of Emma's laughter, he turned, and I almost dropped the planner I'd been carrying.

"No, no, James is at a conference in New York this week. This is my brother, Grayson."

Shock colored his features, mirroring my own for half a second before he recovered and smiled. "I think we're already acquainted. Alaina, isn't it?" he asked, extending his hand.

I gulped, trying not to swallow my tongue in the process, and nodded, accepting his hand. "Good to see you again." I tried to ignore the accelerated thrum in my chest. "The um…sitting room is this way." My hand waved of its own accord as my body's autopilot took over.

"Actually, do you have a restroom?" Emma whispered.

Grayson and I held eye contact for what felt like forever. *What in holy hell is happening?*

"Alaina?" Emma asked.

I snapped out of it. "Sorry! Um…bathroom. It's down the hall, first door to the right."

"Thank you!" Her relief was evident as she skirted down the narrow corridor toward the back of the building.

As we walked into the parlor, I motioned around, "You can sit anywhere you like," I gestured to the chairs and couch along the back wall but noticed my hands were shaking, so

I clenched them into fists and put them back down at my sides.

"Oh, I'm good," he responded, looking around. "It's a nice place you've got here."

"Thanks. It's kind of my brainchild." I took a breath, bracing myself. "So, are you following me now?" I asked, trying to sound flirtatious, but in reality, sounding more like a strangled cat. I'm not one who handles humiliation well, and by some sick twist of fate, my creator put my easily embarrassed soul into a body that trips at least three times a day—and that's on a good day. The fact that this handsome young man had not only pulled me out of the line of fire but was also, apparently, willing to let the whole thing slide was just extra kindling on the flames of mortification.

His eyes, which were previously occupied by the center-pieces on the display table, flashed up to me, and he gave me a small smile. "You know, contrary to what you may think, I don't spend my limited free time stalking random women I meet in the garage area."

"What a relief," I muttered with a wry twist of the lips. My cheeks flushed in embarrassment, and my gaze fell to the floor. "Look, about last week, if we could um…maybe not mention it to your sister?"

He chuckled. "No worries, if I had a nickel for every time I've pulled a woman out of the path of a moving vehicle…"

"A regular occurrence for you, then?" I asked, eyebrows raised.

White teeth gleamed between the pink lines of his thin lips. "No, not at all. I was just trying to make you feel less embarrassed about the whole thing."

"I think saying I was embarrassed would be putting it

lightly." I couldn't help but giggle; his smile was contagious. We were quiet for a moment, hitting a lull in the conversation. I looked at my watch. "Nothing going on at the track this morning?"

"Nah, as long as you two don't get caught up talking about china patterns, I shouldn't miss much."

I nodded. "Well, no promises, but I'll try to stick to the schedule. You and your sister are pretty close?"

He nodded, "As close as one can be to his little sister… women and their secrets." He threw another playful dig at me.

I rolled my eyes. "I suppose I get that. I have a younger brother and I get the impression he'd do some serious damage to anyone who hurt me. But most of the time, I feel like we're thousands of miles apart."

"That's a pretty accurate assessment." This was followed by a real laugh.

"I have the feeling I'm interrupting," Emma offered by way of greeting as she came back into the room.

"Not at all!" I exclaimed, "We're just making small talk. Can I get either of you a glass of champagne?"

"Oh, could you? That would be so perfect!" Emma exclaimed happily. Grayson gave an imperceptive shake of his head, and I walked back out to the office. *Of course he doesn't want alcohol before he jumps into a race car. Dumb. Dumb. Dumb.* I could slap myself sometimes.

Jessica looked up from her computer as I walked in. "Was that Gray—"

"Oh, yeah." I nodded, pressing my lips together tightly. I couldn't even process what was happening. I'd gone from a completely confident wedding consultant to a frazzled mess of a human being in about five seconds flat.

"How—"

"He's her brother," I interrupted to answer her question as I walked over to the ice bucket and grabbed a champagne flute. I poured a glass and threw my head back, pounding it like a shot of tequila.

"No way," Jess muttered with bug eyes as she watched me drain another glass.

"Way."

"I think somebody is trying to tell you something."

"Jess, this isn't karma or kismet. It's just a coincidence."

"Yeah well, *some* people would say you're in denial."

"What? You think he knew who I was when he saved me from getting flattened in the garage area the other day?"

She shrugged. "No! But I think this is an awfully *big* coincidence...even for somebody who believes in that kind of thing."

I rolled my eyes, refusing to dignify that nonsense with a response.

"Does Emma know what happened?"

"No...and I told him I would prefer she never found out."

It was Jess's turn for an eye roll. "I see two plausible options here. Option one, he's stalking you, which doesn't seem likely since he could probably have any girl he wanted. Add in the fact that this is his sister's appointment, and I'm 99.9 percent sure you're safe. Option two, the universe is literally pushing you two together. Being inclined to go with option two myself, if you do not get that boy's number before he leaves here, I'm going to get it for you."

"You will not! That is totally unprofessional!"

"Girl, he's single, isn't he?"

"As far as I know, but…"

"No buts." She thrust Emma's glass of champagne in my hand and shoved me back toward the parlor. "The universe has spoken. Now go."

Sometimes I really hate her.

I began to pick up on hushed conversation as I made my way back toward the sitting area where I'd left our clients.

"—your own business," Grayson whispered.

"She's pretty and so nice…*super* sweet. I think you guys—" Emma murmured, probably a little louder than she thought.

Grayson shushed her just as I walked back into the room. I smiled and handed Emma the glass of bubbly. She smiled back cheerily. "So, Alaina, how do you know my brother?"

I made brief eye contact with the aforementioned brother, not missing the swift kick to the shin he gave her. I grinned. "Uh, we met at the track last week."

"Interesting…" she murmured, giving him a sidelong glance. She had a keen nose for half-truths and falsities, it would seem. "My brother neglected to mention that."

"Maybe because it's none of your business," he grumbled, shifting uncomfortably in his seat.

She turned her green-eyed gaze on me. I knew the look of a rabid matchmaker when I saw one. I had my own in the next room.

I cleared my throat. "Anyway, um…let's take a look at these centerpieces, shall we?"

4

Second Impressions

Copper's obnoxious snoring woke me. I glanced over at the clock—3:00 a.m. "Seriously?" I moaned and flipped over, waking my bedmate as I did. He let out a surprised snort and, as if in retaliation, snuggled closer to me. I shoved him away. "Damn it, dog. You're too hot. Get off." He growled, disgruntled, and gave a soft *wuff* before jumping off the bed. I heard the click of his claws on the laminate and then a soft rustle as he lay on his own bed. *Sweet release...*

And then, of course, I couldn't go back to sleep. After thirty more minutes of tossing and turning, I sat up and looked at my phone, scrolling through social media and altogether avoiding the little piece of paper tucked in my planner. At any time now, we were going to reach the nightmare portion of this dream sequence. Perhaps I wouldn't realize I'd forgotten to put a shirt on until we were in the middle of a nice crowded restaurant, or better yet, maybe I would trip off the curb and get hit by an *actual* car.

Or maybe it ran a little bit deeper than my superficial fear of things being too good to be true. I would be the first to admit I still had issues over how my parents' marriage had ended, and I'd be lying if I said I wasn't avoiding a serious relationship because of it. But I could have a fling with a hot racing driver. Wasn't that every girl's fantasy? *Every girl except you,* a little voice whispered in the back of my head. It was right. I didn't want a superficial, no-strings-attached thing. I wanted a relationship—something built on mutual trust, understanding, and attraction. I wanted to feel something for someone and have it be more than lust. I wanted love and devotion, not a guy who wanted to see how fast he could get me out of my pixie pants. *Is that too much to ask?*

Of course, that's too much to ask... the voice in my head whispered again. *Tell a guy that's what you want, and he'll go running in the other direction.* I sighed and flopped on my side, burying my head in my pillow and stubbornly scrunching my eyes closed, willing my thoughts to leave me alone. The next time I awoke, the sun was peeking through my curtains and my phone was ringing off the hook.

"So, are you coming into the office at all today?" Jess's perky voice came through the phone.

"Yeah," I sighed, sitting up. "What time is it?" I looked over at the clock on my bedside table. "Shit..." *Noon.* "Um...I'll be in," I yawned. "Just give me an hour."

"It's Thursday afternoon, and we don't have any appointments today, so if you want to go to the track, I would be supportive of that."

"Jess...I am not about to—"

"Alaina Aileen Montgomery." I could feel her urge to slap me, and I grinned. "He is into you, and if you're too blind to see it…my God, how could you be *that* blind?"

I couldn't help but give a small smile, but then sighed, quiet for a moment. "I don't know if I want to do this, Jess…"

She was quiet too, and I knew she felt my mood shift. She has been my best friend since childhood, and she knew every doubt and bad feeling I'd ever had when it came to my relationships. "Just because you've had a few bad eggs doesn't mean Grayson will be one too. You have to keep trying or you'll never find one worth keeping."

My throat grew tight thinking about my dad. Right before I'd graduated from college, my world fell apart. One night, I went to bed dreaming of moving out on my own and working for *National Geographic* or *Travel Magazine,* and the next morning, I woke up to a nightmare. My parents were divorcing, my brother was deployed, and I felt like I was the only one attempting to keep the world on its axis. I had been fresh off a nasty breakup myself and, as far as I was concerned, my dad was the one to blame for all of it—well maybe not my breakup, but the rest of it? Definitely.

And yeah, maybe after all this time, it was petty of me to keep avoiding him, but things hadn't been the same since he'd run off to be with that…that *girl.* If I were being honest, we had both stopped trying after the prerequisite awkward period. He was sick of having more of a relationship with my voicemail than with me, and I was tired of getting my hopes up only to have them dashed when he called to cancel our plans at the last minute. Unfortunately, our mutual throwing in of the towel didn't keep me from feeling guilty about the whole situation. "What do I do?" I asked quietly.

"You're gonna go to the track, you are going to talk to that boy, and if you don't come out with a date, I'm gonna go back with you and ask him out *for* you."

I smiled. "You're not kidding, are you?"

"I never said I was."

"If this ends in total disaster, I'm coming for you first." I grumbled, flicking my blankets off me and rolling out of bed.

"For the sake of my best friend's happiness, it's a risk I'm willing to take," she cheerfully allowed before hanging up the phone.

I rubbed my eyes, trying to rid myself of the gritty sandpaper feeling that came with lack of sleep. I stumbled into the bathroom and flicked on the light, groaning as I saw myself in the mirror. My curly brown hair stuck out in a thousand different directions. I had imprint lines across my left cheek where I'd been cuddled into my pillow, and leftover mascara from yesterday's makeup was smeared above one eye. I was going to have to do some serious damage control if I wanted to impress anyone today.

* * *

The track was quiet for a change, and I wondered if maybe I'd gotten the time wrong on the schedule, but the presence of the Yellow Shirt manning the gate assured me there was indeed some sort of activity going on today. I heard the sudden squeal of fresh tires on pavement and the growl of an engine as a car pulled out of the pits. I made my way onto the viewing mounds just in time to see Grayson's teal and charcoal car scream by. There was no doubt about it, racing was a dangerous business. All that stood between a driver and certain death was the competency of his crew, his own skill, and a little bit of luck.

I wondered what fueled such an individual to constantly put his life on the line. Was it the adrenaline, the challenge, or had he just found something he was good at and stuck with it? After a solid install lap, he pulled the car off the track and back onto pit lane. Reluctantly, and with a stuttering heart, I proceeded down the path toward the Pagoda. Tinted with green glass and framed with a black steel skeleton, the monstrous tiered structure loomed overhead like Mount Olympus, allowing the broadcasting gods to observe the activities of the mere mortals below. I grabbed a seat on the bleachers right above Grayson's pit area and waited patiently. Was I completely dense to think I had a shot with this guy?

Jess was right. He could have anyone he wanted. So, why me? What did I have that some model or actress didn't have? Certainly not a six-pack or legs for days. I was the definition of average. Most days, my unruly hair took to the humidity like the snakes on Medusa's head. It was remarkably hard for my skin to hold any color other than the ivory complexion I'd been born with. My eyes were a dull hazel that appeared brown unless the light was just right and were framed with a dark set of lashes that *refused* to curl.

I tapped my foot in an anxious tattoo, fighting every instinct screaming at me to run before Grayson caught sight of me. He was way out of my league, and the longer I sat there taking that in, the more evident it became. I was still warring with myself when he cut the engine and a crew member leaned down to help him unbuckle. Grayson lifted himself out of the car and unstrapped his chrome and teal helmet, saying a couple of words to his engineer as he removed his earpieces and tucked them into his suit for safekeeping.

I rose from where I'd been hiding in plain sight, making

up my mind to get out before I could do anything foolish. Despite the internal running dialogue urging me to flee, my eyes couldn't leave him. I drifted down the aluminum risers, careful with my steps so as not to fall. They were still damp with the morning rain and extremely hazardous. Hopping over the wall, he looked at the computer monitors in their mobile command center, pointing at the screen and gesturing with his hands. After several more animated movements, they hooked the car up and pulled it back into the garage. As Grayson stepped down from the booth and headed for his golf cart, he glanced in my general direction and did a double-take.

*Damn...*I waved shyly before making my way over to the fence. Luckily, it was chilly and overcast, so there weren't a lot of people around. We could speak without being swarmed by an influx of fans begging for autographs and selfies.

"You know, those numbers I wrote down can be tapped into this nifty little device. I think it's called a phone?" He smiled, and all of my worries melted away. He was good at that, putting me at ease and calming all of my doubts.

"Sorry, I've had a lot going on the past couple of days." It was a lame excuse. We both knew it, but it was the best I could come up with on short notice.

He nodded thoughtfully. "Listen, they're going to be working on the car for a bit. You want to grab a bite? The guys are gonna throw some burgers on the grill back at the trailer."

Shocked at his forward invitation, I nodded, not giving myself time to think it through. "Sure, that sounds great!" *WHAT????* My inner voice screamed at me. *This is such a bad idea...*The bolder part of me shoved my insecurities in a closet and slammed the door. *And you can just stay there,* I thought as I forced a smile on my face.

He looked around. "Go ahead and head over to the gate. I'll pick you up in a second."

My stomach fluttered nervously, but I forced my feet to move to my designated pickup spot. The Yellow Shirt on duty looked unconvinced when I told him I was meeting Grayson, and I don't think any version of the truth would have swayed him. Seeing the look on that crusty old man's face when Grayson waved me through made it worth it, though.

It was odd. After a lifetime of watching golf carts zoom through the Paddock, I was actually in one. Of course, who I was riding next to didn't hurt either. It was hard to miss the occasional jealous stares from random women as we passed. We pulled up next to a large RV, and he swung himself out of the golf cart. "I'll be right back." He gestured around to a few lawn chairs and a picnic table. "You can make yourself comfortable, the others will be here in a few."

I smiled. "Okay." I stepped over to one of the camp chairs and lowered myself slowly, looking around the maze of RVs and hospitality tents.

"And who, may I ask, would you be?" I heard from behind me.

I spun around at the new, vaguely familiar, voice of Jack Kinney, another young gun on the racing circuit and Grayson's teammate.

"Oh, um, Alaina," I finally managed, offering my hand to shake. Jack took it, giving two friendly pumps of his arm. "Grayson's inside. He said to wait here?" I claimed, my voice going up at the end in a question.

Jack smiled. "No need to get nervous. Gray doesn't usually

bring girls back here. I couldn't help but be a little curious." He winked at me with a mischievous smile.

I could feel the heat building in my cheeks. *Don't blush. Don't you dare…* I was fair, so the slightest change in complexion was hideously noticeable. Jack threw the door of the RV open without ceremony. "Gray, get your ass out here. Don't you know better than to keep a pretty girl waiting?"

Not long after that, they both emerged shoving each other playfully, reminding me of two brothers. I'll be the first to admit, Grayson looked pretty hot with his fire suit hanging around his hips, baseball cap and Ray-Bans adorning his head.

"So, *Alaina*, how is it you met my friend here?" Jack asked, slumping into the seat next to me.

This time I *really* blushed. "Um, well…we met in the garage area last week."

"And then, she turned out to be Emma's wedding planner," Grayson added, offering more detail to combat any potential questions. Every time he thwarted any inquiries into our meeting, he won more brownie points with me. *Keep on keeping on, buddy.* I thought to myself with a smile.

Jack smirked. "And your first thought was to invite her to a barbecue with a bunch of guys she doesn't know? *Smooth*," he jabbed.

"Okay, I think you can go now," Grayson muttered, pulling his friend up out of his chair and away from the trailer.

"Ow!" Jack yelped. "But, I'm hungry."

Not being monstrous in size himself, Grayson was definitely the larger of the two, and he had no qualms about pushing Jack elsewhere. Grayson bowed his head, saying something in a harsh whisper.

Jack rolled his eyes before punching him in the arm. "I'll see you around, Alaina!" he said with a wave, never losing the devious look in his eye. I got the feeling that boy was always up to something.

I stood up and waved back. "Nice meeting you!"

"Sorry." Grayson rolled his eyes. "He can be…"

I laughed. "It's fine. He seems like a good friend." A shy smile crept over my lips.

Grayson nodded. "The best. He's like the brother I never had," he admitted with a shrug. "This job…it takes a lot out of you. It's good to have somebody who can relate."

"I know what you mean. I doubt I could have made it through the last couple of years getting our business off the ground if it weren't for Jess. She knows me better than anyone. Don't get me wrong, she's a complete pain in my ass, but in a good way."

His smile broke into a full-on grin, and he laughed quietly.

I cleared my throat. "I've actually kind of been…I don't know…not avoiding you, but…" I sighed, playing with my nails.

"Should I be offended?" he asked, feigning outrage.

"No, no, it's not like that!" I sighed and made eye contact with him, feeling his curiosity burning into me. "I'm not a big risk-taker. I think things out…sometimes too much. Jess is a bit more impulsive and free-spirited," I admitted, feeling myself blush. *Damn it.* "Anyway, if it wasn't for Jess, I wouldn't have come today but, um, I'm glad I did." Sincerity coated my voice.

"Enjoying watching Jack poke fun at my lack of skills when it comes to women?" he offered self-deprecatingly.

"I'll admit, I may have misjudged you there."

He got up from his seat and went over to the cooler by the door, pulling out two bottles of water. "What do you mean?"

"I guess I expected you to be a bit more…I don't know." I shook my head and looked down at the ground.

"Oh, come on, now you *have* to tell me."

I sighed, mentally slapping myself. "Okay, so obviously I knew who you were when we met the other day, but I guess in all the interviews and stuff I've seen, you come across as a little more…" I struggled. "…self-confident." *Oh my God, Alaina. Stop talking.*

He snorted. "You mean, I seem like a pompous jackass."

"I did *not* say that!" I shouted defensively, mortified at his accusation.

"Oh, but you meant it," he insisted, playful. "No, look, I get it." His shoulders lifted in a shrug as if it didn't bother him in the slightest. *I wish I could be like that—confident in who I am, the rest of the world be damned.*

"Honestly, though, I figured you were a bit more of a player than you seem to be," I allowed, clarifying my earlier statement. "There's nothing wrong with sowing wild oats, right?" I physically had to stop my teeth from grinding together. I'd spent my entire dating life avoiding pricks who wanted to "sow wild oats," and yet my words made it seem as though social etiquette required me to give this guy a free pass. *Oh, boy.*

He studied me for a moment. "If you really think that about me, then why did you agree to come to lunch?" There was something in his eyes besides inquiry. Fear, maybe? Definitely suspicion.

"Curiosity, I guess. I don't know, for all the rumors and speculation, you seemed nice enough." My shoulders lifted in an identical motion to his earlier shrug. "And to be quite honest, in the few conversations we've had, I didn't really get that vibe from you. Never hurts to be cautious, though." I shifted in my seat. "I could ask the same of you though. Why did you ask me to lunch? You met me at the track after all. I could be some crazy stalker."

He smiled. "Well, I guess you could say 'I didn't really get that vibe from you' either." The air quotes he included in his statement got a laugh out of me, and he continued, "Don't get me wrong, I've been burned a few more times than I care to admit, but I don't know, you seem…different."

I stared down at my bottle of water. "Well, I don't know about 'different,' but I'm definitely no player. I've been out of the game entirely for…quite some time."

"I find it hard to believe you've been on your own for too long," he added, looking at me like I was a puzzle he was trying to solve.

I felt a little color settle into my cheeks and raised my eyebrows. "Well, when you've dealt with the things I've dealt with in the last few years, it doesn't exactly inspire confidence."

"Uh oh." He let out a breathy laugh.

I shifted in my seat and rolled my eyes. "Yeah well, that's life, right? Everybody's got baggage of some sort." We held each other's gaze for a moment and my stomach did flip flops. His eyes were so warm and inviting, I could get lost in them.

Grayson suddenly sat up, snapping us both out of whatever trance we had been in, and looked around. "Well, something tells me Jack has been at it again."

All of a sudden, the lack of people surrounding us stood out like a sore thumb. "Yeah, I thought this was supposed to be a team function?"

"Well, apparently, everyone else got a different memo."

"I'll let you go get something to eat before practice starts back up," I offered, standing from my chair. As if on cue, the sound of a car speeding out of pit road echoed across the infield.

We walked back toward the garage in comfortable silence, and as we approached the open bay door he turned to me, grabbing my hand. "I'd invite you in, but…"

"No, I get it. Appearances and all. Um…I guess I'll see you around."

"No, it's not that! It's just…" He looked down at his feet self-consciously. The more I talked with him, the more I got the distinct impression he was a naturally reserved person who did a remarkable job of pretending to be outgoing. "I wanted to give us a little more time to get to know each other before, um…" He smiled. "It's a very transparent bubble I live in, if you know what I mean," he allowed, shifting and looking back up at me. "I really had a nice time today though."

"Me too," I whispered with a smile, relief flooding my voice as I realized he wasn't trying to pawn me off. I looked up through my eyelashes at him. "Good luck."

He leaned in close and kissed me gently on the cheek. "Thanks, Alaina," he whispered.

A loud catcall sounded from behind Grayson, and I peeked around to see Jack with a big grin on his face.

"I'm going to kill you," he muttered through gritted teeth.

"Oh, stop being so modest, Gray. You would have thought I'd caught you in a compromising position," Jack said in a scandalized and sarcastic tone, batting his eyelashes.

A blush crept up Grayson's neck and his jaw twitched in

irritation. I smiled and squeezed his hand, which I was still holding. "I'm gonna go. I'll call you, though."

He turned back to me. "Okay, sounds good." He squeezed my hand back. I could read between the lines. He didn't want to say more with his loud-mouthed best friend standing in front of us. He was sparing himself a huge headache later and saving me potential embarrassment in the moment.

I started walking toward the exit of the garage cheerily, singing, "Bye, Jack," as I passed.

5

Press Invasion

The smell of scrambled eggs and toast wafted through the air, and my mouth watered. I scooped the contents of my breakfast onto a plate and grabbed the toast out of the toaster, tossing it on top of my eggs before it could burn my fingertips. Copper followed me eagerly over to the table, no doubt hoping I would trip and dump the contents of my meal onto the floor for his own enjoyment. I slid into my chair and picked up my latest edition of *Bridal Bliss* magazine to thumb through as I ate. I dog-eared several pages of decorated venue pictures for closer observation at a later time. Copper rested his head in my lap and gazed up at me with his adorable brown eyes. *How could anyone resist that puppy dog face?* I caved and tore off a piece of bread for him, tossing it a good distance away, giving me time to finish my food before he wandered back over.

I sipped my coffee, enjoying the flow of bitter richness over my tongue as I glanced over the last bit of the magazine. With a sigh, I flipped it shut, took a final sip of my own personal version of The Water of Life, and tossed another bit of toast to the pup before putting the rest in the trash. It had been just over a week since my pseudo-date with Grayson, and we had texted frequently. He'd been extremely busy with work over the past few days, so while I had managed to speak with him briefly at the track, our primary contact had been late-night phone conversations.

Last night, however, no call had been forthcoming. I'd left him a message to call me, and I felt the abyss of insecurity swelling up under me. I was being pulled into an unhealthy cycle of highs and lows that normally came with a new relationship. I would leave a conversation feeling sufficiently satisfied, and then the doubt would creep in. I swatted away any pessimistic stray thoughts and headed for the shower. *God, get over yourself.*

Copper wanted his own breakfast by the time I stepped back out of the shower and stood by his bowl whining. "You are too needy," I fondly chastised as I scooped some food into the dish, and he wagged his tail happily. "Should I be worried he hasn't texted?" I asked Copper as he chowed down. He looked up briefly and went back to his food. I sighed. "Alright, well you have been no help." I paced back into my room in time to hear my phone buzz.

Unable to hold back hope, I jumped on my bed and swiped my phone off my nightstand. *Please, please, please.*

My heart pounded. A text message from Grayson was waiting for me:

Can you talk?

I took a deep breath and slowly exhaled, trying to calm my racing heart.

Yeah, what's up?

Before my mind could run through a million terrible scenarios, his name popped up on my caller ID. I swiped and answered, "Hey, is everything okay?" I was genuinely concerned.

"Yeah, sorry. I didn't mean to worry you. I've just been super busy."

"It's okay. Is something going on?"

I could hear voices in the background of his phone. "Um… yeah." He cleared his throat. "So, here's the thing. My team's social media rep does a routine search for any rogue stories on me or my teammates, and she found something last night."

I swallowed, taking another deep breath. "Okay, if you're trying to freak me out, it's working."

"Somebody saw us together the other day—outside the garages. They took pictures and posted them on their blog. It's spreading like wildfire. My PR team is trying to get a handle on it, but they don't have any grounds to have it removed."

My heart pounded. I could only imagine the awful things floating around out on the Interwebs about me. "Okay. What do you need me to do?" I asked quietly. I was definitely not ready for a press invasion and I was barely keeping the panic at bay.

"I don't want you to worry. We're going to take care of it. Just keep to yourself. Nobody knows who you are. You should be safe."

I gulped. *You should be safe?* This had escalated very quickly. My friends and family would see this. My *dad* would see this. *Well, it looks like you're about to have a couple of* very *uncomfortable conversations.* "Okay." My voice was shaky, and he was quiet on the other end of the line.

"I'm sorry, Alaina. I know this isn't what you signed up for, and if you want out, I understand."

I cleared my throat and took a deep breath, trying to keep that damn quiver out of my voice that made me sound like a little mouse in the sights of a big, yellow-eyed tomcat. "No, it's fine. We just have to ride it out."

He let out a hard laugh. "I had hoped we could get to know each other a little better before you had to ride anything out," he admitted.

"It's not your fault. I get it. Promise."

A quiet chuckle came through the phone. "I'll try to see you as soon as I can. I have to go though, okay?"

"Okay. Bye."

I sank to my bed staring at my phone. This was a disaster. My mom didn't even know I'd been talking to Grayson. My brother, Tucker, was off in God-only-knows-where, and the last thing I wanted was for him to see my face plastered all over the internet in relation to some guy. And my dad, well…don't even get me started on him. How was I supposed to explain this situation?

With the truth, you idiot. It's not like you're hiding anything.

I rolled my eyes at my internal voice. Well, maybe I shouldn't panic just yet.

I sat on the couch for a moment, pausing to gather my thoughts. I knew I had to tell my mom. She would be devastated if she didn't find out from me. With a sigh, I picked up my phone, dialed her number, and listened to it ring. Eventually I heard, "Hello?" in her sing-songy voice.

"Hey, Mom," I murmured

Mother's intuition immediately threw up red flags. "Lainie, what's wrong?" was her quiet response.

I sighed. "Um…" I swallowed, trying to pick the right words. "I don't really know how to…" I was at a loss.

She was quiet for a moment, a million things being communicated between us. "How about you start at the beginning?"

"I…um…you remember I was telling you about almost getting run over a couple of weeks ago in the garage area?"

She chuckled. "Vividly."

I cleared my throat. "Well, it turns out that wasn't the last time I saw Grayson." She was quiet on the other end, waiting for me to continue. "Do you remember me telling you about that big wedding I landed—the one in September?" I asked.

"The one with that big exec that has like three hundred guests?" she asked, curious now.

"That's the one," I confirmed and sighed again. "So, it turns out the bride is Grayson's sister—Emma."

She let out a disbelieving snort. "What are the odds?"

"That's kind of what I was thinking," I murmured to myself. "Anyway, a couple of weeks ago at Emma's appointment, she brought Grayson with her."

"Did he know you were her planner?" She was hooked now.

I shook my head even though she couldn't see me. "No, he had no idea. It turns out her mom couldn't come with her, and her fiancé was out of town, so he got roped into tagging along." I smiled, remembering the story. "Anyway, we've been texting back and forth a little bit—nothing serious— and when I went to the track the other day, we ended up having lunch together. Apparently, there are pictures of us together. Grayson's PR person found them last night. I guess it's blowing up the internet." I was quiet and so was she. "I didn't want you to find out from someone else."

"I'm glad you told me," she murmured, and I could hear a smile in her voice. "How do you feel about all of this?" She knew me well—too well, sometimes.

I shifted in my seat. "I don't know…I mean, I didn't ask for any of this. It kind of seems like a violation to have somebody watching us together, but I think, if I'm serious about pursuing him, I kind of have to accept it."

More silence. "I think you're right. I know I don't have to say this, but make sure you've really thought it through, Lainie, because…it's one thing to make a relationship work when it's just the two of you. Having the whole world attempting to put their two cents in—it won't be easy."

I nodded to myself and sighed. "I know…um…I have to get ready for work. I'll talk to you later?" I asked.

"Of course," she murmured. "I love you."

"Love you too."

* * *

"So, do you have hordes of paparazzi outside your apartment right now?" Jessica asked through the phone.

I walked over to my window verifying what I already knew. "No, Jess, I'm not dating a prince. Grayson's only well-known in certain circles. I really don't think I'm going to be the next Princess Di."

Jess sighed. "So, does that mean you're coming in today?"

"Yeah, I'm getting ready right now." I threw my lip gloss in my purse and unplugged my straightener.

"See you soon then."

45

I clicked off my phone and threw it in my purse as well. Copper watched from his bed as I paced back and forth. He was very confused by my behavior. We had a pretty regular routine, and this was definitely not normal. I looked at him. "Yeah, I know, but we can't go to the dog park until I talk to Grayson. Until then, it's just short walks so you can do your business."

He let out a huff like he understood and was *not* happy. "Hopefully you'll meet him soon. You'll like him, I swear. It'll be worth a couple of missed trips to the dog park, Cops." I really did feel bad. I think that was the best part of his very boring day, and I hated taking that away from him. I'd have to give him extra couch time tonight. I grabbed my bag and my portfolio and headed to work, hoping like hell I wouldn't encounter any errant bloggers along the way.

* * *

"Have you read some of this stuff?" Jess asked as I walked through the door. She was glued to her computer screen, and I had to roll my eyes.

"Jess, you know none of that stuff's true, right?"

"It's so addicting, though. It's like knowing a car accident is going to happen, and you watch anyway out of morbid curiosity." She switched to her phone and started swiping away, falling into the black hole of gossip magazines. "I also would like to throw it out there that if I could get cute pictures like these of me and my hot boyfriend, I would be all for letting somebody follow me around."

I leaned over her shoulder, not being able to help myself. It was a cute picture. They had caught that perfect moment where Grayson had leaned in to kiss my cheek, and convenient for me, my back was to the camera, so the internet was running wild with rampant speculation as to who Grayson Miles's new girlfriend was. And then, of course, at the top in big bold letters was "**GRAYSON'S GIRL.**"

"The actual article—if you can call it that—isn't too bad. The comments are where it gets hairy," Jess offered as she scrolled. I only caught a couple as she went.

There was the very common:

[INDYRAWKS2323 says:] Lucky Bitch!!!

The slightly discouraging:

[JANETHERACINGKWEEN says:] We see him kissing somebody on the cheek, and we immediately assume he has a girlfriend? Get a life, guys. The way he's kissing her, she could be his sister.

And the downright offensive:

[TEALTEAMBABE1 says:] She's not even that pretty. He could have anyone, and he picks that? Wow…bet she's dumb as a box of rocks too…

"Okay, I'm done reading this. It's total crap. Look at this: 'A source close to the couple says they have been dating secretly for weeks and have wanted to keep the relationship under wraps to prevent any suspicion surrounding the mystery girl's previous relationship.' Where do they come up with this?" I paced away, half angry, half disgusted.

"These people are vicious," Jess muttered, continuing to read despite my protests.

"Then stop giving them the time of day. They comment like that for attention." I growled irritably.

Jess turned to face me. "Alaina, you're making sure I know these things aren't true, but do you? Because I'm starting to get the impression they're getting under your skin a little bit."

"Of course they are. These people are rude. Since when did my personal life become their business?"

She crossed her arms and rocked back in her seat, studying me. "Since you decided to date a highly eligible and extremely popular public figure."

I laid my stuff down on my desk, trying to fight back the urge to cry. "I wish I could do something about it."

Jess hugged me. "It will all blow over eventually, Lainie. You just have to ride out this rough patch," she murmured, holding me until she sensed I had enough strength to keep myself together. "I bet in a million years you never thought you'd have a famous boyfriend and have to deal with the tabloids," she said with a chuckle.

Her attempt at humor worked. I laughed.

"Seriously, though, ignore them. They don't know what they're talking about, and in all honesty, they're just jealous they don't have what you have, which is *Grayson Miles*. Let the rest of it roll off your back."

I poured my second cup of coffee and got back to work. My emails were out of control, and I had several arrangements to complete for a wedding in two weeks. To top it all off, I had a venue walk-through with a bride at 3:00 p.m. Today was not the day to be off my A-game.

I went back to the supply closet where we stored our vases, picking out several copper pitchers. I was excited about this particular wedding. She wanted flowers with jewel tones, so we were using sunflowers, blue hydrangeas, and purple snapdragons for her country chic reception. The event was being held in a refurbished barn, and the colors were going to be fabulous with the stained wood. Arms full of copper pitchers, vases, and even a couple of watering cans, I made my way back to my assembly room. I barely noticed when the bell on the front door rang amid the sounds of tearing open packages of flowers.

"Busy little bee, aren't you?"

I shouted and clutched at my heart as I jumped to face the doorway.

Grayson leaned against the door jam, arms crossed, a bemused expression on his face. "You alright?" he asked, barely containing his laughter at my reaction.

"Jesus, don't do that!"

That did it. He burst into fits of giggles, and I couldn't help the little laugh that escaped my own lips. "Stop, it's not funny!"

"It really was, though," he argued through his fits of snickering.

I rolled my eyes and crossed my arms, trying to be serious.

"Sorry, sorry." He tried to compose himself and failed miserably.

Trying my best to ignore him, I went back to unpacking my boxes. After a minute, I felt his eyes on me. He stepped just behind my back, studying the pile of silk flowers I had accumulated.

"So, what's all this?" His voice was closer than I expected, and I took an instinctive step backward as I turned to face him. My pulse pounded in my ears and my knees felt weak, unable to support my befuddled frame as I stared into the clear depths of his intelligent, almond-shaped eyes. I gulped and took a deep breath, hoping the excess flow of oxygen would help quell the feeling I'd ingested one too many energy drinks. "This is all the stuff I need to make centerpieces for a wedding I have in two weeks." My voice was rough, and I tried to clear my throat delicately.

"When I think about weddings, I think white. I like this. It's different," he allowed, fingering the soft silk petals of a flower delicately.

I leaned against the table and smiled at him. "I love it when a couple branches out. As much as I like the classic whites, blushes, and champagnes, I love to use the bright colors too."

He gave me a one-sided grin and stepped closer, fingering my teardrop earring as he gazed into the depths of my hazel eyes. My stomach pitched and heaved nervously. *Butterflies, my ass.* This was more like a flock of birds in my abdomen. "I like seeing you in your element," he admitted as he grabbed my hand gently.

My stomach was doing flips now, in addition to the large number of avians begging to be let out. I watched as his fingers intertwined with mine, and I shivered with sensual pleasure. "So, what brings you all the way out here?" My voice squeaked like one of Copper's stuffed toys.

"I wanted to make sure you were okay. I was hoping I hadn't scared you off after this morning."

I gave a soft chuckle. "It's going to take a lot more than that to scare me away!" I turned back to my boxes and busied myself before he could see the doubt covering my face. I'd be lying if I said I didn't enjoy my privacy. Did I want to give that up for some guy I barely knew? *Valid question. But Grayson isn't just some* guy, *and you know it.* When I was sure my mask was back up, and I was once again exuding confidence, I pulled the last handful of flowers onto the table and threw a glance back at him. "I'm actually a pretty tough cookie, you know."

He moved to lean on the table next to me as I worked. "I'd understand if you had misgivings about it. I know it's not exactly what you signed up for."

I hesitated, the flowers shaking in my hands. Covertly, I sat the batch on the table and pressed my hands into the cold laminate surface to still the nervous tremors. "I wouldn't say it's…misgivings, exactly," I allowed, letting out a deep breath and continuing to trim a batch of sunflowers.

"Okay. What would you call it then?" I could hear the smile in his voice but didn't look up.

I sighed and sat my work down, looking at an infinitesimal speck on the wall in front of me. "It doesn't have anything to do with you." I glanced up at him to see if he was following. He was. "I don't know that I'm ready to have every inch of my life analyzed and picked apart, you know?"

"I know." His voice was quiet, and I realized he really did— probably better than anyone. This had happened before, then. My heart sank.

"I can't make any promises. I wish I could." He sighed and scratched the back of his head. "All I can say is I'll do everything in my power to protect you and your privacy, but I also understand if you want out."

I closed my eyes and took a deep breath, knowing I would

have regrets if I played the coward, turned tail, and ran. I finally turned to him. "I don't want out." I sighed. "I just want to know you've got my back if this goes sideways."

He gave a breathy laugh and squeezed my hand. "Always."

"Okay then," I allowed with a quirk to my lips.

"Okay then," he repeated. "Now that that's settled, I wanted to ask you if you were free for dinner tonight?"

"I…" My mouth felt dry. "I…um…yeah."

He leaned in closer, and my breath caught in my throat. We were only inches apart when a throat cleared in the doorway. I jumped back, and Grayson sighed, eyes closing briefly in frustration before he turned to face the door.

"Dude, we have to go," Jack announced, not bothering to hide his amused grin at being Mr. Interruption.

Grayson looked back over at me. "I'll pick you up at seven?"

I nodded and smiled. "I'll text you the address."

He winked at me and pushed away from the table. "I'll see you tonight," he murmured, and left as quickly as he'd come.

6

Two Little Birdies

I was running around my apartment like a chicken with its head cut off. From his bed in the corner, Copper studied me as though I were a ticking time bomb, his thoughtful eyes following my every move. Meditatively, I stared at my reflection, wondering if something was missing. My long brown locks cascaded down my shoulders in a sea of freshly curled satin, and the base layer of my makeup glowed a flawless cream. Satisfied my setting powder was sufficiently applied, I dug into the makeup bag on the counter in search of my favorite liquid eyeliner. The soft *zzz-zzz-zzz* of my phone drew my eye away from the mirror and down to the illuminated screen of my smartphone.

Amber wants gardenias instead of dahlias.
Can you make that work or do you want
me to tell her no?

I rolled my eyes and picked up my phone.

If that's what she wants, I'll figure it out.

Holding my breath to steady my hand, I swept the felt tip of my eyeliner pen across my upper lids, creating a delicate wing on each eye. After a dash of mascara and a sprinkle of illuminating powder, I brushed my clean fingers across my face to smooth the places where my makeup clung too heavily. *Much better.* The clock on my bedside table read 6:50 p.m., and my heart leaped into my throat in a slight panic. I sighed internally and ran over to the cute fit-and-flare sundress I'd laid out on the bed—an exquisite pale-yellow piece with delicate lace trim along the hem. I slipped in and zipped it up, being extra careful not to get my long hair stuck in the zipper like last time. *That was a nightmare.* As I was putting my dainty teardrop pearl earrings in, there was a soft knock at the door. I walked out to the living room to pull my wedges from underneath the coffee table and shouted, "Coming," as another knock sounded.

Copper was now growling with incessant ferocity—making up for lost time as he realized he'd been slacking in his guard dog duties. He sounded like he was going to chew our visitor's leg off, but in reality, would do about as much damage as a fluffy little duckling. "Copper, no," I scolded in hushed tones as I ran to meet Grayson before he could knock for a third time. Somewhat haphazardly, I flung open the door while managing to grab Copper before he jumped up on my date. He stepped back quickly, startled by the huge dog lunging at him, eyes wide.

"Sorry!" I rolled my eyes. "Copper, stop it!" I insisted a little more forcefully. "Sit." Another stern command. Still fidgety, he sat back on his haunches, and I rubbed the top of his head,

"Good boy." I looked up at Grayson with an apologetic smile. "He's harmless, I promise. He just gets excited when people visit." I grabbed Copper's collar and walked him back to the living room. "Come on in."

Grayson's eyes darted between the charcoal ballerina sketches on the wall and the baby pink throw pillows on the couch before coming to rest on the fresh peonies in the vase on the table. "Nice place."

"A little girlie, I know. But hey, it's just me here, and I like girlie, so…" I shrugged with a sheepish grin. "It's not much, but it's home."

He shook his head as if to disagree with me when Copper moseyed up and sat, staring at him.

Grayson chuckled, staring right back. "What?"

Copper let out a whine and pawed at Grayson's leg, his eager, deep brown eyes never leaving his target.

Grayson looked at me, perplexed, and I had to laugh. "He wants you to love on him a little bit. He's a big marshmallow."

Grayson knelt down and Copper closed the gap, letting him rub his ears and scratch his shoulders. "You're a good boy, aren't ya?" he murmured before patting him one more time on the head and standing up.

"Best friends for life," I joked lightly. "I think he might even forgive you for keeping him from going to the dog park tonight."

Grayson smiled and gave Copper one final pat on the head. "Sorry, Buddy," he apologized before looking up at me. "You ready?" he asked as I grabbed my little purse off the kitchen counter.

"Yep. Let's do this!"

* * *

"Care to share where we're going?" My curiosity was getting the better of me, like always.

He glanced over. "Not a fan of surprises?"

I sighed. "Not particularly."

Light laughter filled the blacked-out interior of Grayson's Nautical Blue 4Runner. "Well, you're in trouble then, because I love to surprise people."

We kept driving further and further away from the city, and when we pulled up at a little diner on the outside of town, I couldn't help but give him a questioning glance. I had definitely anticipated something fancier and felt completely overdressed.

He laughed. "It's only phase one of the plan. I promise. Come on." He stepped out of the vehicle. *Better go with him or God only knows what you'll be stuck with for dinner.* With a sigh, I tugged on the door handle and swung down out of the vehicle onto the rough pavement of the parking lot, cracks zigzagging across it like it hadn't been resealed since it was laid down fifty years ago.

The bell above the door rang cheerily as we entered the old fifties-style restaurant with its chrome fixtures and red leather booths. The only one to give us a second glance was the gray-haired waitress behind the counter, counting her tips idly. A grin split her face from ear to ear, and in a flash, she was right in front of us. "Grayson," she murmured lovingly, patting my date on the hand. "How've you been, hon?"

"Not too bad, Miss Maggie. How about yourself?" The responding smile on his face, more than anything else, clued me in to the fact that these two had a history.

"Can't complain!" she allowed. "Every day's a blessing. You know, my Evie got married last year? She's got a little one on the way now."

Grayson ducked his head, a dimple appearing in his left cheek as he acknowledged her comment. "Well, that's great. Tell her congratulations for me."

Maggie patted Grayson's hand again. "I will. I will," she assured as she prepared to move to the next item on the agenda. "You want this to go, Gray?"

"You know me well." He grinned.

I scrunched my brow, confused, and the matronly waitress laughed. "Grayson's been coming here since he was about knee-high to a grasshopper." The light bulb clicked on in my head. I forgot he was raised in Indiana, and it made sense he would visit his old hangouts when he was back in town.

"Well then, tell me what's good."

He laughed. "Burgers and fries are nonnegotiable. They have *the best* pie here. Maggie makes them herself." With this, he gave her a little wink and refocused on me. "I'd also recommend a milkshake."

"So basically, you're hoping to give me a heart attack?" I asked with a laugh. "Lucky for you, I don't shy away from artery-clogging food." With a glance at the menu, I ordered a bacon cheeseburger, fries, a piece of cherry pie—*wouldn't want to insult Miss Maggie*—and a strawberry milkshake.

Grayson was in the middle of explaining what makes the 'special sauce' on his burger so special when the line cook yelled, "Order up!"

Maggie threw some napkins and plastic cutlery in the bag and handed it over. "You two have a good time!" She shouted as we walked out the door.

When we piled back into the vehicle with our food, he turned to me. "Evie and I dated back in high school," he allowed before twisting to see over his shoulder as he backed out of the small parking lot.

"Her daughter?" I asked, curious.

He laughed. "I'm sure she'd be flattered to hear you say that. No, Evie's her granddaughter."

I nodded along, slowly putting the pieces together as I thought to myself. We continued to drive farther out into the country, where green fields full of young corn and soybeans dominated the landscape. This was the backdrop of my youth, and seeing it again put an absent-minded smile on my face. Living in the city made me forget how much I loved the musty smell of fresh-turned soil and the feeling of a brisk breeze blowing through my hair as I drove down a country road with the windows down.

After several more minutes traversing the countryside, we began to slow, and I felt the small vibration and soft ticking of the undercarriage that meant we had transitioned to a gravel lane. It had been a week since the last rain shower and a white cloud of dust billowed out from underneath Grayson's SUV.

"I'm not gonna lie, this is a little sketchy." I laughed as I pushed open my door and joined him outside the vehicle with my milkshake in hand. He gave me a sly grin and disappeared from view.

"What, you don't trust me?" he half-shouted as he occupied himself at the open back hatch, shuffling items to and fro.

"I don't really trust anyone. It's an annoying character trait," I replied loudly, as I walked around exploring a little bit.

"Well, if it makes you feel any better, I don't find it annoying. I think, in this day and age, it pays to be smart. My Grandpa used to tell me, 'This world is full of people looking out for one person, and you can bet your ass that person isn't you,'" he impersonated in a deep, gruff voice as he shut the rear door, his arms full of picnic gear.

I lifted one side of my mouth in a smirk, "Well, unfortunately, I didn't have anyone telling me that. I had to learn the hard way." Birds chirped in the trees cheerily, their melodies intermingling in a harmonious chorus. I glanced above me where a male goldfinch hopped from branch to branch, flashing his brilliant yellow plumage and chasing a smaller, less flashy female through the foliage.

I pointed up as Grayson joined me, and he smiled. "I think he fancies her. What do you think?"

I laughed. "I think you may be right." I watched for another few moments, hearing a breeze begin to stir the dense canopy of leaves above us before I felt it tickle my skin. With my eyes lingering on the birds above, I slowly turned to follow Grayson through a line of brush. After struggling through the fabric-tugging, skin-scraping layer of shrubbery, we came to a small clearing that overlooked a relatively large stone quarry. "Wow, I never knew this was back here!"

"Family secret." He smiled and spread out the blanket he was carrying. We stood looking out over the expansive body of water, mesmerized as the sun began to sink toward the horizon. A thin haze in the air painted the sky a brilliant shade of pink. He lowered himself onto the blanket, and I joined him. "I used to come here quite a bit when I was younger."

"Ahh, so this is your own personal 'Lovers Lane' then," I

teased.

He let out a boisterous laugh. "I'll admit, I may have brought one or two girls here back in the day, but my Gramps put an end to that pretty quickly."

"What happened?" I asked, engrossed.

He chuckled. "Well, he was out in the field across the way…" He gestured back the way we had come. "One night when I was driving back here, he didn't recognize it was me and came to investigate who was trespassing. You can imagine his surprise when he found me and poor Jenny Devellan… entangled."

I burst into laughter. "How old were you?"

His shoulders shook with mirth. "Oh, probably seventeen. Anyway, that's the last time I brought somebody back here."

"I'm assuming you told him we were back here today? Wouldn't want any unexpected guests." I giggled.

"Yes, he's been well-informed." Our laughter echoed out across the water.

"Were you close to your grandparents growing up?" I asked as I took another sip of my strawberry shake.

He nodded as he finished chewing a bite of his burger. "I lived with them most of my life actually, me and Mom. Of course, we moved out when Mom remarried, but that didn't work out, soooo we moved right back in. This time we had Emma with us, though." He gave me a lopsided grin and swallowed a swig of his soda before continuing his thought. "I grew up right down the road, actually. My grandparents used to own a lot of this farmland, and when my grandpa decided to retire, they sold most of it—kept the farmhouse and some of the more desirable acreage. Good fishing." He gestured to the quarry, and I leaned over the edge to inspect. "So, I grew up working for my grandparents during the summer. Riding tractors by day and go-karts by night. There's actually a dirt track, not too far from here, and that's where I cut my teeth," he said with a reminiscent smile.

"How old were you when you started racing?"

He thought about it. "I was…geez…five, six? I honestly don't remember a time when I wasn't racing in some capacity or another."

"That's crazy. I don't think I was doing anything remotely productive at five." I let out a giggle.

"I think karting was the only thing that kept me focused at that age. I had a tendency to be a little hyperactive," he whispered, in a loud aside.

I snickered. "Okay, well, what five-year-old boy isn't a little hyperactive?"

"Fair point," he allowed, before taking another bite of his burger. "So, you're not a city girl, I take it?"

"No." I laughed. "I think I actually gave my mom a heart attack when I told her I was moving to Indianapolis."

"Really? I don't think Indy is too bad." The smell of French fries wafted over to me as he took them out of the bag, and I picked a couple from the package when he offered.

"No. It's a great city. I love it. I think it was just hard for her to accept I wanted to move at all—even if it was only an hour up the road."

"Sounds like you two are pretty close," Grayson observed.

"She's amazing…so strong and kind. Funny. Smart."

"She sounds great."

I nodded in agreement. "She's pretty awesome."

"What about your dad?" he asked quietly. "Are you close with him too?"

I was quiet for a moment, staring intently at a blade of grass near the edge of the blanket. I shook my head. "No…it's, um…a long story," I replied with a forced smile.

He took a swig of his milkshake, sensing he'd stepped in a proverbial pile of shit, and pinched his bottom lip with his front teeth, not sure how to continue.

I shifted my weight. "My parents were happily married for a long time. It's one of those things that was very consistent for me. That's what I wanted my future to be, you know?"

He nodded in understanding, but let me go on.

"Then one day, I came home to my mom sitting on the floor holding a piece of paper. Dad was gone—picked up and left. All of his stuff was gone, and he didn't even have the sheer human decency to tell us in person." I gritted my teeth, anger seeping into my veins as I recalled the memory.

Grayson sat across from me, his elbow resting on an angled knee. He studied me, surmising what I hadn't yet said, but I soldiered on. "He wasn't happy anymore—said he needed space to 'figure things out,' and apparently by 'space' he meant room to shack up with his twenty-four-year-old gold-digging girlfriend while he contemplated his younger years." I let out a shaky breath and forced the smile back on my face painfully. "That's the abridged version anyway."

"And you haven't talked to him since?" he asked, picking apart a blade of Switchgrass as he contemplated my story.

"No, not really. He came to my college graduation, but that was several years ago. After everything was said and done, he didn't have a good explanation for his behavior. He didn't want to try to work it out with Mom—wouldn't even admit he'd made a mistake." I shook my head, lost in thought for a moment. Fury was swirling deep down in the pit of my stomach, but I took a deep breath and plunged forward, taking a pull on my milkshake to try and squelch the flames. "And then pretty much every time I wanted to do anything with him, he would make up some excuse about why he couldn't hang out, and I got tired of the disappointment. I figured it was better to remove myself altogether and save myself the trouble."

He plucked another piece of grass out of its sheath and bent the shaft back and forth. "It doesn't bother you—not having a relationship with your father?" Grayson asked quietly, the comment wasn't aggressive or nosy, merely curious.

I shrugged. "I mean, it's not like he gave me a lot of choices. I'm not an angry person. I like to leave well enough alone. But every time he would cancel dinner or come up with some excuse to move our plans, it was like he was breaking open the same wound over and over again. I was tired of living my life like that."

He nodded along with me for a second, but I got the feeling he didn't completely agree.

"Haven't you ever been hurt so badly by something or someone that you just wanted to move past it because you felt like if you dwelled on it anymore it would swallow you whole?" I asked, desperate for him to understand my plight.

He nodded along with me for a second, but I got the feeling he didn't completely agree. Finally, he sighed, rolling his shoulders as if setting himself to some insurmountable task. "Well let's just say, if I could have one more chance to talk to *my* dad, I'd gladly take it." His voice was gentle and sad at the same time.

Instant guilt. *Damn it,* I thought to myself, and I knew he saw the emotions shift on my face. "I'm sorry, I didn't realize…"

"No, it's okay. I was really young when he died, so I don't remember him. But I think every kid who's lost a parent has a moment in their lives when they wish they could talk to their mom or dad—out of simple curiosity if nothing else." His mouth curled up in a halfhearted smile, and he shrugged.

"Yeah," I agreed absently, mentally bludgeoning myself for my thoughtless blunder. "I…I didn't realize that about your dad. What happened?" *More like, excuse me while I choke on my own foot.*

"I'm actually surprised you didn't know. You seem well-versed in racing trivia."

I tilted my head, confused.

He bent his blade of grass completely in half, staring at it for a second. "Rick Anderson." His gaze came back up to meet mine. "My dad is Rick Anderson."

My mouth popped open of its own accord. *How did I not know Grayson Miles was Rick Anderson's son?* Rick had been killed in a racing accident back in the '90s. A piece of debris had flown off another car during a crash ahead of him on the track and struck him, killing him instantly. "I had no idea," I murmured, feeling a blush creep up my neck slowly. *Damn fool…* I cursed myself, feeling ashamed at my "woe is me" sob story.

"I was only four when it happened." Grayson shifted and drew in on himself, draping his arms around his knees. "That's probably the toughest part. I have people all around me who knew him, worked with him, loved him, and they all have their stories, but all I have is what others choose to tell me. It's hard not really knowing where half of you comes from."

I swallowed hard, my mouth dry. Here I was with a father who was alive and well but might as well have been dead for all the effort I'd put into our relationship. I let out a slow breath and looked out at the sun, the last bit of it sinking below the horizon. "So, your last name…?"

"It's my mom's name. They weren't ever married."

"Scandalous," I teased and leaned into him playfully.

He chuckled. "If you only knew."

I could feel the mood lighten between us and was relieved. He leaned over and lit a citronella candle I didn't even know was there. A sense of gratitude rushed through me. I could only imagine a cloud of mosquitoes swarming around us in search of an easy meal.

He sighed. "Okay, change of subject, tell me something no one else knows about you. Something good."

"Oh geez." I thought for a moment. "Are we going with serious or light-hearted?" I asked, turning over potential subjects in my mind.

"How about one of each?"

"Okay…" I drifted off, thinking to myself. "Well, when I was little, my brother used to do all kinds of annoying things—you know, little brother stuff." Grayson smiled, and I continued. "And he used to have all of these little action figures on this shelf over his door. So, to get back at him for all of his devilish little deeds, I would sneak into his room while he was sleeping and rearrange all of them. And I kid you not, for three solid years from the time he was four until he was seven, I had him completely convinced they came alive at night—like Toy Story—and moved themselves," I giggled to myself and Grayson laughed too.

"Sounds like trickery runs in the family," he surmised with

a smile.

My head bobbed in assent as I thought about my 'something serious.' Grayson waited silently, sensing I needed a minute. I sighed. "The reason I don't talk to my dad anymore…it goes a little bit deeper than the affair and *how* he left." I pulled at an imaginary thread on the blanket we were sitting on. "I think it's resentment. If that makes sense?" I looked up at him, his expression was unreadable. "I mean, he took off with his girlfriend and got everything he wanted. And there I was, the only one left to comfort my mom and help keep things together. I had to put my dreams on hold to be responsible for a life that wasn't even mine. I don't know, maybe that's selfish," I murmured, continuing to pick at the blanket manically.

Grayson gently placed his hand on mine, stopping my nervous tick. "I don't think that's selfish. I think your dad was the selfish one." I dragged my eyes up to meet his, and he continued. "It makes more sense now, though…the way you feel about him. You were young. You wanted to be independent and just when you thought you were getting your freedom, he dumped all the responsibilities of an established adult on your shoulders and ran. That's not very fair."

I could feel tears clawing at my eyes and looked back down at his hand, now holding mine. *Don't cry. Don't cry.* I took a deep, shaky breath and looked back up. "Thanks." I cleared my throat. "Your turn."

* * *

At some point, as the night wore on, we ended up lying next to each other looking up at the clear night sky. In the darkness, his hand had inched over to lace his fingers through mine. I smiled to myself, butterflies pounding against the walls of my stomach as I continued to stare up at the dark sky. The cool spring air held little humidity tonight, which made for prime stargazing conditions. The atmosphere was so clear that, far removed from any light pollution as we were, even the most remote of celestial bodies could be seen from our perch atop the stone quarry cliffs. It was breathtaking. "Can I ask you something?" I asked quietly after several minutes of comfortable silence.

He turned his head to stare at me. "Of course."

"Is it hard? Being gone so much?" Neither one of us shifted, and he was quiet for a minute.

"Sometimes. I think it was harder moving to Phoenix. None of my family moved with me, so I imagine if I had family or a girlfriend there waiting for me all the time, it would be harder."

"So, no other girlfriends I need to be made aware of?" I kidded.

I could feel his body shake with silent laughter. "Honestly? I haven't had time for a serious relationship. I think that's the story for most racers my age. We work ourselves to the bone to make our careers. It's constant meetings with potential sponsors and investors, team owners and CEOs, and that's just the off-season."

"Sounds lonely," I murmured.

Another pensive silence followed by, "Yeah."

"So, what changed your mind?" I asked with a sigh, turning on my side to look at him.

"What do you mean?"

"What made you ask me out? I mean, you just explained to me—in detail—your reasons for staying single. That, and I didn't exactly make a great first impression." I giggled.

He flipped onto his side, propping his head up with one hand. "First of all, that was an amazing first impression."

"Yeah, if damsel in distress is what you're looking for." My blush heated the air between us.

He gave a breathy laugh. "Second," he continued, "I kind of put you out of my mind after we first met because I figured I'd never see you again. But then, I saw you at my sister's appointment, and I thought it was way too much of a coincidence. Obviously, somebody was trying to tell me something," he admitted, nearly repeating verbatim what Jess had said.

"I was so embarrassed that first day," I muttered, covering my face with my hands.

I felt him grab my hands and pull them away from my face, squeezing them, "Honestly, Alaina," —I admired the way my name sounded in his smooth voice— "Don't be. The look on your face…I could tell you were lost in something. I didn't step in and pull you out of the way because it was the right thing to do," he murmured, then paused.

"Then, why'd you do it?"

"Selfish reasons, I guess." He drifted off, toying with my hand as he thought. "I wanted to know you. I wanted to understand what had you so entranced you would let yourself be run over by a tire cart," he finished with a chuckle.

I smiled, more to myself than anything. "You're kind of deep, aren't you, Grayson Miles?"

He smiled shyly and rolled over. "Okay." He sighed, shoving off my playful jab, and went back to looking at the stars. I knew he felt me staring at him, but he didn't budge. The urge within me kept growing the longer he ignored me. It was like a thunderstorm bottled up inside me with lightning veining out from me in tendrils of attraction. Finally, the tension was too much for me to bear.

I leaned over him, our eyes making contact in a wash of moonlight. We held each other's gaze for a moment, an entire conversation happening without us saying a word. Then, suddenly, he rose up, and our lips connected. A jolt went through us both, making the hairs on my arms stand on end as though there was a static charge between us. His soft lips sucked gently on my lower lip, before forcing my mouth open wider in anticipation. My tongue grazed his lower lip in return, and I felt a second, small jolt as our tongues met. The self-assured exploration of his hands as they drifted behind me to rest on my lower back only added to the feeling of safety and comfort I felt in his presence, and slowly but surely, every wall I had built was dissolving into dust.

After a couple of minutes, he pulled away slightly with a small laugh.

"What's so funny?" I asked.

"Nothing." He shook his head.

I shoved his chest playfully. "Seriously, what?"

"You're kind of impatient, aren't you?" I could see a faint smile on his face, illuminated by the warm light of our citronella candle.

I rolled my eyes. "Well, I wouldn't say patience is one of my strong suits."

He leaned in and placed small kisses all the way across my face from my left ear to my lips and back again, before placing his mouth solidly over mine. The possession of my lips was all the more enjoyable for its unexpected nature, and I yielded to him like a hot knife through butter.

He pulled away, and I found myself following him as he broke the kiss. His generous mouth curved in a mischievous smile, and I could see him mentally noting I liked it when he took charge. "Sometimes…" Another kiss. "Patience…" Another kiss. "Can be a great thing," he whispered.

"Well, I'll bear that in mind," I said breathlessly as he kissed right under my jaw.

He chuckled again and pulled himself back, gazing at me. "I'd love for you to come to the track tomorrow."

I smiled. "You think I would miss it?" Qualifying was one of the best parts of the month of May, and I would rather die of heatstroke or drown in a torrential downpour than miss it.

He let out a breathy laugh. "No." His hand drifted lightly up and down my arm as he thought. "I don't mean just to come. I want you with *me*."

My heart jumped in my throat. "You think we're ready for that? To make this…official?"

He was silent for a little bit, and my stomach clenched with nerves. "I don't want you to do anything you aren't ready for," he said quietly. "The last thing I want is for us to rush this and have it not work out. But…I'm willing to take a leap if you are."

I let out a shaky breath. "Can I…think about it?"

"Of course," he replied, leaning in to kiss my forehead. "I think we should probably head back anyway. Not that it won't be worth it, but I'm going to be trash tomorrow if I don't get some sleep."

I smiled shyly, our most recent conversation fresh in my

mind. "I wouldn't want that."

He got up and offered his hand to help me, which I gladly accepted. I took one last look up at the beautiful night sky and helped gather the remnants of our night together, erasing all traces of us from the small clearing.

7

Personal Problems

I was lying in bed for the second time in a week, reliving my Grayson encounters. I couldn't help feeling the slightest bit guilty over how I had handled last night. I should have said yes immediately when he'd asked me to join him today. Instead, like an idiot, I'd asked for time. I didn't want time. I'd wanted to accept on the spot, but something stopped me. I rolled over and grabbed my phone off my nightstand: three missed phone calls, two voicemails, and ten unanswered texts. A couple were from Grayson. One was from my mom, but most were from Jessica. *Oh boy.*

A knock sounded at my door, quiet at first and then more persistent. With a sigh, I threw back my covers and headed out to the kitchen, Copper at my heels. It had been late when Grayson dropped me off the night before, and I hadn't even been able to shower before face-planting on the bed in exhaustion. Hell, I'd *barely* managed to exchange my dress for pajamas before my eyelids gained ten pounds, and I'd been unable to find the energy to keep them open—a situation that hadn't remedied itself in the past...*what time was it?* I glanced at the clock on the microwave: seven. *Jesus...no wonder I'm dragging*...I'd only been asleep for four hours. I needed coffee, stat. But the fist repeatedly slamming itself into my door made it clear answering my very unwelcome guest was my first priority; unless I wanted to apologize personally to each and every one of my neighbors. I raked a hand through my stringy hair which smelled faintly of citronella and Grayson's cologne and pulled open the door. Blinking rapidly, I tried to compute what was standing in front of me: Jess, disheveled and crying. She looked like she hadn't slept since I'd seen her last and my brow immediately furrowed in concern as I ushered her inside.

"I'm sorry to bother y-you..." she choked, fighting back hysterics. "I didn't w-w-want to wake you." She swallowed hard, fighting for all she was worth to keep it together.

"Hey, no...it's okay. You know you can bang on my door anytime." I murmured with a slight hint of humor. Her lips twitched, but she was clearly too engulfed in her own freak-out session to find anything funny. We sat on the couch, knee to knee, and I rubbed her back in a soothing fashion. "What happened? Are you okay?"

"Lainie..." Her voice squeaked in desperation. "I'm pregnant."

A wave of nausea washed over me like a tsunami, pieces of floating debris whacking me in the head, heart, and stomach in rapid succession. "Jess..." I had no words. My mind was reeling, but the primary question which all my thoughts swirled back to was, *'Who is the father?'*

"I'm freaking out Alaina," she whispered, breathlessly.

You should be! My inner voice shouted at her. Outwardly, I attempted to remain as calm as possible. I let out a breath

I didn't know I'd been holding. "Okay…umm…here's what we're going to do. I'm going to go to the drugstore and get a couple more tests, just to be sure it's not a false positive." I forgot the coffee altogether and paced back into the bedroom in search of clothes. Never in a million years did I think this would happen. I mean, yeah, Jessica liked to have her fun, but she was always *very* careful. I had no idea what she would want to do, but I supposed that was a conversation to be had at a later time when we knew what we were dealing with.

* * *

"How did this happen?" I asked her quietly as we sat on the bed an hour later, waiting for the results to come back on the two tests I'd purchased.

She took a shuddering breath and let it out. "Well, I hooked up with…this guy at a club in Dallas a couple of months ago, and…well, I was pretty drunk; we both were. I don't remember much—only that we woke up together the next morning. As far as I can figure, maybe we were too far gone to remember a condom?" She rubbed her eyes tiredly.

*So, basically, the worst possible time to be hooking up with a stranger—when you are too damn drunk to know your mouth from your…well…*I mentally shoved away any preachy thoughts. I knew this wasn't the time for a lecture, so I kept my mouth shut. At that moment, she needed her friend, so that's who I would be. "But you remembered using protection with every other guy you've been with lately?" I asked, my mouth dry. *This is a perfect example of why I don't gallivant.* I warred with myself. *Stop it, before something slips out you don't mean.*

She nodded. "Definitely. Plus, I got my birth control

refilled when I came back from Texas, so I've been using double contraceptive!" She was at a loss, trying to piece together how something like this could be happening.

The timer went off on my phone, and I let out a steadying breath.

"You do it. I can't." She shook her head, looking away, ashamed.

I sighed and picked up the first test, comparing it to the package, and then the other. "They're both positive," I murmured, looking up at her. She looked like she was going to pass out. "Jess."

"It's um…no, it's because, um…" She closed her eyes and got up off the bed, walking out into the kitchen, wobbling unsteadily.

"Because?" I asked, following her at a safe distance.

"I don't know, okay? I'm trying to get my head around it." She paced up and down the length of the kitchen, biting her thumbnail in agitation.

"What do you need?" I asked, watching her nervously. I wanted to be there to catch her if she fell, but also be far enough away that if she went the other direction and picked up the nearest knick-knack to use as a projectile, I wouldn't be in range.

"I don't even know what I'm doing. I just know I can't sit around and dwell on this all day. I need to keep busy." She continued to stalk back and forth.

"Yeah, I don't know that that's the best option," I murmured.

Her emerald eyes shot silent daggers at me for the briefest of moments before she resumed her pacing. *Okay, we should definitely stick to the "less is more" philosophy, Alaina.* "You should tell your mom."

The phrase "if looks could kill" came to mind. "Right, because I'm not stressed enough as it is. Let's throw my psychotic, judgmental, pain-in-the-ass mother into the mix!"

I sighed. "She's your mom, Jess."

She rubbed her eyes tiredly. "Look, I know you have the perfect relationship with your mother. And if the roles were reversed, you probably would have called her first, but *I* called *you*. You know my relationship with my mom sucks."

I did know. Her saying it made me feel terrible for even mentioning it. I nodded. "You're right. I'm sorry." I walked closer to her. "What do you need? Anything, you name it."

Her eyes were glassy with unshed tears. She was full of panic, and I wanted to help, but I didn't have the slightest clue how. "I need to get out of here. Can you get me out of here?" Her breathing was a step away from hyperventilation, and I needed to act quickly.

I nodded and swallowed hard. I could, actually. My heart thundered in my chest. *Just call him, you big ninny.* "Um…can you give me a minute? I need to…make a call."

"Yeah, sure," she muttered.

I gave a strained smile and walked back into the bedroom to give Grayson a call. It was almost 9:00 a.m.—qualifying started in a couple of hours. I was hoping it wasn't too late.

The phone rang a couple of times, and then a woman answered. "Grayson's phone!"

"Umm…is Grayson there?" I asked, taken aback.

"He's actually in an interview right now. Is this Alaina?"

"Um, yeah," I said with a small laugh. "Is this Cami?"

"The one and only." She laughed back. "Are you coming up for quals? I have your pass in the trailer. I can meet you at the ticket office with a parking pass if you need one!"

"Um, yeah, that's actually what I need to talk to Grayson about."

"Oh, I see. Um.. give me a sec." I could hear her moving now, and then off to the side, "It's Alaina."

"Here he is."

"Oh, okay," I said with a smile.

"I was starting to think you ghosted me," he answered playfully. In all of the madness, I'd forgotten the missed call and text message waiting for my reply.

"No." I literally could not help the smile that lit up my face when I heard his voice. *Man, I have it bad.* "Sorry, I've kind of got a situation I've been dealing with this morning," I murmured delicately. "I was just, um…I was thinking about last night and…"

"Can I get a minute?" I heard him mutter off to the side. "Listen, if it's too fast we can forget I asked," he said back into the phone with a strained laugh.

"No!" I shouted, probably a little louder than was absolutely necessary. I lowered my voice. "No, it's not that. I'd love to join you today. I just…" I sighed. "Jess got some news this morning that's not really the best, and I don't want to leave her alone," I admitted honestly, glancing at my friend who was milling around the living room aimlessly.

"Oh." I heard the background noise on his end diminish like a door had closed. "Is she okay?"

"I think so, or at least, she will be. Time's probably the best remedy in this situation." *Yeah, like nine months of time.*

"You should bring her then!" he offered.

The weight lifted. "Really? You don't mind?" I asked quietly.

"No, not at all. That way you can keep an eye on her. I'll

be busy a lot of the time anyway, so it's better for you to have company. I'll make sure Cami gets two hard cards and a parking pass set up."

I smiled, not sure what else to say. "Thank you."

"It's no big deal. I'm glad you decided to come."

"Me too. Will I see you before qualifying?" I asked, looking at the clock. It was mid-morning by now, and practice started in thirty minutes.

"Maybe. Come to the pits when you get here. We go out twenty-fifth."

"Well, if I don't see you before, good luck."

"Thanks. See you soon!"

"Bye." I clicked off my phone and felt a nervous twinge in my stomach. I'd never been on this side of a race before. Usually, I sat in the grandstands and watched the cars go around like every other fan in attendance. Occasionally, I and a couple of friends put small wagers on the outcome, but I'd never known someone involved. I'd never worried for their safety before and I wasn't sure I liked it.

These drivers were racing around a superspeedway at over two hundred thirty miles per hour, and if one thing went wrong, they were hurtled into a retaining wall and subjected to 130g, maybe more. It was violent and dangerous, and I couldn't allow myself to think about it. I was just going to have to swallow the nerves and deal with it. A lot of people in my life had bigger problems to deal with at the moment.

8

World Class Competitor

The smell of sunscreen and perspiration hit me as a security guard ushered us past a wall of people bordering the lane to the pits. Sweat trickled down my back as the sun beat down, and the unpleasant twinge of ultraviolet rays on my pale skin made my neck and shoulders tingle. I had the strangest feeling as I paraded past the sea of onlookers, feeling the repetitive clack of my credentials smacking my chest as we walked. I guess I was going to have to get used to it. From behind my sunglasses, I stared up at the massive grandstands and all the people in them. The cat would be out of the bag after today. There would be no guessing at my identity on random blogs. My face would be out there for the world to see as I stood by Grayson's side. My stomach did another flip-flop.

"Are you okay?" Jess asked as my pace slowed.

I looked into her green eyes peering over her sunglasses at me. "Yeah." I nodded and took a deep breath. "Just preparing myself. All of those bloggers that were posting about some stranger will have a real person to poke fun at after today."

"I thought you over-analyzed every angle of every possible scenario? How are you just now thinking about this?" she asked incredulously.

I sighed. "I don't know," I moaned. "Of course I thought about it, but…" I sighed. "All I can think about when I'm with him is…him."

"Oh, brother." She made a quiet gagging noise under her breath, and I could practically feel the eye roll she gave me behind her knock-off designer sunglasses. Jess didn't do commitment. The mere idea of it gave her the heebie-jeebies. All she wanted for me was a good lay. Of course, things may have changed slightly in the past twenty-four hours, her finding herself with child by some random bar troll and all. At least, I *hoped* the situation had rearranged her priorities.

I tried to tune out her incredulous babble and my pessimistic inner monologue by naming all the drivers as we passed their cars. *Noah London, Roberto Aguilera, James MaCauley, Alexandra Sabia.*

"All right race fans, we've got five minutes! Five minutes until we get the green flag and *qualifying* for the Indianapolis 500 gets underway!" the announcer broadcasted to the huge arena. Cheers erupted from the fans in the stands, and I found myself smiling. Despite my current situation, I was still a race fan at heart. I loved this day, and I wasn't going to let anyone or anything change that. Jess, on the other hand, was more of the Snake Pit variety. In the past, she had come to the race for the massive rave in the infield rather than the on-track entertainment. Translation: she had no clue what was going on around us.

"This is Jack's car." I pointed to the bright orange machine we were making our way toward. It really was a cool livery—probably my favorite in the field.

As if on cue we heard, "Hey, New Girl" by way of greeting from the thick crowd of engineers, crew members, drivers, and their families. I looked up to see Jack's short but well-toned figure making his way toward us.

We both smiled, and I looked over at Jess, who was blushing slightly. She was definitely attracted to him. "Hey Jack," I greeted. "Are you ready for this?"

"As ready as you ever are for qualifying at Indy," he said with a smirk.

I laughed. "Have you seen Grayson?"

"Yeah, he's around here somewhere…probably down by his car," he motioned lazily down the line as he gave Jess an admiring once-over. Jack was *definitely* more of a ladies' man than Grayson, but he seemed to have a soft spot for my best friend.

"Cool, thanks! Good luck today!" I said over my shoulder as I dragged Jess with me toward the end of the line. Jack was also pretty far back in the group of thirty-seven cars; he would qualify nineteenth. The entry field would only hold thirty-three teams, and today—the first day of qualifying—the fastest thirty teams would be locked into the field for this year's running of the Indianapolis 500. Every team would have an unlimited amount of opportunities to individually go out on the track and run the fastest ten miles they could muster. When the ceremonial gun went off, the slowest seven teams would be left on the outside looking in. They would have to come back and duke it out all over again tomorrow for one of the final three spots in the race, on what we racing enthusiasts affectionately referred to as Bump Day.

As we approached Grayson's car, I immediately caught sight of him standing off to the side with Jenny Kite, one of the pit reporters for the Indianapolis Motor Speedway broadcast team. He glanced away from her for a minute and caught my eye. I gave him a small wave, and he smiled before returning to his conversation.

I saw Jenny move to stand beside Grayson, and then the cameraman motioned. They were live. I looked up at one of the huge TVs looming over the main straightaway.

"Hey guys, it's Jenny coming to you from the Lithgow-Hunt Racing camp with Grayson Miles. Grayson, you've been pretty quick in practice this week. What were you able to find with the car that some teams haven't quite been able to tap into?"

He smiled. "Well if I told you, it wouldn't be a secret, would it?" He laughed, and she reciprocated. "No, I mean, the number 19 car rolled off the truck quick this week. We've been fortunate to have some great weather. I'm super happy with our setup, and we're ready to roll."

"Now you've been on pole here at the Speedway before, what's that experience like?"

"You know, there's no other place on earth where you can go and see three hundred thousand people crammed into one place all at the same time and that, in itself, is a special thing to experience. But to see it from P1 on race day—it's amazing."

"You think you can do it again this year?" she asked slyly.

"We're going to try," he answered earnestly with a smile.

"All right, fans, you heard him. He's got a fast car, and he's going for his second pole this weekend."

Grayson waved at the camera, and the crowd exploded in

cheers as the announcer took over the PA once more. "Good luck out there today, Grayson. All right fans, Race Control is saying one minute until the track goes green. One minute."

When I looked back down from the TV, I could see a couple of people eyeing me as Grayson made his way over to us. I tried to ignore them. "Hey," Grayson greeted me warmly as he wrapped his arms around my waist. "How are you?"

"I'm good," I said with a big smile. "Super excited to be here."

"Good. I was hoping you would be." He leaned down and softly kissed my cheek. "Did you get your crisis taken care of?" he whispered in my ear.

I sighed, my stomach dropping a little bit. For a moment at least, I'd convinced myself this morning hadn't happened.

"Um…kind of. I'll tell you about it later."

We were so involved with our conversation, I'd forgotten Jess was standing behind me until she cleared her throat. I turned to her. "Sorry."

"No, no, by all means, continue being all cute with each other. I'm gonna go, um…use the ladies' room." It was then I noticed she was looking a little clammy.

I stepped out of Grayson's arms and over to my friend. "Are you okay?" I whispered.

"Yeah, I'm just not feeling well," she murmured.

I nodded in understanding. "Do you need to go home? I can take you."

"No, no. It's okay. I'll be back."

I nodded, my brow furrowed in concern as I watched her go.

"Is she okay?" Grayson asked, his concern matching my own as he studied her retreating figure.

"I'm not sure," I admitted, watching her disappear into the crowd.

"You can go with her if you need to. I don't mind."

"No, it's fine. She'll be back." I turned back around, tucking my hair behind my ear. "Plus, I'm excited to be here with you. I mean, I'd be here anyway, but I'm glad you invited me," I elaborated with a smile.

"I keep forgetting you're a gearhead."

My shoulders lifted and fell. "What can I say? It's in the blood."

He gave a quiet chuckle. "It's kind of nice to be able to talk about it with someone and have them understand."

"I think that sentiment might be a little one-sided. I'd like to see you try to put together your sister's centerpieces though."

His eyes widened. "Yeah, I said it was nice to have you to *talk* to, I didn't suggest you jump in the car and try to qualify it." We both laughed heartily.

"Well, don't we look all cozy over here," Jack teased as he walked up beside us, slinging an arm over my shoulders.

"Why do you always have to make a nuisance of yourself?" Grayson asked with a roll of his eyes.

"Gray, you know I love to give you a hard time."

"Yeah, I know." Grayson's tone made it perfectly clear he wasn't fond of the little brother role he'd been given. "Don't you have better things to do?"

"Nah, I could stand here all day if it meant getting to enjoy how much I embarrass you." He turned to me. "Speaking of friends, where's Jessica?"

"Restroom."

"Gotcha," Jack acknowledged. "Well, I wanted to give her this. Would you mind?" He handed me a slip of paper. *His phone number? Shit.*

My heart sank. "Um, sure." I took the little piece of paper and stuck it in my pocket. "I thought you were seeing somebody?"

"Nah. Nothing serious anyway. It's hard finding someone worth the effort."

"Commitment issues are pretty standard in this industry." Grayson laughed.

"You guys really have that much trouble with women?"

They both shrugged. "I think people make the assumption since we drive fast cars, we have a fast and loose lifestyle too, which isn't true. Everyone likes to have someone to come home to after a long week," Grayson continued quietly.

I felt the weight of that statement. Copper was good company and all, but I honestly wanted nothing more than to cuddle up next to someone and tell them how my day was—good or bad. It made me sad to think people made assumptions like that. They were just people after all. I could see getting that kind of impression from Jack, but Grayson was so normal—a quiet guy who'd had girl problems in the past and was a little gun shy.

The cars rolled forward in line again as another car accelerated onto the track. Grayson was only seven cars away from making his first qualifying run, and I could see him starting to shift from foot to foot, nervous energy radiating off him in waves as Jack began the ritual of donning his racing gear: radio earpieces, balaclava, helmet, HANS device. I took his hand and squeezed it comfortingly. He caught my eye and gave me a small smile, squeezing my hand back.

Jess rejoined us with an inconvenienced huff as Jack accelerated onto the track. "I thought you went home," I remarked as I stared up at the big screen across from us, watching Jack smoothly take Turn Three into the short chute for his warm-up lap.

"Well, I thought about it after vomiting for the third time in twenty minutes but decided against it," she allowed. "Jack's out on the track?" she asked, nodding to the screen.

"Yep, let's see what he can do," I murmured.

Grayson had jumped up on the timing stand with his team, watching the numbers as they came in. It was all Greek to me, but he saw something and glanced up at the broadcast monitor as his teammate took the green flag. It wasn't long before I saw what Grayson had seen in the data. A wiggle in the middle of Turn Two sent him drifting up the track, fighting the wheel. He tapped the wall with his right rear and lifted off the gas, decelerating as he came out of the banked turn. It hadn't been a big enough impact to cause any major damage, but by the angle of the steering wheel, it looked like he had a bent toe link. The team owner, Bruce Lithgow, slammed a hand down on the counter in frustration, and Grayson removed his headset, hopping back over the wall.

I looked up at him grimly, and he shook his head. "Trimmed the damn thing too much…he's been dealing with a loose car all week," he grumbled under his breath.

"There's still time…" I comforted, running my hand up his arm. "I'm sure they'll get it fixed and get him back out there."

He nodded. "You're right. I know…" His own nerves were getting to him a little bit and slowly, bit by bit, he drew in on himself so that by the time it was his turn to buckle in, he was completely silent. Grayson slid into his car without a word and waited, pushing all thoughts out of his head except for the job at hand as they rolled him closer and closer to the front of the line. Finally, the engine fired, and I could hear him clutching the car in anticipation of the go-ahead. With the squeal of rubber on pavement, he accelerated out of the narrow lane and up onto the nine-degree banking. Five laps. I just had to hold my breath for five laps. *One warm-up, four fliers, and then it would be over. For today, at least. If he was lucky.*

"The first time is always the worst," Jack said with a smile, eyeing my rigid posture, hands steepled under my chin.

"Really?" I asked, trying to distract myself from the bundle of nerves rolling through my stomach like an earthquake.

"Liar," Cami muttered, nudging him with her elbow. "They're all equally painful."

I rolled my eyes. *Great.* I turned toward Turn Four just in time to see him round the corner and head down the front stretch. The sound of his engine screamed by, and my eyes went back to the video board. *Four more.* "Is it any less nerve-racking for you in the car?" I asked, trying to keep my mind off it as we walked up toward the Pagoda, waiting for him to come back in. I clutched Jess's hand for moral support, but I felt her start to protest at my bone-crushing grip. Forcefully, I pried my fingers loose and gritted my teeth instead.

Jack's crew had taken his car back to the garage, rushing to fix any damage from their driver's brush with the wall, but Jack remained out in the pits, cheering on his friend. He shrugged. "I feel like it's just as nerve-racking inside the car, but you don't have time to think about it."

That was fair. Grayson's car flashed by again, and I looked up to the grandstands. Everyone was on their feet cheering. I looked up at the screen.

"Grayson Miles has set a new single-lap track record!

That's 237.849!" The announcer shouted Grayson's average lap speed excitedly, and the stands erupted with cheers. "Let's see if he can keep it up as he rockets down the backstretch, into Turn Three, now the short chute, Turn Four, and he's turning for home. Another fast lap! That brings his average to 237.701. Two more laps, can he hang on...?" Silence filled the stadium as we listened to his car disappear down the back straight and then get louder as it came even closer. 237.349. *Oh my God, he's going to do it...* I gave a strangled squeal of excitement, my stomach doing somersaults. No one had broken the track record in decades, not since Arie Luyendyk set the record back in the mid-90s.

Everyone on pit road had stopped what they were doing. All eyes were on the video boards, watching closely to see if we were going to witness history. Grayson entered the front stretch out of the final turn, and we all simultaneously moved our eyes to the track, the checkered flag waving.

"Did he do it?" the announcer asked. Silence. "Yes, he did! Ladies and gentlemen, we have a new track record!" And the place went *absolutely bonkers*. "The official time for Grayson Miles driving the number 19 LHR car is an average of 237.309. That is good enough for the top of the pylon and a place at the top of the record books for the young Indiana native."

The smile on Jack's face said it all, shock, joy, and a little bit of envy. Cami was jumping up and down; his team was hugging each other and smacking each other's backs in congratulations, and I just stood there taking it all in. *This is freaking awesome.* My whole life I'd been watching from the other side of the track, and now, here I was experiencing history from a unique and personal vantage point. The next car exited the pits, driving up on the track to start their run, but all eyes were on Grayson's car as it came to a stop in front of the Pagoda on the yard of bricks.

The HANS device was snapped free, the helmet pulled off, and the excitement in his eyes was enough for me to know the crew had radioed him the news. He stood up in his seat and pumped his fist in the air to a scream of cheers from the fans. He slipped his hat over his sweaty hair as Jack squeezed his way through the cameras to give his best friend a huge hug. He said something in his ear, and Grayson laughed, looking over at me. *Great...Did I even want to know?* I was smiling so hard I felt like my cheeks were going to crack.

He stepped forward and grabbed my hand, pulling me through the cameras to give me a hug and a quick kiss. "Oh my god!" he shouted excitedly, still shaking from the adrenaline coursing through his veins, and when I turned around, I felt like the eyes of the world were on me. Grayson had just let the aforementioned cat out of the bag. It wasn't a quick glimpse of me standing by the car during pre-race coverage, this was a kiss on national television after one of the biggest achievements of his career. *Great.* At the same time, I was a little too excited to give a damn.

Jenny Kite wedged herself between us and the cameras. "Congratulations!" she shouted amid the mayhem, and then she got the signal in her headset that we were live. "We are live with Grayson Miles at the Indianapolis Motor Speedway where he has just broken the track record for both a single lap speed and a four-lap average. How are you feeling at this moment?"

He put a hand to the back of his head, in awe. "This is surreal. You know, when I was little, I would literally race around my driveway playing Indy 500. It was a dream of mine to set my own records—to make my own mark on this series—and I'm standing here today, and…oh my God." He looked around, still a little breathless with the physical exertion he'd just put forth. "This is awesome!" He hugged me against him, and I felt like the most important person in the world. He was genuinely glad to have me there beside him, and there couldn't have been a bigger compliment than that.

Jenny took the microphone back. "There's been a lot of speculation over the past few weeks about whether you had what it takes to become an Indy 500 champion because of your road and street course success. Does this make the kind of statement you were hoping for?"

"Absolutely. I mean, it's one thing to *know* you're competitive, but it is completely different to show it. I hope people are looking at us and saying, 'man, I think we underestimated them,' because we're here to win."

I stood there, admiring how handsome he looked in his pure joy. Jenny glanced at me and then spoke into the microphone. "And how has this experience been for you?"

Oh my god...oh god... Panic engulfed me, but I spoke anyway. "It's been great. I grew up in Indiana, and the Indy 500 is very special to me. This is amazing. I'm so proud of him!" I squeezed him around the waist and smiled.

"Going for pole tomorrow?" Jenny asked Grayson.

"Well, who knows what the rest of the session is going to bring. We still have to make the fast nine, but yeah, that's the goal."

"Okay fans, he can hear you, let him know how exciting that was. We have a new track record!"

The stands erupted as the current car on track raced by, for a moment drowning them out. We both waved at the camera, and they cut away. "Nice to meet you, by the way. I'm Jenny!" Jenny introduced herself, shaking my hand.

"Alaina!" I said loudly over the din.

"Sorry to throw you in the limelight, I know people are a little curious about you. Grayson hasn't had a girl on his arm in a while," she teased. She glanced over at him to see if he was listening, but he was busy talking to his crew as they got ready to pose for their team picture. "Full disclosure, he's a good one. Don't let him go." She winked at me and walked away with the cameraman, moving further down pit road in search of her next interview.

9

Down to Brass Tacks

ater that night, I sat curled up on Jess's couch with her while she munched on a bowl of Chex Mix as we talked. Copper and her Border Collie, Layla, lounged at our feet.

"So, I called the doctor, and I have an appointment for Friday. I guess I have to wait until then." Jess informed me. She popped a pretzel in her mouth, her morning sickness finally having subsided.

"What did your mom say?" I asked, taking a sip of my Pepsi.

She shrugged. "I mean, she was shocked. I don't think anybody hopes this'll happen, but she kind of just…took a deep breath and asked how I was doing. She gave me the whole speech about how much my life is going to change and what I'm going to have to give up. She asked me if I'd thought about giving the baby up for adoption."

I studied her carefully. She seemed indifferent to the idea. "And what are your feelings on that?"

Another shrug. "I don't know. I haven't thought about it. I mean, I've literally known I'm pregnant for less than twenty-four hours, and suddenly everyone is expecting me to know what I want to do?" She was quiet for a second. "I wish everyone would give me some time to get my head around the *idea* of being a mom." She pulled her legs up underneath her. "I mean, yeah, I always pictured myself with kids later on—down the road. So that part of it isn't so unbelievable. And when you think about it, I am almost twenty-five, so there's no doubt I *could* do it. I'm financially stable enough that it wouldn't be impossible to manage. But it is a huge lifestyle change, you know? There are a lot of things I would have to give up, and deep down, I don't know if I'm ready for…all of that."

I lifted one side of my mouth in a sympathetic half-smile and reached over to squeeze her knee. "I'm sorry."

She looked up at me with tears in her eyes. "I'm scared." Her voice was unsteady, and I could see the terror in her eyes as she thought about the prospect of impending motherhood.

I could sympathize, but there was no way for me to fully understand what she was going through. "I know…I would be, too." I put the bowl of food on the coffee table and scooted across the couch to wrap my arms around her.

"Yeah, well at least your baby daddy would be a hot, young, rich racing driver. Mine is…" she drifted off, her complexion not reflecting a good train of thought.

After a beat of awkward silence, she switched the subject. "So, let's talk about your TV debut…"

I rolled my eyes. "It was spur-of-the-moment. I didn't even know it was going to happen. She kind of threw a mic in my face and hoped like hell I had a good answer." I laughed.

"Well, can I just say you and Grayson look *ah-mazing* together?" She scrolled through her phone and flipped it around so I could see some of the pictures floating around the internet of us standing together on pit road.

We did look pretty adorable, and I was having a good hair day, so I looked more like a glamorous movie star than a cat who had recently survived a flash flood. "Do I want to know what's surfacing on the blogosphere?" I asked curiously, knowing if anybody had combed all the latest gossip sites, it would be Jess.

"Mostly positive feedback. I think people are better now that they have a face and a name. Last week you were some girl with her back to the camera attached to one of the most eligible bachelors in America." I felt some relief. *Good.* The last thing I needed was some jealous internet troll bashing me and airing all of my dirty laundry to the public. Not that I had that much dirty laundry. I kept my clothes fairly clean of scandal.

I stood up to go refill my soda, and Jess repositioned on the couch to watch me go. "So, am I allowed to ask a question?"

Oh boy. I turned back to her. "Depends..." I knew better than to give her free rein.

"Is he good in bed?"

I almost dropped the bottle of soda and, in the process, managed to spray it all over myself. It's not that I hadn't thought about it. I mean Grayson was quite literally a sex symbol, but we had only been dating a week. "*Jessica!*"

"*What?* I'm your best friend, not your mom. I can ask these things!" she sat up on her knees looking over the back of the couch. "I mean..." She made a face that wasn't entirely appropriate when speaking of someone else's significant other. "His hands and the way he holds himself. He's quiet, but you can tell he's got some fire in him. Always so sure of himself." She bit her bottom lip as she thought.

"Yeah…Easy, tiger. He's mine, not yours." I patted at the soda stains on my shirt and wiped the counter with the towel I'd found. Jess was a very physically driven individual. I'd accepted that as part of her charm.

"Come on! Tell me, tell me, tell me!" she demanded, curiosity eating at her.

I nearly inhaled the soda I'd just sipped. "You think we've slept together?" I choked.

She lost a little wind out of her sails. "Haven't you?"

I coughed, trying to dislodge the carbonation from my windpipe. "No!" I denied, offended. "Even if we had, I don't think I'd be making that anyone's business but mine and Grayson's." My cheeks were flaming. *Oh my God…*

She deflated. "Sorry, I thought…" She shook her head. "Nevermind."

"You thought what?" Now I was the curious one. What had she seen that I hadn't?

"The way you guys are around each other…I don't know. It's hard to describe. It's like you're connected? If that makes sense. He steps closer, you grab his hand. You step closer, he wraps his arm around you. It's this sort of…intimacy a lot of couples only get after…" She was lost in her mental replay, and then she looked up at me. "But I mean, if you guys can have that without…physical relations…well, good for you." She gave me a sly smile.

I hadn't thought about any of what she was talking about. Grayson and I seemed like a natural fit and I'd left it at that. But I thought about my previous relationships and realized she was right. Intimacy in my past relationships had been forced compared to what I had now.

"Do you think it could get serious?" she asked. "Cause I hate to point out the obvious, but he's only here for another week, and then he's off to his next destination."

"I know." I wouldn't say I'd been in denial about the whole thing. I'd been perfectly aware of the reality of the situation, I just wished it wasn't the case. "We haven't even talked about it. I don't know if this is something he wants to pursue…or whether he's just having fun." Based on the conversations I'd had with him, I didn't think that was the case, but one could never be too sure. "Do you think it could work? Being apart all the time?" I almost whispered.

"If you want it to, I think it can, but I feel like there will need to be sacrifices on both sides. It depends on whether you guys are willing to make those sacrifices."

10

Sometimes It Just Works

"So, you're meeting him and riding over together?" My mom asked, nosy as ever, as I continued to get ready. Grayson was due to arrive any minute, and the last thing I wanted was to be running late. He had a million other things to do today but somehow insisted on picking me up since Jess wasn't coming with me.

"No, he's picking me up. He's going to be here any minute, and I'm totally running late," I said breathlessly as I threw all my stuff in my bag and pulled clothes out of my closet. I was worried, now that there were cameras recording my every move, I wouldn't look fashion-forward enough. My Instagram had blown up overnight, and I was panicking. I needed to step it up if I had any hope of survival.

"Honey, seriously, you should take a breather. You haven't taken time for yourself all week. And now with what Jess is going through…I understand, but I'm worried." Her voice was coated with motherly concern, and the last thing I wanted was for her to worry.

"Mom, it's *Pole Day*. I'd be going whether I was dating a

driver or not. It's fine. I'm doing it for me just as much as I'm doing it for him."

She sighed, appeased. "You never gave me any details about your date."

My phone buzzed with a text. Grayson was pulling into my complex. I huffed a sigh, "Mom, he's here. Can I call you tonight?"

"I suppose. Be safe. I love you."

"Love you too," I said quickly, kissing into the phone and grabbing my bag as I dashed out the door. I could see Grayson laughing through the front windshield of his SUV as I came running out of my building.

I jumped in and breathlessly sighed. "Okay, let's go."

"We're not in *that* much of a hurry." He chuckled as he took in my frazzled appearance.

"It's freaking Pole Day. The last thing you should be doing is making side trips to pick up your girlfriend, who is perfectly capable of driving herself to the track."

He laughed even harder. "So, you're my girlfriend now?"

"Well, I don't know what else you want to call a girl you kissed on national television," I grumbled.

His smile broadened. "I'm joking. Man, you're on edge this morning."

I let out a breath. "Sorry, I'm just nervous. It's like I'm experiencing all of this for the first time."

"Well, you kind of are," he suggested, grabbing my hand and holding it as we drove farther into the city. I glanced over at the sure way he held the wheel and admired the toned line of his arms and chest. I hadn't seen a lot of him outside of his fire suit, but I was appreciating it now. I had traumatic flashbacks to my conversation with Jess the night before and couldn't help the blush that crept up my neck into my cheeks.

"What?" Grayson asked, picking up on my flushed face.

I shook my head with a shy smile. "Just thinking."

"About?"

"Nothing," I insisted.

He rolled his eyes heavenward. "You know, you're pretty much the worst liar I've ever met."

"Just showering me with compliments ..." I muttered before insisting, "It's nothing—something Jess said to me last night."

"And why do I get the feeling this 'something' was about me?" he asked, not taking his eyes off the road.

"It...I ..." I stuttered over what I wanted to say and ended up looking out the window with my teeth firmly embedded in my bottom lip. "Jess asks a lot of questions, and they aren't always...appropriate," I allowed. "She thinks she's entitled to more information than she is."

He cocked an eyebrow and glanced at me.

"She thought our relationship was a bit more...intimate than it is ..." I allowed, picking at my nail beds furiously and avoiding his gaze.

"Oh." He cleared his throat and tightened his grip on the steering wheel infinitesimally. "Is that...a problem?"

My eyes flew up to him. "*No.* No. It's not. Which is exactly what I told her when she asked—along with the fact that it wasn't any of her business." My pulse was pounding in my ears, and my palms were slick with sweat. I covertly wiped them on my thighs and took a deep breath, trying to get my racing heart under control.

He stifled a quiet laugh and covered it with a cough. "So, I guess now would be a bad time to tell you my mom and sister are going to be here today?"

My head whipped over to stare at him. "Way to bury the lead!"

"Well, I didn't think you would mind. You've already met them," he said defensively, but always with that damn cute grin of his. He made it so hard to be mad at him.

"Grayson," I groaned. Yeah, I'd met them, but as his sister's wedding services provider, not as his girlfriend. "That's completely different! Did you even tell them we were dating?"

He let out a hard laugh. "Well, I did get a bit of a perturbed text from Emma after the broadcast last night, but she's *fine*. She was upset I didn't tell her. And by upset, I mean, put out she wasn't the first one to know something about my life." He rolled his eyes again, this time in a perfect representation of brotherly resentment.

"What about your mom?" I asked quietly. I'd only met his mother once, but she seemed like a very strong, independent, charismatic individual. Her son was a lot like her in that respect, but I could also tell that underneath, she was also *very* protective of her children. Lord help anyone who messed with her babies.

Over the past week, I'd come to know so much more about her. She'd raised Grayson by herself after the death of his father and then had gone on to marry Emma's dad. Unfortunately, things hadn't worked out, and they'd divorced three years later. I couldn't imagine raising two kids on my own, it physically put the fear of God in me just thinking about it. And trust me, I'd thought about it a lot since Jess had announced her impromptu pregnancy.

He smiled quietly to himself, and I wondered what that

was supposed to mean, but I waited. "Mom's happy I found someone. She's never been vocal about it, but I think she was worried I'd given up on the idea of relationships altogether after my last girlfriend." *There was that elusive ex again.*

"Okay, I have to ask. What *happened* with this chick?"

He was quiet, and I knew this time it wasn't a good kind of quiet. "Well, we met through mutual friends and dated for about a year. She was…social. You know, the life of the party type."

*So pretty much the opposite of me…*I thought to myself as I shifted my gaze to look out the window at the passing traffic.

"About six months into our relationship, I was named *Most Eligible Bachelor in Sports*." He kind of choked out that last part—his shy nature coming through.

Trying to put a time frame to this story, I flipped back through my mental catalog of pop culture. I vaguely re-membered something about him being named *Most Eligible Bachelor in Sports*, but if memory served, that had been almost four years ago. I attempted to keep the shock off my face and tuned back to what he was saying.

"—offered a lot of money to spill the intimate details of our relationship, and she took it."

I jerked upright, floored, and looked over at him—eyes wide with surprise. "Are you *freaking* kidding me? What a bitch!"

He pressed his lips together, suppressing a smile at my reaction. "Yeah, so, needless to say, I broke up with her, and we haven't spoken since. But the damage was already done. She got her five minutes of fame, and I got years' worth of unwanted media attention."

"That sucks…I'm sorry." I squeezed his hand in sympathy.

No wonder he'd been single for so long. I wouldn't want to deal with that crap either.

"I didn't want that to happen to you," he murmured, squeezing my hand back. "I wanted you to have a good experience with the press, and I know, I kind of failed… epically. I hope you know Cami and I are doing everything we can to keep everyone at bay."

"So, that kiss yesterday…" I decided now would be the best time to bring it up. "What was that exactly?"

He looked over at me with a devious grin. "That was just because I wanted to. I *am* sorry I pulled you in like that though. I should have asked first."

I smiled. Well, at least, he was honest. "You're lucky I'm quick on my feet," I muttered with a light laugh. Crawfordsville Road passed by outside the window like the Royal Mall leading up to Buckingham Palace. This time of year, the festivities never ended, and the giant black lamp posts were adorned with checkered flags, like a giant arrow on a billboard reading "This Way" toward the track. I caught sight of the Speedway looming in the distance, a massive coliseum of steel and concrete. We came alongside it, and I gazed up in wonder at the twelve-story monolith built to house over three hundred thousand spectators on race day. The Indy 500 was the largest single-day sporting event in the world, and this facility didn't bear that title lightly.

Our car dipped down into a small tunnel as we passed under the track and into the infield. To our right, we passed the museum full of cars and other racing memorabilia that chronicled the Speedway's long and storied past. "I never get tired of this place…there's something so special about it." I sighed, a wistful note to my voice.

He glanced over as he drove past the security blockade, flashing his credentials, and continued back toward the RV lot the drivers called home. "You know, you mentioned something about that the day we met. I was curious, but I didn't want to pry."

I glanced over at him with a smile. "So, you're wondering why I'm such a nerd?"

He looked up at the roof of the car as he put it in park. "Well, I prefer the word *enthusiast*. I have a reputation to protect."

My hand flew across the space between us, and I smacked him playfully on the shoulder, the car filling with my quiet giggle. "Shut up…My dad used to bring me to the track all the time when I was little. It was kind of our thing." My throat tightened with emotion, but I powered through. "He worked a lot to give us a good life, and I didn't get to spend a lot of time with him because of it, but I always knew when the month of May rolled around, we would get to go to the track." Tears welled in my eyes as I thought about that part of my past. I missed it badly. I took a deep breath and let it out, wiping the tears away quickly.

Grayson reached over and squeezed my thigh. His mere presence was a balm to my frayed nerves.

With my emotions reeled back in, I shook my head and continued. "So, yeah, this time of year, I always think about that. It brings back a lot of good memories, but it makes me sad at the same time."

"Alaina," he said after a moment of silence. "I don't ever want to make you feel like I'm sticking my nose where it doesn't belong, and I know how much of a sore subject your dad is with you, but I can see how much you miss him." He raised his hand up off my leg to wipe away a few tears that had treacherously escaped my eyes. "I have this feeling after all this time a part of you thinks it's too late. Even if you wanted to reach out, so much time has passed, there's no way you could get back to the way things used to be, but he's your dad."

Normally, I got defensive about this kind of stuff. I didn't like to talk about him, and I certainly didn't like unsolicited opinions on the subject. Part of that stemmed from regret. Things had ended horribly between him and my mom. Knowing how much he'd hurt her was a huge catalyst to my own hard feelings. I didn't think I could ever truly forgive him for that. But Grayson was coming from a different place than most. He'd lost his dad at a young age, and he knew what it was like to not know his father—which was heartbreaking to think about. It was hard to be defensive or angry about what he was saying, given where he was coming from.

"You know, I only have one memory of my dad…and it's sitting on his shoulders in Turn Two on the viewing mounds watching the cars go around the track. Sometimes, I wonder if he knew…"

I looked over at him. He seemed at peace, lost in his own happy memory. "If he knew what?" I asked quietly, not wanting to pull him from cloud nine.

"A lot of things. I wonder if he knew who I'd grow up to be."

I smiled, "I'm sure he could only hope you would turn out to be half the man you are." I reached over and rubbed his cheek with my thumb before leaning over to give him a tender little kiss. We rested our foreheads against each other and sat there for a moment, reveling in the closeness we shared. There was a sharp tap on the window, and I looked over to see Jack.

Grayson closed his eyes and sighed. "I love him, but sometimes I really hate him."

I giggled and leaned over to wave at him. Grayson opened the door. "Could you have worse timing?" But the look on his face wasn't the usual playful Jack grin.

"Do you ever answer your phone? Emergency team meeting. Now. We gotta go."

Grayson furrowed his brow. "About what?"

"No idea. Bruce just said we needed to get our asses over to the trailer ASAP."

Grayson turned back to face me, reluctant.

"Go, go. I'll just hang out at the motorhome until you get back," I insisted with a nod.

"Okay, I'll be back as soon as I can." He glanced back at me one last time before hopping in Jack's golf cart and disappearing around the next RV.

I let out an internal sigh of relief. My battery was running low, and I was in desperate need of a catnap. I climbed into Grayson's bus and made myself comfortable on the couch.

The next thing I knew, I felt a gentle hand on my shoulder. I jumped out of my slumber, startled. "It's okay. It's me," Grayson murmured with a smile. "Glad to see you making yourself at home."

"Well, I didn't exactly get a lot of sleep last night," I informed him around a yawn. "I was at Jess's into the wee hours of the morning."

"I remember you said she's going through some stuff..." The comment was matter-of-fact, but his eyes held a deep-seated curiosity, his brows scrunched together in concern.

I pressed my lips together and stared at him. "If I tell you,

you can't breathe a word of it to anyone, especially Jack."

He tilted his head, now more curious than ever. "Of course."

"She's pregnant."

His eyes widened, "But I thought she wasn't seeing any-one?"

I raised my eyebrows. "She's not."

"Oh." He hissed with an intake of breath. "Got it. Does she know the guy? Has she told him?"

I shrugged, deflated. "She says it was a drunken hookup while she was on a girls' trip a couple of months ago. She wasn't overflowing with information on it—to be honest, it seemed like she didn't remember a lot about the evening…" I drifted off in thought, analyzing everything about my short conversation with her. Something seemed off, but I couldn't tell *what* was off. "So, what was the big meeting about?" I asked, throwing the mic to him.

He let out a sigh. "Well, let's say, it's never anything good when they call an emergency meeting."

"Uh oh…" I muttered, scooting over so he could sit beside me. "Am I allowed to know what the bad news is?" I asked quietly.

He gave a hard laugh and slid out of his crouched position to join me. "I mean, it's nothing that won't be all over the news tomorrow. The primary sponsor for my car elected not to renew their contract with us after the conclusion of the season. Sponsoring an IndyCar team isn't exactly at the top of the priority list when you're struggling to make ends meet." He kept his voice low, but I could hear the pain that came with uncertainty. He continued with the second piece of bad news. "And to add insult to injury, Jack's primary sponsor is on the fence."

"Oh no." This was *really* bad news. "So, what are you going to do?"

He shrugged, "What *can* I do? I'm going to go out and do my job and hope everyone in the front office knows how to do theirs. It's kind of above my paygrade at this point."

"But they're under contract for the rest of this season, right? They've already cut the check?"

He let out another hard laugh. "Yeah, I just don't know what it means for my ride next year. Without sponsorship, I'm effectively a free agent." This was the ugly and harsh reality of racing. If the sponsorship wasn't there, neither was the ride in a lot of cases. Grayson was an extremely talented driver and brought money to the table on his own with personal sponsors. However, he was also endorsed by his manufacturer which cut his future prospects in half. It was highly unlikely a team would switch manufacturers to acquire a driver. It wasn't unheard of, but it didn't happen very often.

I sighed. "I'm sorry…that is…" I found myself at a loss for words.

"Yeah," he rubbed his eyes tiredly and sighed. "I'm not going to lie, it's pretty much the last thing I wanted to hear going into media week."

I reached out and squeezed his knee. It did suck. LHR was a competitive team for a lot of reasons. They had great drivers, engineers, and crew members. If news got out they were in financial trouble, it would be like a frenzy of sharks with blood in the water. Instead of promoting "The Greatest Spectacle in Racing," media week would be turned into an excuse to hound Grayson and Jack about their futures at a time when they needed to be focused on the task at hand.

"Anyway, Tuesday morning Jack and I are heading up to New York for a couple days."

"That's cool. Sounds like fun!" I said, trying to put a little more pep in the conversation.

He laughed. "Well, unfortunately, we don't get much time to sightsee. I should be back sometime Thursday night."

This was good. I hadn't been keeping up with the business over the last week, and I needed to get back on track, or I wasn't going to make my deadlines. I'm sure I had a bazillion emails to catch up on. "Well, I'll miss you."

He looked over at me with his beautiful warm eyes reminding me of hot fudge. "I think you'll be just fine." He leaned in to give me another one of those chill-inducing kisses right under my jaw. My eyes closed of their own volition as he worked his way closer to my mouth. My hands drifted upward over his chest, across his shoulders, and around his neck. A small, sensual moan escaped my lips, and I dug my nails in a little bit. His mouth broke into a smile as he continued to kiss me.

"You are driving me crazy." I groaned and moved my head about an inch to the left so our lips brushed, lighting a fire in my chest. Without any further thought, our physical need for each other pulled us together like magnets. Our lips molded around each other, our tongues dancing the steamiest Argentine Tango I'd ever been privy to. If his skilled lips and tongue were any indication of what else he was good at, I was in trouble. I ran my hands up into his short hair and across his chest…pretty much everywhere. My hands and his hands—all over, so much of us in contact it was hard to decipher where I ended and he began.

He laid me back on the couch and positioned himself on

top of me, breaking away to kiss down my neck and across the exposed skin on my midriff. His hot breath tickled the skin above my navel and sent gooseflesh rippling across my body in waves of delight.

Distantly, I heard the door to his motorhome open, and then a gasp, "Oh God! Sorry! Sorry." And then the door shut again with a slam.

Grayson looked back at the door and burst into laughter—body racking fits of giggling. I couldn't help but giggle along even though I was mortified at the entire situation.

After we had collected ourselves and straightened up our disheveled clothing, Grayson opened the door to reveal Emma, her hand covering her eyes. "Is everyone decent?"

"Yes, Em, we're all buttoned up and ready to take on the world."

She removed her hand from her eyes and smiled at me. "Twenty-four hours ago, I didn't even know you two were a thing, and now I find you making out on the sofa in his trailer?"

"Yeah, sorry about that," I murmured.

"How long has this been going on anyway?" she asked, redirecting her accusing stare to her big brother.

"I don't know, like two weeks, maybe?"

"Roughly," I agreed. "Not long!"

"Well, if what I just saw is any indication, it looks a lot more serious than a two-week relationship."

Grayson looked me over briefly with something in his eyes I couldn't quite read. "Well, Em, sometimes, it just works."

* * *

Grayson's schedule leading up to a race was insane. After the team meeting, he had a half-hour break. Then, he had to meet and have a quick talk with some employees from his primary sponsor. He met with another group from his engine manufacturer at the garages around noon, and when that was done, he got exactly twenty minutes to scarf down lunch before a guest spot on a radio broadcast at 1:00 p.m. The radio interview was followed by a driver appearance at the karting track in the infield to support the local children's hospital. Then, he had to go in to do an interview for a sequence on the qualifying broadcast later today. It's a good thing he had Cami to keep him organized because I'm pretty sure I would have major anxiety if I were him.

"Grayson, we're late. We need to go," Cami shouted as she banged on the trailer door. I lounged in one of the chairs outside with his sister and his mom. We had elected to sit this one out.

He opened the door, tucking his team shirt in his dress pants. "My God! Can't a guy get a minute to use the bathroom?" he asked, a little frustrated.

"Sorry, but you know how the producers can get."

"Yeah, I know. Sorry." He walked over and kissed his mom and sister on the cheek before leaning in and giving me a quick peck on the lips. "I'll be back in a few. If you see Jack, tell him he owes me one," he shouted from the golf cart as they drove off. Jack was originally supposed to do the interview, but somehow Grayson had been conned into it instead. To be honest, I wasn't sure I wanted all the details on that one.

Emma shook her head and took a sip of her water. "That boy never stops."

"I told him he needs to slow down. They make these days

way too schedule intensive." His mother sighed. "I wish he had some time to enjoy himself."

"What do you think, Alaina?" Emma asked, bringing me into the conversation.

"Oh, umm…I don't know," I said with a nervous laugh. *Of course, she had to ask me about the one thing I didn't agree with their mom about.*

"No, she's right. You've spent more time with him than we have recently," his mom, Lillian, added. "It must bother you he's never around."

"Well," I started, looking down at my drink and then back up at them. "I think he's enjoying the experience. He seems to embrace his responsibilities, and he's never once complained about it. Being busy is the price these drivers pay to have a full-time ride, and he gets that, so do I. I mean …" I paused, thinking about my next words carefully. "I didn't go into this thinking we would be together every waking moment. I knew there would be times when we were separated because of his schedule or mine, and yes, there are a lot of conversations to be had about that, but no, it doesn't really bother me."

I looked from Emma's face to Lillian's, worried I'd said something wrong. My heart started to sink. If his mom and sister didn't approve of me, I wasn't sure how far Grayson would push the issue. I knew he was a man who, by trade, had to be confident in his choices, but I also knew how much his family meant to him.

Emma's face broke into a sly smile. So did Lillian's and her gaze roamed over me in appraisal.

"I like her." Emma offered matter-of-factly to her mother.

"Me too, but I already had a good feeling about this one."

I tilted my head and gave a nervous laugh. "I'm sorry...what just happened?"

"I hope you understand. We're a little protective of Gray. We wanted to make sure you weren't another girl chasing her fifteen minutes of fame. He deserves better than that," Emma explained.

"I couldn't agree more," I said, shaking my head emphatically.

"There's not a harder job in the world than being the other half of a racing couple. It's long days and even longer nights. There will be times when he comes home and nothing went right that day. It puts a strain on the relationship. But if you can get through the bad days, it makes the wins and championships that much sweeter," Lillian admitted. As she spoke, I hung onto every word. She was the only person I knew who had been in my shoes, and I wasn't taking her advice for granted.

"Is it worth it?" I asked after studying her for a moment of comfortable quiet.

She gave me a soft smile. "Those years were some of the toughest of my life, but out of those tough times I got my son, and I wouldn't give him up for anything," she murmured and shifted in her seat, tears shining in her eyes. "Every time that boy straps into a race car, I hold my breath and say a prayer—especially after what happened to Rick. But, how could I deny him what he loves because of my own selfish fears?"

Emma reached over and put her arm around her mom.

"I'm fine," she murmured, patting her daughter's hand. "I suppose I should amend my statement...being the mom of a racing driver might be equally as hard as being his significant other," she said with a laugh.

I laughed too. "I'm going to get more to drink. I'll be right back."

I was pulling a bottle of water out of the refrigerator when I heard my phone going off. *Jessica.* "Hey, girl," I answered as I twisted the cap off my bottle. "What's going on?"

"I hate being pregnant," she moaned. "I haven't been out of bed all day. My head is spinning. Lainie, I feel awful."

"I'm sorry," I murmured. "Do you need me to come get Copper?" I asked as I rejoined Emma and Lillian outside.

"No, he's been a good buddy. He and Layla have been chilling on the bed with me all morning watching Golden Girls reruns."

I smiled. "Yeah, he's a pretty good lounging partner. If you need me to come take him off your hands though, just say the word."

"Okay. How's your day going?" she asked quietly.

"Pretty slow now. We're waiting for Grayson to get back from the media center, and then we're going to head out to the pits for qualifying."

"That sounds—" her voice cut off as I heard her run to the bathroom and vomit on the other end. *Oh, Lord have mercy.* I cringed at the sound effects, but waited, patiently. After a few minutes, she picked the phone back up. "Sorry."

"No, it's okay. I'm sure the morning sickness will go away soon."

"I hope so." She groaned as I heard her sink back into her bed.

"I'm planning on being in the office early tomorrow morning to get the altar decorations done for the Murphys, and then I'm going to bring my laptop to the track tomorrow so I can answer some emails."

"Good. I think we're up to like one hundred in the inbox.".

I rolled my eyes. *Great.* "Hey Jess, I'm gonna go, but I'll see you tonight. You'll be there when I pick up Cops?"

"Honey, I wish I felt like being anywhere else." She moped. "Seven more months…"

"Ugh, don't remind me."

"Love you," I said sweetly and clicked off the phone.

When I turned around, I froze, shards of ice shearing my stomach. Lillian and Emma were still sitting there, but unfortunately, others had joined them. Grayson…with Jack. The look on Jack's face…Let's just say flabbergasted was an understatement.

"Were you going to tell me Jessica's pregnant or were you going to wait a couple of months and hope I didn't notice?" Jack asked, anger coloring his tone despite the very large part of him still reeling with shock.

"Jack, maybe you should let her explain." Grayson stilled, placing a grip of fair warning on his best friend's shoulder.

Jack rolled out from underneath his friend's touch, glaring at him.

"Jack, I know you would have wanted to know, but it's not my place," I tried to reason with him.

He rolled his eyes, cutting me off. "Right."

"Jack!" I called after him as he stalked off.

I moved to follow him, but Grayson stopped me. "I'll go… It's probably best if I talk to him."

That suited me fine. I wasn't up for getting yelled at again. Protecting Jess was my priority, not soothing Jack's bruised ego. I'd do it again in a heartbeat, and he needed to understand that. Besides, it's not like he was entitled to that information. It's not like they were dating, and if Jessica didn't feel the need to tell him, I sure as hell wasn't going to be the one to break the news. I lowered myself into the chair beside Emma, scratching my temple and feeling a bit at a loss.

"How far along is she?" Emma asked quietly. We could faintly hear Jack and Grayson talking, but couldn't make out what they were saying.

I shrugged. "A couple of months, we think. She just found out yesterday. She's got a doctor's appointment scheduled for Friday, but…" I shrugged again. "I feel bad…I knew Jack was interested in her, but she hasn't even told the father yet. How was I supposed to justify telling a complete stranger?"

Emma put a hand on mine. "It's okay, Alaina. He'll understand. Jack's…fiery. He gets upset easily, but he also cools off quickly. Give him a minute to process. He'll be fine."

I nodded, feeling a little better after talking it out. We sat in companionable silence for a few more minutes, and right about the time I was set on going to look for the duo, they came back around the corner of the RV.

Grayson sighed. "My friend here would like to apologize for his rash behavior."

Jack gave me a half-smile before looking down at his feet and kicking an idle pebble. "Sorry, Alaina. I should have heard you out before I jumped to conclusions."

I smiled back at him. "It's okay. I would have told you eventually, but Jess didn't even tell her mom until last night, and it's a stressful situation right now. I didn't think it was my place to say anything."

Jack sighed. "Well, hopefully, she'll forgive you for telling me, however unintentionally."

"Well, she'll have to get over it," I said as I waved off his concern. "It's not like she's going to be able to avoid the issue forever."

Jack gave me a small smile, but I could tell he was still bummed by the situation. His eyes didn't sparkle like they normally did, and his shoulders were slightly slumped. Maybe he had more of a thing for Jess than I'd initially thought, but before I could get caught up in all the "what-ifs" of the situation, I let out a sigh and turned into Grayson, letting him wrap his arms around me as a shield against all of my troubles for a few more minutes.

11

Burning the Midnight Oil

I t was almost dark outside—much later than I should be at the shop, but I had to get all of this stuff done at some point. It had been a long day at the track, and the fog of fatigue was taking its toll. A stroke of bad luck had resulted in a flat tire on Grayson's last lap of qualifying, landing him in sixth place on the starting grid for next week's race. Nothing to turn his nose up at, but it definitely wasn't what they had hoped for after the morning's news and yesterday's performance.

I sorted another email into the calendar folder. At least twenty messages, so far, were brides inquiring about a meeting to discuss venues, color palettes, and flowers, and I doubted I would have time for half of the requests. Once I had successfully sorted through the inquiries, I pulled my calendar out of my bag and tried to make it work. I already had race weekends marked on my schedule. I sighed. *There aren't enough hours in the day.* By the time I was done arranging sit-downs, my calendar was completely booked through the end of July. Weekends were a nonstarter; those

117

were set aside for events. But during the week, I didn't have a free moment from open to close.

"We might need to hire some help," I muttered to Copper as I sat back in my chair. His ears perked up when he noticed I was talking to him, but then he laid back down, disinterested when he realized I was offering neither food nor physical gratification. "I feel you, Buddy."

We both jumped as someone tapped on the front window, and a grin split my face as I caught sight of my mother standing on the sidewalk looking in. I twisted the deadbolt on the front door and pushed the door open for her, pulling it closed and locking it back behind her. We hugged each other tightly, and I felt some of the tension leave my body. I normally talked to her at least once a day and we hadn't had a conversation of any substance for at least a week. "What are you doing here?" I asked, still surprised to have her in front of me.

"I was on my way home, and I saw the light on. So, I figured I'd stop and see what you were up to."

"Oh, you know…trying to make my whole crazy schedule work." I sighed and joined her where she was sitting on the couch in our waiting area. "I didn't realize how hectic this was going to get. May's a busy time for me anyway, but now adding in all the hours I've been logging at the track, it's getting almost impossible."

"Is there anything I can do to help?" she asked, looking around. I sat up straighter. Having inherited my creative side from my mom, she was probably the only person I could trust to work with me on this kind of stuff.

"I've got an entire altar series to put together, and I've got an order that just came in I need to verify and organize," I suggested, motioning toward the back of the building.

She stood up with me. "Put me to work."

I took her to the craft room where I had laid out all the pieces of this bizarre-looking puzzle. Somehow, I had to take red roses, deep gold sunflowers, and orange Gerbera daisies and make them look romantic.

"Well, this is…"

"A mess? It's a mess," I admitted as we walked in.

"Whose idea was it to use these colors?" she asked as she sorted through the mounds of flowers.

"The bride's, of course. Never argue with them," I offered. "I gave her books, and this is what she picked. She wanted bright and cheery."

"Well, it's definitely bright," she offered. "So, what are we doing?"

I pulled out pictures of the altar. "We need to make rectangular pieces to put together as a set. We're going to place the pieces next to each other so they run the whole length of the altar. She mentioned wanting some sort of decorated trellis as well, but I'm still waiting to hear back on that."

"And when is this wedding?"

"Two weeks," I said under my breath. "I'm not exactly happy with the timing, but we'll make it work for what this chick is paying me."

She laughed, and we got busy. I loved working with my mom. It's like we were perfectly in sync. She would hand me the scissors before I could ask, and I'd hand her the floral tape in return.

"So," she started, "I think we need to talk about this young man you're seeing."

I steeled myself. I knew she meant well and I shouldn't get defensive, but I found myself extremely protective of my new relationship. The last thing I wanted was my mother ripping it to shreds and planting seeds of doubt. I took a deep breath and tilted my head, keeping my eyes trained on my work. "Oh?"

"You never told me about your date. Does that mean it didn't go well?" The sharp snap of wire stems being clipped filled the silence between us.

I smiled. "No! It was…" A blush crept up the back of my neck as I thought about our make-out session on the banks of the stone quarry. "…amazing."

"Wow, that good, huh?" she asked with a smile and a raised brow. "What did you do?"

"We got takeout at this cute little diner, and then he took me out to an old stone quarry. We picnicked while we watched the sun set, and then we stargazed and talked. It was nice."

She simpered. "Sounds romantic." Her voice was almost a whisper.

"It was. He's amazing, Mom. I really think you'll like him."

"What's your favorite thing about him?" she asked. She somehow managed to portray interest while never letting her eyes leave her work.

I had to think about that one. Grayson Miles was not short on good qualities. "He's…warm and sensitive and funny. I don't know. He's just…*him*, and he makes no apologies for that. It's kind of refreshing."

"Did you talk about anything big or was it mainly 'get to know you' stuff?"

I wasn't sure what she was getting at, but I knew there was some conversational strategy involved.

I was quiet. "Umm…yeah, we talked about some personal stuff."

"Like?" She began stuffing flowers into the square blocks of floral foam, intent on her work, but not fooling her audience in the slightest.

I sighed and rolled my eyes. "Mom…"

"I'm just trying to make conversation," she cried innocently.

Riiight. "Well, I told him about Dad and that whole situation."

"And how did he take it?"

I sighed and stopped arranging flowers to look at her. "I don't know. I feel like he took it pretty well, but you know, he had some interesting points as well."

"Well, I don't know how many ways there are to take that whole situation," she muttered passive-aggressively, half under her breath. It didn't take much more than the mention of my father to get her hackles up.

"Mom…" I groaned. She looked at me in contempt, already judging Grayson based on one flippant comment about him not siding with her in the travesty that was my parents' divorce. "It's not the divorce he disagreed with. It's the fact that I haven't talked to dad since."

"Well, don't let him pressure you into something you aren't ready for Lainie. He knows nothing about what you're going through."

My eyes shot to her, the edges of my vision going red. "Considering he lost his dad when he was four years old, I think he probably knows more about my feelings than you do."

She was quiet, and I could tell she was regretting her earlier words. Finally, she sighed. "That's awful. I didn't…" she was quiet for a moment while we continued to work. "What happened?"

"Racing accident," I murmured, never lifting my eyes.

"So, his dad was a driver too?"

I nodded. "A good one. It was a pretty devastating loss."

"That's terrible. I hate the idea of such a young child losing a parent." I looked over and saw tears in her eyes.

"He doesn't really remember him, but sometimes..." I drifted off as I placed and removed flowers to get the right combination.

"Sometimes?" my mother prompted.

The breath left my lungs in an exasperated huff. "Sometimes, I think that would be worse...not remembering. Not all of my memories of Dad are good ones, but at least I know where I come from."

"You've never talked about it before," she murmured as she stared pensively at the wire cutters in her hand.

"About Dad?" I asked, thinking back. *I must have mentioned it at some point.* But I couldn't conjure up any memories of us discussing him—at least not in a way that was related to me. "I guess I figured it was hard enough for you without bringing my own baggage into it," I muttered, shifting to grab more flowers out of the box.

"I feel bad," she whispered shakily. "I was so absorbed in my own feelings I never realized how much you were struggling...and in what way."

I looked up at her, putting my hands on hers. "It's not your fault."

"But it is." She gave me a sad smile. "Part of being a mother is putting your children first, and I didn't do that."

I shrugged, going back to the task at hand. "The truth is, I wasn't sure how I felt about it either for a long time. I knew he wasn't putting much effort into our relationship, and at the end of the day, it was easier for me to walk away."

"And how do you feel about it now—looking back?"

I snipped a few more stems and paired them with wire. "Now, I think I could have done more…maybe?" I sighed. "I don't know…all I do know is, like it or not, I still have a father walking this earth, and it's a damn shame our relationship is in such a sorry state, when—" I thought of Grayson, and the look on his face remembering what little he knew of his dad. "When all some people have is what other people choose to share."

I felt her hand grab and squeeze mine. "I want you to know, when, and if, you do choose to mend fences, I'm not going to hold that against you. He's your father, Lainie. I'm going to have to accept that." Her gray eyes held mine in steady reassurance, and I nodded. We worked in companionable silence for the better part of an hour after that, and as we packaged the leftover flowers, she decided to speak her final piece. "Grayson sounds great. I just want to know you aren't giving up all of your time to be with him. I want to make sure you still have your things, and he still has his."

I smiled. "We've been dating for two weeks. I don't think that's been an issue."

She stopped what she was doing. "Alaina." She sighed, trying to find the right words. "I don't want to see you make the same mistakes I did. When I started dating your father, it was like I lost a part of myself in the process. I became whatever *he* needed me to be instead of being what I needed for myself."

I stopped too. "I know you're worried, but you don't need

to be. Grayson—" I tried to find the right words to describe it. "He's not like that. He wants me to be me. It just so happens that a big part of who I am is a big part of who he is too."

A small smile came across her face. "I see you spending so much time with him, and then I see you here working until all hours of the night, I'm wondering if you've had any time to relax."

"I'll get time to relax this week," I offered. "He's heading off to New York for media week, and I'll be here. No distractions. No track action." My voice held a melancholy note that wasn't lost on her.

She giggled. "You're ridiculous."

"But this is what I'm saying. It's who I am just as much as who he is. I'm not losing anything by being with him," I continued as I shoved the packed box back up on its shelf.

Mom knew I wasn't finished though, so she let me think for a minute before I continued. "I actually feel like I've found something really amazing. It was always the one thing Dad and I had in common. I know you tried to fill that void as best you could," I assured her, "but it's great to enjoy racing again with someone else who loves it as much, if not more than, I do."

She was quiet and nodded. I knew she was worried about me. How could she not be? She was my mom. "And he treats you right?"

"He's very sweet," I assured her.

"Well, from what I've seen on TV, he seems like a very genuine young man. Very honest."

"He is, and he also respects that there are things I'm not ready to share with him yet. He never pushes me about it. There's a level of respect he has for me that..." I was quiet, but she knew what I had been about to say. *That Dad never had for you.*

She nodded. "Well, I'm happy for you, Lainie. I hope it works out."

"Thanks, Mom." *So do I.*

She waited for me to shut off all the lights and walked me to my car. "So, how's Jessica doing?"

I sighed. "I'm not sure. She was pretty sick Saturday at the track. Her doctor's appointment is Friday. I think I'm going to try to go with her."

"She's still holding out on you about who the father is?" Mom asked quietly.

I rolled my eyes. "Yes, the whole situation is bizarre. I'm not sure if she's holding out on me or if she genuinely doesn't know." I shrugged. "I'm sure I'll get the whole story eventually."

She looked up. "I know it's odd for you, but if she's keeping things from you because this man doesn't know yet, then I think that's the right call—as much as you may not like it." I attempted to interrupt her, but she persisted, despite my protests. "It wouldn't be fair—to whomever he is—for him to be the last to know." She stopped at her car, watching me walk to mine in the next spot over.

I nodded. I knew she was right, but that didn't mean I was happy about it. "I'll bear that in mind," I answered. "Thanks for helping me tonight."

She smiled. "No problem. Be careful driving home," she offered and got into her car, ready to head home herself.

* * *

I was crawling into my bed after a long, long, *long* day when I heard my phone buzz. I had half a mind to ignore it and deal with it tomorrow. I'd been up for nearly twenty hours, and my brain was lagging so far behind, it took me a minute to even get my eyelids to open on command. I just…couldn't right now. Whoever and whatever it was could wait until I was in more of a mental state to process things.

Then it went off again.

I sighed and rolled over to see who had the nerve to bother me at this hour.

**Hey Bug, I know it's been a while,
but I'm going to be at the track
tomorrow, and I want to see if
you would like to meet up.
Just let me know.**

My stomach jumped in my throat, and I felt like I was going to vomit. Copper, sensing a weird vibe coming from me, jumped up on the bed and laid his head in my lap. In soft rhythmic swipes, I combed his silky ears with my fingers, measuring my breathing to the length of each stroke. *Why would he want to meet now? After all this time, what could possibly make him decide to contact me?* The curiosity was killing me, but as I sat and stewed about it, things started to make sense. I made my debut on the arm of my new boyfriend yesterday. Anger started simmering as the reality of the situation became more and more apparent.

Really? It had taken seeing me next to my race-car-driver-boyfriend during qualifications to motivate him? *Rude.*

Finally, with fury as my rocket fuel, I rolled back over and picked up my phone.

I'll see what I can do.

It was time I talked to my father anyway.

12

The Girl I Used to Be

"I mean, the balls on this guy!" I shouted to Jess as I paced back and forth in the front office.

She sat at her desk with her chin resting on her palms watching me stalk back and forth like a caged tiger. "Girl, you're giving me anxiety. If you don't want to see him, then don't go!" she said, exasperated.

I sighed. "It's just the idea of it all! 'Hey Alaina, I know I haven't talked to you in three years, but I saw you have a new boyfriend. Would you mind introducing me?'"

"He said that?" she asked incredulously, sitting bolt upright in outrage.

"No, but it was implied!" I cried, mildly embarrassed at my insinuation, but trying to cover it with indignation.

"Through a text?"

I widened my eyes in a look that made it perfectly clear that's what I was talking about and she needed to catch up.

"So, let me get this straight. You *inferred* your dad got in touch with you after three years, not because he misses his only daughter, but because you think he wants to meet your boyfriend?"

"Well, when you say it like that…" I muttered, twirling an ink pen on my desk and refusing to make eye contact with my befuddled business partner.

"Yeah, when I say it like that, it sounds like you're freakin' nuts," she muttered back.

"Well, what am I supposed to think after all this time? It's not as if it's 'proper decorum' to reach out after such a long 'estrangement.'" I crinkled my fingers in exasperated air quotes around my politically correct phrasing. *I'm not crazy damn it! He* has *to want something.*

"Okay, your use of air quotes is *not* working for me." She interrupted my rant. "Alaina." Standing slowly to keep the nausea at bay, she leveled me with a gaze on par with her impending motherhood. "You know I support you no matter what. You're my best friend. You could literally tell me you killed someone, and the only question I would ask is how you wanted to get rid of the body. But girl, you worry too much. He's your *dad*. He probably misses you like crazy!"

I felt tears pricking at my eyes. She sounded like Grayson. *Damn it!* I just hated to admit my stubbornness had cost us three years. "This is so shitty!" I complained as I sank into my chair.

"Yeah, it is, but you know what? At least he's willing to try and work things out."

I sighed. "Yeah." We were both quiet for a little while, and I could tell she was trying to gauge whether she should push the issue or not. "There's something off about the whole situation. Why now?" I wondered aloud, feeling a sense of confusion about the whole thing.

"I guess that's something only he can answer." As if that was the final word on the matter, she plopped back down into her office chair.

"You know, these little sage pieces of advice are really starting to get on my nerves." I growled.

"Well, get over it, sister. I'm practicing my Mom speeches." She cackled and rolled back over to her desk.

I got up and walked back into the craft room, looking at the altarpieces my mom and I had put together last night. Somehow, they had ended up looking pretty fantastic. I couldn't believe it. *Maybe I need to hire mom.*

"Alaina, your phone's ringing!" Jess shouted from the next room. My heart sped nervously. It was probably my dad, and I couldn't deal with him right now. There were so many other things for me to worry about.

"Who is it?" I asked.

"Grayson," she said from the doorway, offering my phone to me.

I took it and tapped the screen. "If it isn't my new favorite driver..." I said making a face at Jess, who mock-gagged herself.

"You mean I haven't always been your favorite?" He feigned surprise. "Who was it? And if you say Jack, you can find a new boyfriend."

"Well, I was always partial to Rick Mears myself..."

"Good pick," he approved.

"Anyway, what's up?" I asked, getting back to the matter at hand.

"I was just letting you know I'm heading out to the track. I didn't know what time you were planning on coming this way."

"Well, I'm at the shop right now, but I was planning to be up there around noon." I continued to fold napkins as we spoke. "Ummm…I kind of wanted to talk to you about something…" I began, not really sure how to broach the subject of my father.

"What's up?" he asked. I could hear the sounds of the garage in the background and knew he was probably going through some last-minute stuff before practice.

"Umm…" I sighed. *Why are words so hard?* I thought as I squeezed my eyes shut.

"Alaina," he chastised softly. "What's going on?"

"My dad texted me last night…he wants to meet up today… at the track."

Grayson was quiet for a moment. "Isn't that a good thing?"

"I wish I knew," I answered with a hard laugh.

"Maybe you should give him a chance. Things could be different now; you never know. Three years is a long time."

"Don't I know it," I said under my breath as I played with some of the rose petals I had scattered on the craft table.

"If you don't want to, I understand. You don't have to do it for my sake."

"Yeah." Another whisper, this one shaky. This was bringing up all kinds of bad memories, and I refused to cry about it. *Refused.*

"Are you okay?" he asked. I heard it get quieter on his end as he shut a door. I could picture him perfectly, standing in his RV, leaning against his kitchen sink, fire suit tied at the waist with his Nomex undergarments clinging to his chest and shoulders in all the right places… I mentally shook myself and rededicated myself to the conversation.

"Yeah, I'll be fine. I'm just trying to get my head around

it." I took a shaky breath and leaned against the nearest wall. "What if… " I trailed off. "What if he's upset with me for how I handled things?"

"Alaina." My name was a gentle caress through the phone. "From what you've told me, he's the one who owes you an explanation. For you to think you owe him anything, it's just not the case."

"It's funny." I smiled in irony. "After all this time, I still care what he thinks."

Grayson was quiet for a moment. "I probably understand that more than anyone," he murmured. "Do you want me to go with you?"

It was sweet of him to offer, but this was something I had to do on my own. "It's okay. I think it would be better if it was just the two of us." I twirled a strand of hair around my index finger absently as I tried to envision what my reunion with my dad would be like. I'd never even tried to picture it before, so the image felt foreign to my frazzled brain.

"Okay." He was quiet. "If you change your mind, text me. I'll see if I can get away."

"Okay, thanks."

"See you soon."

"See you," I murmured back before ending the call.

I hung my head and let loose with my frustration for a minute, not bothering to hold it together. Silent tears streamed down my face, and I gasped for air, trying to regain control. Finally, I managed a deep breath, hiked up my big girl panties, and pulled out my phone.

I can meet in front of the Pagoda at 1.
Will that work?

It didn't take long for his reply.

I'll be there.

"That boy is totally smitten with you, you know?" Jessica smirked as I walked back out to the office.

"Maybe I'm smitten with him," I suggested half-heartedly.

"Oh, you're definitely smitten. I just figured I'd point out he is equally smitten as a kitten."

"Are we turning this into a Dr. Seuss book now?"

She giggled. "Heading out?"

"Yeah, just gotta get my laptop and I'm gone. You're good to pick up Copper from the groomer, right?" I asked as I gathered my stuff.

"Just call me Super Nanny," she said with a smile.

"Thank you."

* * *

I could feel the sweat running down my back as I stood in the shade of the Pagoda waiting for my dad. It was an interesting structure not commonly found in the western hemisphere. The giant edifice was a reimagined version of the original structure that graced the grounds of the Indianapolis Motor Speedway in 1913 and was inspired by the traditional pagodas of Asian architecture. Lined with green glass and outlined with giant overlapping tiers that sheltered half of the layer below, it was an iconic building. No doubt about it. As I waited, I started to regret turning down Grayson's offer to wait with me. I could have used his steady hand in mine to calm my anxiety. It had been a long time since I'd so much as laid eyes on my dad, let alone talked to him, and I could only guess how awkward this meeting was going to be. One part of me was excited to see him. We used to be close. The more dominant part of me was scared shitless. There were so many things I wished I could tell him, and I knew I should probably avoid most of them today. But maybe someday we would have a strong enough relationship that I could be completely candid. Like I used to be.

I paced back and forth in the shade behind the Pagoda waiting for him. The clock kept ticking closer to 1:00 p.m., and finally, I spotted him across the plaza making his way toward me. He looked a little different than I remembered. His hair was grayer and beginning to thin out. He had glasses, and he'd put on a few pounds. I never thought I'd see my dad with glasses. It brought a smile to my face. *Time catches up to all of us, eh, Pops?*

As he caught sight of me his face broke into a smile, and I couldn't help but smile back, even if I did feel a bit awkward about it. When he came to a stop in front of me, he studied me in awe, studying the changes in me as carefully as I'd studied him. I'd lost weight, gained confidence, and was definitely standing on the moral high ground. "Hey, Dad," I murmured, shifting from foot to foot.

"Hey, Bug." He stepped in for a hug, and I couldn't help the tears that clawed at my eyes as we embraced. I buried my face in his shoulder, and he hugged me tightly, the smell of men's cologne and sweat, a powerful combination that threw me back to my childhood. Suddenly, I was six years old again, feeling his big strong arms around me as he taught me how to cast a fishing pole.

I felt a weight begin to melt off my shoulders. I guess

everyone knew what they were talking about when they tried to put their two cents on the counter. We stood holding each other for a lingering moment, and then he finally pulled back. "How are you?" he asked enthusiastically. "You look great."

"Thanks, I've been…" I took a moment to actually process how I was and decided on, "good." I didn't want to start out too heavy. This meeting was to get reacquainted with each other, not lay guilt or blame.

He sighed. "Well, come sit. I'm buying lunch."

I walked over with him to stand in line at the food stand in the plaza. "What are you eating?" he asked as he ordered and pulled out his wallet.

I shook my head. "Oh, a bottle of water will be fine. I already ate with Grayson."

His facial expression didn't flinch as I mentioned my boyfriend. I wasn't naive enough to think he had no idea who I was talking about. He just had a good poker face—like most lawyers. "Okay, a bottle of water it is." He told the cashier and handed her his credit card.

After he got his food, we found a seat at one of the shaded tables and quietly stared at each other. *Awwwkwarrrd.*

"So, how are things?" he asked, taking a bite of his sandwich.

"Busy. Jess and I started up a little event shop, and it looks like business is starting to pick up."

He nodded along. "So, what exactly do you do?"

"Mostly weddings." I nodded. "Brides and event planners pick color schemes, flowers, and fabrics, and then we put together centerpieces, place settings, and decorations and deliver them. They pay me to be creative. I love it."

"Awesome," he said with a smile. "It sounds like a perfect

fit. Still taking pictures?" he asked as he swallowed a bite of food.

My stomach hardened, and I clenched my jaw. "Um, no, actually. Not professionally, anyway." The scabs hadn't completely healed from that particular wound.

"That's a shame. You were pretty good if memory serves." He wasn't picking up what I was putting down.

"Yeah well, when your life gets shattered a lot of things get lost in the process," I muttered, taking a swig of water.

He stared at me, not missing what I'd said under my breath. "I'm sorry, I shouldn't have—" He sighed.

Moving on. "What about you? What have you been up to?" I picked up a fry from his plate and popped it in my mouth, trying to relax.

He smiled as he watched me, "Not a lot, to be honest. I've been working on an environmental case. Turns out this company has been dumping crap in the river for years, and they finally got caught. Now it's a huge suit. We've had ten people working on it for six months, but we're not getting anywhere. That's the worst part of law, whether you agree with your client or not, you have to be on their side."

I listened to him talk about his case for a little bit longer, and then we moved on to other small talk. To an outsider, you wouldn't have been able to tell we had been estranged for so long.

"Have you talked to Tucker lately?" My dad asked as he took a sip of his soda.

I shook my head. "No, actually. I know he's back from overseas, but I haven't heard from him. He's in Texas somewhere, I think."

Dad nodded in deep thought and sighed. *That's weird.* Tuck

knew I wasn't on speaking terms with Dad. I thought he was at least making an effort to keep in touch himself. *Maybe the situation between them was a little more tense than I'd realized.* Technically, Tuck was stationed at Sheppard Air Force Base in Wichita Falls with the 82nd Civil Engineer Squadron, but hey, if Dad didn't know, I wasn't offering. There was a reason Tuck hadn't shared his whereabouts.

Eventually, the conversation faded, and he picked at the straw in his cup absently. I leaned in and rested my chin on my fist, studying him as he redirected his hazel eyes, the same ones I had inherited, and looked at me. *Oh boy! I guess we aren't avoiding serious conversations today, after all.*

He took a deep breath. "Look," he cleared his throat and sat up straighter, "I wanted to tell you I broke things off with Brooke."

My heart skipped. Brooke was the girl he'd left my mom for—and by girl, I mean she was only four years older than me. "Blondie finally got the boot, huh?" I asked with a sarcastic smirk, trying to hide the level of hurt attached to that individual. I sure as hell wasn't about to feel sorry for either of them if that's what he was fishing for.

He gave me a look that warned me to be careful with my words.

I rolled my eyes. "So, what happened? Too young?"

"Alaina, please." He was trying not to get frustrated with me, but I was deliberately testing his patience. *He* was trying to win *me* back, not the other way around, and he needed to try a little harder in my opinion.

I raised my eyebrows signaling for him to continue. "Brooke and I weren't ever going to work, and I know she was a big reason why you refused to come around. I just wanted to let you know…"

"You cheated on Mom with that…that…" I was having trouble coming up with words that were strong enough for how I felt. Finally, I gritted my teeth and continued. "You're downplaying it a bit, don't you think?"

He took a deep breath, and reached across the table, grabbing my hand. "Bug, I know you're still angry, and I'm sorry I hurt you, okay? But I can't undo what's been done. I wish I could take it back, but I can't."

My eyes burned, threatening to tear up. "You have no idea," I started with a shaky breath, "how hard it's been." Tears spilled over as I pulled my hand out of his reach. I hated crying in front of him. It made me feel weak, and if there was one thing in this world I was not, it was weak.

His brow furrowed. "And you'll never know how sorry I am for that. Really, I am." He took a deep breath, trying to hide his emotions, but I could tell this was hard for him too. "Look, I've been seeing someone, and I think it's helping."

"Okay." I rolled my eyes and sat up. I was not about to sit idly by while he touted the benefit of his escapades in the land of the single white male.

"No, not dating someone. Seeing someone, a therapist. She's helped me to sort my priorities and set my feelings straight. I think I've spent the past few years feeling confused. I was unhappy, and I couldn't figure out why. At first, I thought it was my marriage, and then the kind of work I was doing. No matter what I did, I couldn't get rid of this overwhelming frustration I felt, but I've been working through it, and I think talking about everything with an impartial third party has helped."

I nodded along, shell-shocked my *dad* was seeing a *therapist*.

Never in a million years would I have *ever* thought this would be a conversation I would have—especially today. "Wow," I murmured. "Well, that's…that's great, Dad. Really. I'm glad you're sorting through some of that stuff. That's um…that's great."

He nodded. "It's a long process, but I think I'm making progress. When I saw you on TV Saturday I thought, 'Oh my God, that's my daughter.'" He leaned in closer. "I had no idea this was part of your life, and it hit me when I saw you. I've missed so much, Lainie. I don't want to miss anything else. Okay? I really don't."

I bit my lip. It felt like someone had punched a hole through my chest, wrapped their fist around my heart, and was squeezing it with a vice-like ferocity. I'd yearned for this for such a long time, and now that it was here, I was at a loss. "I—" *no words.* "Okay." I sighed. *Wait, what?!*

"Okay?" He seemed as unsure of my reaction as I was.

I sighed. *Well, there's no taking it back now.* "I can try to let go of the past and move on, but Dad, I can't go through this again." I shook my head. "It's taken me years to deal with everything, and I'm finally *happy*. I don't want to lose that. I won't. So, if you're ready to try, I'm ready to let you, but I'm also not going to allow someone else to be the source of my unhappiness again. I won't tolerate it." I shook my head adamantly.

He smiled at me and reached across to take my hand again. "I get that, and I respect it." He studied me for another moment. "I'm so proud of you, Alaina. So proud."

I smiled and got up from the table, grabbing my bottle of water. "Well, you want a tour of the Paddock before you leave?"

He smiled back at me and stood as well. "I would love that."

We slowly made our way back toward Gasoline Alley, and I pointed out a couple of things that were new to the track as we went. I didn't know if he already knew about them, but he never interrupted. A couple of Yellow Shirts stopped us from entering the garage area as one of the teams towed their car out to pit lane. I waved at a couple of the crew members as they went past, earning me a couple of smiles, and a wave back. It was Community Day in the garage area, and people were weaving in and out of the aisles, milling around in search of drivers to take pictures with and get autographs.

We were walking back toward the gate when a young girl, maybe seven or eight, bounded up to me. "You're Alaina!"

I smiled and lifted my sunglasses to rest in my hair so she could see me. "I am! And who might you be?" I asked.

She looked so giddy standing there in front of me. Her cute little T-shirt proudly proclaimed Team Grayson. She shifted on her feet nervously, holding her 1/18 scale diecast car in her hands. It only had two or three signatures on it. "I'm Summer! Could you sign my car?" she asked. Her mom smiled indulgently, knowing my signature wasn't worth anything, but tolerating her young daughter's whims.

"Sure!" I exclaimed and knelt down, taking her Sharpie from her to sign the tail wing in my curly scrawl. She wriggled excitedly as I signed. "I love your name! You know what Summer, I think I can do one better for you." I looked behind me. We weren't too far from Grayon's garage. "Do you mind if I borrow this? I'll bring it right back," I asked, gesturing to her car.

She nodded her head rapidly, letting me know she was

more than okay with me taking it. I had a feeling I could be gone for a week, and that little girl would still be waiting for me when I returned. Honestly, she reminded me so much of myself that I really wanted to make her day. "I'll be right back," I told my dad, holding up my finger. He smiled, knowing what I was going to do as I took off for the garages. With my newfound privilege, I could weave in and out of the garages in search of anyone with an autograph of any value. By the time I made it back around to Grayson's garage, the car was full of signatures—the drivers were happy to indulge my whim when I told them it was for a good cause. I walked into the final garage and found Jack and Grayson chatting animatedly in the back.

"Oh, my God, it was unreal. I've never felt oversteer like that going into Two," Jack marveled.

"Hey, guys," I interrupted lightly, approaching with a skip in my step.

"Hey!" Grayson exclaimed, leaning in to kiss me. "How was your meeting?"

I gave him a smile. "It was…good. But, um, I'll tell you about it later. Right now, I have a favor to ask."

Jack rolled his eyes jokingly. "Always with a favor."

Grayson, ever the chivalrous knight, came to my defense with a swift elbow to his teammate's ribs and redirected his attention to me all in the same moment. "What's up?"

"Jack, I need you to sign this," I shoved the Sharpie-riddled replica in his hands and held out the marker for him.

"Geez, Alaina, you could have asked for my autograph before now, you didn't have to date Grayson first." He laughed as he took his own Sharpie out and went for the big blank spot on the side pod.

I stopped him. "Nope, somewhere else. That spot's saved."

He glanced at me questioningly but signed part of the roll hoop that was still blank. "Thanks, Jack," I murmured as I took back possession of Summer's souvenir. "Okay, now I need to borrow you," I told Grayson, grabbing his hand.

"Alaina, what is going on?" he asked urgently, but not resisting as I towed him toward the mouth of the garage bay.

Before we exited though, I turned to him. "Okay, so outside, with her mom, is the cutest little girl in the world, and she was carrying this car around. It only had like, two signatures on it, and she asked for *my* autograph—"

"Congratulations?" Grayson asked with a chuckle, not sure where this was going.

"No, you don't understand. She's like eight years old, and she's wearing this Team Grayson T-shirt. Oh, my God, it's so cute."

He leaned out around the garage inconspicuously to look at her and leaned back in smiling. "So you want me to go out and surprise her," he surmised.

"Could you? Seriously, I've been in her shoes, and it would make her *year!*" I swore.

"And the big blank spot on the car—"

"For your autograph?" I asked, my voice full of hope as I gave him the sweetest smile I could muster—batting my eyelashes flirtatiously.

He gazed upward as if asking the Lord to give him strength and took the Sharpie and car from me. "You're lucky you're cute," he teased. He took my hand with his free hand, and we walked out of the garage to meet the little girl and her mom.

The look on Summer's face was priceless. It made my

whole month to see the tears of joy in her eyes when she saw us approaching.

"Hey, Summer, I've got someone I'd like you to meet. This is Grayson. Grayson, this is Summer."

"Hey, Summer, it's nice to meet you. Are you having a good time today?" I looked up at her mom who was filming the meeting on her phone.

Summer nodded, grinning ear to ear. "We came on Saturday, and it was so cool how you broke the record!" she shouted as she squirmed with barely contained glee.

Grayson laughed. "Yeah, I thought it was pretty cool too." He took the Sharpie, and signed his autograph really big in the blank space on the car, completing the collage of unique scribbles.

"Summer! Smile!" Her mom shouted, leaning in to take a picture of the little girl with her favorite driver. When Grayson stood up, Summer beamed up at him. "Good luck next week. I'm sorry you didn't get the pole."

He chuckled. "Yeah, me too, but we'll still give them a run for their money," he claimed with a wink. He gave her car back to her, and I leaned in as she took in all the signatures with bug eyes.

"Mom!" she screeched.

Her mom smiled and looked at me. "Thank you so much. You made her day."

I waved it off. "It wasn't a problem. I remember when I was her age. I lived for this kind of stuff. I'm happy to help." Her mom smiled, and I was taken aback as Summer lunged at me and wrapped her arms around my waist.

"Thank you, Alaina!" she shouted happily.

"Aw, no problem. Have a good rest of your day!" I said as

she let go and started to walk away with her mom.

I glanced at my dad who had a weird emotional look on his face, and then I caught a glimpse of Grayson smiling at me with a mix of fascination and affection. "You have a bit of a soft spot, don't you?" He asked, wrapping his arm around my waist.

I shrugged. "Just don't tell anybody," I murmured, leaning into his side as we watched her go. Dad cleared his throat, and I jumped toward him. "Oh, Grayson, this is my dad!"

His posture straightened, and he gave me a questioning look I almost missed before he plastered a smile on his face and offered his hand to shake. "Nice to meet you, Mr. Montgomery. It's a pleasure."

My dad took his hand and shook it. "The pleasure's all mine. That was great how you handled that back there. The sport's only going to grow if you guys keep encouraging the kids."

"That's the goal," Grayson acknowledged.

"Well, Bug, I'm going to get going. I have to stop back by the office."

I smiled and brought him in for a hug. "Okay. Well, be careful."

"I will. I'll call you later this week, and maybe we can get together, maybe catch up a bit more?"

"Sounds good," I agreed with a nod.

"Bye." He waved. I felt Grayson's hand grab mine and squeeze it in comfort as I watched my dad walk away.

13

Hickeys and Hand Grenades

"Okay, my turn. Favorite boy band?" Grayson asked as he chucked a piece of popcorn at me, I promptly threw my head back and caught it. We were lounging on the couch in my apartment after a long day at the track. His flight for New York departed the next morning, and we were basking in each other's presence for as long as possible before the first, albeit brief, separation of our young relationship.

I laughed as I crunched away. "Um, probably...*NSYNC? Although, I'm slightly embarrassed to admit I know any nineties boy bands." It was my turn. "Biggest pet peeve?"

He rolled his eyes, "Oh, that's easy. I cannot stand it when people chew their gum with their mouths open." He mocked the sound and shivered. "It makes me cringe."

I let out a loud laugh and threw a piece of popcorn at him. "Weirdo."

"Don't make fun of me. I'm very self-conscious about it," he teased, popping the piece in his mouth. "Okay, I'm gonna go a little more serious on this one. Biggest fear?"

"Oh, geez." I gave pause, thinking carefully about my answer. "Missing the Indy 500," I said seriously and then broke into boisterous laughter.

"Shut up, I'm serious. What keeps you awake at night?"

"I feel like that's two different questions. Just because it keeps me awake at night, doesn't mean I'm afraid of it."

He tilted his head back and forth before surrendering to my point, "Okay, true. So, what keeps you up at night?"

"Uh, a lot of things," I answered truthfully. "Lately, I'm up at night thinking about Jess. I worry about her. I mean, I know she can do it, and I shouldn't be worried, but still…" I said earnestly, drawing my feet up under me to warm them.

"How's she doing?" he asked as he continued to munch popcorn. I swear he never stopped eating. Of course, he did burn a lot of calories over the course of a workday, so I couldn't blame him.

"She's doing well, I guess. It was just *so* out of the blue. As much as I'm struggling to wrap my head around the entire situation, I have to keep reminding myself she's even more at a loss." I sighed and fingered the popcorn, looking for answers at the bottom of the bowl.

"Do you think she'll decide to—" he insinuated.

"No. No, I think abortion is out of the question. She's not that person, but I think she might consider adoption. Then again, she could come to me tomorrow and say, 'I want to be a mom,' and I'd support her 110 percent. That's just who we are for each other." My shoulders lifted and fell in an offhand gesture.

"What about you?"

"What do you mean?" I asked him quietly, confused about where the conversation had gone. I felt like I had missed something.

"Kids. Do you want them?"

I let out a cough, feeling a kernel lodge behind one of my tonsils. "Kids?" I croaked. He pounded on my back helpfully, and I took a swig from my Pinot Grigio. "I mean, I guess," I allowed as I attempted to gauge how sticky this situation was about to get. To be honest, I hadn't ever calculated kids into the equation of my life. My career path hadn't accounted for them, and I'd never been in a serious enough relationship to debate the pros and cons of having a couple of rugrats.

"Well, that was enthusiastic." Grayson chuckled. "You don't want kids?"

I gave a hard, defensive laugh. "Well, I wouldn't say it's an emphatic no. I've just never really considered it. It's not a deal-breaker or anything. I would have one or two if my spouse wanted them, but I definitely don't have baby fever."

I grabbed his hand off of his thigh and played with it absently as we talked. "What about you? Marriage? Kids? Beach house? What's in Grayson Miles's future?"

"I love kids. If it were up to me, I'd have three or four, but I mean, if life had other ideas, I think I'd be okay with that too."

"That's very sweet of you." I smiled and reached out to tenderly play with the tuft of dark brown hair above his ear. He leaned his head over to kiss the inside of my wrist.

"Trust me, I'm very aware of the fact *my* body is not the one that would be dealing with the birth of those three or four children." He smiled and pulled me closer so that I was practically on top of him, our faces inches apart. "Did you have a good time today?" he asked. "You didn't tell me how lunch went with your dad."

After meeting Summer, and the subsequent high from that adventure, I'd completely forgotten about my lunch date. "It was…okay," I murmured. I pulled back so I was still snuggled next to him, but far enough away from his lips I could have a train of thought independent from what it felt like to have those lips pressed against every inch of my skin. "He's changed…since I last saw him."

"What do you mean?" he asked, keeping his voice non-assuming and intimate.

"He broke up with her…the girl he cheated with."

Grayson hadn't missed my choice of words. "Girl?"

I rolled my eyes. "Yeah, she was a lot closer to my age than his. It was *super* weird."

"Oh my *God*," he muttered in disgust.

"Yeah," I assented with a sigh. "Anyway, he's been seeing a therapist. He said he was unhappy, and no matter what he did, he couldn't make it right, but things are starting to get better. He's feeling a lot more satisfied with his everyday life since he started therapy."

"Did he say what made him reach out?" Grayson asked quietly, resting his hand on my knee.

I let out a breathy laugh. "He saw us…on qualification coverage."

Grayson was still for a minute and then burst into laughter. "Oh my God," he cried.

I slapped his chest. "It's not funny!"

"Oh, but it *so* is." He laughed. "He saw his daughter… kissing a random guy…and he thought…'I should probably see…what she's been up to.'"

His laughter was contagious, and I soon found myself bubbling with my own.

Keys rattled in the door, and I tried to get my giggles under control. Jess swung the door open with a curious look. "I thought I heard laughter. Sorry, didn't mean to interrupt. I was just dropping my main squeeze off!"

"It's fine!" I said cheerily, sitting up to greet Copper as he trotted over to me. "Hey, Buddy. You look so handsome after your bath!" He jumped up on the couch and promptly squeezed himself in the nonexistent space between Grayson and me.

"Well, let me move over now that the man of the house is here." Grayson laughed as Copper leaned into me and gave my companion an indignant stare.

"He's not used to sharing Alaina. It's going to take him a bit." Jessica giggled as she eyed Copper. The massive bundle of fluff had changed tactics and decided he wanted to assume the role of a ten-pound lap dog—lounging across my lap and effectively smothering me.

"Thanks, Jess. I really appreciate you going to get him for me," I offered as I leaned out and around my fur baby's immense bulk.

"Yeah, you only owe me like a hundred favors now," she jabbed playfully. "Anyway, I have to go. I've got a hot date."

Grayson looked at me, surprised, and I shrugged, as if to say, *I've been with you all day, how the hell should I know?* "A date? Really?" The queries I put forth were both genuine and a question of her sanity, and she missed nothing in my inflection.

She studied me for a minute. "For your information, my date is perfectly aware of the situation, and he asked me out anyway. I'm not trying to pull the wool over anybody's eyes," she claimed, resentful.

"You're going out with Jack?" Grayson cried, quickly putting two-and-two together.

I looked at him for a second before reaffirming his sentiments with my own incredulity—though a couple of octaves higher on the register. "What!?"

"You're the one that gave me his freaking number, Alaina! Don't act so surprised. You can thank yourself for spilling my *condition* to him…"

I grabbed her arm and pulled her into the kitchen. "Why wouldn't you tell me?" I asked, a little hurt. I always told her stuff when it happened.

"Well, I kind of just did—or at least, I was going to until Grayson figured it out!" she exclaimed. "Anyway, I don't know why it matters. He seems nice enough, and he knows the whole story about the father and how we're not an item. If he's fine with it, and I'm fine with it, then you two should be too."

"Wait. He knows the *whole* story? You told me you didn't know who the father was!" *Okay, now I was really hurt.* "What is happening here? Why won't you tell me? Jessica, what's going on?"

Her eyes darted back and forth reading my face. She almost looked like she was waiting for me to figure it out on my own, but I was at a complete loss.

"I have to go," she muttered as she hiked her purse up over her shoulder and turned for the door.

I studied her face for another minute, holding her gaze before sighing, and stepping back to let her out the door. "Have fun," I muttered back as I watched her go. I stared at the closed door for a minute before turning back around to join Grayson on the couch.

"Everything okay?" he asked quietly, taking in how tense I was.

I sighed and ran a hand through my hair. "No, not really."

He took my hands and pulled me in for a hug. "You want to talk about it?"

"She's being super secretive all of a sudden. I don't get it. Jess and I have always told each other everything. We don't do secrets. And now…" I trailed off, thinking about how pale she had been when I asked her about this random stranger who had fathered her baby. "I don't know. It's weird." My mental tally of the situation was not adding up, and I looked helplessly to Grayson in the hopes he could shed some light on the cluster fuck festering in my lap.

He was quiet for a minute. "Maybe she feels like she can't tell you—that you'll judge her."

"That ship sailed a *long* time ago." I laughed. "It's just one of those things we leave unspoken between us, but I think it's more than that."

"Maybe it's somebody you both know, and she's afraid of how you'll react," he suggested.

I pondered that thought for a while, drawing mindless patterns on his forearm with my fingers as I thought. "Yeah… maybe…" After another minute, I sat back up.

"I'm just worried about Jack. This sounds like a lot of drama."

"Well, apparently, he already knows everything, so he's probably better off in this situation than any of the rest of us," I grumbled. "Has he ever dated anyone with kids before?"

"Not that I know of, but then again, it's kind of hard to keep track of Jack's escapades." He let out half a laugh.

"Well, what could possibly go wrong?" I asked, putting my

head in my hands.

I felt Grayson shift next to me and put a hand on my back, comforting me. "You know what the beauty of all of this is?" He whispered in my ear, his breath tickling my cheek.

I squirmed and giggled on impulse. "Do enlighten me."

"Well, now that they've found each other, we may actually be able to get some peace and quiet." He chuckled as he leaned in closer to me and kissed my temple.

I let out a single laugh, "Well, I suppose that *is* a plus, but just in case…" I put up a finger as I rose from the couch and walked over to deadbolt the door.

He raised his eyebrows suggestively and met me halfway between the couch and the newly secured door. He ran his hands up my back, pulling me closer to him, and leaned down. "And what are you planning on doing that we shouldn't be interrupted," he replied huskily, applying kisses down my collarbone.

"Well, step into my office, and I'll show you," I murmured, grabbing his hand and pulling him into my bedroom, shutting the door on Copper as he tried to follow.

I fell backward onto the bed, pulling him with me. I let out a giggle as we bounced on the mattress and pulled him to me. He touched his lips gently to mine once, twice, a third time, and then more firmly, opening my mouth to his. His tongue slid against my lower lip sensuously, sending shivers up my spine. Pulling my leg up over his hip, he ran a confident hand over the back of my leg to squeeze one buttock possessively. I let out a little gasp. It had been a long time since someone had touched me like that. His lips curled in a smile, and he continued to move his hands up my back and around to my breasts, cupping one gently.

I moaned, pulling back slightly to lengthen our kiss and slow the excited pace of our make-out session. He was receptive to my body language and rested his hand lightly on the curve of my waist as he deepened our kiss, nipping my bottom lip affectionately.

"You're pretty good at this," I murmured, picking up his hand and dragging my fingers down his palm. We were both lying on our sides, bodies mere inches from each other, and I could feel the sexual energy pulsing around him. He was a twenty-six-year-old racing driver. He lived on the edge as a profession. While most people drank a cup of coffee or went for a run to wake themselves up in the morning, jumping in a rocket on wheels and going two hundred miles an hour was his caffeine jolt. The testosterone practically rolled off him in waves on a normal day, but despite all of that, he kept himself on a short leash and was never presumptive about anything. It was probably the sexiest quality I'd ever seen in a man if I was being honest. He knew who he was and what he wanted, but self-fulfillment and gratification wouldn't come at the cost of someone else's scruples.

"You're not too bad yourself," he observed, leaning over to press his lips against my neck near my carotid artery. I tilted my head away from him to expose more skin there. "Your skin is so soft," he murmured.

I felt his lips tighten on my neck, and I shoved him away as he laughed playfully. "Grayson Miles, I *know* you are not trying to give me a hickey."

"You're adorable." He leaned into me, continuing his pattern of kisses. "And so...damn...sexy." He placed one last kiss right at the base of my neck in the hollow of my collarbone.

We laid on the bed, staring at each other, content. "I can't believe it's only been three weeks since we met," I murmured. "I feel like I've known you my whole life."

His lips curled in a small, equally content smile. "I know. I feel the same way."

I looked at the bedspread, contemplative, and when I looked back up, the smile was gone from Grayson's face.

"What's wrong?" he asked quietly.

"I'm just…" I shook my head, thinking better of airing my doubts. "Nevermind."

He was silent, reading me with his fine-tuned sense of social cues. "Alaina," he murmured, putting a finger under my chin to make eye contact with me.

"I'm scared," I admitted in a timid tone, turning my head so my chin slid out of his delicate grasp. I twisted my body into a sitting position.

"What are you scared of?" he asked, his voice barely louder than my pounding heart.

"I'm not naive. I know it was always the plan. You would be here until Memorial Day, and then…" I shrugged and scooted off the bed, making my way over to the window, arms crossed tightly over my chest.

It was so quiet you could have heard a pin drop three floors above us. It seemed we were both at a loss for words. "Alaina…I…"

"You don't have to say anything," I muttered, continuing to watch out the window. "It is what it is. It just sucks." I felt tears start to claw at my eyes, and I fought back against the urge to let my emotions take hold.

The mattress creaked, and then I felt his arms around me, embracing me from behind. He kissed my shoulder and then nuzzled his head next to mine. "I'm sorry. I know it's hard."

My breath hitched and I swallowed. *Don't cry, don't cry, don't you* dare *cry!*

"Alaina."

I continued to look out the window, tears welling in my eyes.

"Look at me," he murmured next to my ear.

I took a shaky breath and turned to face him, my handsome, sweet boyfriend.

He gave me half a smile and brushed his thumb under my eye, wiping a stray tear away. "We'll figure it out. I promise," he murmured, pulling me into his chest and kissing the crown of my head. We stood there in silence for a moment, both trying to think of something, anything valuable to say.

"I'll fly in on my off weeks." He kissed the top of my head again and pushed me to arm's length so we could look at each other. "I'm not saying it will be easy, but if you're willing to make it work, so am I."

I nodded, biting my bottom lip. "I'll try to make it to as many races as I can, but with wedding season—"

He shook his head, putting a finger to my lips. "It's okay. You don't need to worry about that. I understand." He gave me a lopsided grin and pulled me in for a hug. I felt a bit of the tension I was carrying leave my body at his touch. It was true. If anyone understood what it was like to have work obligations, it was Grayson. I just hoped a mutual understanding of how our jobs worked would be enough.

* * *

The sun had barely begun to paint the morning sky when

155

I groggily opened my eyes. Grayson had his back to me as he studied the north wall of my room, covered in pictures. Once upon a time, I had dreamed of being a professional photographer—not of people, but of places. I wanted to travel, but my lofty aspirations were cut short. That hadn't kept me from photography though. I studied the wall he was looking at. It was covered in foreign landscapes, exotic animals, fast cars, and people I loved. My heart swelled looking at each creation silently. I was proud of my work, even if a publishing body would never see it. I crawled out of bed and wrapped my arms around his waist from behind, resting my chin on his shoulder.

"Did you take all of these?" he asked quietly, his eyes not leaving the images.

"I did."

He reached out, his fingers tracing the air above one of my favorites, a beautiful male peacock looking straight into my lens with his glamorous plumage out of focus behind him. "Wow…Incredible…" he murmured, turning to me.

I gave him a small smile and glanced back at my wall of art. "It's just a hobby."

He sighed. "I can't help but think you missed your calling a little bit." He gestured to a picture I had taken at the track last year of Lozano Antonetti's yellow car zooming into focus through the middle of Turn Four. "These are shots every photographer would kill for."

I gave a breathy, quiet laugh. "Well, three years ago, that would have been the best compliment you could give me." I shrugged. "Now it's a reminder of what could have been."

"You wanted to be a photographer?" he asked, turning to face me fully.

"Among other things," I admitted. "But, you know, life happened. I couldn't stick around to support my mom through a divorce and travel the world to build my portfolio. What magazine hires a photographer with no publishings?"

He was quiet. "Sorry, I didn't realize."

We were at two opposite ends of the spectrum: one who had worked hard and achieved his dream, and one who had worked hard and had her dream ripped away. I waved it off and crawled back into bed. "I wouldn't worry about it. Everything seemed to work out in the end, don't you think?"

He crawled back into bed with me and we lay there together for a moment, staring at each other. "There's so much I don't know about you," he murmured. "I feel like an idiot for not noticing you're a photographer."

"Amateur photographer," I corrected as I played with an invisible thread on his T-shirt.

He let out an exasperated sigh. "Alaina, if those are amateur, I'd hate to think what my photographs would be considered."

I bit the inside of my cheek, wishing he'd stop talking about it. If there was one spot that was a sorer subject than my parents' divorce, it was this. Don't get me wrong, I loved my job, and I loved making other people happy by doing my job, but...

"Where'd you go?" Grayson murmured, leaning in to nuzzle me.

I sighed and looked up at him, forcing a smile onto my face. "Nowhere, just thinking."

He knew I was lying. He could read my face better than most, despite having known me for only a short time, but he wasn't going to press the issue. After letting his gaze linger for a minute more, he sighed and pressed my hand to his lips.

"I have to go."

"Why?" I whined, pressing closer to him.

He chuckled quietly. "I have a plane to catch. I'm working today, remember?" he said, leaning in to kiss the top of my head before scooting off the bed.

"Do you ever *stop* working?"

"Not in May." He sighed. His T-shirt was completely wrinkled from being slept in all night, and it did not look neat *or* professional.

"You're going to change before you go to the airport though, right?" I asked in concern as I sat up and pulled my blanket up over my chilled body. I was freezing.

He laughed. "Yes, I'm going to change. My flight isn't until ten. I have time to stop back by the bus and grab my stuff before I go."

I smiled and swung my legs over the bed to stand. "I had fun last night," I murmured, leaning into his chest and gazing up at him.

"Me too," he admitted sweetly, smiling down at me. "But if Jack asks, I was never here. The last thing I need to hear is all the innuendos and crude jokes to be made in the next forty-eight hours."

I pinched my fingers together and slid them across my lips, mimicking a zipper, and smiled. "My lips are sealed. Let me know when you land?"

"You bet," he agreed before opening the door and tripping over Copper, who had apparently spent the entire night camped in front of my bedroom door attempting to protect my virtue.

I busted out laughing. "There's a dog there."

"Uh, I can see that." Grayson laughed as he righted himself.

"Well, Copper, she's all yours, Buddy."

He unlatched the apartment door and pulled it open, turning to say goodbye.

"I have to take Copper out anyway, so I'll walk down with you,"

"Okay," he waited patiently for me, and then the three of us made our way down the stairs to Grayson's vehicle. We stopped and stared at each other for a second, and then he leaned down and kissed me softly. "I guess I'll see you in a couple of days."

This was going to be my first dose of distance with Grayson, and while it didn't bother me much, I also knew he was returning in two days. Next week, when he left to go back to Phoenix, I didn't know if I would have the same serene philosophy.

"Stay safe," I murmured and watched him go.

14

Implicit Trust

I could feel the glow around me as I walked into the shop later that morning. I smiled as I sat my stuff down and loaded the coffee into the coffee maker. Today was going to be a good day. I could get back on schedule with all of my work and chill in my pj's with Copper tonight. I loved spending time with Grayson, but I felt like, knowing our time was going to be very limited after this week, we had spent nearly every waking moment together lately. A girl needed some space every once in a while.

I was halfway through the massive pile of mail I'd collected on my desk when Jess walked through the door. After a night out, she looked like a weight had been lifted off her shoulders as well. "Good morning!" she sang as she set her things down.

"Good morning," I greeted back, a little more hesitant. "You look like you had fun last night," I surmised, continuing to sort out the junk mail we'd collected.

"I did! We had a blast. We went out to eat, and then we went down to the canal for a walk. It was very romantic. That guy's a charmer, let me tell you."

"You sound perfect for each other," I said with a laugh.

She smiled. "In all seriousness though, I think he's a catch! He was telling me about some of his dating horror stories. Man, that boy's been through the wringer!"

"I know! Grayson was telling me about his ex. Apparently, it's a hard thing finding someone who wants to date you for the right reasons when you're semi-famous." I shrugged and went back to the mail.

"I mean, it makes sense, but it still sucks," Jess muttered as she sat and booted up her computer.

"Yeah." I was glad she'd had a good night last night, but we still had a lot of things to discuss. My next words came very carefully. "So…um…about last night."

She looked up, not bothering to hide her frustration. "Why is it so important to you?"

"Because we tell each other everything! And the longer you hide it from me, the more I feel like you have something worth hiding!" I shouted.

"Well maybe I do," she muttered and sighed. "I'm worried when I tell you, you're going to be even more upset than you already are, and I don't want that."

I walked over to her desk and sat on the corner. "Jess, you should know me better than that. I told you. We are in this together."

Tears glistened in her eyes, threatening to spill over at any moment. I took her hand, squeezing it in reassurance. "Did something happen? I mean, did he take advantage of you, or…"

"No. No, it wasn't like that." She sniffled and ran a hand under her nose. "It was a moment of drunken bad judgment, and I—" She sighed and wiped the tears from her eyes. She pressed her lips together for a moment, let out her breath, and dropped the bomb. "It's Tucker."

My heart stopped for half a second. I thought I was going to pass out. *What?* "Jess…I…I don't…h-how?" I'd apparently lost my ability to form complete sentences. *I think I'm going to puke.* Stomach acid crept up my throat, and I swallowed convulsively to clear the sting of it from my windpipe. I hadn't even known there was an attraction there. Had I completely missed it? Was I *that* dense?

She rubbed her sweaty palms on her jeans and took a deep breath. "He was at the club we went to in Dallas. I had no idea he was going to be there, and we just kind of ran into each other. Then we started drinking…a lot. We reminisced about the good ole days, and he was telling funny stories about deployment. I'd never realized—" she cut off her thoughts, coming back to herself and realizing she was speaking to his sister. "—anyway, one thing led to another, and somehow I woke up in his bed the next morning."

I'm definitely going to throw up. "Oh my God…" I got off the desk and paced away a few strides. "Does he know?"

"I left him messages, but it goes straight to voicemail," she murmured. "I've got half a mind to drive down there and tell him in person, but I don't even know where to begin."

"He'll call. I know he will," I murmured walking back over to her. "When did you last try to get in touch with him?"

"Sunday. I thought he'd be around but…nothing." She shook her head woefully, burying her face in her hands in dismay.

"He's probably out in the field or something. He's not avoiding you on purpose," I assured her. *At least, he better not be.* "So, Jack knows…that Tuck is…"

Jess nodded. "I had to tell somebody. It's been eating at me, and I couldn't tell you…not then."

"And he's okay with it?"

"Alaina," she sighed and walked over to me. "I talked to Jack ad nauseum about it last night. He's never dated anyone with kids before, but he's willing to try it. He's twenty-nine and he's never dated anyone with half a mind to settle down. Plus, he's never met Tucker. Why would he care about that?"

It made me feel a little better to know she'd talked to him about it. Maybe I should have given her a little more credit. "I guess you're right. I just can't help but worry a little."

"You're my second mom, and I love you for it, but I'm a grown woman. I made the decisions that got me into this, and I can make all the rest of my decisions too."

I nodded. "Speaking of decisions—" I trailed off, and she rolled her eyes. She knew what I was getting at.

"I haven't made up my mind about it."

"Can you tell me what you're thinking, at least?" I asked, sitting on the corner of her desk.

She sighed and rocked back in her chair, her hands absently drifting to her flat stomach. "I'm thinking, whether I admit it or not, I will always be a mother after this. I'm always going to think about my child and wonder what kind of life they have. I'll still worry about them, but I won't be in their life to help them." It seemed to make her sad. "But then I think, 'Am I ready to be a parent?' It comes with a lot of responsibility emotionally, physically, and financially. There are a lot of things I will have to give up to make this work. I mean, it's a lot to ask of someone who hoped and prayed for a child, let alone someone who had a one-night stand."

I sat next to her, putting an arm around her in comfort.

It sounded to me like she'd already made her decision, but I knew Jess, and that meant she had to come to terms with the decision in her own time and in her own way. "Well, I'm with you no matter what. I promise."

She smiled and sat next to me on the desk, laying her head on my shoulder. "Thanks, Alaina. Really. You've been great this past week. I'm sorry I didn't tell you about Tucker. I just…well, at first I was a little embarrassed I slept with your little brother." She gave me a sheepish grin and ran a hand through her silky raven-colored hair. "Then, when I found out I was pregnant…"

I laughed. "Well, I guess I can sort of understand that. But to be honest, I'm pretty weirded out about the whole thing."

"But you're going to be an aunt. That's exciting!" She dangled the term "aunt" optimistically, which gave me an alarming image of some pervert dangling candy in front of a naive child.

I tried to clear the image from my brain, but it was rapidly replaced by another equally alarming thought. If I was going to be an aunt, that meant— "Oh my God, my mom's going to be a grandma!" This interjection was followed closely by a sympathetic and very worried groan. "Oh my God…my mom…"

"I know," Jess murmured. "She's going to freak out."

"Well, maybe not…"

"Alaina." Jess rolled her eyes. "I've known your mom nearly as long as you have. Who are you trying to kid?"

"Right." I clipped the "t" with a sharp click of air through my teeth as I pondered what the proper procedure for this breaking news would be. I thought it was a pretty straightforward answer. Tuck needed to tell her, not me.

I'd be damned if I was going to put myself in the line of fire for the sake of my brother's sexual exploits. I shivered in disgust at that particular mental image.

We were quiet as we sat there looking out the front window of the business we had built together. We had come through a lot together in the past few years. Both of our lives had been turned upside down, rebuilt, and then tumbled again. But through it all, we had always had each other's backs. This pregnancy would be no different.

Jessica sighed, "So…" she leaned over and nudged me. "Are you going to tell me what happened last night, or am I meant to guess?"

"What do you mean?" I asked, but I could feel a blush creeping up on me. I'd told Grayson I wouldn't tell Jack, and now that they were dating, Jess and Jack were virtually extensions of each other.

"Well, my friend Heather, who lives in the apartment next to you, said she heard quite a bit of activity over on your side of the wall this morning, and when she looked out the window, she happened to see a certain walk of shame taking place."

Fully blushed now, I put my hand to my face. *Damn it, Heather…* "Okay, seriously, this is getting borderline stalker-ish. I mean, do you have people watching me everywhere?"

"No, but when a neighbor that normally keeps to herself walks out of her apartment with a very handsome young man who *clearly* spent the night—" she spread her hands in a gesture of innocence and continued, "people tend to notice. I just so happen to be friends with a few of those people."

I rolled my eyes. "Okay, look, nothing happened last night. I mean, yeah, we kissed and…stuff, but we didn't…" My cheeks were on fire.

She shoved me in the side. "I don't know why you're so embarrassed about it. Alaina…I know it's been a while since your last boyfriend, and I know you like to take things slow. There's nothing wrong with that. I'm not going to shame you into making a bad choice. At the end of the day, it's your decision. If you want to wait, I commend you on that. If you decide to get your needs met, I'll be supportive of that too. I just want to know what's up with you. I want you to talk to me."

I sighed and got up from the desk to pour myself a cup of coffee. "I mean, don't get me wrong, I want to, but with everything that's happening…" I stared into the dark swirl of liquid caffeine as if answers could be found in the bottom of my mug. "I don't want to rush into anything. He's so great. He is such a gentleman. When I'm with him, I feel like I'm on top of the world."

"So, what's holding you back?" she asked, knowing there was a catch. *There always is with me.*

I was quiet for a minute. "He's leaving. He's leaving in six days, and it scares the crap out of me. Because I never knew I could fall this hard and fast for somebody, and the fact that he has a job that literally takes him across the country every weekend is intimidating!"

"But you'll make it work," she added. "I know you, Alaina. If you want something, nothing can stop you."

I smiled softly. "I guess I shouldn't be so worked up about it. We've only been together two weeks."

"But when you know something is worth fighting for, it's scary to imagine living without it." Her voice was understanding and more emotional than I had expected.

I glanced over at her and saw she wasn't talking to me anymore. She was lost in her own head. I leaned into her gently. "You want this baby, don't you?" She looked over at me, tears in her eyes, and nodded. "Then, we'll do it together," I whispered, determined, as I grabbed her hand and squeezed. She nodded, not having the words to speak as we sat together contemplating our futures.

* * *

Emma had picked a stunning wedding venue. The ceremony would be held outdoors atop a rolling hill that overlooked the lake below. It was rustic, and not at all what I had pictured for such an elegant socialite. She struck me as an upscale, ballroom-type girl, but hey, you know what they say about judging a book by its cover.

"Wow. This is gorgeous," I murmured, walking up onto the platform where she and her fiancé, James, would say "I do."

"Isn't it?" she asked, breathing in the fresh air and admiring the view. "James found it. His company had a corporate retreat here a few years ago, and he fell in love with it. I was a little iffy when he said he wanted me to look at the Lake Club, but I loved it too!"

"It's incredible! I have so many ideas!"

"Well, let's hear them!" she cried enthusiastically.

I jumped up onto the platform and gestured enthusiastically. "Okay, so I want to do a grapevine arch here with lots of greenery and white flowers. I'm thinking, some roses, hydrangeas, and wisteria. Very whimsical." I walked over to where the aisle would be, "And then down the aisle, at the end of each row, we could do a log pedestal and put flower arrangements on them with the same flowers as the arch. We'll want to do a white runner down the aisle too." I turned to her, "What do you think?"

She was looking at the space with glossy eyes as she imagined what I was suggesting. "I think that would be amazing…"

I smiled and walked up to her, putting a hand on each of her shoulders. "Is it what you had pictured?" I didn't want to take over her day by any means.

She smiled softly. "Alaina, I hired you because I trust your tastes and talents to make this the best wedding possible. You are *amazing* at what you do, and I trust you implicitly. Okay?"

I smiled and nodded. "Thank you."

"No. Thank *you*. I'm glad you had the idea to start this company, because brides like me…" She paused, looking for the right phrasing. "We want fantastic weddings, but we have absolutely no idea where to start," she admitted with a laugh. "You have been such a lifesaver, honestly. And your ideas…they are better than I ever could have come up with on my own. I'm so excited!"

Pure relief flooded through me. "Good, I'm so glad!"

We turned around and started back toward the lodge where the reception would be held. "So, let's talk about you and my brother," she began as we walked up the stairs and back into the air conditioning.

"Oh, boy…" I sighed, glancing at her out of the corner of my eye as we continued walking toward the event hall.

She giggled. "You know, he's technically my half brother, but we were always close growing up. I know he's older than me, but I'm pretty protective of him. He's been through a lot."

I was quiet as we continued the nice walk back to the lodge. "He doesn't talk about him a lot…his dad," I allowed, prompting her to continue.

She sighed. "I don't know that anybody gets over losing a parent, but racing keeps him close to Rick. I think that's why he started karting, and then it turned out he was actually *really* good at it. I think Mom panicked a little bit when team owners started to approach her about signing Gray, but she couldn't exactly tell him no, could she?" she said with a smile.

I laughed. I could only imagine how Lillian felt at the time. She'd lost her partner—her son's father—to a racing accident. When her son told her he wanted to race competitively, it must have been her worst nightmare. The whole situation made me admire her strength that much more. I don't know that I could have done it.

"She's pretty remarkable—your mom."

Emma smiled to herself. "Yes, she is. I think about all the things she's been through in her life… I can't imagine going through it. I mean, she was my age when Rick died, and she had Grayson to take care of and support." She shook her head. "It's crazy to think about." After a reflective beat of silence, she sighed. "Anyway, I just wanted to say I'm glad you guys are giving it a shot. He's a great guy. He can be kind of shy sometimes, but I don't think that's a bad thing."

I shook my head. "No, it's not. I'm kind of reserved myself, so it's nice to have someone who doesn't expect me to be the life of the party."

"He really likes you, you know. He hasn't had a lot of girlfriends, especially since he made it to the big leagues— his commitments take a lot of time and energy. The last thing he wants to do is put what little time he has left into a relationship that will never work." She was quiet for a moment. "I know things are good right now, but there will be times when the stress gets the better of him. The distance will take its toll, and there will be a lot of arguments, but Alaina, I promise you, he's worth it."

I smiled at her and nodded. "Thanks, Emma. I really appreciate that."

She smiled back. "My money's on you. So, don't let me down, okay?"

"Okay." I laughed. "So, this ex-girlfriend of his, the one everyone always brings up," I started.

"Oh, Kayla?" she guessed.

I realized at that moment I didn't actually know her name. "I'm not sure. The one who took a payout to give information to the tabloids."

"Yeah, that was Kayla," Emma acknowledged with a roll of her eyes. "What about her?"

"Did you like her?"

Emma laughed. "No, I never liked her. She raised a lot of red flags for me, but the last thing Gray wanted was to listen to my advice when it came to his love life. So, I let it go. It sucked watching him go through it, but there wasn't anything I could do. I just had to watch it all unfold, which, as you can imagine, was very hard for me." She laughed. "I don't like to leave things up to fate. I'm kind of a control freak when it comes to stuff like that."

I laughed too. Most of my brides were typical customers—sometimes rude and presumptuous, but we worked with them because they were cutting the checks. Emma, on the other hand, I really liked. She was sophisticated, intelligent, and had a good sense of humor.

"Okay, so you mentioned you had a lot of lace on your dress?" I asked as we walked into the main hall where the reception would be held. The high-vaulted ceilings had white fabric draped artfully across the exposed beams which accented the crystal chandeliers to perfection.

"Yes!" she exclaimed. "Oh my Gosh, I am on such a lace kick right now. Here, let me show you a picture."

"Oh, wow, that's perfect!" The dress popped off the screen at me, and I could practically feel the soft lace in my hands. It was a gorgeous mermaid-cut gown with a boned bodice that flared out below the hips in a cascade of lace-appliqued organza. It was stunning. "Okay, so here was my thought. To keep with the whimsical, country chic theme, I was thinking we could do lace overlays on the table with a champagne tablecloth underneath. Then for the centerpieces, we can pull in the same flowers from the ceremony and do an arrangement with candles around the main piece to add some warmth. I would like to do quite a bit of greenery in the centerpieces to give it an organic feel. What do you think?"

"Sounds perfect," she murmured, looking around the space. "Seriously, Alaina. Thank you. I never would have been able to do all of this on my own. This is going to be magical," she said, pressing her hands to her mouth, momentarily hiding her giddiness as she pictured what I had explained to her.

"Okay." I looked down at my checklist as we walked to the opposite side of the room. "So, did you decide what table format you wanted? We can do a formal table up front for the bridal party, a King's table, or we can do a Sweetheart table for you and James."

"Hmmm…" she bit her bottom lip. "So, if we did the King's

table, what are you thinking for the layout?"

"Well, I'm thinking we do rounds on either side of the room, and then we could do the King's table in the middle. We can do different decorations on the King's table too, so it stands out from the rest of the tables."

"And the Sweetheart table is just a small round for the two of us?" she asked, trying to keep everything straight.

"Right, so since the Sweetheart table would be smaller, we would probably do a smaller centerpiece like this," I pulled out one of my sketches from my portfolio to show her the very simple LED candle with some ferns splayed around it on top of a mirror.

She nodded, trying to picture it. "Okay, let's do that. And then we can have the bridal party at a round table nearby."

I scribbled in my notebook furiously, trying to write down all of her preferences and thoughts. I took each of my weddings personally. I knew when it came time for my big day, I would want the very best of everything, so I gave each of my brides the same treatment.

"Okay." I sighed. Let's talk place settings."

15

Since We Last Spoke

Feeling inspired by my trip with Emma to the Lake Club, I found myself sitting on the couch sketching the following morning. I was obsessed with the idea of the arch behind them on the platform, and I spent a lot of time thinking of the perfect flower combination to make it all come together. I had the TV on in the background waiting for Grayson and Jack's interview on the Early Morning Show and jumped to the remote as I saw them flash across the screen from their seats in front of a live audience.

"We are back on the Early Morning Show. I'm Carolina Valdez, and today, I have some very special guests with me: IndyCar drivers Grayson Miles and Jack Kinney. Thanks for coming guys!"

"Thanks for having us," they both chimed and laughed as they glanced at each other.

"I think you guys are the first drivers we've ever had on this show," she said, looking to her producer who confirmed. "So, tell us what a normal race weekend is like."

"Ridiculously busy," Jack answered to a laugh from the

173

crowd. "We generally roll off the trucks on a Friday, run through a couple of practice sessions to kind of get a feel for the car, and make some adjustments. We usually qualify on Saturday after another practice session, and then we go racing on Sunday."

"But you guys race at night sometimes too. Right?"

"Two or three times a year we go to some of the shorter oval tracks on the circuit and race under the lights."

"It's a whole different animal," Grayson chimed in.

Carolina nodded. "In what respects?"

"The cars have a lot more grip in cooler conditions. The tires don't wear as quickly because of the lower temperatures. It's really fun."

"I see," she added. "But this weekend, you're not under the lights. As you said, Jack, you are at the big kahuna of race tracks." She led them through the interview with ease, picking up on small details that could be expanded upon and asking all the right questions to keep her audience interested.

"Yeah, so this weekend is the Indianapolis 500. It's like our Super Bowl. We have a field that's a third again the size of our normal field. We've been practicing for it all month, and we're ready to go!" Jack answered excitedly.

"So, this race is five hundred miles. How long does it normally take?" she asked somewhat in shock.

"Well, on a good day with few cautions, it can take about three hours." The producers took this moment to flash some pictures across the screen of the cars racing around the track and the teams on pit road.

"Wow, so you must be going like—"

"I think the fastest race average is around one-eighty-six. On the straights, we top out over two-thirty," Grayson offered. He was so good at remembering stuff like that.

"Unbelievable…" Carolina replied in awe before looking back at the camera. "When we come back, we'll talk more with Jack and Grayson and the lives they lead *off* the track. We'll be right back."

I pulled out my phone, knowing they were off the air, and sent a quick text.

Don't you look all cute in your suit

…with a winky face.

I'm sure you look better than I do

…a winky face and a kissy face followed.

**Two more interviews and
opening the stock exchange
tomorrow. Then headed back.**

My heart fluttered. I was so excited to see him, it was borderline embarrassing.

"We are back with two of the young stars of the IndyCar series as they get ready to take on their biggest race of the season at the Indy 500 this weekend. But can we take a minute to talk about the smile that came over this guy's face while we were off the air?" The camera panned over to Grayson, who was turning red. "He got a text message after we went to commercial. This young woman must be pretty special," the middle-aged woman allowed as she eyed her interviewee with the eyes of a veteran reporter.

Grayson smiled. "She is." A picture of us kissing after he'd broken the record flashed across the screen. I smiled to myself.

"I mean, you two are so cute together!" The very first picture ever taken of us, him kissing my cheek in the garage area, came up in a side-by-side image with Grayson in real-time.

"Thank you," he said graciously.

"But you were telling me a little bit about it. You and… Alaina?" She asked, unsure of my name. Grayson nodded. "You guys kind of met by accident."

"It was one of those random things. We had probably been in close proximity to each other a hundred times and then one day, she was in the garage area walking around, and I was talking to a couple of my guys, and I saw her across the way…" he drifted off, blissfully cutting out the embarrassing part of that story.

She shook her head. "So cool!"

What the hell am I watching right now???

Tucker. "Shit," I swore, squeezing my eyes shut in the hopes I was having a nightmare versus experiencing the reality of this, shall we say, undesirable situation. How had I forgotten to tell him? Instant regret flooded through me. I picked up the phone and called him immediately.

Tuck answered the phone miffed. "I don't even know if I'm talking to you anymore."

"I'm sorry! I totally spaced. I thought you knew!" I stumbled over my words.

"Sorry Sis, that would be a big fat negative. I'm at work,

and one of the guys said 'Hey, isn't that your sister?' as I see you macking with some guy on national television!"

Hand to face. "First off, I'm watching the interview, and there is definitely no *macking* going on. I think it's probably one of the most chaste kisses I've ever seen."

He scoffed. "Chaste? Seriously? Maybe it's because I know you, but you look like you want to find a dark corner with him ASAP."

FUCK. I closed my eyes, certain my face was going to burst into flames at any moment. I put on my best your-comments-aren't-phasing-me voice and said, "I'm sorry I didn't tell you. I suck."

"You kind of do," he agreed, but I could hear the smile in his voice. "How long has this been going on anyway?"

I swallowed. "A few weeks. It's hard to keep anything private anymore…" The last part came out in a grumble. I'd accepted the situation for what it was, but that didn't mean I was happy about it.

"It's going well, I take it? I mean, I doubt he'd be broadcasting it to the world if it wasn't," my brother added as an afterthought.

"Likely he didn't have a choice in the matter, but yeah, it's going well."

"Good."

Our conversation wilted. We hadn't seen each other in months, but we both knew what we had to share warranted more than an impromptu phone call. My heart lurched in my chest as an unsettling thought occurred to me. "Um, Tuck…Listen…" My mouth was dry all of a sudden.

He was quiet for a minute and sighed. "You know, don't you?"

"Tucker." I couldn't help the slightly patronizing tone that came out.

"Look, Lainie, I don't need a lecture, okay? It was one night. We both had way more to drink than we should have, and that's that. I know she's your friend, but I'm not looking for anything serious right now."

"Tuck, I get it, okay? I understand, but it's—" I sighed, trying to find the words without betraying my friend's trust. "Please, call her. It's important."

He was quiet for a minute. "What is that supposed to mean?" His voice went up an octave with concern.

"Trust me. She's not wanting—" I bit my tongue. "Just call her."

"Alaina. What the hell is going on? You have to tell me!" He was scared now, and it took every ounce of my willpower not to break down and tell him everything. *It's not your place. It's not your responsibility. Walk away!* I screamed at myself.

"Tuck. Call Jess. I can't say anything else. Just call her," I muttered, and hung up the phone.

I sighed heavily, not knowing what else to do. I felt terrible. A million emotions were running through me all at once: guilt, fear, sorrow. Copper bounced up onto the sofa next to me, and I wrapped my arms around him, burying my face in his soft and fluffy rust-colored fur. "What do I do?" I asked his silent form. "I feel like a terrible person." At that moment, I understood why Jess had kept me in the dark for so long. Not only had she worried about my reaction to the news, but she had also wanted to spare me the grief of keeping such a massive secret from my own brother. My only hope now was he would call Jessica and hear the news for himself—and as quickly as possible, if he knew what was good for him.

I sighed and rose from the couch to gather my sketch pad and notebook from the coffee table and place them in my messenger bag. I couldn't sit around all day and hope for news. I had a business to run, and unfortunately, that meant shoving my personal issues aside. Copper followed me anxiously over to the door and sat, ever so patiently, as I clipped on his leash and escorted him down the stairs into the fresh air for a quick walk before I headed downtown for my meeting.

He trotted from one side of the path to the other, smelling this and that and squatting to mark some random spot on the ground every once in a while. Living the life of a dog seemed like the best gig ever. Copper always seemed completely at peace, stopping to smell the flowers every chance he got. I, on the other hand, was running around like a nervous hummingbird, flitting from one thing to the other haphazardly. Eventually, we made our way back to the apartment, and my furry friend plopped himself on his bed—apparently exhausted from his twenty minutes of mild exercise. I smiled down at him, "Rough day, huh?" I leaned down and gave him a quick pat on the head. "I'll be back tonight."

I reached out to open the door when I felt my phone buzz. I pulled it from my purse, and felt a weight lift off me as I read the message:

Tuck called. Thank you.

16

A Little Surreal

I sat impatiently next to Jess in the waiting room of the doctor's office, waiting for her name to be called. She'd wanted someone to go with her and did not, under any circumstances, want that person to be her mother. The initial shock had worn off her news, and her mom had ensued with the outlandish accusations, malicious comments, and unsolicited advice that normally came with her mother's reactive nature. I felt sorry for Jess. She was having a rough time, and the last thing she needed was an unsupportive parental figure.

Jess flipped through her magazine aimlessly and tossed it back on the table, tapping her foot nervously as she waited.

I glanced over. "You okay?"

"Perfectly peachy," she muttered, "just nervous," with a little more honesty. Her fingers rippled across her thigh in a drumming motion as she tapped her knee, which bobbed mercilessly.

"It's going to be okay," I assured her as I put a steady hand on her leg to stop the incessant shaking.

I turned to gaze out the window as I waited. The weather was sunny now, but massive storms had slammed the East Coast yesterday resulting in *a lot* of canceled flights, meaning Grayson and Jack had been stuck in the city overnight. They were able to get on the first flight out this morning, but unfortunately, that meant they had to go straight to the track without so much as a side trip to drop off their bags. *Or see me,* I thought to myself.

I was partially relieved because that meant I had more time to work. I was still behind with everything I needed to get done. Also, because of his busy schedule, I didn't have to feel bad about ditching him to come to Jess's doctor's appointment. I felt like she needed me a lot more than Grayson did right now. The only thing happening at the track today was the pit stop competition. As always, there were several interviews to be had and the public Driver's Meeting—nothing he couldn't handle without me. But while I had comforted myself with sound reasoning, there was still a small part of me that was mad. I felt like I was being robbed of what little time I had left with Grayson in Indianapolis.

"Jessica?" One of the nurses called from the door that led back to the exam rooms. She took a deep breath, and let it out before getting up and heading back with the nurse. She turned back to me, motioning for me to come with her, and the nurse—about our age, smiled. "We're waiting on the results of your urine test, and the doctor will be with you shortly."

"Thanks," Jess allowed politely. I sat, relaxed in the corner chair, and watched Jess pace back and forth, fumbling with her hands.

"Jess, calm down. You already know what your plan is.

The worst thing they could tell you is you're not pregnant," I consoled.

She glared, sending daggers through me. I promptly shut up and went back to studying all the models of the female anatomy on display nearby. The door opened, and a slight young woman in her late thirties entered the room cheerily. "Hello, I'm Doctor Adler. You must be Jessica," she said, walking over to introduce herself.

"Yes, hi," Jess greeted, shaking the doctor's hand and forcing a smile onto her face.

"You look nervous!" Doctor Adler surmised. "Don't be. Whatever happens today, we'll take good care of you. You have nothing to worry about, okay?"

I could see Jess visibly relax and she smiled hopefully.

"Why don't you take a seat, and we'll go over your test results," the woman said, motioning for Jess to take a seat on the paper-covered exam table. The paper crackled under her slim figure, and I smiled, trying not to let out a giggle. This was probably one of the least appropriate times in the history of laughter to let one slip.

"Now, who is this?" the doctor asked, looking over to me momentarily.

I offered my hand. "I'm Alaina—the best friend," I said with a smile.

"Nice to meet you. I'm glad you're here. I think it's so great when patients have a strong support system." She turned back away from me toward Jess. "Okay, so here's the deal. We got the results of your urinalysis back, and it is showing elevated levels of hCG, which is indicative of pregnancy." Jess was as pale as a sheet, and the doctor leaned in from her seat to place a hand on her knee. "I know this can be scary, especially for a first-time mom, but I promise you, we are going to do everything we can to help you. Okay?"

I got up from my seat and walked over to Jess, grabbing her hand to squeeze comfortingly. Jess nodded.

"So, tell me a little bit about your situation. Are you married?"

Jess shook her head, fighting back tears as she spoke. "No… it's just me."

"What about the father? Is he in the picture at all?"

Jess looked at me and shook her head, "No, he umm…he's in the military, so he's not around a lot." I glanced at her out of the corner of my eye. We hadn't discussed her conversation with Tucker at all. But if she hadn't brought it up, it probably hadn't gone well, and she didn't want to talk about it.

The doctor nodded. "Okay, well it looks like you've got your friend here with you every step of the way. So you're not alone, okay?"

Jess nodded, tears escaping her eyes as I pulled her in close to me.

The doctor shifted quietly, giving Jess time to compose herself. "There are options we can discuss if you are not confident in this pregnancy. We can terminate—"

Jess shook her head rapidly. "No, I don't want to do that." Her answer was swift and harsh. My heart clenched a little bit at the idea of it. Now that I knew this little nugget was my niece or nephew, the idea of abortion was even more appalling. I would raise that baby myself if I had to.

"Okay," the doctor said soothingly. "I'm not advocating, but it's my job to make sure you are aware of all your options, okay? We can also arrange for you to meet with an adoption agency if you are inclined to forfeit your parental rights."

"No, I want to keep the baby…" Jess said shakily, sitting up from me. "Sorry…I've been really emotional lately."

"It's okay, hon. I understand, believe me. Your body is producing all kinds of hormones it's not used to. That wreaks havoc on your emotional stability," Doctor Adler commented with a sympathetic smile. "Okay, we'll want to run some tests before we go any further. I'm going to ask you to get changed into this gown the nurse laid out for you, and then we'll do an exam. We'll bring Alaina back in for the fun part."

Jess looked up at me, confused. "Fun part?" she asked.

"Well, you'll want to see that baby of yours before you leave, won't you?" The doctor asked, fiddling with the ultrasound machine. Jess looked hopeful at this, and I smiled at her in reassurance. "I'll wait outside," I voiced quietly and made my way to the hall.

I looked at my phone and saw a new Instagram post from Grayson. It was a picture of him and Jack on pit lane, fire suits on, helmets out, and ready for action with a caption that read: Ready for some friendly competition. Come out and see us at IMS today.

I smiled and texted him.

Good luck. Don't beat Jack too badly.

I adorned my message with a flirtatious winky face.

He sent back a laughing emoji with tears rolling down it.

Too late.

It was over already? I looked at the clock. It was almost three o'clock…*aw, man.* Another text buzzed on my phone.

How's Jess?

With the doctor now. Will know more soon.

Call me when you head home.
Can't wait to see you!

I smiled, blushing a little bit.

I will! Can't wait to see you either!!

After making a few scrolls through social media, I saw the doctor step out into the hallway. "Okay, you can come in now."

I shoved my phone back into my pocket and walked in. Jess was laying on the exam table with one arm propped behind her head, her feet resting in the stirrups of the exam table. "You ready for this?" I asked, coming over to stand beside her.

She nodded. "I think so." Her breath was shaky, but her voice was steady.

The doctor squirted a bit of gel on the transducer and placed the oblong-shaped piece of equipment under the paper sheet covering Jess's pelvis with a soft crackle. Jess's hand reached out for mine and I squeezed lovingly as more silence filled the room. The doctor, intent on the screen, made a few clacks on the keyboard by the monitor. "And there…is your baby," she said, turning the screen around so we could see. It was just a little peanut-sized blob of gray static, but we could hear the heartbeat of this little person thrumming away as we studied the small screen before us in awe.

"Wow…" Jess murmured shakily. Tears streamed down her face, silent and shiny as moonlight on her porcelain skin.

"Pretty cool?" I asked as we both looked on.

"Yeah, pretty cool…" she whispered.

The doctor smiled. "I'd say you're probably about nine weeks. That would put your due date at…December thirty-first," she informed us as she looked at the calendar near her. "I'll get some of these images printed for you to take with you so you can share with friends and family. It makes a good gift for grandparents," she explained in an aside as she went back to typing on the keyboard.

This whole situation was still surreal. It was just yesterday that Jess and I were buying our first bras and helping each other pick out lip gloss at the local drugstore. And now, not only was she going to be a mother, but my brother was about to become a father.

* * *

"So…while you were gone there were some…interesting developments."

I felt Grayson sit up straighter behind me. He was ready for the scoop. "Did she tell you?" he asked in a low voice like he was afraid someone would overhear us.

"Um…yeah…" I picked at imaginary lint on my jeans, letting my reply hang there for a minute. It didn't matter how many times I said it, I still could not believe Jess and my brother had…*ugh*…and they were having a baby. It made me shiver thinking about it. Twisting around to look at him, I forced the words from my lips. "Turns out she hooked up with my brother when she was in Dallas a couple of months ago."

Grayson's hot fudge eyes grew to saucers. "No way!"

I pressed my lips together. "Unfortunately."

He leaned back against the window of my reading nook and crossed his arms. "Well, I guess it makes sense why she didn't want to tell you now."

"Oh yeah, her hiding it made the news so much easier to hear." My eyes rolled of their own accord. "I guess she finally talked to him, but as far as I know, my parents are still in the dark." *Ugh...this is a ginormous cluster!*

Grayson sighed but bit his bottom lip like he was deciding whether he should include his opinion in the proceedings.

"What?" I asked, curious to know what he was keeping to himself.

"I know Jess is your best friend, but...I don't know. I kind of feel for Tucker in all of this. I mean, he literally went from having a great night with a girl to finding out he's going to be a dad. That's..." He shook his head mournfully. "I don't think I would wish that on my worst enemy. The emotions that must be going through him..." He tucked a strand of hair behind my ear in silence, but I knew he had more to say. "Everyone is concerned with how this will affect Jess, but is anybody thinking about how Tucker is handling this?"

I suddenly felt horrible as it hit me that I hadn't bothered to make sure he was okay. I'd thrown this pregnancy in his lap and said good luck. I sighed. "Duly noted."

Grayson smiled and put a hand on my thigh. "I think he probably just needs you to be his sister."

I twisted back around, putting my back to him and resting my head against his chest. "I'll call him in the morning."

I felt him twist little strands of my chocolate curls around his fingers absently as we spoke about our time apart. Apparently, the town car hadn't shown up to take them from LaGuardia to the hotel Tuesday afternoon, and they had to take a cab, which had been a death-defying experience. I giggled uncontrollably. "You're hilarious."

"Look, I've traveled all around the world, but that cab ride was the most terrifying thing I have ever experienced—weaving in and out of traffic, cutting across four lanes for the correct exit. And the guy didn't speak a lick of English."

More fits of giggles poured out of me. I told him about Jess's doctor's appointment and how she had decided she was keeping the baby—my little niece or nephew. He seemed pleased and not the least bit surprised. "Well, it will have an awesome aunt, won't it?" he asked as he kissed my temple lovingly.

"Hell yeah, it will!" I enthused. "So, mark your calendars because December thirty-first will be here before we know it!" I sat curled up between Grayson's legs, leaning back against his chest as we watched the sunset from my apartment window. It was nice to sit with him.

"She seems more at peace with it, then?" Grayson asked, his low voice rumbling through his chest and sending goosebumps down my arms.

"I think so…well, I *hope* so. She's coming to terms, at least—whether there's any peace involved, I guess you'd have to ask her about that." I laughed without humor, and he wrapped his arms around me, pulling me closer and eliminating any space between us. He leaned his head down to mine, his cheek to my temple. "I'm going to miss this," I murmured, leaning my head into his, eyes closed. My lungs filled with his intoxicating scent of cedarwood and soap.

"It's not permanent," he murmured, not moving from our embrace. "We just have to tell ourselves that…every time we think we can't stand it anymore."

I brought my arms up to embrace his arms, melding into him. "What if it's not enough?" I asked, already feeling the start of an ache in my heart. We had two more days, but I could feel the distance spanning out before us like a lonely, deserted stretch of road.

"I don't know," he whispered, pressing his lips to my cheek in a lingering kiss. We sat in silence, clinging to each other. "If you'd told me a month ago, I would be leaving a part of myself behind in Indianapolis, I'd have laughed in your face." His voice was muffled against my shoulder as he laid a tender kiss there as well.

My heart squeezed in equal parts torture and elation. *I know what you mean.*

He kissed the soft spot behind my ear, and I moaned softly. When he expressed tenderness there, it sent chills through my whole body, and he knew it. He kissed down my neck, pulling my shirt down around my shoulder to expose my creamy skin. "Grayson," I whispered breathlessly as his lips continued to explore my bare body.

"Hmm?" he murmured, only half-listening to my breathy sigh.

I twisted up onto my knees and pushed him against the window frame. My hands ran up under his shirt, feeling his strong core and the springy curls of his chest hair. Every nerve ending in my body was a live wire, but I took my time, kissing his jawline and down his neck in sultry worship. My hands caressed his strong back, and my nails dragged along his skin with just enough pressure to send shivers through him. He groaned with longing and aggressively pulled my mouth up to his, bowing me to fit the curve of his body as we sat in the window sill. I'm sure we were giving my neighbors across the street quite the show, but I could not have cared less.

He toyed with the hem of my shirt, asking for permission, and I let go of him long enough to throw my arms up to help him remove it. The further along into this little escapade we got, the less self-control I had. I threw my head back, reveling in the sensation of his strong, sure hands cupping my breasts and reached out and pulled his shirt up over his head, letting it fall to the floor silently in a pool of formless green cotton. With his gloriously shirtless form ripe for the taking, my lips found their way to his toned chest and shoulder, leaving a pattern of kisses from clavicle to sternum and back again. My tongue twirled delicately across his nipple, bringing goosebumps out in force across his flawless skin, and he sucked in a sharp breath at the unexpected sensation.

He stood, picking me up with him and carrying me, legs wrapped around his waist to the bedroom. Kneeling, he laid me down gently on the bed and paused for the briefest of moments, his eyes roaming hungrily over me. I felt the burn of his stare as though I had been dying of hypothermia and his gaze was a brazier full of hot coals. Our eyes locked on each other for a long moment, our chests heaving with exertion and anticipation, and then as if the pause had only been an augmented reality, he lowered himself onto the bed, and we resumed our carnal lusting. A single finger found its way under the waistband of my jeans, and I arched my back in anticipation, losing my mind to a rush of hormones. He tugged my pants off in one practiced maneuver and kissed the inside of my leg from my knee up, up, up. I gasped and grappled for a fist full of sheets. Some tiny voice inside of me was trying to say something, but all I could hear was my body screaming for more. The quiet voice grew louder by the second, pleading for reason.

"Grayson…" I murmured breathlessly—easily mistaken for ecstasy versus objection. "Grayson." I put my hand on his shoulder more firmly, trying to catch my breath amid the yearning ache below.

"Are you okay?" He asked quietly, concerned.

I gazed at him, desire warring with common sense. I could easily nod my head and we could pick up right where we left off, but before any of that, I had to be a responsible adult. I let out a sigh of frustration and untangled myself from him, running a hand through my loose hair.

He drew himself up to a sitting position and studied me, waiting for some sort of explanation.

I crossed my arms over my chest. The haze of hormones quickly faded from my brain, and in their place, a sense of self-conscious embarrassment bloomed. He reached out to touch my thigh, and I inched away before he could make contact. I couldn't allow that touch. Things had gone too far already. I wouldn't be able to stop myself a second time.

I saw a flash of hurt ripple across his face as he pulled his hand back. "Did I…do something?" I could see insecurity starting to seep into him as well.

"I—" *How do I explain? What could I say?* "We never talked about this…" I murmured, looking down at my blanket before leaving the bed to grab a sweatshirt from my closet to cover my naked body.

Grayson's head came up and his shoulders rolled back as he nodded slowly, eyes distant with thought. "It's too fast. I'm sorry. I shouldn't have assumed," he murmured as he scooted to the edge of the bed, gathering his hands in his lap.

I pulled my sweatshirt tighter around me. "It's not that," I allowed, pacing over to sit beside him, just far enough apart that we didn't touch. I tucked my hair behind my ear and gave him a small smile. "I'm sorry. I didn't mean to make you feel like…" I began, leaving space in my explanation to account for the myriad of thoughts and feelings that were surely rushing through him at the moment.

He gave me a one-sided smile, somewhat shy. I could only imagine how my reaction had seemed from his point of view, and I wanted him to understand. I took a shaky breath and let it all come out like water over a breached dam.

"I haven't exactly had the best track record with relationships. My last serious boyfriend was almost five years ago, and it didn't end well." I shook my head. "We went to high school together, but we left for different colleges after graduation. I was at IU, and he was up at Notre Dame. We never saw each other—not really. Our breaks didn't line up, and we were freshmen, so we weren't allowed to have cars. The first time we were together again was at Thanksgiving, and by then"—I let my voice trail off as I tried to form the right words—"things were different."

I thought back to the awkwardness I'd felt sitting next to Isaac. We had talked on the phone nearly every night, but as I sat next to him over Thanksgiving dinner with his family, there was an emotional distance between us I couldn't explain.

"He was rushing for a fraternity, and as you can imagine,

there's a lot of pressure on pledges to…" It was weird for me to talk about it even now, all these years later. I cleared my throat. "He wasn't okay with waiting anymore—for sex. And with the growing emotional distance between us at that point, let's just say, I wasn't agreeing with him on much in that department. And he—" I glanced up at Grayson to gauge what he was thinking, but all I saw was a look of mingled horror and regret.

"He didn't—" I sighed, and looked back down, trying to find the words. "It's hard to describe the pressure you feel as a young woman, trying to stand up for yourself, only to be bullied when you refuse. Isaac didn't think it was a big deal, and well…you can only beat a dead horse for so long before…" I shook my head. The memory of giving in to him was a painful one. It was a story only two people in my life— now three—knew. "I gave in, and it's something I struggle with even now. I knew it wasn't the right time, but I was so tired of fighting him." I looked up from my hands but didn't move my gaze to Grayson, who I could feel studying me warily. "And with all that regret between us…needless to say, we didn't last long past that point."

Another deep breath. "So, I went on with my life. I focused on school. The next opportunity I had for a serious relationship was right before I finished college. But he was moving back home to New York, and with my history, I didn't think it was a good idea." My story was starting to draw a pattern, and I knew he saw it too. *Long distances plus Alaina equals no bueno.* "And then, of course, my parents announced they were getting a divorce, which was horrible. Still stings, if I'm being honest. That was pretty much simultaneous with my own relationship woes. So, it was a nightmarish time for me…" I gave an exasperated laugh and glanced up at him for a moment. He was so good at hiding his thoughts—the complete opposite of me. "I'd resigned myself to the fact that it wasn't going to happen; I was never going to find a relationship worth investing in. I've gone out with guys, but it never amounted to anything, and then…" I was quiet and fiddled with my hands. *And then…there you were.* Grayson made me want to forget everything bad that had ever happened to me.

He reached for me, but thought better of it and kept to himself. The small gesture was enough to make me look up at him. "I'm sorry…" he whispered.

I raised one side of my mouth in a weak smile. "I just wanted you to understand. The way I acted, it doesn't have anything to do with you, or how I feel about you. I just…need to take it slow," I murmured, bridging the gap between us by grabbing his hand instead.

He nodded in understanding. "It was selfish of me to assume—"

"You couldn't have known," I murmured, leaning closer to him. I drew my leg up onto the bed so I was facing him fully, and took his other hand too—squeezing them with reassurance. "I don't want you to feel guilty. You didn't do anything wrong."

He wasn't letting himself off that easily. "But I should have read the signs. I should have—"

"That's the thing," I interrupted him, scooting closer. "I want to be with you so bad, it hurts," I insisted. "There's just a part of me that pleads for sanity." I laughed quietly. "And that part won out earlier." I motioned to the bed where we had been deeply involved minutes ago. "So, no. It's not your fault.

There wasn't anything for you to pick up on. You didn't miss anything." I ran my hand up his arm. "But you listened to me, when I wanted to stop, and that means a lot." I gave him another shy smile.

"Of course I did," he responded. It had never occurred to him to do otherwise. I think it was at that moment I realized I was falling in love with him. This wasn't lust. This wasn't a crush. This was something bigger than I'd ever experienced, and it felt good. I cupped the back of his neck with my hand and leaned in, giving him a tender, slow kiss. I kept a hold of his hand and scooted up to the head of the bed, pulling him with me, and curled into him, laying my head on his chest.

Grayson's strong arms folded around me, and the last thing I registered before I drifted off to sleep was the steady thrum of his beating heart.

17

The Greatest Spectacle in Racing

ace Day. It was the first thing to go through my head when I woke up. Just thinking about it made my heart skip a beat. I stared out the window and watched the sun rise as I drank my coffee and listened to the morning news coverage at the track. There were already loads of people there, ready to get their party on, and I couldn't help but smile. Indiana wasn't known for much besides cows and cornfields, but the Hoosier State had it down pat when it came to hosting a city full of race fans. In fact, a survey done a few years ago showed Indianapolis—a city with a humble population of roughly 865,000—becomes the fourteenth largest city by population in the United States on race day.

I heard my phone ringing from its place on the kitchen counter and walked over to answer it, turning the television volume down to a quiet hum as I did so. "Hey, Mom," I murmured, sipping more coffee.

"Hey, babe, I had a feeling you'd be up." She chuckled.

"The better question is, did I ever go to bed?"

"Tell me you did, at least, get *some* sleep last night," she voiced in concern.

"Yes, I slept, Mom. I'm just joking with you," I said with a laugh as I rinsed my cup out and placed it in the dishwasher.

She sighed. "You know I worry about you."

Yeah, like I should be the child you're worried about. The thought came unbidden, and I immediately felt guilty. "I know. That's what makes it fun to tease you." *I'm going straight to hell for not telling her.*

"Well, I wanted to check in on you and see how you were doing." She was clearly distracted as well. I could hear her digging through her makeup bag, and there were lulls in the conversation that suggested she was focusing on something intently while she wasn't speaking.

"I'm fine right now. I can't speak to how I'll be feeling eight hours from now when the race is almost over."

"I'm sure it will be fine," she assured me. "You know I don't know much about racing, but I do know Grayson is good at what he does."

"Yeah, I suppose you're right. That's probably the best way to look at it," I allowed.

"What time is Jess meeting you?" she asked.

"Um…" I looked up at the clock. "She should be here in about forty-five minutes. She's bringing Layla over to keep Copper company today. We have to meet our escort at nine-thirty."

"Escort, huh? *Fancy.* Well, if you need me to swing by and let them out later, let me know." My mom was pretty fond of my big puppy, despite the fact she wasn't a dog person.

"Okay, I will!" I walked back into my bedroom, surveying the final three outfit options I had decided on. "You're chipper this morning. What's up with you?" I put her on speaker and eliminated one of my options, a sunny yellow fit-and-flare, and placed it back in my closet.

"Well, if you must know, I have a date this afternoon," she claimed, and I could practically see the grin that lit her face as she said it.

"That's awesome! Anyone I know?" My hometown wasn't very big, so chances were if I didn't know them directly, I knew someone who did.

"Well, don't laugh, but I'm going out with Rob Hilton."

"Mr. Hilton? My high school biology teacher?"

"Alaina, you've been out of high school for nearly a decade. I think it's fine if I date a teacher!" She was a little frustrated at my reaction, but I couldn't help it.

I never thought I'd see the day mom was dating and dad was single, but that day had arrived, and I was going to have to get used to it. After all, there's a first time for everything. I sighed, getting back to the task at hand and eyeing the final two outfits with care: a lace-trimmed, red halter top romper, or a cobalt blue, square-necked maxi dress with little pink flowers? "I know. So, what is *Rob* taking you to do on this *date*?"

"I think we're going kayaking!" She seemed excited even though my mom wasn't exactly the outdoor type. In fact, if there was one person in this world who could give me a run for my money in the clumsy department, it was her.

"Kayaking? You?" I asked, shocked. "Do you really think that's a good idea?"

"I *am* capable of branching out every once in a while, Lainie." She was straight-up defensive now.

I laughed. "I know, Mom." I stopped myself from exuding

further doubt. This woman had spent the better part of three years trying to get over her divorce. The last thing I wanted was to discourage her from going out and enjoying herself. "Have fun. Let me know how your *kayaking* adventure with *Rob* goes," I couldn't quite stop the laughter building up inside of me, no matter how hard I tried.

"I will," she answered. "Have fun this afternoon. Try not to worry too much."

"Well, I get the worry gene honestly," I said with a roll of my eyes.

"I know, but I have to tell you anyway," she insisted.

I smiled. "Hey, Mom?" I asked, hoping to catch her before she hung up.

"Yeah, babe?"

"Which is my color: blue or red?"

"Oh, red. It makes your hair look black and your skin creamy—gorgeous combination."

I nodded to myself. "Red it is. Bye, Mom."

"Bye, sweetie," she crooned, and the phone disconnected. I sighed and looked at my selection. *Yes: fashionable, practical, and adorable. It would do nicely.*

* * *

Have you ever been asked the age-old question, "Would you rather freeze to death or be burned alive?" Well, after standing on the starting grid of the Indianapolis Motor Speedway during one of the hottest race days on record, I can unequivocally conclude I would much rather freeze to death. It was *hot*. We were standing on the track for pre-race festivities in the ninety-two-degree heat with the sun beating down on us, and I was dripping sweat. Of course, the ambient temperature was in the low nineties, but the track temperature was *much* warmer—probably up around one hundred twenty degrees on the north side of the track where there was no shade to be found.

The humidity and heat were combining in a feat of nature that made the Turn Four spectators look like a mirage in the Sahara, shimmery and faded through the wall of moisture in the air. I didn't know how Grayson was managing in his charcoal gray fire suit, and I definitely didn't envy him. He had been hydrating for the past few days, but somehow, I doubted he'd be anything other than exhausted when he parked his car after this one. "How are you feeling?" I asked him as I turned into him, my hands on his chest.

He smiled down at me. "I'm good. How are you?" he asked, wrapping his arms around my waist.

"Other than dying of heatstroke? Nervous."

He laughed and gazed down. "Well, you *look* gorgeous." He ducked under my floppy sun hat to give me a quick kiss. "Don't be nervous." He rubbed my back comfortingly, but I could feel his own heart hammering in his chest. Knowing he was anxious too did little to comfort me.

I took a deep breath and stood on my tiptoes to kiss him lightly on his cheek, whispering in his ear, "Well, I don't think I have to tell you what seeing you in a fire suit does to me."

His mouth lifted in a smirk. "Really now?" He leaned down to whisper in my ear. "I'll keep that in mind."

"Ladies and gentlemen, please rise and remove your hats for the playing of our national anthem." The announcer's voice came over the public address system. We both straightened from our flirtatious back and forth and Grayson removed his hat, placing it over his heart as we listened to the "Star-Spangled Banner."

I could see four fighter jets coming straight at us, and as the final notes, "and the home of the brave," roared throughout the arena, the cluster of F-22 Raptors soared over us so low my sunglasses vibrated against my face.

I looked over at Grayson, who glanced over at me with a smile. "Promise me you won't do anything stupid," I murmured in the silence between pre-race activities.

He laughed lightly. "Stupid is relative. I drive a car at two hundred thirty miles an hour for a living."

"You know what I mean," I murmured, gazing into the depths of his beautiful brown eyes. He leaned down toward me, and I tenderly brushed my nose against his. "Come back safe." I leaned in and grazed my lips against his. He pulled me in more firmly and gave me a real kiss that sent my heart thundering all over again.

"Drivers, to your cars," came over the speakers in the voice of some celebrity they'd enlisted that I didn't know.

He held my hands tightly to his chest for another second before leaning in to kiss my forehead. "See you in five hundred miles."

"Technically, it's five hundred ten miles, five hundred twelve and some change, if you get a victory lap," I said with a wink, and walked off the grid with the rest of the crowd, leaving Grayson and his crew members to their work.

I met Jess once we were over the wall and back on pit lane. "This is crazy!" she shouted as "Back Home Again in Indiana" reverberated off the grandstands. This was my favorite part of the pre-race festivities, hearing everyone sing along to such an iconic song.

"Back home again in Indiana,
And it seems that I can see,
The gleaming candlelight, still shining bright
Through the sycamores for me.
The new mown hay sends all its fragrance,
From the fields I used to roam.
When I dream about the moonlight on the Wabash,
Then I long for my Indiana home!"

As the final, powerful line rang out, I took a moment to gaze out over the crowd. In a stadium so big, each individual person looked no bigger than a pushpin on a corkboard, but as a whole, they painted a rainbow of color across a gorgeous canvas. I loved this sport with a deep passion that stretched way back before I met Grayson. This race was part of me, and I knew it like the back of my hand. Granted, today marked the beginning of a much bigger adventure for me. I was now a partner—not a spouse, but still one of the lucky few who got to know and love one of these thirty-three drivers. As I made my way up to our suite, I prayed to whatever higher power might be out there that my man would be delivered safely back to me when the race was done.

"And now, for the most famous words in motorsports."

A hush settled over the vast crowd as we all waited.

"Drivers. Start. Your. Engines!"

Thirty-three engines rumbled to life, and the cars slowly rolled from the starting grid for the pace laps. I took a deep breath, said another prayer, and waited for the show to get on the road.

* * *

The last fifty laps of the Indianapolis 500 were, in my opinion, the tensest fifty laps in motorsports. The 500 was an endurance race for the drivers and their crews. Everything had to work out just right, and even if you did everything humanly possible to win the race, it could still go up in smoke. Call it a myth, or a legend, or even a superstition, but in the racing community, it's believed the Indianapolis Motor Speedway chooses its victor every year. After all, how else can you explain years when rookies with no experience win and veterans with ten seasons under their belt wreck in Turn One? Dumb luck? Perhaps, but it's easier for the drivers to sleep at night thinking it wasn't in the cards.

The truth of the matter is, there are thirty-three drivers in the field all vying for the same victory. Despite being professionals, each one is just as prone to human error as the next. They are racing inches apart at death-defying speeds, and it's their job to come out unscathed. Unfortunately, sometimes things don't work out that way. The race itself is a perfect recipe of pacing, strategy, and skill. Teams have to have patience and an extremely competitive drive that allow them to straddle the precipice of perfection, because one mistake could send an entire year of hard work spiraling down the drain.

"I think I'm going to throw up." I groaned, bending over at the waist.

I heard Emma laugh and put a hand on my back. "Honey, join the club."

"How do you do this? I'm losing my freaking mind over here!"

"You're being a control freak," Jess complained as she picked at the food on her plate.

I rolled my eyes. "I honestly can't tell you how many Indy 500s I've watched, and I've never in my life felt this nervous."

"You're thinking about it too much," Lillian murmured, empathizing. "Especially with fifty laps left. Have a drink and relax, save the real nerves for ten to go."

I gave her a weak grin and straightened up a little bit as I peeked down at the track. A whole pack of cars whizzed by in a hurry, and I could almost feel the wind they kicked up—almost. That's one thing I was missing about my Turn Four seats, three rows away from the action. I looked up at the screen across from our stands and watched. Grayson was running in fifth, and Jack was out of contention at the moment running fifteenth. Pit stops would start soon if the race stayed green, but we were praying for a caution.

And then, as if on cue, a car entered Turn Three at an awkward angle, its blue and white livery blurring into a streak of color as it veered out of control, climbing up the embankment and out of the racing groove. In a millisecond, the car had careened across the track, collected another car with the sickening crunch of shattered fiberglass, and slammed into the safer barrier with an impact that reverberated down the track with a wave of released energy. *Ouch.* I'd caught enough of it to know the incident had occurred behind Grayson and Jack. They were safe for now. Although, I couldn't say as much for the two drivers whose race was now over. This caution was a little too early in the game for our final stop, but the guys on the pit crew stood up. I guess they were going for it. I took a deep breath and let it out. *Oh, boy.*

I felt my phone buzz in my pocket and pulled it out to see who it was. *Dad.* I knew he was here somewhere. "Hey, Dad,"

I answered kind of loudly to make sure he could hear me above the noise.

"Hey, kid, how are you doing?"

"Holding it together." My tone said what my words did not: *barely.*

"He's doing pretty well! Are you listening to the radio?"

"No, I wish I had one. I'm completely in the dark."

"He's got a vibration. They called him in for a tire change, and they're topping off fuel."

My heart sank. Vibrations were never good. "Let's hope the tire change fixes things."

The hum of a large crowd and the growl of racing engines passing at low speed nearly drowned out his words as he spoke. I had to close my eyes and concentrate to catch what he was saying. "I'm sure it will. Deep breaths, Lainie. Okay? It'll all work out either way."

"That's what everyone keeps saying. I just hope he gets through this thing safe and sound."

"I understand. Well, I'm going to go. I just wanted to check on you while we had a break."

"Thanks," I murmured. "Enjoy the rest of the race."

"You should try to as well," he answered with a smile in his voice.

"Yeah. I'll try. Bye." I sighed and hung up.

"Look at you, all progressive," Jess teased as she elbowed me in the side. "I'm proud of you!"

I rolled my eyes. "He's trying, so I'm going to try too."

* * *

Two laps. There are two laps left in the Indianapolis 500, and

205

Grayson is back up to fifth. We were now down in the pits waiting to see how the last ten laps would play out while nervously chewing our fingernails, pacing back and forth, and generally freaking out. Lillian was pale as a ghost, and I was pretty sure I was a mirror image. Jack had been collected in the latest caution, and Jess was more concerned with how he was doing than anything else. I was faintly annoyed at her lack of empathy but also understood how unsettling it was to watch someone you cared about plunge into a wall at one hundred and fifty miles per hour. *I think I'd be more concerned if she* wasn't *worried.*

I could hear the cars growing closer as the pace car peeled off the track, and the green flag waved from the flagstand above the finish line, signaling the field to restart the race. I looked around, taking a second to absorb the situation. Every person in the stands was on their feet, and I watched on the big screen as the cars came racing toward us. Grayson went wide to the outside lane entering Turn One, and I jumped up and down, half in fear, half in excitement. I couldn't believe he held on, and he just kept going—passing for fourth, then third, and then, all of a sudden, he was sitting in second as they exited Turn Two heading down the backstretch. The speed coming from his car was unbelievable, and he quickly closed in on Pedro Garza's bright green machine, but that was only half the battle. Everyone watching knew it was one thing to catch the lead car, it was an entirely different beast trying to pass it.

As they shot into Turn Three, Pedro was protecting the inside line well, and he forced Grayson wide entering the final turn of the lap. If Grayson wanted the lead, he was going to have to go the long way around. The draft pulled Grayson right up behind Pedro, but he lifted and tucked in behind the leader as they zoomed past us into Turn One at top speed. They pulled even down the backstretch, and I could tell from the in-car camera footage being broadcast on the big screen that Grayson was giving it everything he had.

He forced the car into Turn Three, daring to take the outside line again, this time on hot tires. He was either going to stick it and beat Pedro, or he would end up in the wall. Either way, he was committed. The cheer from the crowd was deafening as we heard them round Turn Four. I jumped up on a cooler to see them come down the front stretch and watched in disbelief as Grayson whipped around Pedro—the draft sucking him forward like a vacuum. They passed under the twin checkers so close together I couldn't tell who had won.

I jumped down from the cooler and held Lillian's hand as we waited for the replay, and then we both sank down onto it in tears, holding each other. *He did it. He won.* There were a lot of cameras around, and I knew I should have been doing my best to remain halfway composed, but I couldn't help myself. Tears were streaming down my face. The team was celebrating too, and I could see Jack's team running down to meet and congratulate us. *This is insane.* I could feel my phone starting to go off in my pocket already, and I knew there would be an endless parade of phone calls, text messages, and social media notifications for the rest of the day.

We hurried over to Victory Lane as the cars started to arrive back on pit road. I wanted to be there when he got out of the car. Luckily, it wasn't far. We hustled through security, flashing our hard cards to the Yellow Shirts, and ran past the Pagoda as Grayson drove past us to park in the winner's circle. We waited impatiently as his crew members helped him unbuckle, took his steering wheel, and gave him his ball cap. He sat in his car for a minute, collecting his thoughts with his hands over his face. All of the emotions were hitting him at once.

This was a dream his father before him had dreamed, but his life had been cut short and that dream had never been realized. I never knew Rick Anderson, but I knew without a shadow of a doubt he was looking down on his son now with the respect of a competitor and the pride of a father. And for a split second, I felt the overwhelming sadness that came with Grayson's complete elation. As much as it was a dream come true to win The Greatest Spectacle in Racing, it also came with an overwhelmingly bitter dose of reality. He could never share this particular joy with the one person who could have fully understood it. Tears welled in my eyes too as I watched the emotions struggle for dominance on his face.

Finally, he pulled himself up out of the car to stand on the side pod and threw his fists up in the air victoriously. The tears streaming down his face intermingled with the sweat pouring off his forehead, but I could still see them. He jumped off the car and ran to his mom, wrapping her up and squeezing her tight. She was crying too. It was a lifetime of sacrifices and sleepless nights that had finally paid off. But Lillian didn't make it about her at that moment. She leaned close to her son's ear, trying to block out the celebratory cacophony, and said, "He would be so proud of you."

Her son nodded, more tears forming, and squeezed her tighter before turning to me. He leaned in and kissed me passionately, to which I responded in kind. Finally, I broke away and leaned in for a sweaty hug. "You killed it! That was the most amazing finish I've ever seen."

"I can't believe it!" he shouted back. Exhilaration at what he had accomplished was quickly taking over his face, and the aura of self-confidence, pride, and pure joy around him gave me goosebumps. Cameras immediately descended, affording us all the private time we were likely to get for the next few weeks. And then there was Jenny Kite, ready for the post-race interview, cameras already rolling. Grayson wrapped an arm around me and the other around his mom.

"Grayson, you are in your fourth season with IndyCar, and in the past three years, your best finish in this race was seventh. Now we're standing here today, and you are an Indianapolis 500 champion. Can you put into words how you're feeling?"

"No." he denied as he shook his head in wonderment, at a loss for words. "This is insane!" His eyes flitted from one group of people to another before settling back on the small reporter in front of him. "I'm so proud of this team. We came into this month hoping to make a statement. We rolled off the truck strong, and my guys have continued to deliver day in and day out, and man, I had a rocket ship today. I wouldn't be here without them." He glanced back at his team celebrating with reckless abandon and laughed.

"You have these two lovely ladies here beside you. What does that mean to have such a strong support system?"

He shook his head vehemently. "It means everything." He brought Emma into the fold as well, with his long arms, and smiled. "These women are the reason I can do what I do every day. I'm the luckiest guy on earth."

"You've got your mom, your sister, and your girlfriend here, but there's one important person who isn't here today—your dad." She left the comment open-ended and pointed the mic back at Grayson.

He nodded, getting emotional again. "You know, I lost my dad at a very young age, and umm, it's been hard." He swallowed back the tears and trudged forward. "My mom, she did the best she could to give me the tools I needed to succeed in life, but she didn't really have the racing bug." He nudged her, and she gave a good-natured grin. "But, um, it was my dad's dream to win the Indy 500, and—" He got choked up momentarily talking about it. "I know he's looking down on all of this with a big smile on his face."

Jenny smiled, tears in her eyes, seeing the emotion on Grayson's face. "I'm sure he is too. Congratulations, again."

"Thank you," he said with another big smile and turned to bring us all in for a group hug.

My boyfriend is an Indianapolis 500 winner! I repeated that to myself over and over again, but it still blew me away. How could this be my life? I was riding so high, I never wanted to come down. A wall of photographers shouted for Grayson to look this way and that, as they scrambled for the right angle to plaster all over the front page of every newspaper across the globe. He waved me over through the wreath around his neck as he sat atop his car, and I stepped in for several pictures as well. Then it was both of us with his mom and sister, and of course, Emma's future husband. It was a family portrait like no other.

Everything I had ever dreamed of was sitting in front of me.

And then, the world fell apart.

18

If I Lose Myself

"Paging Doctor O'Brien to O.R. three," the loudspeaker squawked.

Grayson started in his seat lost in the eerie quiet of the private waiting room he'd been ushered to. He flexed his hands, picking at the dried blood under his fingernails. He'd picked, and scrubbed, and scratched, and he couldn't get it off. He took in a shaky breath and shot up from his chair. He couldn't sit for a minute longer. He had to do something, anything. He ran his hands through his hair, bracing them against the back of his head, and let out his breath slowly, trying to calm his racing heart and drown out the tick, tick, ticking of the clock on the wall behind him.

"Grayson! Grayson. Oh my God, are you okay? Oh my God..."

Mom. Relief flooded through him. Lillian Miles bull-rushed her son, running her hands across his shoulders and down his arms, scanning for injury and eyeing his blood-encrusted clothes in apprehension.

"Jack called me. I came as soon as I could. Are you okay?"

she asked, her deep brown eyes scanning his face.

Grayson opened his mouth to speak but couldn't. All he could do was shake his head and burst into tears.

Lillian pulled him in tight. "Shhh. Shhh. It's okay." She pulled him down to sit in the chairs resting against the nearest wall and let him compose himself. "What happened?"

"A drunk driver hit her while she was crossing the street." His brow furrowed and his eyes stared hard at the floor, distant. Lillian rested a hand on her son's back, and let him talk.

"We had just said goodbye, and this woman came running. I went to see what was happening…and I saw Alaina's purse… this dainty little gold thing." Grayson's thoughts were flitting around, images dancing in his mind like moths to a flame. "I was making fun of her on the way to the party because she's always got something sparkly on, and when I saw it…" More tears began streaming down his face, and his voice shook like a leaf in a windstorm. "She was lying in the street…so still. I thought—" he ran his hands up his neck and grabbed his hair by the fistful.

"I tried to keep her calm, to talk to her, but she couldn't… she couldn't breathe." Now Grayson was the one struggling to breathe as he fought back the waves of panic that were threatening to engulf him. "I could hear the sirens, but I couldn't look away. There was this off-duty EMT trying to help, but there wasn't much he could do, and I could s-see her…slipping away…" Grayson took another shaky breath. "There wasn't anything I could do. Nothing. And I felt…s-so…helpless…" A sob racked his body, and his mother pulled him back to her, stroking his cheek and kissing the crown of his head.

"Where are her parents?" Lillian asked in a low murmur.

Grayson shook his head. "I don't know. Jess was going to call her mom, but she lives an hour from the city."

"Grayson," she continued to run a comforting hand over his back. Her face was pale, but composed. "Is she alive?"

Grayson dragged his bloodshot eyes up to his mother. "I think so…at least she was when…when they took her. I haven't heard otherwise." He sniffled, and his chin quivered.

A throat cleared from the hallway and they both turned to see Cami. "I went to your trailer and got you some clothes." Grayson stood, gratefully taking the pile of clothes from his friend. "I've been fielding calls for the past hour. Word's gotten out. The press wants a statement. I can…I can do it for you," Cami offered, pale but composed. "Do we have any updates?"

"No, not yet. Just that she's in surgery, and she's in critical condition," Grayson offered quietly.

"Okay. Well, get changed, and I will prepare something. I won't say anything until her family arrives."

Grayson studied the clothes in his hands. "Thanks, Cami." The petite little blonde was one of the sweetest people he'd ever met, but she was also fiercely loyal. Now with her and his mother here, he was starting to feel like he could get through this. He wasn't alone anymore, and that, in and of itself, gave him an immeasurable amount of strength.

Cami rested a hand on her friend's arm and gave him a small smile before turning and heading back the way she'd come.

* * *

After scrubbing at his ruined shirt for a solid five minutes, Grayson tossed the mass of expensive blood-stained fabric in the sink. Frustration welled up inside him, trying to claw its way out, and he gripped the dull corners of the sink wishing it would crumble. He wanted to break things. His reflection stared back at him, eyes bloodshot, face devoid of color, hair askew. At least his new clothes gave him some semblance of poise. He carefully wadded up his ruined clothes and tossed them in the trash. He could buy new clothes. It was the least of his worries. He combed his hair back over into its naturally groomed look and took another deep breath. *Alright. Let's go,* he thought and made his way back to the small waiting room.

When he rounded the corner, his knees went weak. Alaina's parents had arrived and they were speaking with a surgeon who was still in a surgical cap and scrubs. He approached slowly and began picking up bits of the conversation. "...repair her liver lacerations...blood pressure bottomed... transfused twelve units..." Grayson came up next to her parents, arms crossed as if to ward off bad luck. Her mom, whom he'd never met before, put an arm around him in comfort. The embrace felt natural nonetheless.

A flash of recognition lit the doctor's face, but he kept talking. "Right now, our biggest concern is cerebral edema. Traumatic brain injuries are always tricky. There's a great deal of pressure right now. We're working on putting a ventriculostomy in to relieve some of the pressure, but the injury is fairly severe. The swelling is wreaking havoc on her breathing and heart rate, and the longer it goes on the more severe the setbacks will become." He took his gaze from her parents to Grayson. "I want you folks to know we're doing everything we can." He was quiet as he coupled his hands together in front of him. "But I also want you to be prepared for the worst."

Alaina's mother made a weak, strangled noise, and Nathan Montgomery wrapped a strong arm around his ex-wife, holding her up.

The doctor continued with a pained glance in Grayson's direction. "Alaina's condition is severe. It's a miracle she even made it to the hospital. So, take heart in that. We'll work for as long as it takes to stabilize her. I'll come out to update you once she's been moved to ICU."

Grayson felt light-headed. He'd known it was bad. Alaina had barely been able to speak, and most of the time, she had looked like she didn't know where she was or what was going on. It was awful. Regardless of the outcome here today, it was a moment he would never forget as long as he lived.

"Thank you, Doctor Reilly," Mr. Montgomery murmured before helping Alaina's mother to sit down.

The doctor gave a glance in Grayson's direction with a smile that was supposed to be comforting and sympathetic, but actually looked like the tortured grimace of a POW. With one final glance at his patient's loved ones, he turned to head back to the operating room.

* * *

Time passed oddly in the waiting area. Grayson could stare off into space for what felt like hours and look back at the clock to find only seconds had passed. Somehow though, when he thought back to the accident, he would look up and find an hour had passed. "I'm sorry." That's the last thing

Alaina had said to him. "I'm sorry." *Sorry for what? She hadn't done anything to be sorry for.*

Grayson stood from his seat and paced over to the window. The masses of news vans outside made him nauseous. "Any excuse for a story," he muttered bitterly under his breath.

"Sickening, isn't it?" he heard behind him and looked to see Alaina's dad looking out the same window. "The worst moment of a family's life, and all they care about is a scoop."

Grayson turned to look at his girlfriend's father, and Nathan stared back, stone-faced. He was good at that— keeping his emotions to himself. Alaina had told him as much when she explained what her father did for a living. Nathan Montgomery was a corporate lawyer with a formidable presence, and Grayson could feel that presence now, looming next to him like a brewing storm cloud. Grayson's mouth popped open to speak, but no words came.

"It's okay," Nathan muttered. "I mean, it's *not* okay. But, it's not your fault either." The older man said with a shake of his head. "When some drunkard hits your daughter with a car, the least of your worries is a young man with a good head on his shoulders, who clearly cares for her." He gave him a small smile. "I know you did what you could—even if it wasn't much, and that's all we can ask."

Grayson swallowed hard and went back to looking out the window.

"It's a shame. Today should be the best day of your life and instead—" He sighed from behind him. "It's just a shame."

*A shame...what an odd use of words...*Grayson thought as he looked on at the stirring crowd. Cami had arrived to read her statement.

The Victory Lane celebration seemed so long ago now—

decades away. The soft scratch of the wreath around his neck, the excited soprano congratulations from the 500 Princess, the creamy, crisp, and oddly refreshing taste of milk. It was all a distant recall. Even the way Alaina had felt in his arms, soft and vibrant, the way her smile made him feel even lighter on the wave of adrenaline coursing through his body. It was all some murky, distant place, tucked away in the recesses of his mind. He was an Indianapolis 500 champion, and he couldn't care less about it. All he wanted was for Alaina to be okay.

Alaina's words echoed in his skull. *"I'm sorry..."* and he finally understood why.

* * *

"Grayson," a female voice whispered quietly near his ear.

Grayson nuzzled into the blanket someone had provided him with during the night. "Grayson," came the voice again with a shake. He pried one bloodshot chocolate eye open to see his mother kneeling before him.

"Mom?" He looked around the small waiting room with bleary eyes. The sky outside was turning a pale blue, and the brilliant morning sun was painting the clouds nearby hues of pink, yellow, and orange. The birds chirped in the trees, and to everyone outside the room in which he occupied, it was a beautiful Memorial Day. Jack had made an appearance sometime in the night and was now huddled in the corner, serving as a pillow for Jessica, who was sound asleep with her head in his lap. Jack made eye contact with Grayson and gave him a weak smile. Grayson gave a small nod of thanks and looked back to his mother. "What time is it?"

"It's early—about seven thirty."

It had been seven hours since the accident. *Is that all?* It felt like a lifetime. He ran a hand over his sleepy eyes and sat up, feeling the aches and pains that normally came after a race. He rolled his neck to one side and then the other, taking in the rest of the room and noting who wasn't there. "Where are they?" He did a quick inventory of the room again. No. Alaina's parents definitely weren't here. "Mom." His voice was a desperate plea.

"It's okay. Gray, look at me." Her strong voice demanded his attention, and his eyes shot back to her face. "Alaina is out of surgery. She's in the ICU. Her parents are with her now."

Grayson threw the blanket off himself and stood to the protest of his aching body. A bench in the hospital waiting room wasn't the best place to sleep on any night, let alone the night after manually operating a car at high g-forces for five hundred miles. "I have to see her," Grayson muttered and began to walk out of the room. His mom grabbed his arm, warning him without a word, and walked out with him. She clearly had more to say but didn't for fear of waking the other sleeping people in their company.

"What?" the young man asked his mother. "What aren't you telling me?"

"Gray." His mother's eyes shone with tears. "They lost her twice on the operating table last night. They were able to get her back, but she's highly unstable. They aren't sure she's going to make it." Her eyes were full of pain, as though she knew she was stabbing her son repeatedly with her words.

The world stopped. He stumbled back against the wall, his knees turning to jelly. Lillian gave her son a moment to process and get his bearings. "How…how long has she…?"

"Her parents have been with her for a little while. They didn't want to wake you," Lillian murmured, putting a hand on her son's arm. "Come on, I'll take you," she murmured to her child, like a groom coaxing a nervous horse out of his stall. She paused to press the button for the elevator before proceeding with the onslaught of information. "They've repaired all of her internal injuries, and they've placed a drain in her head to keep the swelling down."

Grayson stepped onto the elevator in a daze, trying to wrap his mind around the situation. He felt like he was living a nightmare he couldn't wake up from. The elevator door dinged, and they walked into the sterile environment of the intensive care unit. The harsh scent of antiseptic smacked him in the face, sending flashbacks of past hospital visits running through his head.

Every patient had their own room in the ICU to avoid unwanted contagions, and Alaina was no exception. Lillian began to walk down one of the long white corridors, waiting for her son to join her. "She's on a ventilator. It's the best way to reduce the strain on her body—especially with the brain swelling." Lillian struggled to find the words and finally gave up as she drifted to a stop outside a new set of windows. Her gaze was locked on the occupants inside, and Grayson felt himself drifting toward her, compelled to lay eyes upon the horror inside.

He'd always thought of Alaina as relatively tall, probably five feet seven inches, and she did not have the build of a model. No, he loved the curve of her hips and the faint sun-kissed glow of her skin. He reveled in the silky feel of her chestnut curls and how they smelled like coconuts after she showered. He could lose himself for hours in her beautiful hazel eyes and the warm gleam of her smile. And now… He could feel small fissures webbing their way across his broken heart like a rock hitting a windshield. She looked sunken and small in her hospital bed. Her head was wrapped in gauze, concealing what was left of her beautiful brown locks. Her once lightly tanned, unblemished skin was ravaged with cuts and bruises from head to toe, and the trauma of the night's events had left her swollen and slightly disfigured. Grayson's stomach turned with the shock of her appearance.

"She's in a drug-induced coma," his mother spoke. "The doctors said it's best for her to not have any lucidity with her type of injuries."

Silent tears streamed down Grayson's face as he watched. Alaina's mother…

What had Alaina said her name was? Maura. That was it.

…sat in a chair at her daughter's bedside, grasping her hand tightly. They were close, closer than he was with his own mother, and he pitied her. She was a gentle, loving soul constantly being forced to exude strength. Watching her in profile, sitting next to her daughter, Grayson could see her lonely, battle-worn desperation. Alaina was her eldest child and only daughter. Her son, Tucker, was off in Texas—out of reach at the moment. Alaina's dad stood on the other side of the room, looking out the window but not seeing. He looked as lost as Grayson felt.

After what seemed like hours, Nathan turned from the window and walked over to his daughter's bed, leaning down to kiss her forehead. There were tubes, wires, and machines running from Alaina's face, abdomen, and neck in all different directions. It reminded him a bit of a map of the city, roads converging and diverging all from one central location.

The ventilator was the most noticeable of these with the largest tube running from Alaina's mouth down to the box-like structure with a large digital read-out. More monitors displayed heart rate and different pressures, most of which were beyond his comprehension. Nathan looked at all of the machines hissing and beeping and shook his head. Kneeling next to his ex-wife, he said something in her ear and she straightened to look over her shoulder at Grayson.

He stepped back from the window, shoving his hands in his pocket, unsure where to go from here. Maura kissed her daughter's hand lovingly, and they both stood to come greet their daughter's boyfriend. "How is she?" Grayson murmured, glancing back into the small room.

"Hard to say. The doctors…" Nathan shook his head. "There isn't much more they can do for her other than keep her comfortable and hope she stabilizes."

Maura was silent as she looked at the floor. Any passerby could tell she was miserable. *How could she not be?* When she spoke, she sounded so much like Alaina, Grayson's heart leaped in his chest. "We wanted to give you a minute…t-to…" she bit her lip to keep from losing all control in front of this young stranger.

Grayson swallowed hard, his dry mouth betraying him. "Thank you."

Nathan placed a hand on his shoulder and gave a healthy squeeze before walking down the hall. Maura continued to hold Grayson's gaze. He could see his own tortured soul reflected in her eyes, but for once, a kindred spirit was no comfort. "I've never seen my daughter care for anyone quite like she does you. Alaina is a very levelheaded girl—never done one reckless thing in her life. But the way she—" the older woman shook her head and sighed, swallowing against the lump in her throat. "I don't know, maybe you can reach her in a way I can't. Make her strong, make her want to live." The hope in her eyes was painful to watch—especially when Grayson felt so powerless. He gave a nod of acknowledgment and turned to enter.

The ventilator hissed quietly from one corner of the bed, and Alaina's chest rose mechanically before falling back to its resting place. The sound of her heartbeat echoed against the inside of his head, pulsing behind his eyes like a bad headache, but Grayson took comfort in the feeling. She was here. She was alive. That had to be worth something.

The swelling was even worse up close, but he tried to push it from his mind, instead choosing to see the perfectly beautiful and undamaged girl who had danced with him at the victory party only seven hours ago. Bending over her cautiously to avoid the jumble of tubes and wires streaming out of her, he kissed her cheek. Her skin was cool to the touch with a faint pink hue to indicate some small sign of life. "Hi, baby," he murmured, running a finger lovingly down her undamaged cheek. It was the way he spoke lying with her on the couch. He could imagine that she would turn to him and flash her perfect white smile, her left cheek dimpled, with crystal clarity.

Both of her eyes were black with bruises, and the cut adorning her cheek was sewn, but still ghastly. She would have a scar there for the rest of her life—if she made it through. Road rash covered the right side of her face from temple to chin, leaving her milky skin an angry red blotched with blue and purple bruises.

"I don't know what to say." Grayson took hold of her cold hand, rubbing it between his, willing some life back into it. "Your mom seems to think you've given up, but…I guess she ought to know you better than that, hmm?" His laugh was forced. "The doctors aren't giving you very good odds, but I know you. If you don't come back, it's because your body failed you, not the other way around." Grayson took a deep breath and let out a choked sob. Tears raked at his raw eyes. He'd cried so much in the last twenty-four hours, he didn't understand how he could have any tears left to give. "You have to come back. Please, Alaina." He let his lips press fiercely to her hand, begging her with the silent gesture. "Please." It was quiet for a moment while Grayson struggled to compose himself.

"When my dad died, I wasn't there. My mom had to come and give me the news afterward." His voice trailed off. "It must have been terrible for her…her heart shattered, grieving her loss, and having to put it on hold to break the news to her child." He swallowed convulsively and thought back to that moment of pure panic he'd felt seeing her parents the night before.

"I couldn't even imagine…until I saw your parents last night and thought I might have to be the one to…" Grayson gritted his teeth, his eyes drifting from the bed to her destroyed face. "If you can't or…*won't* do it for yourself, do it for them." He shook his head, wiping his tears with his free hand while still keeping contact with her lifeless form. "Do it for me." He gripped her hand tighter. "I love you, Alaina," he whispered. "I should have told you last night." Regret twisted his already knotted stomach even further. "Maybe you would have stayed, or maybe I'm being cocky. Maybe I would have scared you off." His quiet laughter was dark with irony. "But at least you would have known. Instead, I have to sit here and wonder if I'll ever get to tell you."

A flash of color caught Grayson's attention, and his gaze drifted to the monitor in the corner, which had gone from a normal blue reading to yellow and then quickly to red at an alarming rate as her heart rate plummeted. Alaina's frail body arched upward, her dainty hands curled into fists, her arms rigid as sticks at her sides, and her head thrown back in violent protest of whatever internal stimuli were wreaking havoc on her body now. Grayson's own heart hammered in his chest. Someone was screaming for help, and he realized with a start, it was his own voice he heard.

The room flooded with nurses armed with medication, equipment, and an emergency cart. The cavalry had arrived. Standing against the wall and wishing he was anywhere else, Grayson watched as the army of medical staff swarmed his girlfriend, injecting medications and evaluating her vitals in a flurry of activity. Above the hum, he heard, "I'm worried she's going to herniate, can someone page Doctor Reilly?"

What little strength he had left disappeared at that moment. Some part of him had held on to the hope if she was out of surgery, she was past the worst of it, and clearly, that wasn't even remotely true. Hands pushed Grayson toward the door. "I need you to wait outside. Someone can show you back to the waiting room."

"You have to help her. Please," he begged, not able to pry his eyes from his girlfriend's stiff form, seized in the grip of some unseen force.

With a bit more insistence, the tough young woman in

front of him in lavender scrubs began turning him toward the exit. "We'll do everything we can, but I *need* you to wait outside," the nurse insisted, promptly closing the door on him. He stumbled against the closest wall and slid down it, burying his head between his knees.

* * *

The sun warmed my skin soothingly as I lay with my eyes closed. There was no pain, no grief, no unpleasantness of any sort. I was content. I opened my eyes to a cloudless sapphire sky free of blemishes. There were no sounds around me except the gentle rustle of tall grass in a light summer breeze. The sweet scent of flowers came to me in the wind, and a thrush warbled nearby.

"It's beautiful, isn't it?" A familiar voice with a slight southern drawl asked.

I turned my head to look next to me—not alarmed, merely curious. "Who are you?" I asked.

The woman's auburn curls danced around the creamy skin of her face. Her green eyes held my gaze hypnotically. "So, you don't recognize your own grandmother?" the woman replied with a smile. Those eyes held me in rapture; something about them was so familiar. I was thrown back to a time when I was a small child, visiting my paternal grandparents. My grandma had died of pancreatic cancer when I was ten, a long time ago now. All I remembered of her was a white-haired woman, once strong-willed and able-bodied but worn down by age and illness at the end. Her eyes though, yes, I remembered those eyes. I sat up from my spot in the soft grass and looked around, alarmed. *Where was I?*

"Don't you worry now, my little Lainie bug. I'm not here to take you with me. It's only a brief visit." She smiled at me, placing a hand on my knee.

I gazed at the wildflowers by my feet, playing with the pastel purple petals. My mind was hazy at best, but I was starting to recall some pretty dreadful things from my last few minutes of consciousness.

"Alaina?" the woman's voice was slightly more pressing.

"Granny, am I…" I looked around again, swallowing hard. The hills rose behind me into steep mountains covered in violet wildflowers, and the image was so beautifully vivid and breathtaking I almost wanted to cry.

"Dead?" she asked me, her quiet voice calm. "Nearly so. Your poor body can't take much more. No one would blame you if you chose the easier path, but I suspect you've got half a mind to fight on." Her lips curled in a small smile. "You're my kin, after all. That little fire in your belly will keep you going through almost anything. If you'll let it."

"I suppose so," I murmured, distracted by the light catching in the leafy canopy above.

"You wouldn't be thinkin' to give up now, would you?" she asked sternly.

I shook my head. *Never*, I thought. I had too much to fight for. I thought of Grayson almost immediately. It seemed strange that with all the people I loved in this world, he was the first to come to mind.

My grandma nodded knowingly. "It's a strange thing, love. You hold on to that boy. He knows what he's about."

I smiled at her, wishing I'd known her as a young woman. I had the feeling we would have been thick as thieves. I rose to my feet, looking at the sparkle of water ahead of us, falling at the feet of two mountains.

"Beautiful, isn't it?" she whispered again, the light from above making the entire area glow.

So beautiful I never want to leave, I thought, looking out over the endless wilderness, untouched by time and civilization.

As if divining my thoughts, she replied, "Oftentimes, the hard path is the most rewardin', Alaina. If you go back, it's not going to be sunshine and roses. There will be pain and heartache, anger and sorrow, but you have so much to offer the world. You're much too young to let that fire inside you burn out. Think of all the life you have yet to live." She gazed up at the sky and smiled, "It's best you be gettin' on back, darlin'." She rested her hands on my shoulders. "We'll see each other again."

Then she was gone, and the black closed around me once more.

* * *

I don't know where I had been before, but I was once again painfully aware of my damaged body. I was trapped—suspended in a tomb of misery. This was different from before though. The pain was a dull, aching menace that encapsulated my every nerve ending. My eyelids were still too heavy to open. I couldn't move. Something kept dragging me further and further under. I wanted to surface—badly, but I couldn't fight against this black semi-consciousness. My senses were dulled so much I could barely feel my own heartbeat. Everything was coming to me through a soundproof barrier. It was impossible even to pinpoint what part of me was injured.

I wasn't breathing, that much I did know. Something was breathing for me—an odd sensation. There seemed to be a disconnect between my brain and the rest of my body. I was trapped in a room with no windows and no doors. The intelligent part of my mind where I currently resided seemed completely intact, but my physical shell was left unable to function. I wondered if this was what death was like. I was beating on the front door of a house filled with my friends and family, but no one could hear me. They were completely oblivious to my presence.

* * *

Alaina was back in her small little room after a successful emergency surgery. Her earlier episode had been the result of increased pressure in the brain. The drain from the first surgery had malfunctioned and, without immediate intervention, could have been fatal. Doctor Reilly had been confident they made the repair in time. She'd had no further posturing, and her vitals were steady. She wasn't breathing on her own yet, but the doctors were hopeful she would begin to improve soon.

Steam swirled up from Grayson's cup of coffee, and he breathed in the intoxicating, bitter scent. It sharpened his dull senses considerably. He wasn't sure if it was possible to inhale caffeine, but it was a balm to his fried nervous system regardless. He'd only had short spurts of sleep in the last forty-eight hours and felt like a zombie. A warm hand rested on his shoulder, and he looked up, startled out of his daze. "Grayson." It was Maura Montgomery.

He gave her a weak smile and took a sip of the coffee he'd

been staring into. "How is she?" He knew she must be doing all right if Maura was here and not with her daughter. She'd barely left her side.

Maura nodded slowly. "She's okay, I think. You should go home. Get some sleep."

He shook his head. "I can't. She wouldn't leave me. I won't leave her." He rubbed his eyes, exhausted, despite his argument.

Alaina's mother stared at him, sternly. He suspected if she'd been standing, she would have put her hands on her hips. "And what good will that do you?"

He scrutinized her own exhausted face. "Are you going home to sleep?"

Her eyes widened. "Of course not."

He gave her a tired smile. "Well then, I guess I'm not going either."

She closed her eyes and gave a quiet laugh. "I didn't understand what Jess meant when she said you were an even match for my daughter but," her head wagged back and forth, "you have her stubbornness, that's for sure. Nobody's going to make you do something you don't want to do, are they?"

He let out a hard laugh. "There's probably only one person on this earth that could."

"Your mom?" his companion asked with a smile in her voice.

He let his chocolate gaze drift over to take in the middle-aged woman next to him. "Your daughter."

She was quiet for a moment, taking his meaning. "It worries me—how strongly you feel for each other already. I don't want her heart broken."

He stared down at his coffee again. The billows of steam

had turned to occasional wisps. "I'm pretty sure she'd break me long before I had the chance to break her," he allowed carefully before taking a healthy gulp of his drink—wishing it was something a little stronger than coffee.

"You think you care more for her than she does for you. Is that it?"

Grayson shrugged and kneaded the back of his neck to release some of the tension there. "I couldn't say. She's not the best communicator."

She laughed lightly, "Or maybe you should learn to be a better listener."

Grayson's head shot up. "She said I'm a bad listener?"

"That's not what I said," the older woman denied. "But a woman can tell a man a lot without coming right out with it. Although, I'm willing to bet you already knew that. Growing up with a single mom and a little sister must have had some effect on you."

She sipped on her own coffee, taupe with cream and sugar. *Extremely forthright, that one.* With a start, Grayson realized the woman reminded him a great deal of his own mother. Her steely gray eyes studied him. "You're in love with her." It wasn't a question but a statement of fact.

No sense in denying it, then. "She's an amazing woman."

"Yes, she is." She gave him a small smile and picked up the red plastic stirrer in her coffee cup, toying with it absently. "She's going to have a long road ahead of her after this."

They both sat in silence, knowing the truth of it. Her doctors had been open with them about her recovery time regarding physical injuries: broken pelvis, broken ribs, incisions from several major surgeries. The one thing they couldn't put a finger on was her neurological recovery. She'd suffered a traumatic brain injury, and while it had been assessed and treated, there was no guarantee she would be the same if and when she woke up. She could live the rest of her life on a ventilator in unconsciousness. The thought soured his stomach. Alaina was a vibrant soul. He couldn't imagine her life ending in a hospital at the mercy of a machine.

Grayson squared his shoulders and took a deep breath. "I think she's a lot stronger than they give her credit for, but whatever happens, I'm here for the long haul."

Maura reached over and patted Grayson softly on the knee, no more words needed.

* * *

Everything was so loud. The beeping of the monitors. The hiss of the ventilator. An incessant clicking noise that Would. Not. Stop. Even the TV someone had turned almost all the way down felt like a jet engine beside my ear. It rattled around in my head, banging against my skull. I didn't know how long it had been since the accident. I had no concept of time. I got brief moments where I was aware of my surroundings before I slipped back under, but I never regained full consciousness. I had yet to open my eyes or breathe for myself. I couldn't even begin to think about walking or talking.

I felt so helpless in those moments of darkness, and I feared this would be the rest of my life—dependent on those around me for everything. Sometimes, I thought I would rather die than live out the rest of my existence confined to a bed with a machine breathing for me. But when I thought about death, the will to live grew exponentially. I wanted to hug my mom. I wanted to see my little niece or nephew be born. I wanted to kiss Grayson. I wanted it all so badly.

19

Sleeping Beauty Awakens

"Did you try Tucker again?" my dad asked.

"I've called him a hundred times. It keeps going to voicemail," my mom's shaky voice answered. "A friend of mine got me the number for the Red Cross. She said they could get in touch with his C.O., and I called, but I still haven't heard from him." It was quiet except for the sound of the machines and her tortured whisper. "What are we going to do, Nate?"

"It's going to be okay," he murmured. "The doc says she's improving. We just have to have faith. We have to trust she's going to wake up."

"They also said if she does wake up, she could have major deficits. We're not prepared for that. She won't understand. How am I supposed to tell her everything's going to be okay when I can't even tell myself that?" My mom's muffled sobs reverberated in my skull as the ventilator pushed more air into my chest. I hoped Dad was hugging her. Someone should be.

There was a shuffling sound from farther off by what I

imagined to be the door of my room. My mom let out a strangled sound, and I wasn't sure what that meant until her next words. "Tucker!" Relief. Pure relief.

"Mom, I'm so sorry. I came as soon as I could." There was a pause while he consoled our hysterical mother. "Shhh…It's okay."

I felt relieved myself. At least he was here. I had no idea how long I had been unconscious, but I knew things would be better for my parents with him here.

"Hey, Dad," he murmured. They patted each other's back with a sharp smack as they embraced.

"Hey, kid."

"How is she?" He stood next to me as he asked this.

Dad sighed. "Her body is healing from the surgeries. They had to put some pins in to stabilize her pelvis, and they had to repair some internal bleeding."

"She's still unconscious?"

My dad sighed. "She hit her head pretty good, and it's caused a lot of swelling on the brain. She had an episode of some sort yesterday, but they said it was a drain malfunction they were able to fix. She's still not breathing on her own, but she's stable—which is progress. It was pretty bad the day after the accident." The tone of Dad's voice made me think horrible things had happened that day.

Tuck had noticed too. "Bad like…?"

"She coded twice. They were able to get her back, but it was touch and go for a while."

Tucker let out a breath—something he did when he was trying to stay calm and process things. I could envision perfectly the way he would run his hands through his thick, sandy hair. "But she's doing better now?"

"A lot better, but she's still not out of the woods. They keep waiting for the rest of the pressure to ebb, thinking she'll wake up when it does."

A familiar hand grabbed mine. I could feel everything like I was awake. I was mentally there. I just couldn't force my eyes open or move my limbs.

"Hey, Lainie."

Tuck. I wanted to hug him. It had been so long since I'd seen him—almost a year. All I wanted was to wrap my arms around him and squeeze him to death.

"She's strong. She'll wake up." His words were confident, and I let them sink in. *Yes, I was strong. I could do this. I would wake up. Soon.*

* * *

"...a week with no change. We need to get you back in the car." A stranger's voice materialized into my thoughts like someone was turning up the knob on a stereo.

"I can't leave her. Not like this." Torment coated these words.

The first voice replied with exasperation. "She's unconscious. This team needs you. Our sponsors need you. *I* need you. You've known this girl for a month. I've given you your whole career!" It was quiet for a moment, and then the man continued more calmly. "This team is losing ground and every single one of us needs to do our part or it won't survive."

"I guess I was naive to think if I needed anything, you would be there for me. It seems you're only there for me when it benefits you."

"Grayson." A sigh. "You know you're like a son to me, but the sponsors are down my throat. They're threatening to pull the plug. The 500 rallied some support, but how am I supposed to keep them interested when the driver they want in the car isn't even racing?" There was a beat of silence. "You know I would move mountains for you if I could, but you're my lead driver. I can't...*I can't* allow you to be gone for an unlimited number of races when we're trying to draw in sponsors and partners to create rides for you and Jack next season. I need you, kid."

What? It sounded like the situation was in dire straits over at the LHR camp. This was so much worse than I'd originally thought.

"Bruce." Grayson's voice was a bit of a moan.

"I know this is difficult for you, okay? I know you care about her, and you want to be here for her and her family. But she's not going to know if you're here or not. And if she cares for you, like you do for her, she's not going to want you to throw your career away over this."

A heavy sigh.

He was right. As much as I appreciated him being with me, Grayson needed to put his career first. The last thing I wanted to be responsible for was him losing his ride. I wanted to scream, *"Listen to him, Grayson. Listen. You can't do this, not now, not after everything you've worked for!"*

"The car's ready to go?" he asked after several moments of silence.

"The guys have been working with one of the test drivers, and Jack tested earlier this week."

Another sigh. "I'll be on the last flight out tonight."

More silence. "I promise you, you're doing the right thing."

"I wish I knew you were right," he muttered as Bruce opened the door and walked out. Grayson sat next to me and grabbed my hand. "I really wish you would wake up," he whispered. "I need you to tell me this is okay. That you won't hate me for leaving you."

Me too, I thought. I wanted to touch his face. I wanted to kiss his soft lips. I wanted to say his name. I wanted it all—badly.

"The doctors say we shouldn't worry, but…" There was a pause in his narration as he shifted his weight closer to me. "Your mom…she's not doing so good either. I think she needs you more than I do. Maybe you need *her* more than you need *me.*" He gave a chuckle as he mulled over that thought. "I hope so…considering I'm pretty much guaranteed to lose my job if I don't get my ass to Wisconsin this weekend." His hands enveloped mine, squeezing them.

"I'm sorry, Alaina. I can't…" he struggled for the right words. "You have no idea how much I regret talking you into going to that party." I felt something wet hit my hand. Was he crying? *Don't cry.* All I wanted was to hug him. I didn't want him to feel the way he was feeling. It wasn't his fault. "If you hadn't been there, none of this would have happened." He lifted my hand to his lips and kissed it desperately. More tears hit my hand, and I listened as he cried quietly.

My heart wrenched in my chest. *I don't want this. I don't want this! Why is this happening?* I screamed internally, but despite my inner fury at the higher power that had decided my fate, my body remained immobile. And then, my fingers twitched.

His hands stiffened. I knew he'd felt it too. "Alaina?" He squeezed my hand. "Come on, Alaina. I know you're in there.

Can you hear me?"

If I can just... I mustered everything I had left—every ounce of willpower in my weak and exhausted body and felt my index finger move slightly.

"Please, wake up. Come on," he murmured.

My eyelids flickered, and the restraint I'd been feeling released like a broken rubber band. An analysis of my surroundings went no further than the stippled ceiling tiles before a blinding pain resembling an ice pick to the brain coursed through my temple.

Oh my God, I panicked. My heart took off at a record pace, and I shifted. *What is happening? What is this?* I tried to move my head, but the brace around my neck was still there to inhibit my movements, and I didn't get very far. The tube down my throat shifted though, and I gagged.

Grayson stopped breathing, and his hand went completely still in mine. "Alaina?" I felt my bed go down on one side as he sat next to me and pressed his hand to my face. "Shhhh. Shhhh…Alaina. It's okay. Shhh."

A stranger's voice came from the doorway. "Is everything okay in here? Should I page someone?"

"Something's wrong. She's in a lot of pain."

"I'll see if I can find her nurse," the voice acknowledged.

My heart rate had slowed a little but was still fast. The ventilator was uncomfortable at best and wouldn't allow for vocal cord movement, making the situation even scarier. *How is someone supposed to fix me if I can't tell them what's wrong?*

"It's okay," Grayson murmured in my ear, stroking my cheek repeatedly with his thumb. "Can you squeeze my hand if you understand me?" I squeezed with a force that couldn't knock a feather over, but he expelled a puff of air in relief.

He took a shaky breath. "It'll be okay. Someone will come. They'll figure out what's wrong."

I tightened my grip on his hand and decided not to let go. My thoughts were clear. *Please don't leave me.*

He squeezed my hand back, feeling the weight of my gesture. "I need to go tell your parents you're awake. I'll be right back. I promise." It wasn't an enthusiastic statement. I understood he would rather stay with me than leave, but I also understood my mother was likely to skin him alive if he failed to tell her I was conscious.

Reluctantly, I let him pry his hand from my grip. The pain in my head was taking its toll, and the strain on my body was too much in my weakened state. I barely felt his soft lips press to my forehead as he removed himself from the bed and had fallen back into the void before his footsteps faded down the hall.

20

Working Hard or Hardly Working

My eyelids flickered, and with tentative hope, I drew them back. *Big mistake.* My head felt like it was going to explode as murky gray light filtered through my optic nerve. I wrinkled my forehead in pain and tried to groan, but I was still hooked up to that abominable machine. I was breathing now, but it took some effort, and I could feel the tube pushing extra air through my lungs to help them inflate. My eyes fluttered open again, and it hurt a little less, but my vision was merely dim light with a few shadows. My head pitched and heaved like a dingy in a storm, and my eyelids fell back shut of their own accord as more air pushed into my lungs. I felt a stab in my abdomen as my rib cage expanded. All of it hurt like hell. I couldn't even describe the feeling fully. It just was, and it sucked. I dragged my eyelids open one last time and looked to my other side.

I was groggy from my meds and all I could think about was getting that tube out. I raised my hand, wanting to yank on it, but another hand shot out and seized my wrist before I

240

could do any damage.

"No, no, no. Lainie, no. It's okay. Hey, it's okay."

My eyes closed drowsily and flickered back open. *Stay awake, damn it!* The room was dark, but I could make out shadowed objects surrounding me. I wasn't prone to migraines. I'd only ever experienced one in my twenty-four years on this earth, but I knew without a shadow of a doubt, that's what I was experiencing now. The voice sounded again, and my muddled brain tried desperately to place it. The shadow to my right leaned closer, and through my squinted lids I could barely make out facial features. *Tucker.*

"Hi," he murmured as he leaned over me. "Can you see me?" he asked quietly, noticing my eyes wander in his direction.

My head hurt too badly to even think about shaking it. Something as simple as raising a hand felt like an impossibility, but I managed to reach out ever so slightly. His hand met mine three-quarters of the way across the short distance and clasped it with relieved fervor. The calluses of his strong hands rubbed against my palm with a quiet protectiveness that made me feel completely safe, despite my severely damaged state. I tried to smile at him in the reassuring way that big sisters often smile at their younger siblings and hoped he got the idea. I didn't want him to be worried or scared. That felt wrong to me, but the energy I was expending on reassuring him was drastically draining the fuel in my tank.

Besides that, I couldn't take the light, however dim. It made my eyes feel swollen, and my head throbbed uncontrollably. So, I closed my eyes and dreamed of better days.

* * *

Air whistled in and out of my lungs in a clean, smooth rhythm. *Thank you, Jesus.* The breathing tube was gone. *One hurdle down, a bajillion to go.* I braced myself and let my eyes come open. It was startling. My surroundings were crystal clear, and by some miracle of God or pharmaceuticals, the pain in my head was gone. All of my limbs felt like giant sandbags, and even the simple act of holding up my hand took a great deal of effort. Slowly, I was able to move my head enough to see my mom, who was seated next to me, and my dad, who was asleep in the green faux-leather recliner near the window.

A croak emanated from my vocal cords, no more than a whisper. My eyes were already starting to close again, but I struggled against the weight of my lids wanting to stay awake as long as possible.

Her eyes shot up from the book she was reading, and she leaned over my bed. "Alaina? Alaina, it's Mom…can you hear me?" she asked quietly. The sound of chair legs grating on linoleum rattled in my head, and I winced. She placed her hand on the top of my head, and her thumb caressed my forehead tenderly.

"Mmmm…" I muttered sleepily. My tongue felt weird in my mouth, and it prevented words from taking shape.

"Are you in pain? Do you want me to get a nurse?"

The longer I was awake the worse I felt. I was starting to feel like every bone in my body had been beaten into shrapnel with a baseball bat. I shook my head with a sharp pain resembling an axe through the skull.

"Easy," she soothed as she steadied me. "You've got a head injury, sweetheart. You need to keep still."

I slurred something incomprehensible as I looked up into

my mother's gray eyes. There were small wrinkles next to each of them, and the wrinkles in her brow seemed deeper as well. I wanted to reach up and smooth them away. She'd been through so much. The last thing I wanted was to add this whole mess to the pile. But the more I racked my brain, the more I realized I had no idea what had happened. My memory was a huge blank page.

Mother's intuition allowed her to divine my thoughts. "You were leaving the victory party after the race, and a drunk driver hit you."

Well, I certainly *felt* like I'd been rolled over by a piece of heavy equipment. My eyes continued to grow heavier and heavier, and I struggled to keep them open.

"It's okay, babe. You can sleep." Her soprano voice was soothing to my disquieted mind, and I found it hard to protest against its peaceful lull.

I desperately wanted to see Grayson and vaguely wondered why he wasn't here, but the drugs were too powerful for me to fight, and I quickly fell back into oblivion.

* * *

When I woke up the next time, I was alone. It was dark outside, and I finally had control over my own consciousness. I was able to think with a clear enough head to take stock of my body. A pulsing pain came from one side of my head. My entire abdomen and hip area throbbed in discomfort, and I felt the uncomfortable pinch and pull of stitches across several areas of my body. The remnants of road rash littered my right side, and the scabs were beginning to peel, leaving pink blotches of new skin in their wake.

The fading bruises and fresh skin were my only indicator of how much time had passed since the accident. My mom said I'd been hit by a car, but exactly how long ago had that been? I wanted my phone. I wanted to talk to Grayson. Footsteps sounded at the door, and I turned my head in that direction with deep-seated instinct. My dad came in, coffee in one hand and a stack of manila file folders in the other. A grin spread from ear to ear when he met my eye. "You're awake!" he shouted gleefully, plopping back down in the chair he'd recently vacated. The faux leather of the chair next to my bed creaked under his weight, and he grabbed my hand as he leaned closer to me. "How are you feeling?"

I opened my mouth and tried to force my tongue to work with a horrid false start that sounded like tires on gravel. I swallowed, my heart thumping anxiously. I clenched my jaw in frustration. I couldn't project my voice. It was a rough whisper at best, and I sounded like a chain smoker.

He gave me a sympathetic smile and patted my arm. "It's alright. It may take a while to get it all back. You've been asleep for a while. Probably twelve hours or so."

Twelve hours? Whoa. I had no concept of time anymore. "What day…is it?" The raspy strain of my once clear and melodic voice grated on my already fragile nerves, and I blushed furiously, tears coming to my eyes.

My dad's hand clamped down on mine. "It's okay, Alaina. It's normal. You're doing great, sweetheart."

I shook my head slowly, tears streaming down my face. *I might as well still have that damn tube down my throat for all the good it does to have it out.*

"It's Sunday night. It's been a week since the acci—" My father, rarely at a loss for words, had none now, but he valiantly tried again for my sake.

"You were leaving the party last Sunday, and while you were crossing the street for your rideshare pickup—" He cleared his throat against the invisible chokehold he was experiencing. "You were hit by a truck. You're at IU Health Methodist Hospital and still in ICU. They removed you from the ventilator yesterday. You had what's called cerebral edema. Your brain started to swell."

He continued to give me the catalog of my injuries, but his words faded into the background. It was all too overwhelming for me to process. It didn't take a remarkable IQ to know there were things wrong with me beyond my control, and the fear of what that meant for my future was almost too much for me to bear.

"Grayson?" I whispered, afraid to butcher his name. It was sacred to me. I could hardly bear to say it, but I had to know. My vocal cords rattled and grated against each other—raw from the ventilator I'd been on for six whole days.

"He had to leave for the race, but he should be on his way back by now. I think he's supposed to get in around midnight. You'll be excited to see him, then?" There was a smile in my dad's voice. Clearly, *somebody* was excited to see him. The past week must have given the people in my life time to get to know each other. I wasn't sure whether that was good news or bad.

I felt my eyes widen in what was unmistakably fear. Grayson couldn't see me like this. He couldn't.

"Bug." Dad moved to sit on my bed, never loosening his firm grip on my hand. "Listen to me." Tears were streaming down my face by now, and it was evident by the pulsing of my ribcage that I had a few broken ribs to go along with the list my father had already given me. "It won't matter to him. You hear me? It won't."

I sniffled. "It…matters…to me." The more upset I got, the more impossible it became to speak at all. My throat was sore. My vocal cords felt like someone had run them over a cheese grater, and I was so out of breath I was gasping between words. All of which combined into a speech hurdle akin to climbing Everest.

He pulled me into a gentle embrace. "Bug."

"Please," I begged into his chest.

After a long moment of consolation, my dad pulled back and eyed me evenly. "Hell or high water couldn't keep that boy from you, and I think you know that. Aside from that asshole of a team owner threatening litigation if Grayson didn't get back in the car, he hasn't left your side."

I closed my eyes and clasped my hands in my lap, unsure how to proceed. My dad was right. When Grayson got a mind to do something, there wasn't much that could stand in his way. *Do I really want anything to stand in his way?* I was embarrassed about my voice, but the more rational part of me argued that that was no reason to punish him. He had probably been worried sick this entire time, and I did want to see him—badly. There was no help for it then. I would have to suck it up.

* * *

I'm not sure at what point I drifted off, but the sound of quiet rustling brought me back to the edge of the waking world. I felt light fingers on my temple, playing with my hair. The fingers trailed down the left side of my face, relatively undamaged from the accident, in a gentle caress, rousing me to sleepy consciousness. I tilted my head instinctively to nuzzle the hand as it cupped the side of my face. A pair of lips pressed to my temple and then quietly said, "Are you gonna wake up for me?"

"No," I whined quietly, burrowing further into my pillow.

He let out a breathy chuckle and sat on my bed, careful not to jostle me. "I spent six hours in a car with Jack to get all the way back down here. The *least* you could do is open those pretty eyes for me to see."

I cracked one eye open, guarded against the light in the doorway. And there he was. My heart fluttered. I opened my other eye and adjusted my head so it was slightly propped on my pillows.

"Hi," he murmured with a smile, reaching to grab my hand. He pressed it tenderly to his lips.

"Hi," I whispered back. *If we keep it to one-syllable words, I should be okay.*

"How are you feeling?" His eyes traveled over my injuries wearily and his Adam's apple bobbed with an apprehensive swallow.

I looked down at my hands. *Okay, clearly, he did not get the memo about the single syllables.* I swallowed, testing the limits of my very fragile voice. My throat ached a little less than it had earlier, but it was still incredibly sore. I was guessing my vocal cords weren't in much better shape. There were so many things I wished to say, but could I get them all out?

A long finger found its way under my chin and lifted my face. "It's okay. Your dad told me."

I turned my face, letting my chin slide out of his grasp as my cheeks took on the color of a ripe tomato.

"The only thing that matters to me is that you're alive, you're awake, and you're healing. The rest…it's not important."

I looked up at him but kept my mouth closed. *Not important? Was he joking?*

"You're really going to let your pride make you a mute?" A single dark eyebrow rose in inquiry.

I worked my tongue over my teeth, debating his questions. He was baiting me, and he could see it was working.

"It's not going to just go away. You're going to have to work at it."

"I know," I retorted with more force than I had previously used. A cough erupted from my lungs, sending flames ripping up my throat.

His brow wrinkled in concern, but once he realized I was okay, he placed a hand on my thigh and squeezed. "Come on, Lainie, it's not that bad."

My eyes fell to my lap. He'd never called me Lainie before. I'd always been Alaina—sometimes Sexy or Babe, but never Lainie. "Lainie?" I asked, raising an eyebrow to emphasize my surprise.

He tucked a strand of hair behind my ear with a smile. "I like Lainie. It suits you."

"Okay…Gray," I teased in return, letting another cough slip through my lips, this time with less violence.

His smile widened into a grin, and he leaned in to kiss me tenderly. "I missed you." An odd emotion leaked into his words as he spoke.

I wasn't as good at reading him as he was with me. "What's…wrong?" My fingers intertwined with his, desperate for contact.

He looked at our joined hands for a little bit before looking up. "I'm really glad you're awake." The beautiful, warm brown of his eyes was murky with something he'd left unspoken.

I struggled to rise, wishing I could look him square in the eye. It felt as though someone was stabbing me in the stomach and the deep-seated ache of broken bones radiated through my body. I hissed in pain but didn't cease my efforts, however futile.

"Alaina—" he protested but decided to help me sit up rather than watch me injure myself further. He raised the back of my bed so I was lying slightly angled and helped adjust my pillows. "Better?"

I nodded with as deep a breath as I could manage through my broken ribs and intolerant lungs. "Tell me," I insisted, holding both his hands in mine. My voice was weak but stern, and he knew he wasn't going to get out of telling me whatever was bothering him.

I'd been so involved in getting myself adjusted I had missed the brace on his left hand and wrist. I gawked, twisting it slightly to get a different angle. His thumb looked swollen. I swallowed hard and glanced up to see him staring at his hand too.

He shook his head slowly. "Stupid. Got loose in Turn Five, over-corrected, and ended up in the wall. I didn't get my hand off the wheel fast enough."

I sighed and held his hand closer for inspection. "Is it… serious?"

"Nah, just a sprain. I should be good for practice on Friday."

I lifted a hand to his face and used my thumb to caress his cheek. The injury wasn't what was bothering him, and my question still lingered between us.

"Can I just sit here with you for a little bit?"

I managed to scoot over without causing too much discomfort, and he situated himself, so I could lean into his chest. He wrapped his arms around me and rested his cheek on the crown of my head. Slowly but surely, I felt him begin to relax and my own body subsided into a contented stupor as well.

* * *

Now that I was conscious, everything concerning my recovery was in overdrive. When I wasn't in occupational therapy, speech therapy, or physical therapy, I was bounced between consults from my orthopedic surgeon, neurosurgeon, and general surgeon, all of which had separate post-operative care instructions and questions concerning my comfort level and recovery progress.

As if it wasn't overwhelming enough waking up to my body being broken in a million different ways and having to relearn how to function with my new restrictions, I was also dealing with the aftermath of a moderate traumatic brain injury. Luckily, I had escaped with little to no harm concerning my motor skills and speech, but my memory was spotty, and that's something I was becoming more and more aware of on the rare occasion I had to internalize.

A week had done wonders for me. My speech therapist had given me some new breathing exercises and techniques. With his help, my voice sounded almost normal again. I still lost my breath easily and couldn't project my voice, but it didn't have the quiet raspiness from the week before either, which allowed me to feel some small semblance of progress.

My migraines, however, were a different problem entirely. I'd had three good days in the last seven, which my doctor didn't seem overly concerned about, but it severely hampered my optimism on a full recovery. The headaches were debilitating, and when one came on, all I could do was lay in bed with the lights off and the door closed to inhibit as much sound as possible—a nearly impossible feat with how noisy a hospital is.

Grayson had been gone all weekend. Another city, another race. Today, however, I found myself tucked into his side, enjoying his natural state of being—similar to that of a portable space heater. The hospital was so cold. I always felt like my toes were turning blue. We had such little time together these days that we were nearly inseparable in the time we did have together.

"Can I tell you something?" I asked quietly. The memory, one of the few things I could actually recall surrounding the accident, had been bothering me for a few days, and I needed to talk to someone about it, even if he did think I was crazy.

"Hmm?" he murmured drowsily. I wondered if he'd been asleep.

"When I was…unconscious…" I took a deep breath, trying to figure out how to say what I was mulling over in my head. "I think I had…an out-of-body experience," I murmured, thinking back to my encounter with Granny. I was fairly confident I hadn't imagined or dreamed of her. The memories were so vivid. It couldn't possibly have been a hallucination.

Grayson lifted his head off mine and shifted out from under me so we could face each other. "What do you mean?" That haunted look was back in his eyes.

I squirmed under his gaze, not sure how to explain the experience. "I don't know. It was dark, and I could feel my body, but I couldn't control it. Then, all of a sudden, I wasn't in my body anymore. I was on this beautiful hillside with wildflowers all around me. The sun shone on my face—I could feel it on my skin…" I drifted off, basking in the memory. It had been so long since I'd felt the sun on my skin.

I glanced up at Grayson shyly, but he was introspective—looking but not seeing. When he noticed I was no longer speaking, he glanced up. "What makes you think it wasn't a dream?"

"It was so real. I'd never been to this place before. I'm certain of that." I shook my head, instantly regretting the movement when a wave of nausea and pain rolled through me. I closed my eyes. *Deep breath.*

"Are you okay?" he asked.

I let out a steady, calming breath. "Yeah." I glanced back up at him. "About the time I get used to not doing that, it won't matter anymore."

He gave me half a grin and chafed my arm gently. "What do you mean, you've never been to this place before?"

"It was gorgeous—absolutely untouched wilderness," I murmured, remembering the feel of the flower petals between my fingertips and their aromatic, herbal scent.

"You probably saw a picture or something," he argued, fighting back with logic. I knew he'd have a hard time processing something like this.

I moved out from under his touch. "So, I suppose you'll tell me I imagined my grandmother too?"

"Your grandmother?" he asked, unsure now.

"Granny Aileen," I murmured, lost in my memories. Her

deep auburn hair had flowed around her wildly, and when the sun caught it, I could see streaks of copper, gold, and darker strands of burnt sienna. "She died when I was ten—cancer...but when I saw her, she was...younger, probably my age, maybe a little older." I met Grayson's gaze levelly. "I was scared. She told me I was hurt badly, but I was still alive. It was almost like I had a choice," I murmured, letting my fingers trail up and down my arm gently. "She said no one would blame me if I didn't go back, but she had her suspicions I wasn't about to give up." I smiled, remembering the drawl of her Carolinian accent. "'A little fire in my belly' is how she put it." I smiled, and Grayson smiled too.

"So, that was your dad's mom?" he asked, trying to piece together the branches of my family tree.

"Yeah." I was still lost in thought. "You believe me, then?" Hope was evident in my tone. I'd been coddled for most of the past week, and the last thing I needed or wanted was to be treated like the newest resident of the loony bin.

He sighed. "I...I don't know what I believe. I know people claim to have out-of-body experiences when they—" He cut off his train of thought. There was that look again. I'd seen it off and on over the past few days. For the most part, he was his normal, cheery and optimistic self, but sometimes I would catch him deep in a memory I wasn't privy to.

"Grayson." I took his hand and squeezed it. "What happened?" My words were as soft as velvet. I reached up and traced his cheekbone in tender encouragement.

His breath was shaky. "After the accident...you were in surgery for hours, and they lost you twice. They weren't confident you would make it. So, your parents," he swallowed hard, his eyes watering. "They let me sit with you...and—"

his voice cut off. His normal olive complexion was ashen, and his lips pressed together in a contemplative line. "There's no way to describe that feeling." He held my gaze, emotions roiling under the surface like a rip current.

"What feeling?" I asked, squeezing his hand, hoping by talking, he could shed some of his burden.

"The feeling you have when you're sitting next to the person that means the most to you, and you know they're fighting for their life, but there's absolutely *nothing* you can do to help them."

I didn't know what he was going through. I could only imagine what I would feel if something like that had happened to him. The feeling of helplessness would be overwhelming. And the fear, well, I didn't even think I could conjure up that level of terror. I would live with the accident forever, but so would he.

21

Lost and Found

I watched silently as the morning sun caused the sky to change colors from deep navy to lavender, to pink, to orange, and finally to a brilliant blue. Grayson was out like a light, and I didn't want to disturb him. I knew he probably hadn't had a lot of sleep in the last few days, and the last thing I wanted was to interrupt what little rest he did get.

A nurse quietly came into the room to check all the readings on the machines by my bed and looked a bit startled when I turned to greet her. "Good morning," she murmured quietly.

"Morning," I whispered back, stifling a yawn.

"How are you feeling?" she whispered, glancing at the iPad in her hand as she read over my medical updates.

"Pretty good."

"Good. Looks like they changed your pain medication yesterday. What's your rating this morning?" she asked, looking at me.

I shifted and winced. "Maybe like a four." Anything was better than the pain I was starting to remember from the accident. I would wake in a panic some nights, my heart beating like a trip-hammer, but with no memory of why. The memories lurked under the surface of my conscious mind like a terrifying sea monster stalking its prey.

She nodded. "Okay. I'll see what I can do about that. Your doctor should come by in about an hour or so for rounds."

"Okay," I murmured, feeling Grayson stir beneath me. We had fallen asleep embracing one another, and the few hours I'd spent dozing in his arms felt more restful than all the sleep I'd accumulated over the past week. That feeling coupled with the change in pain medication brightened my outlook considerably. The idea of leaving the business in the sole hands of my best friend for another second had me riddled with anxiety, but I couldn't very well resume my role as a full-time entrepreneur when I was sleeping eighteen hours a day.

"Good morning," Grayson murmured, tightening his arms around me.

"Morning," I whispered back.

I traced imaginary patterns across his chest quietly. "If you need a place to shower and stuff, you can go to my apartment. I think my keys are in the cabinet." I gestured over to the meager storage facility in one corner of my room.

He laughed. "Are you trying to tell me something?"

I giggled. "No! I just wanted to tell you before I forgot."

His chest shook with another laugh. Grayson sighed and rolled off the bed, stretching out to his full height and groaning with a yawn. "I might go and shower then. I think Jack and Jess are going to come by this afternoon, and I'll want to be back by then."

I gave him a serene smile. "Okay."

He paced over to the cabinet, fished through what little had survived the accident, and grabbed my keys. "I'll be back in a bit," he murmured, leaning in to kiss my temple before making a hasty departure.

I hadn't been alone for more than fifteen minutes when my mother graced me with her presence. I looked up from my phone with a smile when I sensed her standing in my doorway. "You just missed Grayson," I stated, leaning in to kiss her cheek as she did the same to me.

"No. I passed him on the way out. He said he's heading over to your place for a shower?"

I didn't miss the conservative disapproval coating her voice and gritted my teeth. "Yes, I gave him my keys. Where else is he going to shower and sleep?"

"I don't know, a hotel?" she huffed as she sat in the chair next to my bed. "He won the Indy 500, for goodness' sake. I think he can afford a hotel room for a couple of nights."

"I'm not going to argue about this with you." I didn't bother telling her he'd already spent quite a few nights at my apartment—with me. I spared that for her sake more than my own. I wouldn't want her having a stroke and ending up in the bed next to me. Looking for a redirect on the conversation, I asked, "I never got a chance to ask you how your date with Mr. Hilton went."

A blush tinged her cheeks a delicate rose color, and she toyed with an imaginary thread on my blanket. "It went… well," she allowed. "Rob has called several times to check in on me—and you—during this whole mess. He's so sweet. Honestly, though…" she drifted off and cleared her throat, suddenly remembering to whom she was talking.

I furrowed my brow in confusion. "What?"

With a tight smile plastered on her face, she shook her head and paced to her purse, digging around for an imaginary item. I knew the signs well enough. She was avoiding me. It was odd, though, she usually told me anything and everything without hesitation.

"What's going on, Mom?" I asked in a semi-patronizing tone. "You can tell me. I'm not going to flatline."

Her face went from flushed to pale in a millisecond.

"Poor choice of words. Sorry," I murmured. "But really, you don't have to worry about me."

She sighed and looked up at me. "I know, sweetheart. It's just…complicated. The last thing I want is to bring you into it when I'm still sorting things out."

What the hell did that mean? "Okay…" I drew the word out, making it clear I wasn't sold on her excuses, but her lips were sealed.

* * *

The next day I was on the edge of sleep after an early morning PT session when I heard Grayson's voice come to me softly. These words weren't for me, though. Then I heard my brother's voice join the conversation. I relaxed even further. They seemed to get along well, and I took comfort in that. Their dialogue, however, put me on edge.

"You're lucky as hell. I saw that crash. Man, that was nasty," my brother muttered, "I mean, the impact alone, but then when—"

My eyes flew open, and Grayson's eyes drifted to me, guilty. I wasn't sure if he regretted their conversation had woken me or that the story I'd been eavesdropping on was a much different story than the one he'd bothered to share with me earlier. "What are you talking about?" I asked, trying painfully to sit up.

He came to help me, gently placing his arm behind my back. "It's nothing," he muttered with a shake of his head.

"It doesn't sound like nothing." I challenged, holding his gaze and daring him to deny it again.

He sighed. "It's a racing accident, Alaina. They happen, you know that." He soothed, rubbing my thigh softly as he spoke.

"You told me you hit the wall and got your hand caught on the steering wheel." I was getting a strong suspicion a lie of omission was rearing its ugly head.

Grayson glanced over his shoulder at Tucker, irritated. Guilt coated my brother's face, and he dropped his gaze to the floor. "I did," he claimed, straightening up his posture as he spoke in defiance of my accusation.

"And then what happened?" I asked, glancing from face to face. Something deep inside me was simmering right below the flash-point. It wasn't a comfortable feeling.

Grayson surveyed my face for a moment longer, his deep-set eyes like pools of hot coffee, nearly black in shadow. I wasn't going to flinch from this silent war of wills, and finally he caved, typing something into his phone for several moments before handing it over to me. I glanced up, but Grayson wouldn't meet my eye. He simply handed the device to me and removed himself from my bedside, striding over to the far side of the room to look out of the window.

I glanced at my brother briefly before playing the video. Race coverage from Wisconsin ensued for thirty seconds before the footage cut to Grayson's charcoal and azure car careening over the curb of Turn Five and slamming into the barrier wall. Then, without warning, another car shot into view, slamming into Grayson before coming to rest atop the windscreen of his car, preventing escape. It wasn't until I saw the smoldering of a fire caused by hot brakes that my heart began to race. My eyes could not leave the phone as I watched replay after replay, my stomach roiling with acid and nerves as I watched how close Grayson had come to serious injury, or even death. Finally, I stopped the footage. "Tuck…can you give us a minute?" I asked, my voice low under the strain.

Without so much as a word, my brother gave us the room. I studied Grayson's strong figure, silhouetted against the light of the window. His arms were crossed in front of him, his hands clamped between his biceps and his chest. "Grayson." The muscles in his back gathered with tension, but he remained silent. "Grayson, look at me," I voiced in a slightly more demanding tone.

He turned slowly, bracing himself. For what, I wasn't sure.

"Why did you lie?" I inquired, barely-contained anger seeping into the words. Waiting for his response was not a task I was up to at the moment. "I'm not some delicate little flower. I'm not going to wilt if the conditions aren't right."

His eyes narrowed, fire burning deep in their depths. "I know that!" he bit, regret flashing across his face before looking back out the window. It was the first time he'd shown anything other than kindness, tenderness, or patience toward me, and I was taken aback. I wasn't naive enough to think he had an endless fuse, but it was still jarring to experience. My hands wrung absently in my lap. I wasn't sure what to say.

His head hung limply against his chest. "I'm sorry," he

murmured, turning back to me. He took a few hesitant steps toward the bed, arms still crossed in front of him. The quiet was almost too difficult for me to take. I could handle arguments, but I wasn't good at silence.

"I know you can handle it. That's not—" he sighed and dropped his arms from his chest. "I just feel like—with everything that's happened, you shouldn't *have* to handle it. Not now," he muttered, scratching the back of his head.

My brow furrowed of its own volition. "You think I don't feel those problems—that I don't know they're there, even if you choose not to share them with me?" Tears welled in my eyes and clouded my vision. *Why are you crying? This isn't a tear-appropriate moment. Be mad, but don't cry!*

"No. I—" he was trying to find the right words, but it was proving more difficult than he thought. "You nearly died, Alaina, and the last thing you need to worry about is me."

The impulse to laugh was too strong, and an unhinged cackle escaped my lips as tears flowed down my cheeks unabated. "But I worry about you anyway! Don't you see that?" Realizing I was yelling, I paused and took a deep breath. "Grayson." His name was quiet on my lips as I attempted to rein in my emotions and wiped away the tears. "We can't keep things like this from each other. Besides, did you honestly think I wouldn't find out?"

"I *hoped* you wouldn't," he admitted. "It was a close call, but I'm fine." He defended himself as if I were going to lay into him again.

I put a hand to his cheek. "I know. You're sitting right here. I can see that for myself." I gave him a small smile and pinched his ear lobe playfully before withdrawing my hand and becoming serious again. "Crashes and accidents, they're part of it. I know what I signed up for. I'm not saying I won't be scared out of my mind when they happen, but I don't think anyone can promise that."

He picked up my hand, rubbing our palms together. "No. I don't think anyone can promise that." His thought was absent-minded, and I clenched my jaw. I knew what he was thinking. My fingers laced through his and squeezed tightly to catch his attention. His eyes flitted to mine in response.

"I'm going to be fine."

"I know." He assured me in return and leaned in for a kiss.

* * *

"Have you ever Googled yourself?" I asked Tucker a few days later as I sat in bed messing with my iPad. I only had a solid ten to fifteen minutes of screen time before my head started to throb like the ground under a herd of elephants. The more time passed, the more frustrated I became. How was I supposed to get anything done without being able to look at the computer? I couldn't answer emails. I couldn't verify invoices. Hell, I couldn't even watch an entire IndyCar broadcast. *At least the radio isn't wholly obsolete.*

He looked up from his phone with a comical look on his face. "No, I can't say I have."

"Well, check this out. It's a picture of the truck that hit me." I turned the iPad around for him to see.

"Oh my God," he swore under his breath as he took the tablet and swiped through the stories.

"It says he ran the red light a block down and then ran another red light when he hit me." I shook my head, feeling a distance between myself and what I had read. It was like I was looking at someone else's life. When I tried to remember that night, it was like it never happened.

"You okay?" Tucker asked as he handed the tablet back.

"Yeah. Just trying to remember."

"You *want* to remember?" he asked, shifting closer to me.

"I don't know. I mean, everything after Victory Lane is this blank page, and I know there are probably a lot of good things that happened." *How could there not be?* It upset me having a hole in my memory on such an important day, and it wasn't just an important day for me, but for Grayson as well. I wanted to be able to share that with him.

Tuck broke eye contact and looked at the floor, shaking his head. "I…" He sighed and looked back up at me. "Alaina, I've seen a lot of terrible things on deployment in Afghanistan, things I wouldn't wish on anyone, and I think I have a pretty good idea of what that night was like for you—and for the people with you. Trust me. Some things are better left alone. I just hope they crucify that son of a bitch." His eyes were cold with barely contained rage.

"The article says he's being charged with a felony DUI resulting in great bodily harm. Whatever that means." My shoulders lifted and fell in a quick shrug.

"It means the dumbass almost killed you, and they're going to send him to prison," my brother muttered as he got up from his seat and paced to the window. It was a warm, humid morning and the shock of the moist, hot air stippled the cool window with tiny beads of condensation. Tuck stared at the moisture running down the window in rivulets, deep in thought.

"I didn't mean to upset you."

He continued to stare at the window, but his eyes were

blank, thinking back to a distant memory. When I called his name, he snapped to attention. "No, you didn't…I was just…" He shook his head to clear the remnants of whatever unpleasant thoughts he'd been having. "Talking about it makes the horror of it hard to ignore."

I let out a hard laugh. "Must be nice—being able to ignore it, or at the very least, push it to the back of your mind," I said bluntly as I looked down at the gash running down my arm. Obvious injuries like the one on my arm and the six-inch incision down my stomach aside, there were other things—internal things—I wouldn't be able to push aside for much longer.

One of the many downsides of being stuck in the hospital for weeks on end was the limited amount of entertainment at my disposal. On one such occasion when I was knee-deep in the lonely abyss of spotty Wi-Fi, I'd picked up the stack of papers my legally obligated medical professionals had left for my perusal. I didn't understand half of the medical terminology in the document, but when it came to the potential side effects of my fractured pelvis, the two bullet points at the bottom of the page stuck out like sore thumbs.

- *Sexual dysfunction and/or vaginal discomfort during intercourse*
- *Complications in childbearing, childbirth, and fertility*

I gritted my teeth and forced the thought to the back of my mind. Before meeting Grayson, I'd thought an icicle in hell had a better chance of survival than any notion of me becoming a mother. I really had no desire to procreate, but I couldn't help feeling bitter about the whole thing. I'd nearly had my life taken from me because of one person's hare-brained decision. I'd only been dealing with the reality of my injuries for one week, and I found it extremely difficult not to feel overwhelmed, frustrated, angry, or hopeless. I couldn't even manage something as simple as getting out of bed, walking across the room, and taking a pee on my own. It was infuriating.

Earlier in the day, my mom had helped me wash my hair and brush it over the shaved area and incision on the side of my head. Occupational therapy had given me the skills to bathe on my own, but it wasn't without its struggles, and my mom saw that—*bless her.* It had taken me half the time to shower with her help, and being clean allowed me to feel somewhat human again. I inhaled deeply and leaned back into my pillows, basking in the feeling. *You can only take so many sponge baths in a row before they just don't cut it anymore.* I sighed and looked at my brother's back for a minute as he stared out the window at the city beyond. "Have you talked to Jess since…"

He turned to me, his face looking distant. "As soon as I knew you were out of the woods, she was my first stop."

I bit the inside of my cheek. "And?"

He rolled his eyes and leaned against the windowsill. "It's a bit of a touch-and-go situation."

"What happened?" I asked, knowing it probably hadn't been a civilized conversation.

He let out a hard laugh. "Well, at first, she slammed the door in my face, but after a few minutes of groveling through the door with her neighbors staring at me, she let me in."

"No offense, but you kind of deserved that." He'd behaved

like an asshole with the whole baby situation, and I wasn't about to pretend his behavior had been acceptable.

He scratched the back of his head and smiled. "I know. Trust me. I'm pretty embarrassed about how I reacted, but it's like I told Jess, all I can do now is try to be better. I wasn't planning for this to happen, and I know she wasn't either. So, we'll deal with it. She says she wants to keep the baby, and I support her decision." He shrugged and gave me a small smile. "It's kind of crazy, right? Me being a dad?"

I nodded slowly. "A little bit." We were quiet for a moment. "Have you talked to Mom and Dad about it yet?"

He let out a sigh and rolled his eyes. "Oh, yeah. They weren't pleased, but I think they're dealing with it, same as everyone else, I suppose." One day I would get the whole story, but I could sense he wasn't up for it right now.

"So, when did you get in?"

He sighed and came back over to sit next to me. "It took a couple of days for someone to track me down." He rolled his eyes. "I was out in the field, and my phone died. After Mom called half a dozen times, she got the Red Cross involved, and we got a call over the radio." His face was washed out completely as he recalled the situation. He shook his head and looked down at the floor. "That call… God… it was awful. They couldn't give me many details. All I had to go on was you'd been in an accident, and you were severely injured. I knew it had to be bad if the Red Cross was calling me in." His blue eyes were clouded in memory as he continued to share his story. "It was late at night. I couldn't get on a flight until the next day, so I got in my car and started driving." He let out a shuddery breath. "It makes me sick thinking about it."

"I'm sorry you had to find out like that," I murmured.

He shrugged. "It's not your fault. I'm just glad you're okay," he allowed with a smile.

"It's good to see you, Tuck. Even if it did take *great bodily harm* to get you here."

He laughed. "Yeah. I'd prefer it if we skipped the whole bodily harm part next time." He paused and gazed at me for a minute before earnestly adding, "It's good to see you, too, sis."

* * *

"Wake up, hon. It's not your time. That's it. Open your eyes." The voice was gentle and familiar, coaxing me back the way I'd come—whatever that way was.

There was nothing but me and a brilliant white that wrapped around my soul like a warm blanket, comforting me and making me content to stay right where I was for the rest of time. I struggled against the firm foot in my backside, kicking me toward a much colder, harsher reality. All I could process was a dull ringing; it stretched on infinitely as I fell. I had an empty weightlessness in my stomach. Then, with the force of a freight train, I slammed back into my body and wished I could go back to the comforting white surround.

My lungs begged for a reprieve, but no matter how much air I tried to suck in, they refused to inflate. My eyes rolled in my head blindly. The night sky was black, tinted with the strange amber glow of street lamps. Something green was shining in the distance. *A traffic light?* Horns everywhere blared, and the wash of headlights over my face was blinding. *Am I lying in the street? Why am I lying in the street?*

"Alaina?" Someone called from far away as if inquiring after

267

a familiar face. The murmur of a gathering crowd filled the air like white noise, a constant rumble but nothing distinct. Closer this time, a more urgent, panicked shout sounded as footsteps charged closer. "Alaina! Oh my God..."

A more feminine screech echoed these sentiments.

I convulsed as my brain began to process the trauma. An unbelievable amount of pain was beginning to course through every inch of my body. *Oh my God, make it stop!*

"Call 911!" the girl screamed. Someone's hands touched me, and I let out a whimper. I couldn't move. I couldn't even speak. There were no words. *How could there be?*

"Alaina, can you hear me? Alaina?"

Grayson. Grayson was here. The ability to make my lips and tongue function, however, was not. I was a newborn baby squalling with the inability to make my needs known.

I laid on my side, my face pressed to the rough asphalt, sticky with oil. Hands reached out and touched my exposed side but didn't move me.

"I'm here, I'm here," he assured me as I squawked.

Someone ran up to us. "Ambulance is on the way." I couldn't see anything. It was hard to breathe, and every mindless muscle spasm sent white-hot pokers through me. I felt like I had been steamrolled by a piece of heavy equipment. "Somebody get those cameras out of here!"

"I need everybody to get back! Give them some space!"

"Alaina, please," someone sobbed brokenly from nearby as they grabbed my hand.

"Don't move her!" Grayson bellowed and then away from me, "What the hell happened?"

I kept trying to talk, but all I managed were a couple more agonized screams. My vision was blurry, which only added to my mounting sense of panic. The oil slick I was lying in was growing by the second, and I realized with detached clarity, the shiny black liquid I was lying in was not oil, but blood. If something weren't done soon, I would bleed out right here in the middle of the street.

More feet pounding on pavement. "I'm an EMT. Can I help? What happened?"

"I…she…" Grayson struggled for words, his steady hand still on my upper arm. "I think she was crossing the street, and somebody hit her. I don't know. I was inside, and I—" Grayson's strangled reply was agonized, and he was fighting down the claws of panic with every ounce of self-control he could muster.

"What's her name?"

"Alaina."

"How old is she?" As the guy asked Grayson questions, he continued to work.

"Twenty-four."

"Any health conditions or allergies?"

"I…I don't…" Grayson's voice trailed off helplessly and another voice provided the answer.

"No, nothing like that." Jess. My head moved toward the familiar sound, trying to find her through the murky water of my sight.

"No, no, no." The helpful stranger's soothing words came to me. "Stay still. Shhhh…" He rested his hands on the sides of my head firmly. "Okay, I need you to hold her just like this. Keep her still, alright? If she has a spinal cord injury, we don't want to aggravate it," he clarified. I felt hands restraining me, and I whimpered, my heart pounding out of my chest.

"Shh, shh. Alaina. They're coming, okay? Hold on." He

sounded terrified, and while I certainly understood his panic, I was finding it harder and harder to care. The whole world was moving like a tilt-a-whirl at the fair, and as the pain started to fade, an odd tingling sensation filled its wake.

"Stay with me." I felt Grayson's arms go rigid as I continued to drift further and further away, riding the waves of painless euphoria. My eyes kept rolling to the sides or back of my head. I couldn't keep them fixed on anything. It took all the effort I could muster to even focus on Grayson's voice. He had such a rich, warm voice, full of passion and tenderness.

"No, no, no. Alaina. You have to stay with me. Come on!" Sirens were growing near, and the closer they got, the further from shore I felt. I was adrift in the calm of a tropical sea. Warm waves washed over me, lulling me into a peaceful state of bliss. I barely even noticed how hard it was to draw a breath.

I managed to drag my eyelids open one more time, wanting to catch a final glimpse of Grayson's fathomless, dark eyes. One more time, that's all I needed. His thumb was stroking my cheek as he braced my head. "You're going to be okay," he murmured. I couldn't differentiate my hands from my feet anymore. All the muscles in my body had been replaced with cotton balls and sandbags—motionless, unfeeling masses.

"Grayson," I rasped so quietly I don't think he heard me so much as saw my lips move with the effort.

"I'm here. I'm right here." A tear rolled down his cheek and landed on my face as he leaned over me.

"I'm…s-sorry…" My voice was weak with fatigue and physical damage, making the words slur together.

He shook his head, eyes going wide, terror taking a solid hold on him. I was barely hanging on, and I wasn't sure if it was blood loss or a traumatic brain injury, but neither option boded well for me, and we both knew it.

Sirens wailed nearby. The alternating red and white lights hit the glass of the city's buildings in a beautiful, fractured pattern. "So…pretty…" I breathed and surrendered to the current trying to pull me under.

* * *

I came back to consciousness, gasping desperately for air. My face was coated in a cold sweat, and my heart was pounding at such a frenzied pace I thought it would leap out of my chest. As I came back to my senses, the scent of antiseptic began to fill my nostrils, chasing away the remnants of fresh blood and motor oil. I put a hand to my forehead and took several deep, calming breaths, letting the oxygen fill my system and slow my pulse. *It was a dream. Just a dream,* I thought to myself as I wiped the cool perspiration from my forehead and glanced around the room.

I was alone for the first time in three weeks. The majority of the tubes and wires had been removed earlier in the day, and I was now the proud owner of my very own recovery room. A nurse peeked her head in the room. "Everything alright, hon?"

"Fine," I answered shakily. "Just a nightmare. I'm okay."

She nodded in understanding. "If you need anything, just press your call button."

I nodded back and pushed into my pillows, trying to get comfortable again. Cautiously, I began to examine the nightmare, and as I began to dissect, I realized it wasn't fiction at all, but a very, *very*, true story. The shuddering of my body as waves and waves of agony had washed over me made my blood run cold. When I'd told Tuck I wanted to remember, I hadn't meant I wanted to remember *this*. Whoever was upstairs pulling the strings had an extremely dark sense of humor.

Despite all of the earth-shattering recollections of my physical state after the accident, there was one thing that haunted me more than anything else—Grayson's voice, so completely desperate and helpless. The far-away look that had clouded his eyes so much lately was rapidly beginning to make more sense. As I'd lain on the streets of Indianapolis bleeding out, I'd been resigned to dying, and as I let that sink in, I realized that night haunted Grayson for all the same reasons, and the amount of guilt I felt welling inside of me was enough to drown in.

22

Bound for Life

Since I was on the mend, my family didn't feel the need to be here with me every second of every day anymore, which was both good and bad. Grayson was gone again—off to another weekend in the fast lane. I had been in the hospital for close to a month now, and while the doctors were amazed at my progress, they didn't feel comfortable releasing me since I lived on my own. *A minor detail in my book, but they're stubborn old farts.*

My body, admittedly, felt exhausted most of the time. Each day I got a little bit stronger, and Jess often stopped by after work to monitor my progress. While she used her stops as an excuse to mother me, I used her visits to bombard her with questions about the shop.

"What about the Neeses? Are they okay with the centerpieces I had made already?"

Jess sighed. "Alaina, stop worrying. I've got everything under control. All of the immediate weddings are fine with what you have finished, and I've referred everyone else to Once Upon a Time for anything else they need."

I cringed at the thought of giving business to our competitors, but I didn't have a choice.

Jess saw my reaction and rolled her eyes. "I know you don't want to refer anybody, but you are physically incapable of working right now. It's the right thing to do. You know you can't depend on me to get all the creative things done."

"Yeah," I whispered, looking down at my hands.

"I know. Okay? I do, but you don't need to worry about that right now."

"You know, I'm really tired of everyone telling me what I do and don't need." The words were sharp. Bitter. Almost mean.

Hurt registered on Jess's face for a millisecond before she took a breath and continued quietly. "Everyone I spoke to was completely understanding of the situation. They want what's best for you, Lainie. The shop will still be there whenever you are ready for it."

I gave a slight nod and wiped away a tear of frustration. She gently sat on my bed and pulled me in for a hug, which only made me cry harder. "Look at us," she said with a laugh. "Just a pregnant girl and her gimpy friend, taking on the world."

I let out a weird half-sob, half-laugh. "I keep thinking, four weeks ago, you were the one with all the problems."

She stroked my hair, cognizant of the side of my head that was still healing. "It's all going to be okay. In six weeks' time, you'll be good as new, and I'll still be pregnant," she chuckled darkly.

I gave her a tight smile and let out a deep breath, endeavoring to persevere though the subject matter was a bit heavy for me at present. I took a deep breath and wiped the remnants of a few stray tears from my face. "I talked to Tuck."

She sat up a little straighter, starting to raise her guard at the mention of my little brother. They'd spoken about the baby and the general situation, but things could still be considered uncomfortable at best.

"How do you feel about that?" I asked her quietly.

"About what? His apology?"

I nodded in assent but kept my lips pressed firmly together.

"I don't know," she said with a roll of her eyes. "How am I supposed to feel about it? He avoided me for two weeks before he found out I was pregnant, and now he wants to pretend like it never happened?"

I took her hand and squeezed it. "I'm with you. You know that, but he's my brother, and I feel a little obligated to hear him out. Neither one of you planned on taking this past that one night."

"He knows me, Alaina. He should have known I wouldn't have bothered him if it wasn't important." She was quiet for a minute. "After I told him…about the baby…" She got up from the bed and paced to the window absentmindedly. "He was terrified—we both were. And I don't blame him for being scared. I get it. I don't need a big strong man to come and save the day. I can do this on my own. I'm not saying it won't be hard—only an idiot would think that, but I can do it. I can be enough." She was nodding her head, assuring herself. "But knowing all of that…I also have to admit our baby has a right to know its father, and Tuck, for all his faults, is a good guy." She gave me a half-smile. "I mean, I may be liberal with my choices, but I don't sleep with anyone, even if I *am* six tequila shots deep." She laughed. "All I want is for him to think about it—truly think about it. And if he decides he doesn't want to be a father to this child, I won't say another word." She shrugged.

"Did you tell him that?"

She turned back toward me from the window and nodded. "I did. He says he doesn't have to think about it, he wants to be a part of his child's life—unconditionally."

I didn't reply for a moment, confused. It sounded to me like Tucker had said all the right things. At least if I were having that conversation with a man I'd had a one-night stand with, that's what I would want to hear. "That's good, right? That's what you want?"

"Is it?" she asked. "When he showed up at my door, I thought…" She had tears in her eyes. "I was prepared to hear he didn't want anything to do with me or the baby. I was ready for that, and when he told me, not only did he want to be a father, but that he would take care of me too, for as long as I needed…" She took a shaky breath. "I should have felt relieved—happy even. And instead, I felt…trapped." The words were strangled in her throat.

For Christ's sake! I may not even be able to have children, and she's complaining that having this baby may permanently associate her with its father? What the actual fuck?

Confusion and emotional baggage were quickly turning into something darker and more explosive. "You *want* to do this all on your own?" I tilted my head to the side and eyed her, trying to put all the pieces together.

Jess was oblivious to my change in mood, too absorbed in her own problems to notice or care. "I'm forever tied to him. I can't change that. This child…it links us forever, but the one thing I have left in this world is the ability to find a man who chooses me *and* my baby, not one that's stuck with us. If I accept Tucker's help, I'm tying myself to him and limiting my options in the process."

I closed my eyes and pinched the bridge of my nose between my thumb and forefinger. "He…didn't *propose* to you, did he?" *Surely he's not that stupid.*

My best friend looked down at her feet. "No, no…I just… what guy is going to want to put himself in the middle of all this crap?"

I studied my best friend and gave her an incredulous look. "Someone who wants you for the *right reasons?*" My friend looked up, confused at my tone. "I don't know what more you want me to say…" I added. "You've got one really great guy following you around like an infatuated little puppy, and you've got another who just wants to be accountable for his actions, and make sure you're taken care of. I get that it's a change of pace from the type of guy you're used to sleeping with, but I still don't understand what the problem is."

"Why are you acting like this?" Jess had tears in her eyes now. "I thought you would understand."

"Understand what? That you're feeling trapped by a situation that I warned you about time and time again? 'You need to be careful, Jess. You probably shouldn't sleep with random strangers, Jess. What do you mean you don't refill your birth control regularly, Jess?' Seriously, what more do you want from me?" The edges of my vision were beginning to turn red and my pulse was pounding against my temples in an unrelenting throb of barely contained anger. Suddenly, I snapped. "My brother is trying to do the right thing. I'm sorry if that doesn't jive with your lifestyle choices."

"What the *fuck*, Alaina?" Jess jumped back like she'd been stung. "Where is this coming from?"

I shrugged, unflinching as she glared at me through the

tears welling in her eyes.

"Wow." Without another word, she turned and fled the room, barely pausing to gather her purse in the process.

* * *

It was Saturday night. I felt a quiver of excitement in my stomach. The IndyCar race at Texas Motor Speedway was one of my favorite races of the year: high banks, high speed, and lots of passing. *What isn't to love?*

While my heart and soul yearned to be there, my body wasn't quite up to the challenge. And if I couldn't be there in person, the next best thing was to watch it live. I had to wait a few minutes for the previous program to end, but then they were showing helicopter views of the wide-open Texas countryside. The massive grandstands of the track seemed to have fallen straight out of the sky, landing somewhere between blue sky and rolling green fields, like God himself had desired a little racing action. I couldn't help but smile, remembering how I'd felt the first time I'd happened upon this particular track. I looked down at my phone. Knowing Cami would soon have possession of Grayson's phone, I sent a quick text.

**I know you're going to knock 'em out.
  Good luck. Stay safe. Can't wait to
  see you.**

I also sent a couple of kissy emojis for good measure.

My phone buzzed almost instantly, like he'd been waiting for me to text.

Thanks, babe. See you soon.

I looked up from my phone to see Tucker step quietly into the room to join me and my dad, as we watched the start of race coverage via the small TV mounted on the wall opposite my bed. Part of me wondered if he was intentionally avoiding Jess. *It couldn't be a coincidence he was always showing up after she left, could it?*

I watched as the broadcasters spoke about the weather, tire degradation, and the like as they prepared for the race. They interviewed a few of the drivers and made small talk, including Makenna Armstrong. The only woman in the field of twenty-four had won the pole for today's race, and that was big news, so they were interviewing her at the moment. They flashed to a recap of last week's race at Belle Isle.

"Can you turn it up?" I asked, curious to know what had happened last week.

Tuck happily obliged. The Detroit doubleheader was always a brutal affair. A temporary road course built on the streets of Belle Isle, the course was bumpy and physically demanding. After the accident at the start of Race One that sent three drivers into the tire barrier in Turn Two, it had been a fairly uneventful race. Other than a couple of debris cautions and the resulting on-track action, nothing too interesting happened. Pedro had rebounded from his 500 loss beautifully, leading nearly the whole race and swiping the win. They did a brief interview with him and then flicked to the recap of Race Two—which had taken place completely under rainy conditions. My heart leaped anxiously at the thought of it. Rain tires were required on a wet course, but the constant mist that was kicked up made visibility extremely poor, and conditions were treacherous at best. The race had been called early on account of unsafe racing conditions when lightning had been spotted. *Well, that's boring.*

The camera switched back to the announcers in the booth. "Before we send it down trackside, we want to take a moment to touch on something that has hit the IndyCar community and some of its most notable members hard since the Indy 500. Take a look." The screen faded to black, and I looked sideways at Tucker, who was watching with mirrored rapture.

The familiar sounds of a high-speed engine echoing off the empty grandstands at Indy came through the speaker. "Indianapolis." A man's baritone voice began. "It's the birthplace of modern motorsports…and the Indianapolis 500." Timelapse footage of the sun rising over the track on race day filled the screen. "For over one hundred years, the greatest racers in the world have endeavored to make their mark on this hallowed ground. For Grayson Miles, that dream is in his DNA. Son of the late Rick Anderson, competitors and spectators alike have watched this young driver grow into a champion." Old pictures of a small boy in a go-kart filled the screen in a slideshow as the commentator kept speaking. "So, when a new face made her appearance on his arm this May, they took the internet and the racing world by storm."

Pictures of Grayson and me from our earliest encounters bloomed on the screen, and I felt a twist of longing in my stomach for the simplistic nature of six weeks ago. More pictures floated into view: us in front of the media on Bump Day, Grayson's enthusiastic kiss after he broke the record, us walking hand in hand through Gasoline Alley during the pre-race festivities, and me leaning in to kiss the front of his helmet before he strapped in for the 500. "A couple brought together by their passion for racing—nearly torn apart by tragedy." The recap continued as it showed Grayson drinking the milk, hugging his mom, and kissing me. The screen, showing all of us posing happily around the Borg-Warner Trophy, faded to black.

Sirens sounded. News coverage from outside the hotel where the victory party was being held flooded the screen, and sound bites of different news footage resonated. "Breaking news out of downtown Indianapolis this evening where a young woman has been the victim of a hit and run... We are now getting reports the victim is none other than Alaina Montgomery, the girlfriend of today's Indianapolis 500 winner, Grayson Miles..."

And then a video of a stone-faced Cami making a statement at a press conference. "At approximately twelve-thirty this morning, while leaving the Indianapolis 500 Victory Celebration, Alaina Montgomery was struck by a driver under the influence of alcohol. She has been taken into emergency surgery at IU Health Methodist Hospital with life-threatening injuries. Her condition is unknown at this time. Miss Montgomery's friends and family want to thank everyone for the outpouring of support they have received and ask for privacy at this time."

"She's a great girl, always has a smile on her face. She's a lover of this sport and a great supporter of Grayson. We all love her and are hoping for the best." Grayson's team owner Bruce was speaking, and then the announcer took back over as "#AlainaStrong" flashed across the screen, making me smile.

"An overwhelming amount of support has flowed out of this community in the past several weeks for both Grayson and Alaina. You can see those hot pink logos on every car in the field today in support of Alaina as she continues to recover." Several images of different cars sporting the sticker came across the screen as the announcer spoke. The pre-race segment cut to a reporter standing on pit road. "In a week where the schedule is normally grueling with cross-country interviews and tons of flight hours, you didn't end up doing any of those things," the reporter said, looking at his interviewee. The camera panned over to Grayson, and I smiled.

He let out a hard laugh. "No…I'd say I had a very abnormal post Indy 500 victory. But um…yeah…fortunately, all the networks have been really understanding and supportive of my need to be with Alaina and her family. So, we've been able to reschedule most of the interviews for next month."

"That's great," the reporter commented. "You're obviously here now. Take me through a little bit of what your schedule has entailed over the past few weeks."

"Yeah. I was at the hospital pretty much the entire week after the accident. The doctors determined Alaina was stable enough for me to race at Road America, so I flew up there Friday morning. We drove back down to Indy immediately after the race that night to be back with her and her family. She's been steadily improving since then, but I've been racking up the frequent flier miles. I normally fly up to Indy on Sunday nights and then in for the race on Thursday afternoons." He gave a tight smile to the reporter while twisting his water bottle in his hands in a gesture I recognized as agitation. The fact that Bruce had forced him into racing the past three weeks had come as a shock, and while Grayson hadn't felt the need to vent his frustration to me, it was still very clearly there.

"How's Alaina doing?" the reporter asked, in a tone that was more like a concerned friend than a gossip-hungry journalist.

He gave his typical half-smile. "The first few days were touch and go. She didn't stabilize until the Thursday after the accident, but she's alert and responsive now and on the mend," he informed the audience with a small smile, repeating the agreed-upon status update we, along with Cami, had come up with earlier in the week.

The announcer smiled. "So, she's doing well?"

"She's pretty banged up, has lots of broken bones, and she's recovering from several major surgeries, but she's definitely on the mend. And, I'm sure she's watching now," he informed with a wave.

"That's what we like to hear. Good luck today, and best wishes on a speedy recovery for Alaina."

"Thank you." Grayson thanked the reporter and blew a kiss to the camera as they cut away.

"Amazing," my dad said, looking away from the TV to me. "It's pretty cool how much of a family everybody is over there. I guess you're a part of that now," he claimed with a smile.

"I guess so." I leaned back into my pillows and rested my head against them gently as the pre-race festivities continued on TV.

"I can't believe that's your boyfriend." Tuck threw himself on the bench near the window and settled in to watch the race with me.

I gave a hard laugh. "I know, right? And you were worried

I'd be single forever."

He rolled his eyes. "I guess patience pays off."

"Yeah, and to think, if I'd dated one of your Air Force buddies like you wanted, I probably wouldn't have been single when I met Grayson."

"Yeah, yeah, yeah. You told me so. Is that what you wanted to hear?" he said as he waved me off.

My phone lit up with a push notification, and I swiped into my Instagram. Grayson had posted a picture of his #AlainaStrong sticker right next to his name on the side of his car. "Strongest woman I know. You're amazing, @LainieBug. I'm racing for you tonight. #AlainaStrong."

I smiled through my watery eyes.

"What's that smile about?" My mom asked as she walked back into the room with bags upon bags of food. I twisted my hand around so she could read the post, and she smiled too. "He really cares about you."

"Yeah," I murmured, smiling more to myself.

"What?" she asked softly as she ran her fingers through the stringy tendrils of unwashed hair at my shoulder and gave a brief questioning look at my brother.

"I really care about him too."

* * *

My physical therapist, Monique, was a beautiful, young woman—fresh out of college from the looks of her. Her black hair was pulled back from her face in a puff of tight-knit curls, and her dark skin had a healthy, sun-kissed glow to it that I'd once had on my own skin. I stared down at my pasty complexion in revulsion. These morning sessions always put me in an abysmal mood. Each morning at the ass crack of dawn, an orderly would burst into my room with an insufferably cheery smile that said, "I woke up at five a.m. to go for a five-mile run, and I didn't even need an alarm clock." Like clockwork, I'd then be torn from my cozy cocoon of wrappings and hurled into the forthcoming wheelchair, which would shuttle me down to a gym full of ten more morning people, all grinning from ear to ear like the worst forms of sadists on planet Earth. *Good morning, Alaina! Ready for your morning torture session, Alaina?*

"How are you feeling today?" Monique asked with a smile as she helped me out of my wheelchair and onto the seated stepper machine, where I always began my PT sessions.

"I'm ready to get the hell out of Dodge," I grumbled.

She laughed and smiled. It was amazing how she took my bad moods in stride. *I'm probably not her only grouchy patient. This place makes me want to kick puppies, and I love puppies.* "Has your nerve pain subsided since our session yesterday?" she asked.

The memory of the burning, shooting pain down my right leg made me shudder. It had been ten times worse than my post-op pain, and medications hadn't been able to touch it. Blessedly, after my session yesterday, it had dulled and was now completely gone. I nodded in response, and she shook her head. "Good, good. Okay," she murmured. "Let's start with seven minutes on this, and then we'll move to the mat table."

I nodded, trying to "embrace the suck," as Tuck always said. *Suck it up, or you're never getting out of this place.* My muscles were always tight and painful in the morning, which made getting out of bed even more difficult. I supposed that was the point of it all, though. Warm up the muscles, work out the kinks, and hope like hell your body was functioning enough that day to make any sort of progress. As more and more time passed without an end to my incarceration in sight, my moods were becoming more volatile. I was falling into a depressive state—something I'd never had trouble with before. *Hey, who says you can't teach an old dog new tricks?* I smirked to myself. My dark humor was definitely on point these days. Honestly, I'd found my sense of humor was altogether different since the accident.

My time in the hospital was a torrential downpour on my usual good nature and perpetual optimism, but I couldn't blame everything on my extended stay. No, there was something fundamentally different about how my brain functioned now. People, in general, annoyed the piss out of me. My temper was an ever-present demon lurking just under the surface, waiting for somebody to say or do something wrong. And then, sometimes, my emotions would get the better of me altogether, causing me to burst into tears for no good reason—one of the more disdainful new habits, in my opinion.

Surprised, I looked up to see Monique standing next to me. "Time's up. Let's get you over to the table." Slowly and carefully, she helped me up off the seated stepper machine so I could transition back into the wheelchair and over to the mat table, ready for whatever torture she saw fit to put me through now.

Monique proceeded to lead me through heel slides, bridges, and a plethora of other exercises geared toward priming my muscles and preparing my body for what this session was really all about. When she finally called out the third and final box squat of my third sequence, I slid down onto the table in exhaustion. *God, I'm such a wuss.* She offered me a paper cup of cold water and smiled. "You're doing great. I know it seems like you're barely treading water, but trust me, you're way ahead of where your doctors thought you would be three weeks ago."

I nodded, trying not to let the disappointment show. My neurosurgeon and orthopedic surgeon had both raved about my recovery, but if I had to hear one more person marvel at how quickly I was bouncing back, I was going to hurl my water in their face. It wasn't about my recovery time. It was the fact I had to recover *at all*. Four weeks ago, I'd had everything I ever wanted and more, and now I couldn't even stand on my own two feet for more than ten seconds without some form of support. *Jesus fucking Christ! What did I do to deserve this? There are terrorists, rapists, and murders running around, and I'm the one who gets to be maimed for life?*

"Ready?" Monique asked, a nude gait belt dangling from her left hand as she approached.

My mood bounced up and down like a Geiger counter that had hit on a uranium deposit because of what was next. I'd graduated from the parallel bars a few days ago and found the idea of a walker *and* a gait belt a bit humiliating. *Did I want to be able to walk again? Yes. Did I want to walk around healthy young people using a walker like a ninety-year-old grandma? No. Was I going to suck it up and do it anyway? Absolutely.* Because I wanted out of this damn hospital and being able to walk on my own two feet precluded that result.

"I don't need that thing," I grumbled as I scooted forward on the table to plant my feet firmly on the ground.

"Yes, you do. We've been over this," my ever-patient

physical therapist insisted.

"It's embarrassing," I whined.

"Alaina," she squatted in front of me so we were at eye level. "Your pelvis is broken in two places, and you were in a medically-induced coma for nearly a week. Your muscles are atrophied, and you need the gait belt."

"Fuck this shit," I muttered under my breath as Monique fastened the belt around me. A week of unconsciousness had thrown a wrench in the works. Typically, someone with my type of pelvic injury would have been mobile within a day or two of surgery, but alas, no dice. So, now I was paying for it in stiff ligaments and tendons and stamina equivalent to that of a koala.

"Look, I know this is your favorite activity of the day," Monique mocked playfully. Maybe this is why she was my physical therapist and not one of the others. She had thick skin and was fluent in sarcasm, which I could, and did, appreciate. "So, if you do three laps around the gym with the walker today, I'll give you a surprise, and I'll upgrade you to crutches tomorrow."

"A surprise? What on earth did I do to deserve this celebrity status?" I asked, trying to fight the smile twitching into view at the corner of my lips. "If I ask nicely, can I have the surprise in good faith?"

She let out a bubbly laugh. "You know what, I think an improvement in mood is enough incentive for me. So, if you *promise* not to give me any more 'tude, I'll fork over the goods."

I made a criss-cross pattern over my chest as I spoke. "Cross my heart and hope to die." It wasn't too much of an ask after all. The haze of sleep was starting to wear off enough for me to at least put on the mask of civility.

Monique reached behind the counter and handed over the contraband—a medium Dunkin' Donuts Extra Extra iced coffee. My mouth watered embarrassingly, but I found it hard even to care. I snatched the coffee out of her hands and sucked down a mouthful of the sweet elixir. "I'm not even going to ask how you knew."

"I don't give away my sources anyway." She laughed. "Alright." She seized the coffee back out of my grasp with a 'down to business' look and said, "Let's see what you've got."

Three laps later, exhausted and drenched with sweat, I lay on the table as Monique helped me stretch my muscles out before the conclusion of our morning round of exercise. As she pushed my wheelchair back within range and prepared to help me transition off the table, I cradled my iced coffee and debated whether to ask her about the pamphlets I'd been reading. I cleared my throat, and she turned around, raising one well-sculpted, black eyebrow, her warm, brown eyes searching. "Umm…can I ask you a question?"

The smile reappeared. "Of course!"

"In the packet you gave me to read…I saw that pelvic fractures can cause issues…sexually." I blushed an unflattering shade of red and dropped my eyes.

"Oh…" she murmured and sat lightly on the table next to me. "It's not very common to have any sort of permanent dysfunction in women," she allowed. "You might experience some pain and discomfort," her voice was soft, soothing. "I think the biggest issue—and you'd have to talk to your obstetrician about this when you decide to have children—is that a high percentage of women, who suffer pelvic fractures like yours, have problems with childbirth. They may recommend you deliver via cesarean if you decide to have kids."

I nodded absently, thinking to myself. Just add it to the list of things I already had to worry about. *Ask about the fertility thing. Do it. Come on you, ninny. Don't be a baby!*

Monique could see the thoughts rolling through my head and misread my reluctance. "It will be sometime yet before you're cleared for any sort of…activity." Her blush was harder to see through her dark skin tone, but it was there. "Your boyfriend…Grayson? He seems…understanding. I'm sure it won't be an issue."

"No." I shook my head. "I don't think it will be…I just…" I sighed, chickening out at the last second. "The last thing you want is complications with…that stuff," I muttered.

A small giggle escaped her lips that she quickly clamped down. She removed herself from her seat next to me. "Like I said, I'm sure it will all work out. And when your doctor clears you, we can take some time out of our last session to go over positions that may be less weight-bearing and more comfortable for you. With all that in mind, I would just tell your boyfriend everything. If he knows how to avoid hurting you, everything should be fine."

I nodded, taking some comfort in her words. "Thanks, Monique."

The smile widened past one of professional courtesy. "You're welcome."

23

Repercussions

The day before, Jess had managed to smuggle my laptop past my mom, and I was anxious to get back to work. Things were more than a little tense with my best friend after my explosion. She was pretending she was fine, but I knew her better than that. *Better add an apology to my ever-growing list of crap to do.* With some trepidation, I opened my Outlook inbox. My breath caught, and my heart stuttered. *Five hundred emails?* "Sweet Lord, what has she been doing the past four weeks, her nails?" When I got into business with her, I knew I couldn't rely on her to pick up the slack, but I'd never thought of it being an issue, primarily because I'm a bit of a control freak and prefer to hold the reins. But now, looking at the neglect my inbox had suffered, I was beginning to think I'd made a severe error in judgment.

My first order of business was emailing back the brides and event planners who emailed with concern for my welfare. They were clients, but I also considered many of them friends. It touched me deeply to know they felt the same. After I'd reached out to them, I began to divide my inbox into folders.

Anyone that was inquiring about an event within the next three months got a mass email explaining the situation and referring them to other companies in the area. Despite the anguish I felt at sending them to my competitors, I knew it was the right thing to do. As Jess had argued, I wasn't physically capable of helping them, and I shouldn't commit to something I wasn't up for.

To my surprise, the majority of my emails were from people wanting to set up meetings or get quotes from us for events six to eighteen months away. I was knee-deep in proposals when I heard footsteps stop at my door.

"Uh, oh. Your mom is going to hurt someone."

"What she doesn't know, won't kill her. Will it?" I asked rhetorically as I shut my laptop and looked up at the handsome figure standing in my doorway. Though he was a sight for sore eyes, it was the gorgeous arrangement of flowers he was holding that took my breath away. "Grayson," I murmured as he stepped closer and sat them on my side table for closer inspection: peonies, gardenias, gladiolus, and hydrangeas. It was a beautiful display. "They're amazing. Thank you!"

He leaned down to kiss me, and I gleefully reciprocated, not letting my lips leave his as he gingerly sat on the bed. Breaking away, I lingered close to him for a moment brushing my nose tenderly against his before pulling back to appreciate my newest flower arrangement.

"How was the race?" I asked, nonchalant as I fingered the delicate petals.

He raised his brow in shock. "You mean, you don't know?"

"I may have fallen asleep," I admitted with a shy grin. "But in my defense, I'm still recovering."

"Uh huh. Milk it while you can," he teased. "No, it was good. No accidents for me this time," he grinned. "We managed a top five. Although, by the time it was all said and done, there were only thirteen cars left, soo…"

My mouth popped open, and my eyes bulged in an expression that resembled a surprised goldfish. "What happened?"

"Two guys behind me touched wheels in the corner and caught a bunch of cars in the process. It was like an eight-car pile-up on the freeway."

"Shit," I swore. "Was anybody hurt?"

"Nah, nothing but their pride anyway. How was your weekend?"

"Oh, you know." I gestured around. "There's so much to do around here. I wouldn't even know where to start."

He chuckled and tucked a strand of hair behind my ear, lightly tracing the pink scar on the side of my head. My hair grew fast, and my bare scalp was slowly fading under a patch of brown fuzz.

"Has the doctor said anything about when you can be released?" he asked, shifting on the bed.

"Not really. He says it's day-to-day. They want me on oral meds, so we're working on that, and I think if I have one more morning session with my physical therapist, we *may* kill each other, but other than that—" I lifted my shoulders in a shrug that belied my consistent frustration with the situation. I didn't want him to see how much I was struggling. It would only make him feel worse about how little time he was spending here.

He squeezed my hand and chuckled, "You know, constantly dwelling on it won't make it get here any faster."

I let out an unintelligible grumble and took a deep breath,

still feeling the ache of broken ribs as I inhaled. "So, what's your plan for this week? I know you mentioned something about going back to Phoenix to check on things."

"I'm not worried about it. Cami's out there. She said she'd keep an eye on things, and she's overnighting some new clothes and stuff for me."

"Are you planning on staying at my place then?" I asked, wishing I could join him.

He sighed. "I should probably get a hotel."

"What? Why?" I asked, suspicious at his sudden change of heart. "Did my mom say something to you?" My eyes narrowed, scrutinizing his features.

He gave me a weak smile. "It's fine, Alaina. I shouldn't depend on your generosity. It's not my place, and it's not like I can't afford to stay somewhere else."

I could feel anger bubbling up in me, making my heart rate spike. He glanced at the heart monitor, hearing my reaction, and I blushed furiously. *Damn thing.*

He ran a hand up my arm. "It's okay. Honestly."

"She has no right. None!" I clamped my mouth shut, gritting my teeth together before I said something I'd regret.

That half-smile returned to his face. "She's trying to protect you."

"From what? News flash: I almost died. What else could she possibly be protecting me from?"

He glanced down at our entwined hands. "I think we both know the answer to that."

Silence filled the air between us, and I let out a shaky, calming breath. My heart slowed as the silence dragged out. "She's never been this way before. I don't understand."

"Alaina, if there's any truth to what you told me about your relationship history, she's never been put in this position before."

A heavy sigh of discontent melted out of me. "What am I going to do?"

He leaned in and kissed my forehead. "Nothing. I can take it. I promise."

I gazed up and saw the truth of it in his fudge-colored eyes. He would handle a lot more than this if it meant being with me. A rather large yawn escaped my mouth as I settled back into my pillows, appeased for the moment.

"You can close your eyes," he assured me.

"I feel guilty sleeping when you're here," I admitted. "I know you said you have a test out at Gateway—" Another jaw-popping yawn took over.

He shook his head. "No, I'm going to talk to them about getting a test driver so I can be here wi—"

"Grayson," I interrupted with disdain. "No."

"But I—"

I put a hand on his arm. "You can't put your life on hold for me. I'm not going to let you." I shook my head.

"But…it's not *that* important. And besides, you wouldn't even be in this place if—" his words cut off.

I knew what he'd been about to say, and it felt like he'd reached into my chest and wrapped his fist around my heart. "If it weren't for you?" I whispered. "You really believe that?" I asked, tears in my eyes.

"How could I not?" He choked. "You didn't even want to go that night, but I guilted you into it because *I* wanted you there." He left his seat on my bed and paced over to the window, clearly not wanting me to argue against the lies he'd been feeding himself all this time.

"So, you talked me into going to a party instead of going home and going to bed like a grandma. There's absolutely no way you could have known what would happen. You were high on your win. You wanted to share that with me. That's not a crime!" I scooted to the edge of my bed. I wasn't supposed to be on my feet without my walker, but I'd be damned if I let him continue to beat himself up.

He whirled around, rushing to stop me from standing. "Alaina, stop. Stop." He put a firm hand on my shoulder. "You're going to hurt yourself," he murmured. Prolonged emotional turmoil had etched wrinkles into his forehead and the corners of his eyes. How many times had he sat next to my bed that first week, brow crinkled in worry, eyes squeezed shut in anguish?

"More than it hurts knowing you blame yourself for all of this?" I cried, tears welling in my eyes.

He squatted in front of me, ducking his head and holding my hands in his. "Who else am I going to blame?" was his quiet reply.

"Literally anyone else," I said in frustration. I couldn't understand—couldn't possibly fathom how he saw this insane turn of events as being in any way his fault. "Blame me for not looking both ways before crossing the street. Blame the drunk for driving the car. Blame the police for not having sobriety checkpoints set up on the night of the *Indy 500*. But for God's sake, don't blame yourself!" I paused, trying to calm myself before I continued. If I let myself go any further, my irritation at the situation would morph into a full-blown bomb of fury, and I'd be damned if Grayson caught a piece of shrapnel in the process. It was bad enough Jess was already recovering from her share of battle scars. *Deep breaths.* "I know this was…terrifying, but you couldn't have prevented it."

When he pulled his head up to look at me, tears were streaming down his face. "I was petrified, Alaina. I've never been more afraid in my life," he murmured before looking back at the floor.

In the span of a heartbeat, all of the anger drained out of my body, and I was suddenly filled with an overwhelming need to protect him from the pain he was experiencing. "I know," I murmured. "I'm sorry."

He lifted his eyes to mine, his chestnut hair catching in the light as he did so. Gently, he joined me on the bed and pulled me into his side so we could lay together and let the comfort of each other's presence envelope us.

"I need to tell you something," I whispered, not wanting to look him in the eye. For some inexplicable reason, I was embarrassed to admit what I was about to say.

He shifted underneath me, "Okay…"

"We haven't really talked about the accident. I mean, the repercussions of it." The words were so awkward—so formal. I hadn't been honest about any of it with Grayson. Mainly because I didn't want him to harbor any more guilt for the things I was experiencing, but there was no avoiding this. I couldn't lock it up and throw away the key. *Well, I could, but what good would that do?*

He tightened his arm around me. "What is it?"

"When I hit my head, I—" I squinted my eyes shut and took a deep breath. My head was starting to feel like an elephant was standing on it, and I wasn't sure if it was the photophobia or the stress of the situation that was bringing it on. "I lost some of my memory."

Grayson was absolutely still. So still that I was relatively sure he wasn't breathing. I turned toward him, worried. He was gazing at me with a look of mingled confusion, horror, and fear in his eyes, and it seemed as if he was unsure which of those emotions was worse. After several more seconds, he finally managed two choked words. "How much?"

"I remember everything until…"

"…until?" he whispered. Something was eating at him. I thought it had been the shock of the news. I knew it would be hard for him to hear. After all, that's why I hadn't told him. Wasn't it? Or was it that nagging feeling in the pit of my stomach, that unshakable dread that I forgot something vital to life as I knew it?

"Everything after Victory Lane…it's just…blank." I stared down at my hands, not able to handle the look of devastation in his eyes. He looked like a man on the edge of a cliff who had been prepared to die, only to watch someone shove the woman he loved off the edge in his place. "It's been coming back in pieces, but most of the memories are from after the accident. I had hoped they would reappear before anyone could notice they were gone, but the more time that goes by—" I swallowed hard, the pain behind my eyes pulsing with every beat of my heart. "—the more I'm afraid they aren't ever coming back." I took his hand, feeling tears beginning to sting my eyes. "And the way you're looking at me right now proves I'm right. Something happened. Something important."

His brow was wrinkled in distress as he studied me, and his hand reached up to cup my jaw, his thumb caressing my cheek. "I wish you'd told me."

"I'm telling you now."

"Because you want to know?"

"I want to know," I confirmed, my voice low and pleading. I hated to make him relive that hellish night, but I had to have the blanks filled in. It would drive me mad if I were always left to wonder what happened in those hours between Victory Lane and waking up broken and alone on the street.

Reaffixing his tight grip on my hand, he moved out from underneath me and prepared to tell me what I'd missed.

* * *

Grayson put the vehicle in park and sat back in the padded driver's seat. His body felt completely drained. Even that tiny reserve of energy most people called adrenaline was gone, and his head was spinning. The past few hours had flown by, but at the same time, there were images embedded in his memory that would last a lifetime. He knew that without a shadow of a doubt. He closed his eyes but hesitated to relax too completely for fear he would fall asleep where he sat. His night was far from over, and he couldn't afford to take his foot off the gas now. Then again, he'd done the hard part. He'd won the race. How much more difficult could it get?

I just won the Indy 500. No matter how many times he said it to himself, it still didn't seem real, and he had the feeling it would be days, if not weeks, before it truly set in. His life's work, his father's dream, it was all coming to fruition. He'd never understood the phrase "walking on cloud nine," but if he'd ever come close to walking on a cloud of any sort, it was happening right now. With visions of cheering fans and ice-cold milk dancing in his head, he hauled his eyelids back open and looked up at the building in front of him. Alaina was waiting for him. He would have to resume his walk down memory lane later. Otherwise, they would be late for the victory celebration downtown. The black-tie banquet with every member of the IndyCar organization and cameras galore would be tomorrow night. Tonight was for friends and family—the best sort of celebration in his opinion. He'd never been one for the spotlight.

With a short walk and a one-story climb that felt like the final leg of the trek up Everest, Grayson lifted his fist to knock on the door, but it opened before he could get that far.

"I'm so sorry! I'm not ready. Five minutes," she sputtered as she held up a handful of digits and zoomed back into her room, the tails of her satin dressing robe fluttering in her wake.

He smiled and shut the door behind him. "Don't rush. I'm the guest of honor. The party doesn't technically start until I get there." He raised his voice slightly so she could hear him in the next room. Copper plopped himself at Grayson's feet, demanding the attention he felt he deserved after a lonely day at home. "Hey, Buddy," Grayson cooed, massaging the Golden Retriever's ears. The dog let out a contented sigh that made his state of bliss perfectly plain. Grayson removed his feet from underneath the large dog with one last pat and made his way toward the doorway his girlfriend had disappeared through moments earlier.

He walked into her bedroom to find Alaina in nothing but her underwear, searching through her closet haphazardly for a particular item of clothing. His first reaction was to step back and give her natural modesty some room to breathe, but like an industrial-grade magnet to a pile of iron shavings, he felt himself drifting closer and closer until he stood just behind her. He reached around her and tugged on an emerald green number that would bring out the green flecks in her hazel eyes, whispering, "I like this one."

For a span of two heartbeats, there was nothing but silence and electricity pulsing between them, and then she turned and was in his arms, soft and warm, pliable to his all-consuming need for her. "God, I want you so bad," he murmured, feeling adrenaline and testosterone flood his veins with the hardening of his arousal.

"Then, come get me," she growled, pulling him with her as she backed toward the bed. The intense ache he felt was enough to knock him over. Alaina's soft lips smashed into his with a desire nearly as intense as his own as she reached up to undo the buttons of his neatly pressed dress shirt. To hell with creases and wrinkles. *Why the hell are you thinking about creases and wrinkles at a time like this? Get your shit together, Miles.*

They collapsed onto the bed in a flurry of linens and loose clothing, their lips never parting from each other as Alaina continued to undress him with single-minded ferocity. His hand reached around to run along the delicate skin at the small of her back and drifted up to her bra clasp, springing it open in one deft maneuver. It wasn't until she reached for his belt buckle that some semblance of reason sunk its claws into his balls. "I—" he swallowed and struggled for breath as he fought to recall the fleeting thought that had crossed his mind. "I don't have any protection."

An ironic smile began to curl her lips, and she reached back to the bedside table. The drawer slid open to reveal a box of condoms. He wasn't prepared, but she certainly was. She must have thought of their conversation earlier in the week just as often as he had, but clearly for different reasons. The story of her past relationships had made him ashamed of the way he'd behaved, but it was becoming more evident by the second that that hadn't been her intention. She'd shared her story because it was part of who she was, and he wouldn't be able to fully appreciate what sex meant to her unless he knew everything.

"You didn't think I'd let an opportunity like this slip through my fingers a second time, did you?" She giggled and pulled him back down to her.

What was it he'd heard Emma say during one of those TMI moments she was famous for? *"If a girl has matching undergarments, you aren't the one that decided to have sex that night."* Grayson caught a glimpse of rose-patterned lace from the bra Alaina had carelessly flung in the corner as he moved lower to slip his finger under the elastic band of her identical panties.

Part of him wondered if she'd planned it this way in the hopes of luring him in like a siren to a lost sailor. Not that he cared. Alaina let out a sensual moan that drew all of his attention back to her in an instant. She was ready, and holy hell…so was he. But he also remembered the last time they had been down this road. He didn't know if the experience with her ex had been her first and only time, but he certainly wanted to make this one more enjoyable for her.

He laid a gentle trail of kisses down her neck, across her collarbone, and between her breasts before taking a nipple in his mouth and sucking tenderly. She pressed up into him and gasped as his tongue swirled around her areola. One of her hands tangled in his hair as she lost herself to the sensation. His dick was throbbing. He wouldn't be able to—

Her other hand reached out and wrapped around him. She was in control now, and with an inexorable tenderness full of yearning, she guided him to her. Fireworks went off. It was like each synapse in his body was exploding all at once. The sensation was something between pleasure and pain, and he'd never experienced any feeling more addictive in his life.

Alaina arched up to meet him, wrapping her legs around his hips to draw him in further as they rocked together, riding the waves of passion to a climax that had them trembling in each other's arms, hearts pounding, breathing heavy. Two hours ago, riding around the track in the back of a convertible with the wreath around his neck, waving to hundreds of thousands of fans in the stands, he'd thought life couldn't get any more perfect. He'd never been more wrong.

"Grayson." His name came to him, quiet, tender. A finger caressed his cheek lightly, and his eyes fluttered open. Alaina was kneeling in front of him, fully dressed, hair perfectly curled, makeup flawless. Had he dreamed it? No. He was lying naked across Alaina's bed, barely able to move, the fatigue was so strong. How had he managed to have sex in his state? *Well, that's evolution for you.*

"You looked so peaceful. I didn't want to wake you, but we have to get to the party. Everyone's waiting." Her perfume was so intoxicating he felt the stirrings of arousal once again. *You have* got *to be kidding me.*

He reached out and pulled her closer. She was wearing the green dress he'd picked earlier. He was right. It *did* bring out the green in her eyes. "I can cancel. I'd rather stay here with you," he persuaded as he raised himself up to press his lips to hers.

Her lips curled upward, but she let him kiss her. "I would

love to stay here with you and do that all night, but we can't. Everyone is waiting."

Grayson groaned and flopped back down onto the bed.

"Come on, sleepyhead. We don't have to stay long. I can't anyway. I have an early meeting tomorrow."

"Tomorrow? But it's Memorial Day. Nobody works on Memorial Day."

"I have to meet with a bride. She wanted to meet today, but with the race, I couldn't, so we compromised. I'm supposed to meet her at the venue at nine a.m. to do a walk-through, and then I'll have the rest of the day to do whatever you want." She didn't seem bothered by the prospect of working on a national holiday, so he shrugged it off and sat up, rubbing his eyes and yawning.

"Well, if I *have* to..." He moaned and heaved himself out of her annoyingly comfortable bed. The only thing that presented something of a silver lining was the prospect of sleeping in that bed later tonight with her beside him.

* * *

The pounding in my head had escalated to the point it felt like someone was flattening it with a steam roller. A state made even worse by the revelation I was trying to process. *I think I'm going to puke.*

"Alaina?" Grayson's call to me came from a long way off, like the distant whistle of a train preparing to come across a trestle in the dead of night. My throat felt like it was swelling shut. If I could have run, I would have. *It's too much. Too much. Just too much...*My mind was jumping around like a tree frog on meth. One minute I was ashamed, then I was embarrassed, then I was mad, then I was sad, then I was back to square one and more confused than ever.

"Alaina..." This time his voice came with concern.

Tears were clawing their way free from the cage I'd hitherto kept them locked in, and the elephant on my chest was gaining weight by the second as I gasped for air. *As if this God-damned accident hasn't taken enough from me! I should never have asked. Ignorance is bliss, right? I could have gone the rest of my life without knowing, right? Oh god...Oh god, oh god, oh god...*

This was a massive commitment I had decided to make. Sex was sacred to me. Especially after what I'd been through with Isaac, it wasn't something I gave lightly. Grayson knew that, which told me how special that night had been for him too. The devastated look on his face when I told him of my lost memories should have been my first clue on that account. *Well, hindsight's 20/20.*

"Alaina, talk to me," Grayson pleaded. "I need you to tell me what's happening."

That's the problem, isn't it? I have absolutely no clue what's happening. I gave an unhinged cackle through my restricted airway. *Was this what insanity felt like?*

A passing nurse, hearing Grayson's distress, came into my room. One look at my labored breathing and pale complexion set her in motion. "Okay, honey, I'm gonna need you to take a deep breath for me." She kindly directed as she inserted a syringe into my IV port. She turned to Grayson. "It might be best for you to take a walk."

Not one to argue with a professional, Grayson nodded and, with a hesitant glance in my direction, walked out of the room.

* * *

The familiar scents of ethanol, hot brake pads, and fresh rubber engulfed Grayson as he made his way down pit lane at a brisk walk. He was going to be late for practice if he wasn't careful. Bruce would have his head on a silver platter if they didn't get their laps in. Of course, if he was late, so was Jack, so that lessened the pressure a little as Jack struggled to keep pace with Grayson's longer legs.

"I mean, look, Alaina's great and everything, but she's a hot mess, Gray. Are you sure you want to—"

"What am I supposed to do, break up with her?" Grayson's harsh whisper cut through to Jack despite the general din of practice preparation. He didn't *want* to break up with Alaina, and a sudden surge of panic filled him at the thought.

"Nobody would blame you. It's not what you signed up for." Jack shrugged, making it perfectly clear he didn't see any issue with breaking the heart of a thoroughly broken and hospitalized invalid.

Grayson stopped and stared at his best friend. "There is something seriously wrong with you."

"What, you *want* to have a lead weight tied around your ankle? Grayson, the girl is barely even conscious, and when she is conscious, she bounces around like a fucking Ping-Pong ball. One minute she's happy, the next she looks like she's going to rip your balls off and feed them to the wolves."

"Okay, I think you're being a *little* dramatic..." Grayson rolled his eyes, but resumed his mission toward their respective pit boxes, nodding to a few fellow drivers as he went.

"Jess said the other day when Alaina found out Copper is only being fed once a day instead of twice a day, she lost her mind and threw her phone at her." Jack stared meaningfully at his friend.

Okay, so maybe Alaina wasn't the most emotionally stable person right now, but that didn't mean—

"Look, we have enough stress right now with this whole sponsorship deal. I think anything that adds more stress to your life needs to be cut loose."

The guys drifted to a stop next to Jack's car and Jack hopped up onto the pit wall in one deft maneuver, looking for his helmet bag.

"How am I supposed to prioritize that kind of decision when—"

"When you're too sympathetic for your own good?" Jack asked as he gathered up his balaclava and prepared to dive headfirst into it.

"When I love her," Grayson murmured.

Jack raised his eyebrows in surprise. "Seriously?"

"Yeah. I do. I love her." Grayson stood up straight with more confidence than he felt and gazed levelly at the slightly shorter man in front of him.

"Well, Forrest, I think that's a whole other box of choco-lates."

* * *

"Don't tell me you're hiding too."

Grayson jumped out of his reverie, mouth downturned in a guilty frown. "Not hiding, per se, just—"

"Avoiding her altogether?" Jess's lips twitched at her own joke. The hand tightening around her coffee cup was the only indicator she wasn't being entirely facetious.

307

Grayson's brow furrowed and he sat up straight on the cushioned bench he'd been using as his refuge, scooting over to make room for his new companion. It was a beautiful day outside and the sun came through the atrium windows with a blissful glow full of vitamin D and warmth. "She's having a bad day, so I'm giving her some space." He held up his reading material in illustration, though he'd barely looked at it. The book was a convenient excuse more than anything. The only thing he could think about was Alaina's confession.

She didn't remember. None of it. Jess plucked the thin blue book from his grasp, *A New Normal: Living With Your Loved One's Traumatic Brain Injury*. Her eyebrows lifted and she offered the novel back. "A little bit of light reading?"

Grayson took the thing back in a defensive gesture and rolled it into a tube to hide the cover. "I just…" he sighed and closed his eyes, gathering his thoughts. "I don't have any idea what she's going through—none of us do."

Jess shrugged and took a sip of her latte. "I figured if she wants us to know, she'll tell us."

"Maybe *you* should read this." Grayson offered the book back to her with a smirk.

Jess pushed it back at him, her nose wrinkled in distaste. "How 'bout you give me the Cliff Notes version?"

"Well, obviously, I haven't read it all, but…" Grayson ran his hand through the pages, fluttering them thoughtfully. "There's a lot more to this than the physical injuries. Yeah, the migraines and sensitivity to light factor in, but the mood swings, the lack of communication…" *Memory loss…* He added silently. If Alaina hadn't bothered to share her problems with Jess, he wasn't about to put a stack of kindling on her already short fuse. "They're all part of it too."

Jess was quiet, not sure what to say.

"When people think of TBIs, they think of speech problems and physical handicaps, and while those are common, it's not always like that. Look at Alaina. She almost died, but she seems relatively okay. On the inside though…I think she's…"

"Not okay?" Jess concluded.

"Well, she's definitely not the same Alaina we knew before the accident, is she?" Grayson shifted uncomfortably. He hesitated to say it out loud. He should be grateful she was alive. For a long time, he'd thought that was maybe too much to ask, but after the last few days, he'd begun to realize Alaina's physical setbacks were the least of their concerns. He still loved her, that was never a question, but there was also a good bit of doubt bouncing around in his head at the moment.

Before, Alaina had always been an open book with him. There had never been a day when he felt she wasn't telling him the whole story, and if she felt the need to withhold information, the topic of discussion generally wasn't herself. Jess's pregnancy was a vivid example of that. It wasn't that she hadn't *wanted* to tell him, it's just that protecting her friend came first, and he understood that. Now, it was like there was a wall between them. Her affection for him was still there. She still lit up when she saw him, true, but when it came to expressing her feelings, most of the time her responses came down to one or two words. He knew she was in pain. He knew she was confused, but she couldn't express that herself, and it was frustrating beyond bearing—not only because he *needed* that open dialogue, but because he knew she did too.

"They call it 'the new normal.'" Grayson shuddered at the impending prospect of a life with Alaina that was nothing like he'd originally envisioned. There would be no going to the movies because the lights and noise would trigger a migraine. They wouldn't be able to go on long hikes without irritating her pelvic fracture. They wouldn't be able to lay in bed and reminisce about the first time they'd—

"Is it *always* going to be like this?" Jess asked, just as horrified as Grayson, but not hiding it nearly as well.

He lifted his shoulders in a shrug. "The lady who wrote this book, she suffered an injury pretty similar to Alaina's. It took her years to get back to a place where she felt somewhat like her old self. To this day, it's a struggle. The migraines and photophobia will more than likely go away, but there will also be a tendency toward depression as time progresses."

"Poor Alaina…" Jess whispered. "God…that's…" She ran a hand through her dark, silky hair as she stared down at her feet.

"I know." Grayson sympathized. "It's a lot…" *A lot for her. A lot for me.* There was no denying the world had been a much simpler place before the accident. As if he hadn't had enough problems… His grip on the book tightened and he wasn't sure whether to cling to the thing like a life raft or toss it in the nearest garbage can.

"The other day she snapped at me and…and I yelled at her." Tears welled in Jess's emerald eyes, and she glanced up at Grayson, shame crinkling the features of her face. She wasn't what he considered classically beautiful, but she had the unique ability to draw the eye of even the most unavailable man like a moth to a flame.

Grayson, resolutely in the unavailable category and proud of it, put his arm around Jess in comfort. "It's not your fault. It's hard. Trust me, I know. I think we just need…patience."

He sighed the last word and gave her a final squeeze before releasing her and moving to stand.

She joined him. "Headed back to the lair?" she asked with a small smile.

He gave her a smile back. "Maybe in a little bit. I think I'm going to stretch my legs first."

Grayson pushed open the nearest door and stepped out into the humid June day. The condensation in the air clung to his skin and made his clothes feel heavy with dampness. Perspiration instantaneously sprung onto his face, and he wiped it away with his forearm. Unsure what else to do, he started pacing up and down the sidewalk, hands shoved in his pockets as he groped for answers he didn't have.

* * *

Whatever the nurse had given me was working. My breathing had slowed, and it was a little easier to think. I wasn't exactly sure what had just happened. Generally speaking, I was a composed individual. I didn't freak out or lose my cool often, or at least I hadn't *before* the accident. I'd definitely never had a panic attack either. So, what was I supposed to make of this?

I laid back and closed my eyes, focusing on my breathing and letting everything else melt away. Growing up, I'd heard the phrase "roll with the punches" on more occasions than I'd cared to admit, but damn it, I was tired of rolling with the punches. These days it felt more like I was stuck in the ring with a heavy-weight prizefighter, getting the shit pummeled out of me every time I could muster the strength to pick myself up. Right now, Grayson was one of the best things in my life. I knew I could depend on him to protect me and take care of me no matter what. Clearly, pre-accident Alaina agreed with that assessment if I'd felt comfortable enough to not only have sex with him but to instigate the encounter.

It was an altogether unsettling story, and I was floundering. What did this mean for me, for Grayson, for *us*? If I didn't remember the encounter, did it really even happen? *It takes two to tango, Alaina. I don't think there are any backsies on this one.* I sighed and rubbed my face vigorously. A light knock sounded at the door to my room, and I turned to see the handsome man in question, hands awkwardly stuffed in his pockets.

"Hey," I greeted, pushing myself into a more upright position as he walked over to reclaim his spot on the corner of my bed.

"Better?" he asked with a small smile, unsure what to say.

I nodded. "Yeah, sorry. I just wasn't expecting...*that*." A blush crept up my neck and flooded my cheeks. I dropped my gaze and picked furiously at a loose thread on the hem of my white bedsheet. I hadn't felt this humiliated since the day Grayson and I met, and I wasn't entirely sure why *embarrassment* of all things was taking center stage. Perhaps it was a front for the myriad of other things bubbling under the surface like a mudflat full of poisonous gases.

He put a cool hand to my flushed face and flashed a genuine smile. "It's okay. You don't scare me."

I let out a breathy laugh and reluctantly lifted my gaze. "Grayson...I..." I thought carefully about my next words. "I feel like..." *No, that wasn't right either.* "I don't know why I'm having such a hard time with this," I muttered.

"You sound dangerously close to a breakup speech," he

suggested with a furrowed brow. His voice held the pretense of jest, but I could hear the worry underneath his bravado.

My heart pounded nervously. "No, I'm in love with you!" I blurted without thought. *Oh no. Oh God... shit, shit, shit.* I pulled my hands out of his and threw them over my eyes incredulously. "I'm sorry...I didn't mean for that to come out," I muttered.

He was quiet for a minute, and I was scared to pry my hands from my face long enough to look at him. The blackness behind my hands was comforting, even if it was an *illusion* of safety. After a lengthy moment, probably to compose himself, he wedged his fingers around mine and pulled them from my face. His feelings were easy enough to analyze: creases in his forehead, slightly downturned lips, eyes moving side to side as he analyzed me in return. He was confused as hell.

I know the feeling.

"You don't seem..." He swallowed, buying time. "I mean..." He gave me his patented smirk, and I could see an emotional wall starting to go up behind his eyes. I'd hurt him. *Shit!*

I opened my mouth to speak but couldn't find the words. "Gray...I..." I sighed and squeezed his hands, which were still holding mine, but with less conviction. "What do you want me to say?" I whispered, pleading for him to guide me through this like he so often did.

He sat up straighter and pulled his hands from mine, running them through his carefully coiffed brown hair so it stood up on end like the quills of a porcupine. The bed sprung in relief as he removed himself. "What I want?" he muttered incredulously. "Because anything about this situation is the way I *wanted* it? Alaina...I..." He squeezed his eyes shut and stood still, trying to think, to process. "I don't think what

I want matters in this situation." His voice was sad, but the words had an honesty to them that shattered my heart into a million pieces.

Whoever's dealing this hand clearly doesn't give a shit about us.

"I didn't *want* it this way," he whispered, kicking his tennis shoe against the linoleum of the floor to remove an invisible scuff from the shiny white and gray flecked surface. "It was perfect...race day. It was...*perfect.* And then everything fell apart, and I don't know if it will ever be the same—whether I'll ever see the world with quite the same optimism I used to have. I feel like...like it's gone. And for you to sit there and tell me one of the most perfect moments in my entire life doesn't *exist* for you—that for all I know I could have *imagined* it—" He looked up at me, tears welling in his dark eyes and spilling down his pale cheeks in a stream of emotion so violent, I could see his hands shaking with the will to control it. "That's not what I want." He shook his head, fisting his tears away.

A throat cleared near the back of the room, and we both jumped like we had been electrocuted. "Sorry, kids. I um, I can...come back."

Grayson sniffed and ducked his head in an attempt to conceal his tears. "No, it's fine. I was just leaving Mr. Montgomery." He turned on his heel and left the room silently—not even sparing a glance in my dad's general direction.

My dad shifted uncomfortably, knowing he'd interrupted something but not sure what else to do.

"Grayson!" I cried after my boyfriend as I watched him exit so quickly, he was almost running. I lurched after him and fell back in shock as a wave of nausea hit me. I was still weak and injured. *Damn this broken body of mine.* Tears of emotional anguish and physical pain rolled down my face.

My dad quickly made his way over to me, holding me close. "Shhh…" he murmured, rubbing my back. "It's okay, Lainie."

I shook my head and let out a hitching sob. "It's not…"

His arms tightened around me, and we sat there together until I was calm enough to speak. "What happened?"

I wiped at the tears still streaming down my face. "I'm not the same person I was four weeks ago, Dad. My emotions, my responses, my sense of humor, it's like they belong to a different person. And my memories…" More tears spilled over, and I sobbed.

My inherited hazel eyes stared me down for a long moment. "It's an adjustment, Lainie. It's going to take some getting used to, but it will get better." Levelheaded as ever, my father took a deep breath and continued. "I know you've had your struggles in the past, and this may be the biggest challenge you'll ever face, but Alaina—" He shook his head and brushed my cheek affectionately with his thumb, wiping away the wetness there. "You're using whatever this is between you and Grayson to create space. You've been hurt so much you don't want to hurt anymore, and I get it." He chaffed my upper arms to warm me as I shivered. "But you need to trust him. He cares about you—a lot."

"I know," I whispered shakily. "I didn't mean to hurt him." My voice trembled with emotion.

"I think he probably knows that." My dad comforted me as he smoothed down my hair. "But just because you didn't mean to hurt him, well, that doesn't take the sting out of it, does it?"

I gave him half a smile. "No, I don't suppose it does."

"Let him lick his wounds." He chucked me under the chin. "He'll be back."

I took a deep breath, sniffling as I took in my visitor's casual appearance. "What are you doing here anyway?"

"I thought I'd come and keep you company for a little bit," he allowed.

"What, no work to be done at the office?" Yes, it was Sunday, but that had never stopped him before.

My dad's warm laughter radiated through the room. "It's my assignment for the week—from my therapist. Separate my personal and professional lives. Give equal opportunity to both."

I smiled, "Well, I'm glad you're here."

We conversed for what felt like hours, catching up. Three years was a long time to go without someone, especially a loved one, and we had plenty to talk about it. He'd just finished telling me a rather hilarious story about a client who had unwittingly incriminated himself when I felt his fingers grip my thigh. My head had been bent in laughter, and I quickly looked up to see what he was signaling. Grayson was standing in my doorway, looking abashed. I glanced at my dad, who gave my leg another squeeze and winked before excusing himself.

Grayson and I held each other's gaze for a moment, unsure what to say, and then, "I'm sorry!" came flooding out of both of us at the same time. We smiled shyly, and then he came over to sit next to me.

"I'm sorry," I murmured, running my hand up his arm. "I didn't mean to..." A sigh made its way out of me in a burst of processed air. "I can't seem to get the right words out," I muttered and glanced up. "It's not that I regret what happened or that I didn't mean what I said. I just…" I let out an exasperated huff. "I'm sad, and I'm angry, and the last thing I wanted was for you to find out like that." I clenched my teeth, frustrated at my inability to form a sentence worth saying at such a critical moment. "I'm trying to be honest with you, but I feel like something's been stolen from me…something I can't ever get back!"

"I know." He nodded. "I know."

My bottom lip trembled, and I bit down on it. Hard. "I've never said 'I love you' before—to anyone. And…I think I've known for a while, at least that there was the possibility of it with…us." I swallowed hard. I wasn't sure at what point I'd looked away from him, but I suddenly found myself studying the blotches of fresh pink skin on my left hand and arm with rapt absorption. *For the love of Christ…speak!* "Some days, I look at you and see forever, and other days, I look at you and see the one person with the ability to break me. The problem is…I don't remember making a conscious choice to take the good with the bad."

His brow was furrowed. "I think, maybe…that's what love is—an unconscious choice to place your heart and soul in someone else's keeping." He finally took my hand, bridging the gap. "It's giving everything to someone, knowing they alone have the power to ruin you, but trusting they won't." His eyes searched mine for an endless eternity, saying so much without saying anything at all. "When I look at you," he began, "all I have ever seen is *you*…not the witty you, not the you that makes me want to throw things, not the you that makes me laugh so hard my stomach hurts…I just see…*you*. The good, the bad, and the ugly."

I gave him a weak, halfhearted smile. His words caressed

me into complacency and calmed my inner storm as he continued to speak.

His breath was shaky. "You are…perfectly imperfect, Alaina Montgomery…and I'm here to say I'm not going anywhere…and I love you, too." The last four words of his monologue made my heart jump into my throat.

"You love me?" I whispered, feeling tears brim my eyes.

His lips turned up in a warm smile. "Of course I do," was his whispered reply as he leaned in to kiss me. "I don't think I ever had a choice."

24

Visiting Hours

I pulled my cardigan tighter as the chill from the air conditioning hit me again. "Bloody cold in here," I muttered as I inhaled the scent of antiseptic and acetone. Jess giggled from her spot at my toes as she painted them a loud shade of pink. "Been reading historical fiction again?"

I raised my brow and offered a grumpy rebuttal. "You say that like it's a problem."

My companion sighed in exaggerated patience and bent back to her work. "I cannot wait for you to get out of here. You're so cranky."

"The best part of my day is watching old Matlock reruns. It's freaking torture!" I cried in exasperation. She continued to spread the thick lacquer on my toes, diligent as ever. I bit my tongue for a minute, wanting to tell her what had happened yesterday with Grayson, but I wasn't sure how it would be received after my outburst over her own personal drama. I let out a long breath. *What the hell?*

I focused my gaze pointedly at the toenail she was currently working on and blurted, "I slept with Grayson."

Her hand paused above my half-painted toe and then purposefully shoved the brush back in the bottle before looking up at me. "I'm sorry. Come again?"

"We...*slept* together."

Her moss green eyes traveled my wrecked body with doubt. "When?"

"After the 500...before the victory party." I shrugged in indifference, recalling the story Grayson had shared.

"Why didn't you tell me?" she asked with something between hurt and anger simmering under the surface of her words.

Silence filled the space between us. "I'm telling you now."

She rolled her eyes. "Alaina."

I picked a nonexistent piece of lint off my sunny yellow dressing gown and swallowed. "I don't remember it happening."

Her eyes widened and her eyebrows went up, but her voice remained calm despite the shock. "What?"

"I lost most of my memory from the night of the accident, including—"

She threw her arms around me and held me to her. "Alaina..."

With that single sigh of my name, the dam broke loose, and I cried. I shed tears for the pain and the heartache, but mostly, I cried for everything I'd lost. It was the most painful thing I'd ever experienced—attempting to maneuver through this mess of a world I'd woken up to, and the situation with Grayson only made it worse. We had left last night in a good place, and I felt confident in him as a partner, but that confidence didn't stop the self-doubt I was feeling. I knew it was a physical issue that was causing my memory loss, but that didn't make me feel any less responsible for the strain I was putting on our relationship. I could only hope someday that missing piece would come back and I could fill in the blanks, for both our sakes.

When I had calmed myself, Jess pulled back and looked at me, brow furrowed, black lashes glistening with tears. "How did you find out? Oh God…you're not—"

"No! God, no." I shook my head fervently despite the wave of dizziness that ensued. "I just…I felt like I was missing something." I paused for thought and continued. "Grayson and I, we've always been on the same page about everything… and when I woke up, it was like there was this shift between us—not in a bad way, it was like he was a page ahead of me. So, I asked him." I shrugged, my body language belying my actual feelings on the matter.

She sighed. "I'm sorry. This must be…" She trailed off, not able to conjure a word powerful enough to encompass the situation.

"He was pretty upset."

"I'm sure," she sympathized, squeezing my hand.

"I don't think my reaction helped matters."

"What happened?" she asked, hungry for more details.

"I told him I loved him."

There was a pause while she tried to wrap her head around that little nugget. "You—"

"Well, not on purpose," I interrupted defensively. "He thought I was breaking up with him, and…I panicked."

My best friend exchanged confusion for humor and let out a raucous laugh. "Oh, my *God*, Alaina! You are a freaking train wreck."

"Takes one to know one…" I muttered, picking at my

fingernails.

She snorted but didn't lose her train of thought. "Did he say it back?" she asked. I could see the curiosity burning deep in her eyes. Jess was possibly the only person more invested in my love life than myself, and she desperately wanted my relationship with Grayson to work.

I rolled my eyes. "Well, initially it ended up being a bit of a catastrophe, and he left—can't say I blame him on that front—I was not doing a good job of…communicating." The last word was said with a sigh and an eye roll. *The heads on Mount Rushmore are better communicators at this point.* While my inner voice chastised and poked fun, part of me felt as though I wasn't entirely to blame. Sometimes, the right words weren't there. It's not that I didn't want to say them. I just couldn't find them.

"That doesn't seem like him."

"No, I think I caught him off guard. And then, to make matters worse, I wasn't very happy about letting it slip… and…" I shrugged. "I think he was hurt by my…lack of enthusiasm," I remarked carefully.

"I see…" she allowed, setting the bottle of nail polish on the tray over my bed. "Is there a reason you didn't want him to know?"

My insides did a somersault. The easy answer to her question was no. I didn't have a good reason for not telling him. My declaration was true whether I'd paused to think about it or not. "It's not a matter of loving him. I do. It's just…hard."

"What's hard about it?" she asked, tapping my knee playfully, but I could see the curiosity burning in the tight set of her reluctant smile.

"Not having control," I admitted. "I haven't felt in control of anything since I woke up," I admitted with a hard laugh. *Leave feeling out of it. There has been no control. Nada.*

She gave me a sad half-smile, not sure what to say.

"I'm sorry," I murmured, allowing my eye contact to linger and illustrate the depth of my apology.

"I know," she whispered back, her smile warming a bit more. "It's not been easy for you, and hearing about my problems that don't really seem like—"

"It's not that," I objected, "I mean, it *is*, but—"

"It's part of the brain injury, isn't it?" Her voice was quiet, almost confidential.

I nodded slowly. "I think so."

She sighed. "Is it always going to be like this?" The thought saddened her. I could see it in the slump of her shoulders and the furrow of her brow.

"I hope not."

She studied me for a long moment and then nodded once, resolving to forge ahead and conquer the unknown. "Well, we'll deal with it as best we can, right?"

I nodded in return, frustration making unshed tears sting the backs of my eyes. *I'm so fucking tired of dealing with it. So tired.*

Before I could respond, Grayson knocked on the door frame of my room by way of greeting. "Hey!" I exclaimed, sniffing to clear the stuffed-up sound from my sinuses.

"Are you up for some visitors?" he asked quietly, noticing the tell-tale glisten of unshed tears.

I forced a smile onto my face. "Of course!"

Grayson glanced toward Jess for confirmation as Jack poked his head around the corner, followed closely by Cami.

"Hey!" I greeted, now genuinely excited. Jessica smiled and got up to greet Jack with a quick kiss.

"How are you?" Jack asked as he came in for a hug.

I hugged him back gingerly. "I'm ready to get out of here," I answered truthfully with a hard laugh.

"I know the feeling. You look good, though!" He made his way over to the small bench near the window where Jessica was sitting and plopped down next to her.

I rolled my eyes. "Well, thanks." Most of the cuts and abrasions on my face were freshly healed. The one noticeable exception was the angry scar across my right cheek where my face had been cut open.

Cami walked over and hugged me. "Hey, Alaina. How are you feeling?"

I shrugged. "A little worse for wear, but pretty good."

"If you need us to go," she hiked a thumb over her shoulder, insinuating they would leave if they were being a burden.

"No, no! Please stay!" I insisted. "It helps to take my mind off it."

She nodded with a smile. "Okay. It will be good for you to finally get home! Have they given you any idea when that will be?"

"Two hours, two days, two weeks…I *wish* I knew. This bed is so uncomfortable…and I want to see Copper." I sighed, thinking about my furry friend. I missed him dearly—his slobbery kisses, soft russet-colored fur, and that mouth that always lolled open in a goofy grin.

"About that…" Cami murmured, glancing over at the door as Grayson came back around the corner with Copper in tow.

"Copper!" I shouted excitedly. Cops almost lost his mind,

dancing in little circles and wagging his tail like a madman. Standing up on his hind legs, he put his front paws on the bed beside me. His familiar, faint musky scent filled my nostrils, and I ran my hand through his shaggy blond mane, soft as goose down. "Such a pretty boy," I whispered, admiring the play of light in his fur. His coat ran the gamut of copper colors from a bleached blond on his chest and hindquarters to rich cinnamon across his back and up onto his ears—thus his name.

"Easy," Grayson murmured as he tightened the tension of the lead in a vain attempt to calm the enthusiastic eighty-pound ball of fluff on the other end, but as Copper sniffed at me, his demeanor changed considerably. He knew I was hurt and gently nudged my hand.

I lifted my hands to cup his face and rubbed his ears. "Hey, Buddy, I'll be okay," I murmured, tears welling in my eyes.

Grayson lifted him onto the bed, and he crawled up next to me, laying along the length of my body, with his head resting on my lap as I stroked his head repeatedly from occiput to nose. I looked up at Grayson, barely able to contain the emotions roiling through me. "Thank you," I whispered.

He smiled. "Thank Cami. She's the one who sold her left kidney."

Cami, resourceful as always, had worked her way through college as a nanny for a member of the hospital board, and after promising him a meet and greet with Grayson and Jack at the track next May, as well as two suite passes for the race, said board member had agreed to pull a few strings of his own and allow my puppy onto the premises for a whopping thirty minutes.

I turned to her with a bubbly laugh and joyous smile. "Well, thank you, too, then."

"He's a sweet boy," she murmured as she stroked the silky bronze fur atop his head. "And it looks like he missed you just as much as you missed him."

"Oh, yeah. He's done nothing but mope around my apartment for the last four weeks," Jess sighed with a roll of her eyes. "He'll be happy to have his mama back, that's for sure."

Copper sighed contentedly and snuggled closer, accidentally tweaking my legs in the process.

I whimpered, the color draining from my face. Tiny black spots filtered into my vision and nausea had my stomach flip-flopping like a landed fish.

Grayson jumped to me. "No, Copper," he said sternly, and then to me, "Are you okay?"

"I'm fine…" I moaned, trying to be reassuring, but my left hip was pulsing.

"Do you want me to get a nurse?" Grayson whispered, stroking my face tenderly.

I shook my head with a deep breath.

"Alaina, maybe you shouldn't push it," Jess quietly suggested as she began to pull my pup off the bed, much to his and my protests.

"He's fine," I objected. "He didn't know. It's okay," I insisted and went back to stroking Copper's ruddy fur.

After a couple of moments of uncomfortable silence, Jack spoke, "So, do you have any awesome battle scars?"

"Jack, she got hit by a car. She's got more scars on her body than she'd probably ever care to admit," Jess muttered with a roll of her eyes at his childish question.

He shrugged and smirked, his slate eyes sparkling with a

boyish playfulness that was never too far away where Jack was concerned.

I laughed at her protective tone. "It's fine. To be honest, I haven't looked at the ones under my hospital gown. I have this one—" I showed them the one running down the underside of my arm. "—and this one," I allowed, as I pulled the sheet up off my legs to show them. The one on my right thigh earned a gasp from Cami. Jack shook his head. "I have a six-inch incision down my stomach, and I've got a couple of smaller ones where they had to go in and put pins in my pelvis to stabilize it. And then, of course, this one," I said as I lifted up my combed-over hair to show them the side of my head.

"Ouch," Jack said with a grimace. "I know it doesn't feel like it, but you're lucky."

"I know," I murmured. "I think about it a lot. There's no reason I should have survived. Even my doctor said when I was inbound, they didn't expect me to make it, but somehow…here I am," I managed a smile as I spoke.

"That's crazy," Cami muttered in awe. "You must have some pull with the man upstairs."

After a beat of agreeable silence, Grayson said, "Well, regardless, we're all very happy you're still here with us."

"Oh, um," a throat cleared. "Sorry. I didn't realize you had company. I'll come back later."

I pulled back from Grayson to see Tucker turning around to exit, the vibrant pink of a blush creeping up his neck as he ducked back around the corner. "No, Tuck. It's fine. Come back!" I shouted.

Jess's eyes were wide with surprise at Tuck's appearance, and she glanced uncertainly at her boyfriend before darting a glance in my direction. I furrowed my brow, wordlessly pleading with her to go after him. "I'll be back," she squeezed Jack's thigh and trotted after my brother.

Jack looked after her for a bit and then glanced over at me, rubbing his palms on his thighs. "I shouldn't be worried about that, right?"

"What? Jess and Tuck?" I smiled and shook my head. "Nah. They've got some issues to work out, but I don't think there's anything there."

He nodded absently. "Besides the fact they slept together and are now having a baby?"

I bit my lip and sighed. "It was just a case of bad judgment amplified by alcohol."

"Yeah," he answered, still sounding unsure.

"Sorry, kids, I don't mean to interrupt, but I brought these for you to try!" Janet spoke cheerfully from the door. By far my favorite nurse, she was a middle-aged woman with mousy brown hair that showed lighter streaks of blonde and white. Her sparkling blue eyes were accented with crow's feet that hinted at a lifetime of smiles. She was a beautiful, vibrant woman, and it was easy to see why she worked in the recovery wing. She'd been born with the innate ability to lift the spirits of others—mine included.

My heart stuttered as I saw she came bearing gifts— crutches, to be exact. "The doctor cleared me?" I asked, hopefully.

"Well, Doctor Reilly told me to drop them off for you. He spoke with Monique and is satisfied you've regained enough strength to try them out—not until PT tonight, though. Doctor's orders!" She wagged her finger in a stern matronly command. *It's like she knows me or something.*

I nodded in reluctant assent, and with an encouraging smile, she departed to her next destination. I looked around at my crowd of visitors, and Cami let out a sigh. "Well, that's good news, right? One step closer to home sweet home!"

I nodded and smiled back, but mine wasn't as genuine. I hadn't been out of this bed unassisted in nearly a month, and I had some serious doubts about my abilities. "Lots of work left to do, but slow and steady, right?"

She seemed to notice the tension in my face and the shift in my mood. "Well, sounds like you've got physical therapy coming up shortly, so I'll let you rest. I'm glad to see you doing so well, Alaina." She squeezed my arm and smiled.

"Thanks for coming, Cami. I really appreciate it."

Jack stood too. "I should probably head out too…since Cami's kind of my ride."

I couldn't help the laugh that escaped my lips. "You're such a dork."

With another good-natured yet cocky smile, he continued, "We'll take Copper with us so Grayson can stay with you…you know, for…moral support and stuff."

I snorted and gave him a small wave. "Thanks for coming, Jack. It was good to see you."

"Same here. Get better soon, okay? We miss you out at the track." His warm hand rested on my shoulder in farewell as he gave me a wink.

I smiled and nodded. "As soon as I can travel, I'll be back."

"That's what I like to hear!"

I sighed sadly and hugged Copper to me. "Bye, Cops. I'll be home soon, okay? You be good for Jess." I kissed his nose and gave him another hug before Grayson lifted him from the bed, and Jack tugged him toward the door. He looked back at me, whining as Jack encouraged him from the room, and as the last remnants of his fluffy blond tail disappeared from sight, I thoroughly went to pieces.

My breath hitched in a strangled sob, and I hugged myself, willing the convulsive breaths to stop. Hot tears blurred my vision and streamed down my face. Grayson's strong arms wrapped around me and he kissed the top of my head. "Shhh, it's okay…" he soothed, rubbing my back in a hypnotic rhythm that lulled me into complacency.

I sniffed. "I have to get out of here. I c-can't be h-here anymore…" I sniffed again, willing my voice to sound less pathetic.

"You will. You just have to hang in there." He hugged me closer to him, my cheek pressed against his chest so I could feel the steady thump of his heart.

* * *

I sighed and smiled with something resembling contentment as Grayson pulled the wheelchair to a stop next to my bed and locked the break. I pushed up off the chair, stood under my own weight before shifting onto the bed, and carefully pulled my legs up over the side. I closed my eyes and a jaw-cracking yawn came over me. I was exhausted after PT, but it was the best kind of exhausted.

I'd made two laps around the room without any assistance, and Monique had been ecstatic, encouraging me every step of the way with her subtle remarks of "Good" and "You got this." So, at the end of therapy, when she sat down with me and said, "I think it's time to talk about outpatient sessions," I almost stood up and did a happy dance—almost.

I felt the bed go down beside me and opened my eyes to see Grayson's dazzling smile. "You were great today."

"I was, wasn't I?" I chuckled and looked up at the sound of approaching tennis shoes on linoleum. My night nurse, Molly, entered, her blonde ponytail swinging behind her with the bounce of her step. She was never far behind me when I returned from a physical therapy session, and her youthful energy was contagious on days like today when I felt completely drained. "Hey girl, how are you tonight?" she asked, scrolling through her iPad before glancing up at me.

"Exhausted," I replied with another huge yawn and pushed myself up. I blinked rapidly in an attempt to reinvigorate my drooping eyelids.

"She walked two laps with crutches at PT just now," Grayson bragged, squeezing my thigh in affection.

"Congratulations!" she crowed. "Looks like no more heart monitor or saline drip…and moved to oral meds! Wow, big progress," she allowed with an appreciative nod. "So, question of the hour. How's the pain?"

I sighed, stopping to think about it, and the fact I had to think about it made me smile. I was getting stronger. "Maybe a three," I finally replied.

She made another note on the tablet in her hand. "Ok, I'll get you some Tylenol then; it looks like you're due. Doctor Reilly will be making rounds around eight tomorrow morning. I think you've got good news in your future!" she replied with a smile.

Yes, yes, yes, yes!

"How are you feeling?" Grayson asked as he tucked a strand of hair behind my right ear. His fingers traced the scar there with tender affection that stippled my skin with goosebumps.

I slowly leaned into him, and he wrapped his arm around my shoulders. "I'm okay…a little sore, but I'll live," I murmured.

"You tired?" His voice was quiet, and I let my eyes shut as I rested against him.

"Yeah…I feel like a total wuss." My voice was full of disdain.

"Nah, you did well today. I wouldn't worry about it."

"I'm not worried, not about that at least." I sighed, drawing silent patterns on the blanket covering my legs.

"What?"

I shook my head. It wasn't just that I didn't want to admit my insecurities. I also had the additional problem of not being able to articulate exactly what I was feeling at the moment.

"Alaina," Grayson's voice was full of frustration and pleading. He wanted to know—at least he thought he did.

I sighed, not looking up at him. "Are you going to get tired of taking care of me?"

He shifted his weight and stared at me, surprised by my question. "What?"

"I'm just…" I sighed. "I'm completely dependent on others right now, and I'm worried that—I don't know—that you'll maybe…get bored?"

His chest shook with laughter, and he kissed the top of my head. "I mean, give me a little credit. I've made it twenty-six years on my own. I think I'll be alright until you can get back on your feet. Besides, I've never seen you as an inconvenience, Alaina. I *want* to be here for you, and I know you would do the same for me."

He was right. I would be there every waking second with him if he'd been in an accident. Why should I expect less from him? I relaxed a little bit more. "I don't know what I'm going to do when they release me. I mean, I'll be happy to go home, but I live by myself, you know? I probably won't be able to do it all on my own."

"Well," he pondered the thought for a few moments. "I could stay with you…"

"What?" I asked, shocked at the suggestion. That's not where I had intended on this conversation going. "After how my mom reacted to you merely sleeping in my apartment by yourself?"

He gave a half-laugh. "Well, I'll admit, it's not ideal. She'll be upset about it, I'm sure, but it seems like a reasonable solution. I mean, I'm not in town a lot, but when I am, I'm with you anyway. And when I'm out of town, maybe Jess or your mom could stay with you? At least until you're back on your feet."

I considered what he was saying. It was true. He might as well save himself the hotel cost if he could. "I don't want you to feel like you have to come back here after every race. I know you're busy."

"Trust me, I doubt Cami will let me forget my busy schedule, but hopefully, we can work everything out to where I can at least be here a couple of nights a week."

"And maybe after I start to be a little more mobile, I can come to a couple of races."

Grayson went completely still under me in that way he often did when he had something on his mind. I waited, nuzzling into his chest. "So, I have something to run by you."

"Mmmm," I murmured as sleep loomed nearer.

"The network wants to do an interview with us…when you feel up to it."

My eyes shot open in alarm. "Both of us? Why?" It was one thing for me to be so disheveled in front of close friends and family but broadcasting it to the world? *Hell no*.

"Everybody loves you, Alaina. They're curious to see how you're doing."

All I could think about was my face and how screwed up it was. I couldn't help but be self-conscious. "Grayson, I don't know if I feel comfortable with that," I mumbled as I looked down at my lap.

He sat up so he could look at me. "Why? What's wrong?"

I was quiet as I stared down at our entwined hands. My palms were beginning to sweat profusely, and a dull ache started to throb at my temples.

"Alaina…"

I pulled my hand from his at the same time he spoke, chastising myself for the defensive gesture. "I don't want to do it, okay?"

He was a little taken aback by my reaction, and he furrowed his brow. "Okay…I'll let them know."

I nodded, not meeting his eyes. I knew he was confused, but I also knew he would think less of me if he knew my true motivations. He was a very attractive, popular, young guy, and I swore he'd come out of the womb looking perfect. He'd never had to worry about his appearance a day in his life, but I'd felt firsthand the judgment people threw at me for simply holding his hand. I didn't want to think about the mean things they would say if they saw my scarred face.

There was a bit of awkward silence, and then we had visitors. My mom and grandma walked in carrying loads of flowers between the two of them. "Hey, honey!" My mom chimed.

"Evening!" I voiced brightly, hoping she wouldn't pick up on the vibe we were giving off.

Grayson pulled back from me gently and got up off the bed. *Modest to the end, that one.*

"Well, you're a looker, aren't you? Nice job, Lainie." My grandma announced her approval.

"Grandma!" I shrieked, red as a cherry.

Grayson laughed. "Nice to meet you. I'm Grayson." He offered his hand, and she took it politely.

"Charmed," she replied with a smile. Grandma Rosie didn't really have a filter anymore. She kind of just said whatever she wanted, the rest of the world be damned. It was *super* embarrassing.

"Who are those from?" I asked with a yawn as my mom sat the flower arrangements on the counter alongside Grayson's. I was getting quite the collection. *It's starting to look like a gift shop in here.*

"These are from the Ladies Guild," she said, gesturing to a pink display with Gerbera daisies and carnations, "and these are from the people at work." she gestured to the smaller bouquet of lilacs, white roses, and lilies.

"They're all gorgeous. Tell everyone thank you for me," I insisted.

I looked back over to see how Grayson was fairing with Grandma, but he seemed to be charming the heck out of her. She was laughing and smiling as he told her something. Not that I blamed her. *I think Grayson could charm the stripes off a zebra.*

"How are you feeling today?" Mom asked as she walked over and moved a couple of strands of hair out of my face.

"Good! Cami pulled some strings and was able to bring

Copper in to see me this morning," I beamed.

"Aww," she cooed. "I bet he was excited to see you."

"Yeah." I smiled, "I was pretty excited to see him too. I can't wait to get home."

"Speaking of which…" she glanced over at the crutches resting next to my bed.

"Yeah, I worked on the crutches today with Monique—and Molly said the doctor might release me in the morning."

"Wow," she let out a nervous breath. "That's…soon."

Nothing like taking the wind out of my sails. "Mom, I've been in the hospital for twenty-nine days." I couldn't help the bit of temper that flared in my voice.

Grayson glanced over at me, hearing a bit of the harshness back in my tone that he'd heard earlier.

"I know, babe, but you were unconscious for five of them and only semiconscious for *two more* after that! Plus, can you really take care of yourself?" she asked. I knew she was looking out for me, but the fact she thought I hadn't already considered every angle annoyed me. "Grayson said he would stay with me," I answered quietly, looking out of the corner of my eye at my grandma. She may be loose with her words, but she still had some pretty ancient ideas about living together before marriage.

"Grayson," my mom said, deadpan. *Here we go.* She looked over at the other two people in the room and cleared her throat. "Grayson, can I get a moment with my daughter, please?"

He glanced at me, questions all over his face, and I nodded, my stomach balling up with nerves and irritation. Grandma, getting a look from Mom, walked out with him.

"You cannot let Grandma be *alone* with him!" I whispered

feverishly.

"Would you rather her be in here for *this* conversation?" she asked back with the same tone as she moved to shut the door.

I rolled my eyes again. *She did have a point.* "Whatever you have to say, Mom, I don't want to hear it."

"Well too damn bad," she muttered as she whirled around with her hands on her hips. "Alaina, I think this whole...*thing* you've got going on with him—"

"*Thing?* You don't like him?" I asked, a little hurt. I thought things had been going well between them. I mean, yeah, there had been a few overprotective scuffles on her part, but nothing major.

"No, it's not that! He's perfectly lovely, and I think he's got a good head on his shoulders."

I bit down on my lip, fighting the urge to say something hurtful, mean, sarcastic, or otherwise counterproductive to this conversation.

"I think this is moving way too fast, honey. Honestly, you've only been together for six weeks, and now all of a sudden, you want to move in together?"

I sighed. "First of all, we aren't moving in together. He's just going to be staying with me on the nights he's in town until I get back on my feet. We were going to be together when he's here anyway. What difference does it make if he's sleeping at my place or at a hotel?"

"Because he's *sleeping* at *your* place!" she cried.

"*Mom,*" I growled, feeling the stirrings of rage at my core. "Look at me. Do I look like I'm going to be rolling around in the sack any time soon?"

"Alaina," she put a hand over her eyes.

"Well, I'm just being honest. If you want to tell me what you think, that's fine, but I'm sure as hell going to do the same!" Between my clenched jaw, blazing glare, and stark complexion, the word "rage" was written all over my face. "I love him. Okay? And he loves me, and if he wants to help me, why is that a problem for you?"

"I'm not saying it is a problem! I'm glad you found someone who's willing to help you when you need it. I just think you need to step back from this and see the bigger picture."

"Which would be?"

She sighed and crossed her arms. "You're twenty-four, Alaina. He's your first serious boyfriend in years. I think you're throwing yourself into this with a little more gusto than you should be."

I was trying not to let my emotions get the best of me, but she wasn't making it easy. "I can't keep up with you people! Jess is telling me to let go and have fun. You're telling me to hold on for dear life and not fall too quickly. How am I ever supposed to make a decision for myself around here?"

"Alaina, I love Jess like she's my own, but she's not the most responsible individual. I think this pregnancy is evidence enough of that."

"Is *that* what this is about? We've already got one illegitimate pregnancy in the family, and God forbid we have another?" My voice climbed an octave as I inquired into my mom's motives.

She sighed. "You know that's not what this is about."

I glared at her, eyes scathing, "Then, *what*? What *is* this about, because I've been trying to figure it out for weeks now!"

Her eyes softened with emotion. "Bug…I just don't want

to see you make the same mistakes I made."

"Well, if I was going to limit myself to other people's relationship successes and failures, I guess I'll be spending my life alone. Because all I've learned in the past few years is getting close to people only gives them the opportunity to crush you in return!" I took a shaky breath, my blood boiling. "I have tried…so hard," my voice wavered, and I forced it to harden. "To let go of all the hurt and anger. But *damn* it!" I shouted. "You can't let me be happy for *once*? It's all about *your* mistakes, *your* unhappiness. Jesus Christ! *I'm. Not. You!*"

My mother's face went from a furrowed brow and flushed cheeks to a stunned, ashen complexion. For a moment, she stared at me, unblinking, and then without a word, she turned, picked up her purse, and walked out.

Remorse flooded through me, and I felt like lead sinkers had been tied to my wrists and feet, weighing me down as my adrenaline began to wane. "Mom…" I murmured as she walked out the door, not looking back.

Tears filled my eyes. I didn't mean to hurt her, and I hated it. But how else was I supposed to get it across? She couldn't baby me forever. I was an adult, and if there were mistakes to be made, I had to be the one to make them. She couldn't wrap me in bubble wrap and protect me from everything. A couple of tears dribbled down my cheeks, and I quickly swatted them away as Grayson popped his head around the corner.

"Are you okay?" he asked, stepping into the room now that I was alone.

I shook my head. "Not really," I muttered, more tears replacing the ones I had just wiped away.

He sat on the bed and wrapped his arms around me, letting

me cry into his shoulder. My ribs ached as I sobbed, and he held me tighter. "What happened?" he asked quietly into my hair when I was able to calm myself a bit, not bothering to move from our embrace.

"I told her you were going to stay with me when you were in town until I could start taking care of stuff again, and she started going on and on about how I was moving too fast, and she didn't think it was good for me. She *really* has a problem with us living together. God, you'd think we were living in the eighteenth century or something by the way she's acting!"

He was quiet. Too quiet, in my opinion. I glanced up at him, but he was a million miles away.

"Hey," I murmured, reaching up to touch his face and bring him back to me.

His eyes came back into focus. "Well, we knew she wasn't going to like it, right? It shouldn't come as a surprise. I could hear the disappointment behind his words. Despite his mental preparation, he had still hoped she would come around.

"I don't know," I murmured. "We don't argue, you know? Not very often anyway. I wish she would stop giving me this holier-than-thou routine and be honest with me."

"I'm sure she will," he replied, distracted. His mind was wandering again.

"I wish she wouldn't worry so much! It's suffocating. I already feel caged in by this place. The last thing I need is my mom hovering over me like a freaking helicopter."

"I know," my companion muttered, only half-listening.

"Grayson," I called, trying to bring him back.

There was a ten-second delay followed by a "hmmm?"

"What's got you so distracted?" I scrutinized his face,

struggling to find answers when there weren't any to be found.

Grayson sighed, and I glanced up at him, curious to know what he was thinking. "I'm wondering if I should go back to Phoenix with the rest of the team."

I sat up a little straighter. "I thought Cami was going to check in on everything."

"Yeah. That was the plan, but if my being here is causing issues with your family…"

"They'll get over it. You don't have to go." *Translation: please don't go!*

"But I don't want to get between you and your mom, Alaina. Seriously. I can't be that person."

Yes, you can. You can totally be that person. "She's the one that's making it an issue!" I was getting upset again, as much as I was trying to avoid it.

He hugged me to his side. "Listen to me for a second, okay?" His request was gentle, his voice as smooth as a hot knife through butter. He took my silence as a go-ahead. "I know how important your family is to you. Never in a million years would I *ever* want you, or them, to feel like I'm standing between you. I feel like, right now, I need to go home and let you guys figure everything out." He hugged me to his side tighter and kissed the top of my head before standing up.

I looked up at him from my spot on the bed, tears in my eyes. I didn't want him to leave. I felt like he was the only one on my side right now, and if he went… "Grayson, please don't go."

I knew he was torn. He didn't want to leave me, but I could tell he thought it was the right thing to do. I didn't care about the rights or wrongs of it. All I knew was I needed him with me. I could see the indecision in the grim set of his mouth and read the war of emotion in the tense set of his shoulders. Grayson knew I needed to be recovering, not worrying about all of this drama. The stress created by all of this tension was not a good conduit for that recovery. What he wasn't factoring in was that this attempt at resolution was making my stomach go sour in a way my mother's shenanigans never had.

After a moment, he leaned back in. "I love you," he whispered in my ear and kissed me on the temple.

All of a sudden, I was thrown back to the night of the accident, laying in the street, immobile, unable to speak, trying to process the agony coursing through my body. It was happening all over again, except instead of lying in the street, I was in a hospital bed, and the source of my pain wasn't physical this time but emotional. All the same, I was rendered speechless, unable to do anything other than helplessly watch the world spin madly on.

25

Good for the Soul

With a sigh, Grayson placed his 4Runner in park and sank back into his seat. The smooth leather enveloped him like a hug and his eyes sank shut of their own accord. Today hadn't turned out at all like he'd planned, but then again, wasn't that par for the course? These days everything seemed ten times harder than it needed to be. He pried his eyelids back open and stared out the windshield at the old white farmhouse. The flowerbeds in front were in pristine condition, each weed plucked out by the roots the second it dared to pop its tender green head above ground. The assortment of marigolds, petunias, and geraniums were all carefully manicured and deadheaded to make the landscaping look like something out of *Country Living*.

Picking up the bouquet of sunflowers from the passenger seat, he pulled the lever to open the door and set his feet on the gravel of the driveway with a soft crunching sound. The air smelled of fresh-cut grass, lilacs, and the musk of recently turned earth. Suddenly, he was a little boy again, running

343

through the crisp white sails of his grandma's bedsheets as they blew in the wind from their place on the clothesline. Despite the conveniences of a dryer in perfect working order, she always said sheets that hung out to dry in the sun smelled better. Grayson, on the other hand, thought her unwillingness to use technology said more about her stubborn nature than the benefits of old-fashioned wash habits, but he wasn't about to tell *her* that.

He rapped on the porch door quickly and then opened it to an empty kitchen, completely spotless from floor to ceiling, the retro appliances gleaming like new. Nothing had changed in this house in twenty years and if he closed his eyes for a moment, he could imagine none of his problems existed and he was back to being that carefree little boy. "Hello?" he called out, hearing the susurrus of far-off television. He followed the sound from the kitchen into the living room. "Helloooo?" he called again at a louder volume.

"Marty? Is that you?" His grandmother's voice called from up the stairs.

"Did you say something, Evelyn?" His grandpa's voice came from the other end of the house near the garage. Grayson's mouth twitched at his grandparents' back and forth. They were both in their eighties and hard of hearing, despite their hearing aids. He was half-tempted to park it in the brown leather La-Z-Boy recliner in the living room and wait to see how long it would take them to realize they had company, but then thought better of it. If he waited for that, he'd miss his flight.

"Grandma! It's me!" He shouted up the stairs.

Her white-haired head bobbed around the door jamb of the bedroom just off the staircase, face full of suspicion as she realized the voice she was hearing wasn't her husband of sixty years. Then, her face lit in a beatific smile. "Grayson!" she shouted with uncontained glee before slowly making her way down the stairs. "I didn't know you were coming today! You should have called. I would have put a pie in to bake." She swatted at his shoulder in disdain as she landed on the final step, looking him over.

"It's okay, I can't stay long. I have a flight to catch. I wanted to say goodbye before I left. I don't know when I'll be back."

A look of disappointment flooded her bright blue eyes for a split second before she mustered a smile and reached up to pat his cheek. "Well, I'm glad you're here nonetheless." With a gasp of delight, she lighted on the sunflowers Grayson held at his side and grinned.

"You know I always come with flowers," he murmured, handing them to her.

"And you know I'm a sucker for them. They're beautiful, Gray. Thank you!"

He brought her in for a hug, resting his head on top of hers despite the fact she still stood on the bottom stair of the staircase. She was a tiny woman, and age had made her once spry form frail. He couldn't help but worry for both of his grandparents as they aged, especially since he wasn't around to take care of them.

His grandma stepped down from the final step and made her way into the kitchen in search of a vase, absently fingering the bright golden petals of her gift as she went. Grayson turned to follow her and noticed a slight limp to her step. He sighed. "Did you fall *again*?"

"Are you worrying about me *again*?" she quipped back, putting the same emphasis on "again" that he had.

"I just—"

"It's nothing, Gray," she interrupted and then shouted, "Marty! Grayson's here!" at the top of her lungs in a volume fit to burst Grayson's ear drum. Momentarily stunned, he shook his head to clear the residual cobwebs and leaned against the kitchen counter as the little old woman rummaged under the kitchen sink for a suitable vase. "So, how's your young woman doing? Audrey was it?"

"Alaina," he corrected with a good-natured roll of the eyes.

"Right, right. Alaina. Is she still in the hospital?"

"Yeah. She should be released soon. No word for sure on when, though." The subject of his girlfriend was one he had been hoping to surreptitiously maneuver during his visit, but apparently, that wasn't going to happen.

"She must be doing alright if you're heading back home." She ran her hand under the running tap water to ensure optimal temperature before running her newly acquired cut glass vase under the stream.

Grayson was quiet, not sure what to say, and his grandmother looked up at him, smelling a rat.

"You want to talk about it?" she asked as she took the sunflowers from their wrapping and began to snip the stems in a methodical fashion.

"Not really," Grayson allowed, his tone saying more than his words. Alaina hadn't wanted him to leave. That had been perfectly obvious, but what was he supposed to do? Her parents—particularly her mother—had made it clear he wasn't wanted at this juncture, and the last thing he wanted was to cause a rift between Alaina and her family.

"What are we talking about?" Martin Miles was like a dog with a bone when it came to gossip. In fact, Grayson thought he was probably worse than half of his grandma's book club ladies in that regard. Grayson gave his grandma a meaningful look which she promptly internalized, mulled over for half a second, and spat back out.

"Gray's having lady trouble."

Seriously, what good is nonverbal communication if nobody takes the hint?

"Ahhh, trouble in paradise, eh?" The older man elbowed his grandson in the ribs and winked before plopping down at the kitchen table in anticipation of some juicy news.

Cornered between the eager eyes of his grandfather and the expectant stare of his grandmother, Grayson sighed and acquiesced, letting all the sordid details of his encounter with Alaina's overprotective mother flow freely.

By the end of it, Grayson had finally admitted to himself he was more than frustrated with the situation. "Where does she get off trying to manipulate her like that? I think Alaina is old enough to make her own decisions, don't you?"

"Well, I'd say so, but then again…you left, didn't you?" Marty voiced. "So, whether you meant it or not, you gave her exactly what she wanted."

Grayson's jaw clenched. Well, he certainly hadn't thought about *that*. "I didn't want to cause Alaina any more stress by arguing with her mom. She gets awful migraines when she's stressed."

Evelyn reached up and patted her grandson's shoulder. "That must be difficult," she murmured in sympathy. The elderly couple gave each other a meaningful look, and then his grandmother excused herself, leaving her husband to deal with the situation.

"Sit down, Gray," he scooted out the chair opposite him

with his foot and turned toward Grayson, who checked his watch, doing the mental math on how long it would take him to get to the airport.

"Now, why don't you tell me what's really bothering you?" Marty asked, studying his grandson with a patient gaze that encompassed all his years of life experience.

Grayson's shoulders slumped. He should have known better than to show up at his grandparents' doorstep in such a state of emotional dishabille. He really *was* going to miss his flight.

26

Building and Burning Bridges

The next morning I was dressed in street clothes and ready to roll, thanks to the kind nurse who had brought me my crutches yesterday. I shuffled around my room, picking up the rest of my belongings and shoving them in the duffle I'd found in the closet. Slowly, I turned around the room, studying wall-upon-wall of flower arrangements. There was no way I would be able to take them all. At the very least, I wanted Grayson's arrangement and the bouquet from the Ladies Guild.

"Hey, Bug, you ready to bust this joint?" My dad asked as he arrived in the doorway to my room.

"Absolutely," I replied as I lowered myself gently into the recliner for a breather. I couldn't believe how easily winded I was. I mean, it's not like I'd been an athletic person, but I took for granted how much activity I did on a daily basis—pre-accident.

My nurse rolled in a wheelchair, ready to escort me to the front where my dad could pull up and get me. *Thank God.* I had no idea where I would have summoned the energy to make it all the way to the front entrance on my own. "Ready, hon?" she asked with a smile.

I nodded with a smile of my own but didn't feel it deep in my bones. Too much had happened in the past twenty-four hours for me to feel good about anything.

I laid my bag across my lap, and with one last look at the room I'd called home for the past eleven days, I was whisked downstairs to be loaded into the car.

"Thanks for coming to get me," I murmured as Dad put the car in drive and headed for the exit.

"No problem. I'm surprised your mom or Grayson didn't volunteer, though," he wondered aloud as he looked both ways for traffic and pulled out onto the main road.

I bit the inside of my cheek. I'd tried not to think about the whole situation, but it kept coming up. "Grayson went back to Phoenix, and…I sort of got in a fight with mom, so…"

"A fight?" he asked, glancing sideways at me. "I thought you two were thick as thieves." He glanced sideways at me with an impish grin that quickly dissolved when he saw I wasn't interested in laughing. "What were you arguing about? Or should I not have asked?" he inquired, not wanting to pry but knowing it had to be a pretty big deal for us not to be speaking.

"No…I just…" I sighed. "She thinks I'm spending too much time with Grayson and not leaving any time for myself. That, and she's totally against my plan to have Grayson stay with me when he's in town to help me out until I'm fully mobile again." *Paraphrased, but not untrue.*

He winced like he'd unintentionally swallowed a mouthful of broken glass. It was extremely awkward for him to think about me living with anyone of the opposite sex, let alone a serious boyfriend. *But who else can I talk to?*

Eventually, he cleared his throat and continued the conversation. "So, did that have anything to do with why he left? I thought he was supposed to be in town for a couple more days?"

I sighed, fighting back tears as I stared out the windshield. This unending stream of waterworks was getting on my last nerve. I gritted my teeth and fisted the moisture from my eyes before it had a chance to spill over.

"Uh oh, trouble in paradise?" Dad asked, trying again to make light of the situation but that only made the tears more imminent.

"Freaking Mom…" *Yep, tears were definitely coming.* "…had to cause a scene, and he's worried about it. He doesn't want to come between us. He says we need to work things out, and he'll see me when he gets back." My breath hitched with the effort of trying to keep my emotions inside, and the resulting ache in my still-healing ribs was overwhelming.

"Bug, I know it's frustrating, but your mom wants what's best for you…and isn't she usually right?" he asked, taking his eyes off the road to look at me.

I rolled my eyes. "I just wish she would realize she's not right about this. I'm an adult. She needs to accept that."

He laughed. "Alaina, do you know how many times your mom told me that about your grandma? Being frustrated with your parents is a rite of passage. You want to be independent, and we want to hold on for as long as we can." His fingers thrummed on the steering wheel to the beat of an internal debate. "If Grayson is willing to give you space to figure this out, then it sounds like he's a better man than your mom thinks."

I rolled my eyes again. "She said she doesn't have a problem with him. She thinks *he's a perfectly nice guy.* She just thinks I'm too attached."

"Well, are you?" he asked.

I stared at him, caught off guard by his direct question. "I…we…" Flustered, I found myself at a loss for words. "We like to spend time together. I didn't think that was a crime!"

"There's absolutely nothing wrong with mutually choosing to spend time together. If I had to guess, that's probably what she's worried about. Relationships are hard—especially when you lose sight of who you were in the beginning."

I sighed. "I was kind of mean when we were fighting," I admitted, ashamed of my behavior. More and more these days, I was beginning to realize my mental filter was no longer present ninety percent of the time. It was an annoying revelation. I needed to constantly think ahead about what I wanted to say, but in instances where my emotions got the better of me, I wasn't always prepared to think before I spoke.

My father was very good at hiding his emotions. In his profession, he had to be, but he wasn't bothering to hide them now. His hazel eyes stared ahead at the road, and a wave of regret washed over his strong countenance. When he spoke again, his voice was soft and measured. "Take it from a guy who was too proud to apologize for most of his marriage. Apologies go a long way."

I glanced at him out of the corner of my eye. "Do you think things would have turned out differently…if…" my voice was soft, non-assuming, and curious.

His shoulders sagged, and for a moment, he was a young man again, trying to find answers to the millions of questions inside of him. "I don't know." The smile on his lips was a sad one. "That's just it, isn't it? For better or worse, every decision you make shapes the rest of your life, and I made some *bad* decisions, Alaina. I lost my family because of it." His breath was shaky, and he fixed his eyes back on the road.

When I was little, my dad had been larger than life to me, but sitting in that car with him, I saw something I'd struggled to grasp all my life. He was human, just like me. He'd made a mistake, and it had cost him dearly. I reached over and squeezed his arm, giving him a shy half-smile. "I forgive you, Dad."

Tears welled in his eyes, and he reached over to squeeze my hand in return. "Thanks, Bug."

* * *

I might as well have been climbing the Great Wall of China. It felt like it took hours for me to get up the stairs to my second-floor apartment, and the only thing that kept running through my mind was *I am never leaving my apartment again.* By the time we reached the top, my whole body was shaking like a mold of Jell-o in an earthquake. The keys jiggled in my hand with a soft jingle, and after missing the keyhole for the third time, my dad walked up next to me.

"Here," he murmured and took the keys from me to get the door open.

"Thanks," I muttered, slightly embarrassed.

"No problem." He pushed the door open for me to get inside and followed with my duffle and flowers. I inhaled deeply. The slight, musky scent of dog and the sweet smell of my sugar cookie air freshener welcomed me home. It was amazing how many things had turned upside down in four weeks, and yet, so much had remained the same. I ran my hand through the soft, hairy fibers of the blanket on the couch, remembering the feel of it on my skin as I'd cuddled beneath it. The refrigerator kicked off with a thud and startled me back into reality.

"Wow, nice place!" My dad exclaimed as he took it all in with a spin.

My chest puffed with pride at the compliment. It might not be very big, but it was furnished and designed to perfection. "Thanks," I slowly walked over to the couch, hoping I could sit before my legs gave out underneath me. I was ready to take a nap after all my morning exertions. "Could you sit those flowers on the counter? I'll move them around later." Slowly, I moved my legs up to recline on the couch and hissed with the ache in my hips and torso. Everything was starting to hurt. "What time is it?" I asked my dad as I laid back against the pillows, my eyes reduced to slits as fatigue overcame me.

"It's about eleven o'clock…probably time for your meds, isn't it?"

I let out a hard laugh. "I should've taken them about an hour ago." A stifled groan escaped my lips as I shifted. "Can you get them for me? They're in my purse," I gestured to where I'd sat my purse on the counter.

I heard the water running, and then my dad appeared with a glass and my pill bottle. "Thanks."

"Are you sure you're going to be okay on your own here?" he asked, looking around at the quiet apartment.

I put on my best smile. "Yeah. I'll be fine!" I popped a capsule into my mouth and took a swig of water.

He sighed. I could see him warring between paternal instinct and his unwillingness to hurt my pride. So, he nodded. "Okay. I'm going to take off then. If you need anything, call me, okay?" he asked as he gave me a hug.

"Thanks, Dad," I murmured as I hugged him back.

"Anytime, kid."

I watched him go and sighed. I honestly wasn't sure what to do with myself. I flipped my TV on and balked at the number of shows I had flooding my recordings list. I made a selection at random and laid back on the couch, propping my feet up so my hips were flat and I was slightly more comfortable. Jess would drop Copper off sometime tonight, which meant I had some time to snooze. *Thank God for small mercies.*

* * *

The cry of children, the buzz of quiet conversation, and the whir of luggage wheels all mixed together in an indefinable hum of activity that lulled Grayson into a hypnotic state, far away from the anthill of humanity in which he currently resided. He was far too distracted to pay any particular attention to the crowd surrounding his gate at Indianapolis International Airport.

"Seems to me like you're struggling with this whole situation." Grandpa Marty had said the day before, as he leaned back in his chair and crossed his arms in front of his chest. He had opened the gate. Now it was up to Grayson on whether he would bolt or not.

Grayson, finding the comment ironic, snorted. "You could say that." The air between them went silent for a while, the older man refusing to get in the way of his grandson's thoughts. "Am I a completely terrible person if I decide…" He closed his lids trying to quell the overwhelming frustration clawing at his innards. "I have this little voice in my head that keeps telling me this is too hard, that it shouldn't be…*this* hard." Shame ran through his body from head to toe.

Marty looked at his grandson in an appraising fashion, but without the judgment Grayson had expected to be there in his warm brown eyes. "Kid, I hesitate to say you've had it easy because you haven't. You've worked a hell of a lot harder than most men your age to achieve what you have, but…" His grandfather sat up and leaned forward with his elbows on his knees, "having doubts doesn't make you a terrible person, Grayson. It makes you…normal."

Grayson ground his teeth together. If he didn't find some relief soon, his molars would be nubs of tender root embedded in his gums. What did *normal* have to do with it anyway? "I just don't know how to sort my fear from what I actually want," he whispered, wringing his hands.

"Bullshit."

Grayson's eyes snapped up to his grandfather. "You think I'm lying?"

"Not to me, but definitely to yourself." Marty stood and stretched his back in the slow way of the elderly and gazed down the bridge of his nose. "You forget, I know what you do for a living. You, more than any other person, are capable of making a decision and sticking to it, fear factor be damned."

His pocket buzzed with an incoming call, and he shook the remnants of the conversation with his grandfather out of his head—or tried to. Stepping away from the busy airport gate and its noisy PA system, he gazed at the unknown number and hesitated before answering.

"Hello?"

"Grayson, it's Nathan Montgomery."

Nathan Mont—Alaina's dad? What the hell? The bottom fell out of his stomach like he'd driven over a cliff. He certainly didn't sound crazed with grief or overtly angry, just…normal. *Calm down, you idiot. Preferably before you give yourself a heart attack.* Apparently, his silence was enough for Nathan to read between the lines.

"Sorry, I didn't mean to worry you. I swiped your number from Alaina's phone when she wasn't looking."

Grayson let out a sigh. "Well, I suppose that answers one question."

Nathan let out a quiet chuckle in response.

"So, she's home then?"

"She is. Just left her apartment. Came as quite a shock when I got the phone call to come pick her up this morning. I thought for sure she'd ask you or Maura."

Shit. He knows. Grayson rolled his eyes heavenward and prayed for strength. "I figured I should give everyone some space. It seemed to be getting a little tense, and my presence clearly wasn't helping matters."

Nathan was quiet for a long moment. "Look, I know a lot of people in the racing community here in Indy, and I know you've got a lot on your plate right now. This whole situation with Alaina's injury and Maura being…well, I know it's not been easy for you."

Grayson could feel a ginormous "but" waiting in the wings, and nervous energy tickled his stomach.

"All that being said, my daughter has a lot going on right now too." There was a hard edge that had come into his voice, and it made the slight tingling in his abdomen grow into a full-on clenching of his bowels. "I haven't been around the past few years, and that's on me, but I'm here now, and I'll be damned if I watch you tug her around like a rag doll when it's taking everything she has to put her life back together."

Grayson felt a stab of anger crash into him at the idea he was being treated like some teenager in need of an attitude adjustment. The line was quiet for a moment and Grayson took a deep breath, willing his voice not to shake when he spoke again. "I love your daughter."

"I know that." Alaina's father's voice was a little softer now. "But Alaina's going to need more than love to get her through this." The voice on the other end of the line was almost sad, but Grayson knew what he meant. She needed strength. Certainty. If he couldn't give her those things, well…shit or get off the pot, as his grandfather was so fond of saying. "Alright, I'm going to get off here. I'm about to head back into the office, but umm…" He paused for a moment in silent debate. "As far as I know, Alaina still isn't speaking to Maura, so my guess is she'll probably be bored stiff in a couple of hours." Another pause, and then a final thought meant to sound offhand. "Oh, well. I'm sure she'll find *something* to do."

Grayson's lip twitched at the man's innuendo.

"I'm sure she will," Grayson replied, glancing across at the gate and its line of people. The flight was boarding. He would have to make a decision, and soon.

"Alright, kid. Maybe I'll see you soon?" There was a smile in his voice Grayson grudgingly admired. It was the voice of a man who seldom lost an argument.

"Yeah, maybe."

* * *

A knock at the door startled me into consciousness. I gingerly pushed myself upright and looked at the clock on the wall. I'd only been sleeping for thirty minutes. *Who the hell is bothering me at this time of day?* I leaned over and grabbed my crutches from their place against the end table as another knock sounded, a little more urgent.

"I'm coming!" I growled as I slowly got up. *Jesus, don't people know I'm a cripple?* I hobbled over to the door and struggled with the stupid deadbolt for a minute before I was finally able to open the door.

I blinked stupidly, attempting to clear the mirage from my vision. "Grayson?"

"Sorry, I didn't mean to wake you…I was just having these images of you having fallen and—"

I mentally shook myself and smiled flirtatiously. "Were you worried about me?"

His gaze dropped to our feet, and a delicate blush colored the back of his neck. "Maybe."

"What are you doing here?" I asked, eyeing the bag he had slung over his shoulder.

"Well, I was about to board my plane when I realized I didn't want to be in Phoenix. I want to be here with you."

My heart stuttered, and I smiled, feeling a blush warm my cheeks as well. Leaning on one crutch for support, I pushed the door open for him to enter.

"You brought the flowers with you!" he exclaimed, taking in my counter display.

"I told you I liked them!" I added as I slowly moved back toward the couch.

He put his bag down on the kitchen table and came over to join me as I sat, picking my legs up to drape them over his lap. With a touch as light as an insect's wing, he rested a hand on my thigh. "How are you feeling?"

"Well, about forty-five minutes ago, I was pretty miserable, but my meds have kicked in, and I'm feeling pretty good now."

"Good," he commented with a nod. "Copper's not here?" he asked, looking around.

"No," I sighed. "I think Jess is planning to bring him back tonight."

He squeezed my leg. "Well, I'm sure he'll be thrilled to see you."

"Yeah." A smile crept across my face as I thought about being reunited with my boy. "What?" I asked as I caught him gazing at me.

"You're beautiful, you know that?"

The blush that had faded from my cheeks rebounded with abandon, and I looked down at our hands. "I don't feel very beautiful right now." My voice was quiet, almost indiscernible amid the hum of the air conditioner.

His brow furrowed. "Alaina." His baritone voice was filled with both incredulity and gentle chastisement. "Why would you say that?"

I shrugged. "I don't know." I sighed and looked up at him. "I just feel a little self-conscious about my face." I drew circles on the back of the hand that was still resting on my leg. "That's why I didn't want to do the interview when you asked me yesterday."

Understanding lit his eyes. "Well, it's not that big of a deal. I told Cami you weren't up for it, and she's going to let the producers know."

I bit my lip. "I'm sorry. I don't want to be a baby about it. I just can't, not now." I lifted my gaze from the nearly hairless backs of his hands and up into the chocolate depths of his beautiful brown eyes, full of compassion and love.

He wrapped his strong hand around the back of my neck and massaged it. "You don't have to apologize. I understand," he assured me. "But, for what it's worth, I still think you're beautiful." He put a finger under my chin to drag it up. "With or without this," he said as he lightly touched my cheek.

I gave him a tentative smile and squeezed his hand. "Can we talk about what happened last night?"

"I think we probably should," he agreed, shifting his weight carefully to avoid hurting me.

I sighed. "At the risk of sounding like a high maintenance brat, I was kind of hurt you left like that. I didn't feel like you were listening to me."

He closed his eyes and sighed. "It's not bratty. You're right. I wasn't listening to you." He let out a sigh. "I'm sorry. I'm trying to make a good impression on your family, and as dumb as that may sound, I didn't want to rock the boat."

"You don't have to *try* to make a good impression, Grayson. You're as good as they come, and any misgivings my parents have, they've never stemmed from any doubts about your character."

After a quiet moment, he gave me a tight smile. "I felt bad about leaving. I stood in front of the hospital for a good fifteen minutes debating whether or not to go back up and apologize."

I wasn't about to tell him his actions were okay because they weren't, but I understood why he did what he did. "We can't just walk out on each other. There are a lot of things that are going to try to tear us apart. I want to know when push comes to shove, I can count on you to be on my side." My eyes were cloudy with emotion, and I sucked my lower lip between my teeth, biting down on it in an effort to keep it from trembling.

His hand had migrated up my leg and now squeezed my thigh. "I will *always* be on your side, Alaina. *Always.*"

I nodded and leaned in to kiss him, feeling like a weight had been lifted from my chest. There weren't many people in my life I could trust unconditionally, but somehow, I knew Grayson was one of them.

* * *

Several hours later, I woke from a fitful doze with my head in Grayson's lap. The final scenes of Fast and Furious were playing out on the television, and I groaned. "I cannot do this for another two weeks. I'm going to lose my freaking mind."

"What? Watch movies and sleep all day? I think I could get used to that." Grayson laughed, but catching wind of the ferocious scowl on my face, he changed course. "Well, what do you *want* to do?"

"Anything but this. I can't take another minute of boredom. Emma's wedding is two months away, and I haven't even started on the arch and centerpieces!" I cried. "This is the epitome of a disaster." I rubbed my eyes, gritty from sleep, and eased myself into a sitting position.

"Come on, if anybody is going to understand, it's Em," Grayson's dark eyes rolled in exasperation.

I bit the inside of my cheek and searched for some way to make him see. "It's not just that it's your sister's wedding— although that's certainly enough stress. This is the biggest wedding of the year for me. *Three hundred people.* Celebrities and CEOs. Grayson, this could make or break my career."

He studied me for a long time and brushed his fingers across an errant strand of hair to tuck it back into place. The corner of his mouth curled up with reluctant amusement. "I was afraid you were going to say that."

I laughed. "What is that supposed to mean?"

"It means…I guess I will go load up the 4Runner with all the shi—stuff—you need tomorrow morning and bring your shop to you."

My face lit up. "Really?" I sat up, jerking my legs, and the sudden movement shot pains up through my left side. I closed my eyes, taking deep breaths until the stabbing pain subsided.

Grayson rubbed my leg in comfort and waited for me to resume my previous line of thought. "Okay?"

Another second and a few deep breaths later, I nodded. "Yeah, I'm alright."

"Sorry, I didn't mean to startle you."

I shook my head. "No, it's not your fault. I just need to remember I can't do that." I gave a dark laugh and scooted to the edge of the couch, groping for my crutches.

"What do you need?" he asked, sitting up now that he didn't have to worry about disturbing me.

"I just need to stretch. I'll be okay," I assured him and used my crutches to pull myself up off the couch. Laboriously, I made my way over to the kitchen counter, going through all the mail that had built up over the past month. "All bills…yay," I muttered.

Grayson walked up behind me and kissed my shoulder, wrapping his arms around my waist protectively. "Have you talked to the hospital? Is your insurance going to cover everything?" His adept fingers shuffled through the thick envelopes with ease.

"Well, my insurance has a 3,500 dollar deductible, and then eighty percent coverage after that, but I think that still brings my bills to well over one hundred thousand dollars," I whispered through my suddenly dry throat.

"Goddamn," Grayson muttered. "Don't they have anything better to do than rob their patients?"

"Yeah, I know." When they'd gone over everything with me before I'd been released, I'd almost had a heart attack. I was doing okay monetarily. I had savings, and I had insurance, but that didn't mean I could afford the black hole of unplanned medical expenses I was headed for. My breathing was quick and shallow as my mind raced. "I don't know what I'm going to do," I whispered, tears rushing to my eyes. My breath hitched. "I really...don't." My chest was beginning to hurt, and I could feel the start of a migraine coming on.

"Shhhh...hey, it's okay. I'm not going to let you drown, okay? I promise. We'll figure it out." His arms came around me without hesitation, and the solid warmth of him eased some of the tension welling inside me. When my breathing had slowed back to normal and the tears had subsided, he released me, squeezing my upper arms in reassurance. "After the accident, we all figured you would have quite a few medical expenses...if you—" He took a shaky breath and shook his head, not saying what he was really thinking. *If you survived.* "Anyway, Cami helped me start a fundraiser page for you." Now that he mentioned it, I vaguely remembered hearing about the page in the pre-race coverage last weekend.

"A lot of the teams and drivers pitched in—family, friends, and fans, too. You've got a nice little nest egg."

"How much of a nest egg are we talking about?" I asked hesitantly, eyeing him as he pulled back from me and pulled out his phone to scroll through the content on his screen. After a moment of searching, he turned his phone around so I could see, and I gasped. "A hundred and twenty-five thousand dollars?" The words came out as sharp squeaks of surprise and more tears began to flow.

His soft pink lips curled up in a warm smile. "I told you. People love you."

"Grayson…I…I don't even know what to say." My knees wobbled, and I realized I was dangerously close to collapsing with the shock of his revelation.

"You don't have to say anything." Noticing my compromised state, he took my arm in a firm, yet gentle, grasp and guided me to the barstool a few feet away. "The page closes out tomorrow, and then we can get the funds transferred. From there, you can do what you want with it. Pay the hospital, pay the phone company, pay a massage therapist… whatever," he shrugged with that impish grin I loved so much.

"Oh my God," I didn't know whether to laugh or cry and settled for both. The sense of relief I felt now was unbelievable. "You're amazing. Thank you. Thank you so much. You have no idea what this means."

"I wanted to help. Everyone was so concerned about whether you would make it or not, but I…" His brow furrowed, and he looked down at his feet, shuffling them awkwardly as he searched for the right words. "I couldn't bear the thought of losing you, Alaina. So, instead of thinking about…about *that*, I thought about what would happen if you lived. And when I realized how many medical bills you would have..." He let out an exasperated sigh. "I just wanted to help," he said again with another shrug.

"I think you help me a lot more than you realize," I said as I drew him closer and placed my head on his chest.

"I love you," he replied simply as if those three words encompassed every action he'd ever taken and every move he had yet to make.

"I love you, too," I whispered back, feeling the words so deep in my bones, I knew I would never be the same again.

* * *

I woke up to the smell of bacon, and my stomach growled. *My man is making me breakfast.* I winced and rolled slightly to see my alarm clock. Ten-thirty. *Wow.* It had been difficult to sleep hooked up to a hundred different machines with people constantly coming in and out of my room, but at home, in my own bed? It was like my own little piece of heaven. I laid back and smiled, feeling the soft caress of high thread count sheets on my cheek. The soft variation in pitch of quiet singing floated to me from the kitchen, along with the delicious smells of food preparation. *And he sings.* I chuckled. Copper's tags jingled as he walked around the living room restlessly. He wanted to go for a walk, that much was clear. I felt more rested now than I had the whole time I'd been in the hospital, but I didn't see how I was going to manage a trip to the dog park in my condition.

I lay in bed for another minute and then summoned the courage to take on the day. I pulled my covers back and gently scooted my legs over the edge, leaning for my crutches. I hopped over to my en suite bathroom to brush my teeth and run a brush through my hair. Looking in the mirror, I studied the three-inch pink line across my right cheek. It didn't look bad. I hadn't tried, but I doubted it would be anything my foundation couldn't cover. I smiled and was happy to find I couldn't even feel it anymore.

Quietly, I pulled the bedroom door open. Grayson had his back to me, whistling as he cooked. Copper, who'd been laying up against the island, perked up when I opened the door, and I smiled at him and slowly walked closer to the kitchen, careful to avoid putting more than half of my weight on my good side.

Grayson turned to me, spatula in hand. "Good morning!" he greeted as he flipped one of the pancakes he was cooking.

"Morning," I murmured as I grabbed a seat on the barstool behind him. "I had no idea you cooked." Copper sat next to me with his chin resting on my knee, prompting me to pet him.

Grayson smiled at me over his shoulder. "Well, it was either learn how to cook or live on fast food, so…" he gestured to the counter full of eggs, bacon, and pancake mix—none of which looked familiar.

"Did you go to the store?" I asked incredulously.

He laughed. "Yeah, well…all you had in your refrigerator was some sour milk and a couple of questionable fruits and vegetables. Your pantry didn't look much more promising, and you were still sleeping. So, I went and got a few things after my run."

I smiled and rolled my eyes. "Well, thanks. This smells amazing, by the way. I'm starving."

"Well, don't let me stop you!" he exclaimed. "What would

you like? I've got bacon, eggs, and pancakes. Yogurt and fruit in the refrigerator."

"Wow. Umm…surprise me," I suggested. In no time at all, I had a plate full of food in front of me. My stomach rumbled. "Oh my God," I groaned, letting a piece of bacon crumble between my teeth. Saliva flooded my mouth at the introduction of savory hickory smoke and grease. "Ambrosia…"

He laughed. "Bacon is good for the soul. I think that's an ancient Chinese proverb or something," he claimed with a chuckle. "By the way, I think Copper officially likes me more than you." He nodded to where Cops was sitting on his feet, leaning into his legs.

I gasped. "What method of bribery were you using?"

He rolled his eyes. "I may have slipped him a couple of pieces of bacon."

Copper licked his chops as he stared at the plate of pork on the counter.

"Yeah, you better watch it, or when you turn back around, that plate won't be there." I laughed.

He made a face and picked up the plate, dropping it in front of me.

I picked up another piece and chewed in ecstasy. I could feel the salt coursing over my tongue. It was *so* good. Grayson finished filling his plate with pancakes and eggs and joined me at the island with two glasses of orange juice. "Did you get pulp?" I asked, referring to the orange juice.

He glanced over at me, no longer chewing the piece of bacon he'd stuck in his mouth. "No, you like pulp?"

"You don't?!" I asked incredulously.

"It gets all stuck in your teeth and crap…" he whined as he

swallowed his mouthful of food.

I rolled my eyes. "First, you steal my dog. Now, you don't like pulp? I don't think this is going to work out…"

"Well, fine. I'll take my bacon and go!" he said as he pulled the plate of meat closer to him. We both burst into laughter, and I grabbed my stomach. My incisions were mostly healed, but my broken ribs were still sore, and it hurt when I coughed, sneezed, or laughed too hard.

We finally managed to get our giggles under control, and I leaned over to take another bite of food. The shorts I was wearing had ridden up my leg, and Grayson studied the nasty scar on my thigh. I wasn't sure what had cut me in the accident, but it wasn't pretty. He reached out and ran a thumb up the scar, sending tingles down my spine and making me shiver.

"Does it hurt?" he asked quietly.

I shook my head, taking a swig of pulp-free OJ.

"That's crazy," he murmured.

"My face doesn't hurt anymore either. I just realized it this morning."

He raised his hand from my leg to my cheek, running his fingers lightly over the mark there. Our eyes met, and we held each other's gaze for a long time. I wanted to know what he was thinking at that moment. The look in his eyes was hard to describe. It wasn't necessarily a bad look. It was contemplative, knowing, desirous even. Eventually, he smiled at me, and with one more rub of his thumb up my cheek, took his hands back and finished his breakfast.

After the meal was cleared away, Grayson took off for the shop to bring me more goodies. I was beginning to wonder if the man ever slept. Boxes were already piled in every nook and cranny of spare space my apartment had to offer. It was clear his day had started several hours before mine. He'd had time to go for a run, go to the grocery store, *and* bring a truckload of wedding decor to the apartment before I'd managed to lug my battered carcass into the world of the living. My living room was starting to look like the house of a hoarder. It was mind-boggling to think this was all for one event. Everyone else on my calendar had been refunded and sent to a competitor, but I flat out *refused* to allow anyone other than myself to design Emma's wedding. Not only was she my boyfriend's sister, but her wedding was possibly the highest-profile wedding I would ever design for, and I wasn't about to let it slip through my fingers. Luckily, I had been ahead of schedule prior to the accident, and I already had all of the flowers, vases, and fabrics ordered.

Now, I had the exciting job of sorting through the afore-mentioned boxes in search of the vases. Before I could put any floral arrangements together, all of the dust and bits of Styrofoam had to be painstakingly wiped from all surfaces. *Easier said than done.*

"Seriously, I'm never going to get used to how much shit it takes to put together a few flower arrangements." Grayson grumbled as he stumbled through the open door and eyed his surroundings, searching for an empty space to dump his latest haul.

I laughed. "What did you think you were getting into when you volunteered?"

He looked at me for a minute. "Not this…that's for sure. This is…chaotic." Beads of sweat were dripping down his flushed face, and for a moment I felt terrible I couldn't help him. It was unseasonably hot for July, and with jeans and a black team polo adorning his slim frame, he wasn't exactly dressed for manual labor.

I opened one of the boxes he'd just brought in and found it brimming with ribbon, floral tape, wire, and pins. Another box had carefully packaged blush roses for the bridal party's accessories. If nothing else, I was going to knock out these bouquets and boutonnieres. They were important, and if I had them ready to go, I was sure a bit of the pressure I felt would ease. By the time Grayson made it upstairs with his second load of boxes, I was knee-deep in unpacked flowers and floral tape.

"Well, at least you won't need to work out today." I giggled as I watched him wipe the sweat from his brow.

"No shit." He huffed as he caught his breath. "I think I should be able to get it in two more trips," he said as he came over to see what I was doing. "What's that going to be?"

"Bridesmaid bouquet…I figured if I could at least get these done, I wouldn't be totally useless," I joked as I dragged my eyes up from the flowers to his face.

He only gave me half a smile, eyes distant. *Something is wrong.*

"Grayson?"

"It's nothing." He shook his head. "Just, um…you know, keep doing what you're doing. I'll be back."

I started to object, but he'd already headed back downstairs for more boxes.

My stomach turned. I didn't like this. Something had happened between this morning and when he'd come back, and it wasn't good. I paired the rose stems with wire and wrapped them in floral tape while I stewed on the myriad of things that could have caused his mood swing. I pulled the bunch of flowers back to observe from afar. It was pretty, but something was missing. *Greenery.*

I'd seen a box of eucalyptus stems somewhere…*Oh, that's specific.* I eyed the sea of boxes apprehensively and slowly made my way over to the boxes closest to my bedroom. Leaning heavily on my crutches, I pulled back the packing tape of box number one and started digging. It wasn't until lucky number seven that I found what I was looking for. Unfortunately, my living room now looked like it had exploded. Dismayed, I stepped around a pile of packing paper and stooped to pick up the corresponding invoice. As I bent to retrieve the paper, I glanced out the window, wondering where on earth Grayson was. It had been at least an hour since he'd disappeared.

Searching for his familiar blue 4Runner, my heart clenched when I finally found it. He was sitting in the passenger seat of his SUV, legs hanging out the open door with his elbows resting on his knees. His head was bent, and his shoulders slumped as though the world had come crashing down on top of him. His cell phone hung loosely in one hand, and I knew instantly whatever news he'd just received on the other end hadn't been good. I sighed and tightened my grip on the rubbery handles of my crutches before hopping toward the door.

When he heard me hopping toward him, he sat up, wiping his face quickly. If I was worried before, I was uneasy now. He jumped out of the car and forced a watery smile onto his face. "What are you doing out here?" He reached out to help me slide onto the passenger seat in his stead, and I gave him a grateful smile. I certainly wasn't about to argue over his chivalry. I was exhausted, and it was hotter than Hades outside.

"I could ask you the same question," I allowed between gasps. My winded state didn't keep me from noticing his red-rimmed eyes and blotchy forehead. He hadn't just been shedding a stray tear. He'd been crying—hard. "Grayson, tell me."

He sighed and looked past me into the distance. "I don't... um..." he cleared his throat. "I just got off the phone with Bruce, and um..." He was fighting against the tears in his eyes. When he spoke next, it sounded as if someone had a hand around his throat and was trying to choke the life out of him. "They're closing the doors on the shop after this season."

"Oh my God." I leaned forward and put a hand on his arm. "Why? What happened?" I asked urgently. What he was telling me wasn't computing. *He'd just won the Indy 500, for God's sake. How could this happen?*

"I don't know. I guess the debt's been mounting for a few seasons, and they're in over their heads. The 500 winnings helped, but without primary sponsors for next season, they decided to cut their losses." He shook his head, still a little dazed by the news. "He said they're going to do their best to make sure Jack and I have a good rest of the season, but both our contracts are up anyway, so it made sense to close shop after Laguna."

I put a hand over my mouth for a minute, and when I heard his breath shake, I pulled him in for a hug. "I'm sorry...I'm so sorry," I murmured as I ran my hand up and down his back in support and sympathy.

He squeezed me back, holding me tight for a few more minutes before pulling away. "We'll figure it out. We always do." His voice was a little stronger, but the facade of his tell-tale optimism was brittle at best. I could see the cracks, and he hardly had the heart to hide them. He sniffed and wiped at his damp face. "But um…nobody knows about this yet. Bruce just wanted to give us a heads-up so we can put out feelers for other rides. Okay?"

Translation: I couldn't breathe a word of this to anyone.

27

Slow and Steady

Two weeks later, I sat quietly on the exam table watching my doctor study the x-rays they had just taken. It was cool seeing where they'd placed the pins in my hip, but I'd been sitting in this doctor's office for the better part of an hour, and all I could think was *Can we hurry this up? I don't have all day!* Finally, after another couple of minutes, he turned around to me. "Well, your x-rays look good. I'm very happy with your progress. You want to hop down from there and try to walk for me?"

My heart fluttered. *Yes!* I lowered myself down off the table and stood on my own two feet. Something was off, though. I didn't know quite what it was, but it felt like my entire left leg was made of pins and needles. I could still feel it, and I knew I could move it if I tried, but it still felt abnormal. I looked up at my doctor, unsure. "Something feels weird," I admitted to him as he studied me.

"Can you describe it to me?" he asked, sitting on his little stool and scooting closer to examine my hip.

"It feels like…I don't know, almost like my leg is asleep."

He sighed and nodded, looking up at me. "With injuries like this, nerve damage is always a possibility. There are a lot of nerves, arteries, veins, and organs nestled in your pelvis. Your accident caused some massive internal injuries—most of them will heal with time, but nerve damage is impossible to predict until the patient has recovered enough to test movement and sensation."

I studied him, horrified and unable to help the cold sweat that broke out on the back of my neck at the thought of never being normal again.

He gazed back at me calmly, taking in my reaction. "It may not be permanent. Some nerve injuries heal completely with time, and others are—"

I rolled my eyes heavenward and leaned back against the table. "Great. So, I'm going to be a gimp for the rest of my life." I crossed my arms stubbornly and glared at him.

"I don't think you realize how lucky you are even to be alive, Alaina." He seemed baffled by my reaction, and he took a deep breath, summoning as much patience as possible.

I closed my eyes and sighed. "I'm sorry. Of course, I do. It's just…an adjustment…"

He nodded in understanding and patted my knee. "I know, but the only way you're going to get better is if you keep working. So, can you try walking again for me?"

I gave him a doubtful look, but he nodded reassuringly. Despite the odd sensation in my leg every time I put my full weight on it, it felt good to stand on my own two feet again. I lifted one foot and planted it solidly back on the ground before lifting my bum leg with a little less success. This created a dramatic limp in my step, but the doctor didn't seem concerned. I repeated the movement and looked at him for his thoughts.

He nodded. "It's a start! I'm going to send you home with a cane. You can use it when you feel you need to, but I definitely want you to focus on strengthening those hip and leg muscles. That will help a lot, I think. There's a good chance the pins-and-needles sensation is temporary, but if it gets worse for any reason, don't hesitate to reach out."

I nodded along with him. *Sure, send the cane. I won't be using it, but you can send it.* After another short wait for the doctor's assistant to dredge up the cane in question, I hobbled out into the parking lot, face upturned to the sun. I felt like I had an iron ball attached at the ankle and a hot air balloon tied around my shoulders. The resulting sensation was like being pulled in two directions: optimism that things would eventually return to normal and the cold, darkness of fear that things would never be the same.

It wasn't the pelvic fracture that weighed on me. It was the crushing emotional despair I felt eighty percent of the time. I tried to pretend it wasn't there, but it was, and when I was alone, it was hard to ignore the demon on my shoulder.

You're just a washed-up mess. You'll be old news soon, and then you'll be alone for the rest of time.

I closed my eyes and pushed the thought aside, telling myself the voice was wrong. The people around me loved me and would always be there for me. Besides, I was making progress. Every day I was less and less dependent on others.

Which just makes it easier to pretend you don't exist.

"How did it go?" my dad asked quietly, snapping me out of my inner turmoil.

"Well, he said I might walk with a limp for the rest of my life. So, that's encouraging," I informed with sarcasm that made him wince as I yanked my seatbelt down and across my lap to click it in place.

He sighed. "Lainie, you know they have to tell you those things. He wouldn't be doing his job if he didn't prepare you for the worst possible outcome."

He had a point, but that didn't make the situation any less frustrating. "I'm having trouble feeling my leg," I mumbled.

He looked over at me, not saying anything, just studying me, and then he snaked his arm around me and pulled me in for a hug. "It's going to be okay."

"Will it, though?" I croaked, gazing up at him with a mix of desperation and panic.

His eyes flicked back and forth as they studied my face in an effort to unveil what was truly bothering me. "Lainie…" He hesitated, not sure how to broach whatever subject he wanted to discuss. "When we spoke with the neurosurgeon after your accident, she said you might suffer from depression, even if you never have before—"

"You think I'm depressed?" I snapped.

His brow furrowed, and he was quiet for a moment. "Aren't you?" he finally replied in a voice barely above a whisper.

I broke away from the vice-like grip his hazel eyes had on my own, unable to accept his demand for honesty. All I wanted was to go home, crawl under my covers, and hide from the world. And yet…

I gave a minuscule nod of the head and redirected my line of sight to my hands, unsure where to go from there.

"Well, then, we'll get you help. Any and all of the help you need, Bug. I mean it." He reached over tentatively and grasped my hand, squeezing gently. "I can't say I understand what you're going through because if I did, I'd be a liar. But

I know what it's like to think you can't talk about what's going on inside you—to think you need to be tough and soldier on because nobody wants to hear about your personal problems."

"It's lonely," I whispered. My throat felt swollen, and it was hard for me to breathe. I'd never been one for secrets, but several weeks of poor communication, depression, anxiety, and ill-advised web searches had compounded into the mother of all cluster-fucks.

"I know," he sighed, patting my knee. "I know." We sat in the car for a moment longer, not feeling the need to speak. Finally, my dad shifted in his seat and gripped the steering wheel as he put the car in drive. "Let's get you home, and then we can deal with what comes next."

I took a deep breath, the scent of the Febreze vent clip calming me considerably. "Actually, Dad…would you mind taking me by the shop?"

He glanced over at me for a second, surprised by my request. "Uh…yeah, Bug. Sure." Instead of turning left at the light to take me home, he turned right, heading toward the downtown strip where the shop was located. When he pulled up to the curb, my heart stuttered. It felt like it had been forever since I'd walked through those doors. "You okay?" he asked me quietly as he placed the car in park and turned to look at me.

"Yeah," I answered as I cleared my throat. "I'll…be right back," I murmured as I opened the door and lifted myself out of his car. I used the railing to slowly make my way up the three steps to our navy-blue awning, and I glanced up at the sign that cheerfully read Decadent Designs in elegant white script. I couldn't help but feel a sense of both pride and sadness at what I had accomplished, but before I could dwell on it too much, I went inside. The little bell above the door jingled merrily in my wake, and I heard the wheels of an office chair rolling against a plastic mat as Jess pushed back from her desk.

"Welcome to…Alaina! Oh my God! You're walking!" She rushed over and threw her arms around me in a celebratory hug.

I squeezed her back, and we held each other for a long moment. The shop felt like a faraway, exotic land after the confines of my apartment, and the familiar smell of clean linens, printer ink, and carefully packaged silk flowers combined to make a unique and familiar bouquet. It smelled like home, but in that peculiar way of a faint reminiscence—like remembering the smell of your childhood house versus the familiar scent of your residence as an adult.

"You didn't tell me the doctor cleared you!" she accused, hands on hips.

"I just got back from the doctor," I informed her with a knowing grin that said, *hold your horses.* "He's happy with my progress, but I'm a long way from being *cleared.*"

"Well, it's a step in the right direction," she encouraged, absently caressing the little bulge of her belly.

My eyes bulged at this sudden chrysalis shedding. "Whoa!"

She grinned back. "Yeah…I wasn't sure when I would start showing, and then, all of a sudden…there it was." Her eyes brightened considerably. "Oh, I got the results of the genetic test this morning!"

My eyes widened. "Oh my God. I forgot!" I twisted over to face her, ignoring the twinge in my lower abdomen down through my legs. "Soo? Pink or Blue? Niece or Nephew?" I clapped my hands together, feeling more myself than I had in a long time.

"I feel like I should tell Tucker first," she whispered confidentially, hesitant to divulge her top-secret information.

I rolled my eyes and sighed dramatically. *"Fine*...well, can we video chat with him or something? I'm dyin' here."

Jess gave me a patronizing smile and pulled out her phone. "Do you realize how ridiculous you sound? You've got to be the most impatient person I've ever met."

"Yeah, yeah, so I've heard," I dismissed, creating a circular motion with my hand to hurry her along. Tuck had gone back to Texas the day after I'd been released from the hospital, but I'd made a point to keep in touch. If the accident had taught me anything, it was the importance of family and friends. The little wheel spun on the screen for what seemed like an eternity, and then suddenly, his smiling face filled the phone. "Hey, what's up?"

I glanced at the clock, suddenly realizing what time it was. *He's still working...crap.*

"Sorry to bother you, but *Alaina* had to know the sex of *our* baby, and I couldn't tell her before I told you. That wouldn't be fair." Jess giggled and bit her bottom lip, blushing a delicate pink. *What is that about?*

Tuck's face lit up. "Shit, I forgot! Hang on." There was significant scuffling on the other end of the phone as Tucker made his way to a more private area. "Alright, lay it on me! Is it what I thought? Wait, no. Just...just say it."

I bit down on my lower lip to keep from laughing. I don't think I had ever seen Tuck more flustered than he was at that moment. I, myself, was waiting with bated breath.

"It's a boy." Her voice was quiet with the millions of

emotions I could see playing across her face, and I couldn't help but feel like an intruder at the moment of intimacy they shared across the video chat.

Tuck's eyes went wide. "A boy. It's…it's a boy?" Tears sprung to his eyes as he let out a joyous laugh and shouted, "We're having a boy!" Whoops and hollers resounded from the next room, and I couldn't help but laugh as I pictured a bunch of tough Airmen standing on the other side of a closed door, ears pressed up against it, just as anxious as I was.

My hands were shaking, and I realized with a start that I had tears running down my face as well. I was going to have a nephew. "That's amazing! Congratulations, you guys, I'm so happy for you!" And I was. I was *so* happy for my best friend and my brother. This child may not have been planned, but that didn't mean he would be any less loved.

Despite my complete joy at the prospect of impending aunthood, I also felt a wave of grief and sadness. I didn't begrudge the budding family in front of me their happiness, but a small part of me also mourned for what I may never have. I mentally shook myself and plastered a smile on my face. Tucker seemed thrilled, and I was glad things had worked out for them.

"Wow," Tuck muttered. "That's awesome…I…couldn't be happier."

After another moment, he shifted. "Well, listen. I'll let Mom and Dad know tonight, but I have to get off here. Thanks for calling, though. I appreciate it!"

"Of course," Jess assured him, shaking her head. "He's your son, too."

Tuck smiled wistfully, as though the idea of being a father hadn't truly sunk in yet. "I'll call you later, okay?"

"Okay," she said with a smile.

"Bye, Lainie. Love you!" Tuck voiced a little louder.

"Love you, too," I said, my enthusiastic smile still carefully locked in place. This whole conversation had confused the hell out of me. And what was that whole "I'll call you later" comment about?

The line disconnected, and I stared at my feet for a long moment before glancing up at Jess.

"What?" she asked, sensing I wanted to say something.

I sighed and stared out the window. "Is there something going on between you two?"

"You mean besides the bun in my oven?" she asked with a smirk. Her eyes were telling a completely different story, though.

"Jess, I'm not blind...and Jack's not either." My mind drifted back to my brief conversation with her boyfriend in the hospital.

She closed her eyes and turned back around in her seat, unsure where to start. "Jack is great. He really is. I just..." She took a shuddering breath and focused her gaze on me, tears glistening. "Tuck wants to try to make it work." Confusion, doubt, and fear all warred for dominance across her feminine features. She'd never had a serious relationship—never even wanted one, and now she had two sitting in her lap. The trouble was, she had to pick one. "We never thought about it, you know? Tuck thinks we owe it to our child, and ourselves, to at least *see* if there could be something there, and...I—I think I agree with him."

I felt sick. I'd told Jack there was nothing to worry about. *He's going to hate me.*

"Don't you think so?" she asked softly. She wanted my

opinion, even though it didn't really matter at this point.

I thought about my life now. As much as I still struggled with my parent's divorce, I wouldn't change a thing about my childhood. For better or worse, Tucker and I had grown up in a happy family, and of course, I wanted that for my nephew. "I just want you all to be happy," I murmured, thinking words as non-committal as those should give her the freedom to make her own choice without worrying what I thought.

She gave me a grin. "Thanks, Alaina." She sat there for a while before sitting up and clearing her throat. "Okay, I have to go."

"Go where?" I asked, surprised.

"Jack and I have a Skype date."

I nodded in thought. *So, Tucker knew she was breaking up with Jack. That's what his comment had been about. He was going to call and check up on her later.* "Well, let him down easy. He's a good guy."

She nodded solemnly. "I hope he understands."

"I'm sure he will. If not right now, eventually," I assured her.

I walked out with my friend as she locked up the shop and kept to myself on the ride home. I had so much going on, and I wasn't even sure where to start. Maybe my dad was right. Maybe I *did* need to speak with a therapist. If nothing else, it would give me a chance to voice some of the things I didn't have the courage to tell those closest to me.

"Are you okay?" Dad asked. Now that I had confirmed it, I felt his concern for my mental health radiating through the car.

I looked up. I had been so lost in my head, I hadn't realized we were parked outside my building. "Yeah. Yeah, I'm fine."

I was going to be sore tomorrow. I could already feel it. In the past week, I'd rarely used my crutches but had them for support when I was feeling tired. Today, I'd supported my entire body weight three times as much as the prior week.

And what have we learned here? The sardonic gremlin on my shoulder questioned.

"Take your time. Be patient. You're doing great." I mocked in a sing-song voice under my breath.

"Hmm?" my dad asked, glancing over at me in curiosity.

"Nothing," I quickly denied. If he thought I was unstable before, I could only imagine the fallout if he discovered I'd taken up talking to an imaginary friend.

My dad studied me for another moment and, evidently satisfied with what he saw, let me out of the car with a pop of the automatic locks. "If you need anything—"

"I'll call," I finished with a smile. "Thanks for the ride."

"Not a problem. Have a good night, Bug."

* * *

As I collapsed on the couch, all I could think was how much I wanted a glass of wine, but sadly, I wasn't allowed to have alcohol yet. I sipped at my soda disappointedly as I flipped through the channels, each click of the remote echoing through the speakers with a quiet *boink, boink, boink*. Copper jerked to an upright position and let out a menacing growl approximately a millisecond before a light knock sounded at the door. I shushed the ferocious Guardian of the Couch and limped over to the door, looking through the peephole. "Shit," I swore under my breath and rolled my eyes. I stood there for a minute, debating whether I was going to answer, but another persistent knock sounded.

"Alaina, I know you're in there."

I took a deep breath, steeling myself, and pulled the door open. "Mom, what are you doing here?" I asked as I forced my face into a halfway cordial expression.

She sighed. "Can we talk?" Her arms were folded uncomfortably in front of her chest, and she looked uneasy. It had been two weeks since the explosion at the hospital, and we had barely spoken since. Clearly, it had been on her mind.

I motioned for her to come inside. *I wish I could tell you no.*

She placed her purse on the island and turned to study me as I shut the door. "You're walking!" she exclaimed happily with a smile.

"Yeah, the doc approved full weight-bearing at my appointment today," I allowed, arms crossed in front of my chest defensively.

"Oh…well, you should have told me you had an appointment. I would've taken you!" she assured me.

"That's alright. Dad was able to take me."

She nodded, pursing her lips in thought. "You seem to have patched things over with him."

My brow raised in surprise, and I cleared my throat, stalling for time as I thought about what I should say. "Um…yeah…I suppose I have." Slowly, I made my way back to the sofa, dodging the manic Golden Retriever at my feet, along with the contents of his toy basket and the odd piece of furniture. I wasn't about to spend another minute standing on my already exhausted legs. I'd be lucky if I could get out of bed in the morning.

"That's good." She nodded, more to herself than me. "Anyway," she walked over and sat in the chair opposite of me. "I...I wanted to talk to you about...everything."

I gazed at her levelly and let her continue.

"Alaina...I hope you know I have only ever wanted what's best for you...truly. And when I got that call from Jessica...that you'd—" her words choked off. "I've never been more scared in my entire life...ever." She emphasized by shaking her head. "I thought for sure I was going to lose you." There were tears in her eyes now, and I could feel my icy resolve melting as I listened. "When you woke up...you were still my little Lainie, but...you weren't. Seeing that for the first time...that was hard..."

"Mom." I was confused. The doctors were impressed with my neurological deficits or lack thereof. In reality, my mood swings, migraines, and depression were all very minor compared to what I *could* be dealing with.

"Alaina, I realized—seeing you with Grayson—you were a different person than I'd ever thought of you being. You were a young woman, in love, and...ready to leave me...and that was scary."

I didn't speak—I couldn't. Her honesty was shocking, but I knew she had more to say.

"As a mother, you know in the back of your mind it will happen. One day, your child is going to find someone, and they are going to be everything you could never be for your...beautiful, strong, successful daughter...and when I look at that young man...I see all of those things." Tears were thick in her voice, making her light soprano shake unsteadily. "So, when you told me he was going to move in with you—to help you..." she took a shaky breath. "The old-fashioned part of me was having an issue with that, sure, but the selfish part of me was upset because I felt like what might have been my last opportunity to nurse you back to health was being taken away from me by someone I barely knew." Not wanting to cause more agitation between us, she hurried on with her thought. "I know it sounds crazy, but…love is irrational sometimes, you know?"

I gave her a laugh through my watery eyes. "Mom, no matter what happens with Grayson, you're always going to be my mom." I reached over and grabbed her hand. "I love you."

"I love you, too, Bug…so much," she murmured and leaned in to hug me tightly. "I didn't want you to think I don't like Grayson, or think he wasn't good enough for you because I think he's wonderful. It's just that…I'm not quite ready to lose you yet." Her lower lip trembled as she struggled with the effort not to break down completely. I couldn't imagine the amount of strength it had taken for her to come here and admit these things to me.

"You're not going to lose me." I held her for a while. "It's not like I'm getting married."

"No, not yet anyway," she laughed and pulled away from me. We both spent a quiet moment collecting ourselves and wiping at the tear stains on our cheeks. I gave her a quiet smile and her lips quirked up in response, her cheeks flushed a rosy pink as she studied me tenderly. She reached out and grabbed my hand, squeezing it gently. "I know you've been going through a lot here lately, and the last thing I want to do is add to that, but…"

She stared down at our linked hands, searching for the right words. I gave her a reassuring squeeze of my own. "Whatever it is…you can tell me."

She took a deep breath and lifted her head to look at

me. Her forehead was scrunched under the weight of a million questions, and her gray eyes danced across my face, communicating what was left unspoken. *Can I really tell her?*

"I don't think it would come as a surprise to you for me to say we've grown closer since…since your father left. Perhaps, I've leaned on you too much, given you too much of a role to play in my recovery. I think—beyond the idea of losing my daughter—that was perhaps the scariest thing for me, about your accident, I mean. Because I had to contemplate a world without my best friend."

My stomach twisted in knots listening to what she went through after the accident, and I wanted to say something to comfort her as she drifted off in thought, but what exactly *could* I say?

"Do you ever get the feeling everything happens for a reason?" her voice was barely above a whisper as she stared off into space, eyes focused on something I couldn't see.

"Not a lot here lately, no," I answered in that brutally honest way I now responded with when caught off guard. "I don't see the point to any of this. Seems like a lot of pain for no gain, if you ask me."

One side of my mom's thin lips quirked up in amusement and her eyes refocused on my face. "It was late, maybe two, three in the morning on the second day you were in the hospital. Your poor face was so swollen…you looked like an alien. Well, what little we could see of you through all the tubes and bandages. I don't think I'd said more than ten words to your father the entire time we'd been at the hospital."

The room was deathly quiet. So quiet, I could hear my neighbor's refrigerator kick off with a wheezing rattle and the delicate rush of the sprinklers on the lawn outside.

"We were both so terrified, Lainie…so, so scared. You'd had an episode earlier that day, and we thought, with you being so weak, another one would surely kill you. And suddenly he looks up at me and says, 'I'm sorry.'"

I furrowed my brow. "Sorry for what?"

"That's exactly what I asked him. I mean, not to say he didn't have anything to be sorry for, but he's not exactly the type to apologize, you know?"

Confronted with the reality of mortality, watching me struggle to live, my father had sat on the edge of my bed and looked my mom straight in the face and said, "I'm sorry for all of it. For my bad communication skills, for my inability to put you first, for my refusal to work on our marriage, and for walking out the way I did. You didn't deserve any of it, and I'm sorry."

I raised my brow again in shock. "Wow."

My mom nodded vigorously. "You're telling me! I couldn't believe it. Never in a million years would I *ever* have expected him to apologize. You could have knocked me over with a feather."

"What did you say?" I asked, leaning forward in rapt attention.

"I said, 'You're right. I didn't deserve that, and it took me a long time to realize it.' At least the man had the grace to look ashamed." She spoke with some amusement at the idea of my father, the embodiment of pride, apologizing for a wrong he had done to someone. "It was easier after that, like a weight had been lifted off both of us. Then, one night, he told me he didn't want to waste any more time wondering what could be, because if your accident had taught him anything, it's that tomorrow may never come to pass." Her voice drifted off for a moment. Then, in a voice barely above a whisper she said, "...and then, he asked me if I would ever consider getting back together."

If my jaw hadn't already been on the floor, it would have been after that statement. "I...I," *Words, Alaina. Use your words.* "What...um...did you...?"

She gave me a small smile and looked down at her steepled hands. "I told him if he would consider couple's therapy, I would think about it."

"And he agreed," I surmised, seeing what I had so plainly missed for the past few weeks. "Why didn't you tell me?" I asked, dumbstruck by the latest news. *This was like...Stop the effing presses...*

"It's not that we didn't *want* to tell you. I just...well, you know." She gestured up and down at me as if that was the answer to all of my questions, and I did get it—to a certain extent, at least. I hadn't been the easiest person to talk to lately, especially after our argument in the hospital.

"So, things seem to be going well?" I finally asked, deciding to let her omittance slide. After all, what did it matter in the long run? She was telling me now, wasn't she?

Her small, contented smile told me everything I needed to know, but she spoke anyway. "They are. We're taking things slow—going to therapy every week, and speaking on the phone, dates every now and then. He's promised to spend less time at work, which was always a problem for us. He seems to be taking this seriously."

I nodded along. "Good. I'm really happy for you, Mom. I hope it all works out."

"Me too." She breathed it as a sigh, and I could see she

still had her reservations about the whole thing. How could she not after being burned so badly the first time? She gave me a genuine smile, one I hadn't seen in a very long time. "Goodness, between you, your father, and your brother, you'll put me in an early grave!"

I laughed and wondered if Tuck had told her yet about them having a boy. *Best not to mention it.* "How are you doing with Tuck and all of that?" I asked, leaning back into the couch.

She gave a hard laugh. "How do you think I'm doing? I'm a wreck. My twenty-one-year-old son is having a baby with my daughter's best friend, who I've known since she started walking." She threw her hands up. "I don't know how they are going to make this work! It would be one thing if he lived here, but...I don't know...I feel awful for Jess having to do this all on her own."

I shifted and shook my head. "She's not doing it on her own. She has us, Grandma."

My mom rolled her eyes toward the ceiling and squeezed them shut. "Yeah...I guess she does, heaven help us." And after another beat said, "but if you ever call me *Grandma* again, I'll kill you."

28

A Fresh Start

It's perfect. I smiled contentedly and stepped up onto the platform at the head of the ceremony space, seeing the entire picture for the first time. It was a gorgeous September day—seventy-five degrees and sunny with a light breeze. The lake glistened merrily, and the birds chirped in the trees. Off in the distance, I could see several small sailboats dotting the far side of the huge body of water to the north, like tiny butterflies lighting on a field of flowers. Slowly, my gaze lifted to the beautiful arch overhead full of wisteria, roses, and gardenias nestled into the woven grapevines. I sighed and walked over to one of the pieces lining the aisle and adjusted the vase on the pedestal, so it was centered. This was my favorite part of my job—taking it in after it was all finished, when it was just me and the space and none of the guests had arrived yet. This wedding, Emma's wedding, was spectacular. I don't think I'd ever been more proud of a finished product in my life.

"Well, look at you." I heard from behind me and smiled. His voice sent chills up my spine in the best way. With a thrill of anticipation, I turned to get my first glimpse of Grayson. *Damn.* I admired him silently in much the same way he was looking at me. His eyes smoldered with a deep look of appreciation that told me just what he'd be doing to me if we weren't standing in broad daylight with a crowd of witnesses nearby. My stomach clenched into a bundle of excitement and nerves at the prospect. I hadn't seen him in almost a week, and I didn't realize how badly I'd missed him until I saw him standing in front of me. He wore a light gray tuxedo with a white shirt and pink blush bowtie that matched my own attire perfectly. His dark hair was flawlessly coiffed to one side, and he had his hands shoved in his pockets, which only added to his casual elegance. He looked like he'd just stepped out of a bridal magazine.

He shook his head slowly back and forth, stunned into speechlessness as he took in my sequined, pale pink organza gown. His eyes lingered on my plunging neckline for a moment before drifting back up to meet my gaze. Not willing to spend another second apart from him, I closed the gap between us and wrapped my arms around him, taking in his heady scent of cedarwood, freshwater, and musk with a welcoming moan.

"You look gorgeous."

"Likewise." I'd had this dress picked out for several weeks, and it was the first time since the accident I truly felt beautiful. I sighed contentedly, eyes closed, resting my head against his chest and enjoying the feel of his strong arms around me.

"You did all this?" he asked quietly, grabbing my hand to hold before taking a step back to do a three sixty and take in the venue in all its glory. Edison bulbs hung from the large pin oaks and Eastern white pines on either side of the ceremony space, draping across in lazy arcs that would give the clearing a cozy feel as night approached. The reception would technically be held inside, but I had the feeling a few couples would take advantage of the quiet night to enjoy some alone time away from the party.

I smiled. "Yeah, do you like it?"

"It's amazing, Alaina…really. I would never have imagined this from the pictures Em showed me. You are crazy talented." He fingered the clean white petals of a gardenia in the planter nearest him and then turned down the aisle to admire the ten identical arrangements lining the path ahead of it.

I felt myself blush. "Thanks. I wanted it to be special."

"Has Em seen it?" he asked with a twinkle in his eye.

I shook my head. "No, not yet."

"She'll love it," he assured me. It was exactly what I wanted to hear. I longed to make dreams come true. It was the driving factor that kept me coming back for more. *Just call me Fairy Godmother.*

* * *

The ceremony had gone off without a hitch, and the weather was so perfect we all now stood outside, enjoying the sunshine and faint breeze rather than fleeing for the sanctuary of the air-conditioned reception hall. Birds chirped cheerily from their roosts in the giant Eastern white pines bordering the lake, and with a vague sense of déjà vu, I watched two flirtatious chickadees hopping back and forth across a nearby branch and thought back to my first date with Grayson.

Absently, I crossed my arms, tracing the sharp angles of my elbows in a meditative fashion as I thought about my conversation with my therapist earlier this week.

"Don't you think Grayson deserves happiness?"

"Of course, I do!" I cried, fighting back the urge to go full crazy bitch and chuck something at her. "It's just…it's more complicated than that." I reached out and straightened the spread of magazines littering her coffee table.

"What makes it complicated?"

"Well…" I drifted off, trying to come up with a solid enough answer that she wouldn't come back at me with more incessant questions. I tapped my toe in agitation. I understood her questions were part of the healing process—reflection, introspection, and all that jazz—but being asked the tough questions was not one of my favorite activities. "I guess I'm just…" I took a deep breath and spoke my mind. After all, lying defeated the purpose of coming to these appointments. "I'm scared."

She was quiet, giving me room to breathe and divulge on my own terms.

"For the longest time, I wasn't even sure I wanted kids." I sighed, the urge to break down into tears growing stronger by the second. "I couldn't picture it. I liked my life the way it was—being able to pick up and leave at a moment's notice, not having to worry about anything but myself."

"What changed?" She probed gently, encouraging me to continue.

"I did," I whispered, staring off into space, envisioning a future for myself I was fairly certain would never exist: two young children, scurrying around the living room in a crazed game of cops and robbers, the dog barking madly in the background, and Grayson and me sitting on the couch, laughing at the frenzied activity before us. "After the accident...I don't know, it was all...different. Like I had a better appreciation of life, maybe?" I glanced at her, brow furrowed as I tried to unravel the tangled threads of my existence.

"Do you think you're the only one who has changed as a result of your accident?" My therapist, a middle-aged woman by the name of Colleen, studied me over the top of her horn-rimmed glasses, the end of her ink pen pinched between her teeth.

I paused to think about that for a moment. There was no question I had changed both physically and mentally as a result of my accident. Whether or not those closest to me had changed had been of little or no consequence to me. *And therein lies the point, Dumb-Dumb.* I shrugged. "I mean...probably. I know it's been hard for everyone."

"Perhaps, before you make assumptions on what others think and feel, you should ask yourself if this accident has made them see things differently, too. I think you're scared if Grayson finds out you can't have children, he'll no longer want to be with you. Does that sound about right?" She sat her notebook down on the coffee table with a gentle thump and brought her hands together, leaning toward me in anticipation of my reply.

I swallowed against my constricting airway. "I...guess?"

"You guess? Or you know?"

So, apparently, we've arrived at the tough love section of this after-school special.

"Okay, I know. What's that got to do with anything?"

"Being afraid of a situation's outcome is not a good enough reason to avoid honesty. Grayson deserves to know the whole truth. By not being honest with him, you've taken away his choice in the matter."

My stomach was turning over on itself. I'd known keeping my potential infertility to myself had been selfish, but having someone else throw it in my face did not feel good at all.

She sat back in her rich brown leather wingback chair and eyed me shrewdly. "Infertility is a painful thing to deal with. There are many avenues for you and your significant other to pursue if and when you choose to have children. From what you've told me, your concern may not even hold water at the end of the day. Your doctors have given you a potential prognosis given your injuries, and you've immediately gone to the worst possible outcome. It's understandable, and it's human, but it's not necessarily the healthiest frame of mind to have when you're trying to maintain a serious relationship."

I sat quietly, picking at my cuticles ferociously in an absurd attempt to distract myself from the painful truth currently being presented to me.

"Our time is almost up for today, so I'll leave you with this. I can't force you to tell him the truth, but when you do tell him—and I have every confidence you will *eventually*—I think he'll surprise you."

* * *

"They look vomit-inducingly happy." Grayson chuckled as he approached from behind.

I thought he was talking about the birds for a split second, but then I realized his eyes were on the newlyweds on the shoreline just beyond the trees. I laughed. "I would hope so. It *is* their wedding day."

"Vomit away!" Emma shouted at her brother as she laid a

big kiss on James, and the photographer clicked off several shots.

"You know I have to tease!" he shouted back, smiling from ear to ear as he watched his sister attempting to remain composed and failing miserably. Emma laughed against her new husband's lips, and the awkward action made him laugh in turn. The photographer in me itched for the feel of a camera in my hand. *The pure joy on her face...and oh, that smile.* Emma was a radiant bride if ever I saw one.

I turned into Grayson and wrapped an arm around his waist, drawing him nearer. I felt more than I saw him look down at me in turn. A weight had been lifted after the stress of this past week. Emma's wedding was my first wedding back, and there had been times when I had wondered if I'd bitten off more than I could chew.

"Alaina! There's someone I'd like you to meet," Emma called to me, snapping me out of my reverie.

I looked to see her waving over a young woman around our age, and with Grayson's hand firmly in mine, I slowly made my way over to the bride and her guest.

"Alaina, this is my friend, Genevieve. She's a columnist for *Bridal Bliss.*"

My heart stopped for a moment, and I plastered a smile on my face, throwing my hand out to shake hers. "Nice to meet you."

"Emma told me you were a wedding planning prodigy, but I didn't really believe it until today. You did all of this?" she asked incredulously, taking in the wisteria-laden grapevine arch and elegant aisle accents composed of blush roses, white gardenias, and pale green eucalyptus leaves.

I swallowed convulsively, not wanting to say the wrong

thing, and felt the reassuring squeeze of Grayson's hand. "I had to do it all from my living room, but I got it done."

"Your living room?" she asked, confused. "Don't you have a studio?"

I froze, panicking. *Great, now she thinks you're a low-rent fraud.*

Grayson, well attuned to my occasional bouts of anxiety, stepped in. "Alaina was in a pretty serious accident back in May. She's been recuperating, so she's had to work from home."

"Oh, well, I'm sorry to hear that, and I'm glad you seem to be on the mend." She went back to admiring the space. "Well, Alaina, I'd like to do a spread on Emma and James's wedding. Is it okay if I mention you and your company in the credits?"

My heart stuttered into double time. "Uh…" *Words. English. Jesus fucking—* "Absolutely!" I shouted, perhaps a bit too enthusiastically, but it was a step in the right direction.

"Great! I'll contact you when I get back to the office Monday, and we can iron out the particulars." She didn't seem to pay any mind to my lack of social skills, and I heaved an internal sigh of relief. *Well, we can't all be social butterflies— traumatic brain injury notwithstanding.*

I nodded like a bobblehead, not containing my glee very well. "Sounds great!"

She smiled again and waved. "It was lovely meeting you, Alaina. This place is amazing. Keep up the good work!" She congratulated me and stepped away with Emma to continue catching up.

I bit my bottom lip and grabbed Grayson's hand. "That was painful," I muttered under my breath, already replaying the encounter and scrutinizing every detail.

He smiled and said, "You did great." Then, leaning closer, he whispered, "Walk with me?" He gave my hand a gentle but certain tug that brooked no argument, and we slowly made our way down to the dock outside the Lake Club. The sun was beginning to set, and the sky had gone from the brilliant azure of a cloudless day to the muted powder blue of a hazy summer evening. The lightning bugs were out in force, their bright yellow bellies glowing orbs of summer cheer across the lakeshore. I lifted my dress and kicked off my shoes, anxious to feel the cool water on my skin. With Grayson's help, I lowered myself to the dock and draped my legs over the edge, toes dipping into the silky water. He lowered himself down as well, removing his socks and dress shoes before rolling up his pant legs and joining me.

I closed my eyes and lifted my face up to the sky, breathing in the combination of aquatic life and pine sap. "This is amazing…" I murmured. "It's so beautiful up here."

"Yes, it is," he agreed as he intertwined his fingers with mine. For a moment, we simply enjoyed the sound of the loons singing to each other across the water and the crickets and frogs creating a beautiful accompaniment to the melancholy melody. Across the shore, a group of children played in the water under the careful supervision of an older woman sitting up on the bank under the shade of a giant sugar maple. A young girl screamed in delight as an older boy splashed her with the brisk water.

I took a shuddering breath and let it out slowly, drawing courage as my pulse slowed. "You know I love you, right?" I whispered.

Grayson turned to me, filled with apprehension at the tone of my voice. "Of course," he replied, reluctant to disturb the pocket of peace we found ourselves in.

I continued to stare out at the water, watching the soft disturbance of the water's surface as the wind picked up, creating gentle waves in its wake. The dock creaked under my weight as I dragged my feet back and forth, pondering how to begin. "I haven't been completely…honest with you." My voice was shy, and I stared intently at the expansive ripples on the water as they slowly fizzled out. I couldn't look at him. If I was going to get this out, I *couldn't* look at him. I swallowed the navel orange-sized lump in my throat and pressed on. "My injuries from the accident are a lot more…complicated than I let on."

"More complicated than a fractured pelvis and a brain injury?"

I threw a warning glance in his direction, and the left side of his mouth, previously curled in a playful smirk, fell back into a serious line. "I had some internal injuries I haven't been able to talk about. It's not…*easy* for me to discuss—with anyone," I amended, not wanting him to think I didn't trust him. "Not my mom. Not Jess."

"Alaina," Grayson murmured, taking my hand in his and squeezing hard. The fact I'd been suffering in silence all this time pained him more than words could express.

"I'm only telling you now because…because I think you…" I paused, feeling my throat constrict with a mixture of guilt, grief, and anxiety. "You deserve to know the truth." My breath hitched as I struggled to retain control of the situation. "Grayson, I…" I glanced up at him then, unable to bear the thought of not looking at him. "There's a…a *good* chance I…I may not be able to have children." The last words hung in the air, barely loud enough to be heard over the din of the wildlife orchestra surrounding us.

His face was devoid of all color, his mouth set in a grim line, and his dark eyes were wide fathomless pools of black in the dim light. A muscle in his jaw twitched, whether in agitation or to conceal his feelings, I didn't know.

I blinked against the tears in my eyes, feeling them spill over and pour down my cheeks unabated. I looked back out over the water through the blur of my vision and then up at the sky, observing the cotton candy swirl of sunset-dyed clouds against their aqua backdrop. When I finally dared to look back at him, he, too, was staring into the distance— not looking at me as I'd previously imagined. I let him sit like that for a while longer, not poking or prodding, but simply letting him process the pipe bomb I'd just dropped in his lap. *It's a hell of an ultimatum. Me or kids. Pick your poison.* I'd had months to process and was still having trouble with it. Bitterness, depression, and anger were my constant companions. I could only imagine how he was feeling.

We sat on the edge of the dock for an interminable moment, both of us afraid to speak. What was there to say, after all? No number of words could fix the problem, that much was abundantly clear. I looked up at him, gazing at the man who had represented calm and stability for me in a time when nothing had been remotely calm or stable. *How am I supposed to let him go?* Through no fault of mine or his, we had suddenly been thrust onto divergent paths, and my heart was breaking because of it. Wasn't this the very thing I had agonized over all those months ago? I had been afraid Grayson wouldn't live up to the standards I'd set for myself. It had never crossed my mind I may not live up to his. *Karma's a bitch.*

Finally, with a deep sigh, he turned to me, squeezing my

hand tightly. Looking down at me, he gave me a small smile. There was a sparkle in his eye I hadn't expected. His lips twitched in elusion to some sort of mischief, but before I could contemplate further, my center of gravity shifted, and I was suddenly flying through the air and into the water. I gasped and spluttered, water running into my eyes and blurring my vision. I squealed and kicked to elevate my head and shoulders above the cool water. "What—,"

Grayson's head broke the surface near me with a smile of angelic innocence before dissolving into hysterical chortling at my outrage. Fizzing with mirth, he shoved a spray of water in my face and ducked back below the surface as I shoved water back at him. He reappeared, as if by magic, several yards away out in the deeper water, and ran a hand through his dark hair, nearly black with damp as he waited for me to catch up. Slowly, I kicked my way toward him, noting the twinkle of mischief still plain in his eyes.

"You suck," I gasped, all the while trying to avoid swallowing a mouthful of water as gentle waves lapped around us. "How are we supposed to attend your sister's reception now that we look like a couple of drowned rats?" I asked, wiping under my eyes in a feeble attempt to prevent raccoon eyes.

"Trust me, I think if they saw us out here, she and James would be the first to join us." Grayson dismissed my worries with a flippant wave of his hand. I let my head fall back into the water, my hair floating out around me in lazy tendrils carried by the current of the underground spring that fed the lake. How was it he always knew exactly what to do or say to make me feel better?

Tenderly, he reached out, wrapping his arms around my waist to hold me to him. "I knew you'd been struggling with something these past few weeks, but I never imagined it would be something like this." His words were quiet and his Adam's apple bobbed as he swallowed. "It's a shitty situation. I won't deny it. And I'm sorry you felt you couldn't come to me with it, but it doesn't change anything, Alaina…not for me."

I turned my face away, looking back toward the shore. The lingering guests that were still enjoying the outdoors were completely oblivious to our impromptu swim. "What do you mean it doesn't *change* anything? It changes everything! You *want* kids, and if I can't give them to you, then—"

"No. Listen to me." He pulled me even tighter to him, holding me so the entire lengths of our bodies were pressed against each other, nothing but our submerged clothing separating us. "There are a thousand ways to make a family. Alaina, what I *want* is you. Always."

My heart stuttered and skipped, and I felt cool beads of perspiration pop up on my neck despite the cool breeze. *There's no way he's thought this through. I'm not enough, not worth it—not worth giving up a chance at having kids.* "Grayson…I…I can't let you—"

He snorted. "You're not *letting* me do anything. I'm perfectly capable of making my own choices, and I choose you. No matter what. I. Choose. You." His hands drifted from my waist, up my back, to rest just below my shoulder blades, his hot fingers burning through the thin fabric of my dress. "Someday, if we decide we want children, we can get consults from all the best doctors, or we can foster, or adopt. It makes no difference to me." He lowered his head so his lips were only an inch or two from mine. "I mean it. I'm not going anywhere." Gently, he pressed his lips to mine, once and then twice, before leaning in to kiss my cheek in a gesture of exceeding tenderness. In his arms, I felt beautiful and strong, courageous and worthy. Through thick and thin, through good times and bad, he was my rock, and I loved him so much it hurt.

I wrapped my arms around his neck and leaned into him, pressing my lips to his in a heady mixture of tenderness and desire. I parted his lips, and his tongue met mine in a welcome rush of passion as his arms tightened around my midsection. Panting, we parted, and he gave me that crooked smile I loved so dearly.

"I, um…" he bit his bottom lip and gazed down at me, water dripping from his hairline, down his temple, and into the cleft between his neck and earlobe. "I have something to tell you, too."

"Okay…" The cool rush of the invisible current swirled around my legs, raising goosebumps on my arms, but I listened attentively.

"I got an offer this morning…from a team."

The resulting grin on my face was so huge. I felt as though my cheeks would pop with enthusiasm. "That's amazing! Who is it?" My body tingled with excitement, and I readjusted myself in his grasp, using his shoulders for leverage.

"Apex." The name was voiced in a whisper of reverence that got my own heart racing.

"Shut up," I whispered. "Shut up!" I shoved my hands into his chest with a sharp smack of enthusiasm. Ryan Steele and Jason Litko were two huge names in the racing industry. Several years ago, they had decided to pool their collective efforts into a race team that was a force to be reckoned with. For fifteen years now, Apex Racing had dominated the league, winning championships, 500s, and at least a third of the races every season. And now they were calling Grayson's number.

"Ow!" he cried. "Why are you hitting me?" His complaints turned to laughter.

"That's amazing, Grayson. I...wow...I'm so proud of you!" I couldn't contain my glee anymore and leaned over to give him another slow, deep kiss.

He was beaming with a mixture of pride and happiness as he pulled away. "I mean...that's all I've ever thought about. They've been *the* team since I was a kid, you know? And now, I'm going to race for them. It's amazing!"

I ran my fingers through the hair near his temple as I stared at him, his giddiness seeping into me. Tiny droplets of water sparkled in his hair, and the faint smell of fish wafted up around us.

"You want to know what the best part is?" he murmured, leaning in so our mouths were mere inches apart.

"Always," I murmured, biting my bottom lip in anticipation.

"They're relocating after this season...to Indianapolis."

My heart stuttered to a stop, and my eyes went wide. "You're moving to Indy?"

"I'm moving to Indy," he confirmed with a brilliant smile. His white teeth gleamed in the final rays of sun before it sank behind the trees surrounding the lake.

I let out a loud squeal of delight and wrapped my legs around him as I drew him in for an even tighter embrace. No more late-night phone conversations. No more long-distance relationship. We could be together.

"I'm so happy right now. I feel like my heart's going to burst." I put my hands to my rosy cheeks, trying to process all of this news. *Good* news. I honestly could not wipe the smile off my face. *My company is being credited in a national bridal magazine,* and *Grayson is moving to Indianapolis with a full-time ride next season.* All of that, coupled with the relief of complete and utter honesty between us, I felt like I was walking on sunshine.

It could have been minutes, or it could have been hours, but sometime later, with hardly any light left to guide our way over the rock-infested shores of the lake, we hauled ourselves onto dry land, laughing. Standing in the ceremony space with the Edison bulb decor twinkling in the night air, he lifted our woven fingers and kissed my hand. "You make me so happy," he murmured. "Honestly, Alaina…happier than I ever thought possible."

The words were so unexpected they brought tears to my eyes.

In all my life, I'd never had anyone tell me that. I'd heard them say 'I like you,' and even 'I love you' a couple of times. They'd given me all the compliments in the world, but I'd never had anyone tell me I made them happy. A smile of complete and utter bliss lifted the corners of my mouth. "I love you," I murmured, feeling the weight of those words. When I'd said them in previous relationships, it had been because I had thought I *should,* but now, I meant them more than I'd ever meant anything. I'd been going through the world with my eyes closed before I met Grayson. For all my talk about being happy and successful, a part of me had always felt incomplete…until now, and man, I'd had no idea what I was missing.

"I love you, too," was his quiet, happy reply. The sounds of romantic jazz floated on the wind from the balcony adjacent to the ballroom where the reception was being held. Silently, he offered his hand to me and pulled me into a slow dance, our bodies swaying to the music as if the notes themselves filled our souls. With one of his hands holding mine close to his heart and the other resting on my lower back, I laid my head on his damp chest and lost myself to the faint melody. I let out a deep breath I hadn't realized I was holding and felt him look down at me. "What's wrong?"

I looked up at him through half-closed eyelids, exhausted but content, feeling completely at peace as I let the sights and sounds of this perfect moment wash over me. "Nothing…" I sighed, nuzzling further into his shoulder. *Absolutely nothing.*

Epilogue

I have seldom set my eyes on anything more beautiful than Paris in the snow. There was something so majestic about the Gothic architecture, draped in a blanket of clean white fluff, that lulled my busy brain into a quiet calm. The icicles above our fifth-story balcony at the Shangri-La Paris dripped meditatively with soft pit-pats that only added to the serenity of the morning. The sun was beginning to make its way over the horizon, turning the muted gray sky to a delicate shade of purple as it went. I breathed in the frigid air and pulled my fluffy white bathrobe closer, enjoying the rush of the brisk December breeze as it swirled around me.

The sparkle of diamonds caught my eye as I rearranged my covering, and I automatically glanced down to admire the fractured rainbows that sprung from my new ring. It was my first time seeing it in daylight, and it was absolutely gorgeous. The large center diamond was a one-and-a-half carat emerald-cut beauty surrounded by an array of smaller stones that ruffled around it in an elegant antique setting of white gold. I wiggled my fingers in delight. If someone had told me a year ago I would be happily engaged to Grayson Miles by Christmas, I would have laughed in their face, but somehow, here we were.

The Eiffel Tower sat off in the distance, shadowed and serene, waiting for dawn to break. On the street below, the general populace was beginning to stir and go about their daily lives. The scent of brewing coffee and fresh pastries came to me in the wind, and my mouth watered.

It hadn't been an easy decision to give operational control of the shop to Jess, but with an extremely talented new hire, fresh out of college, I felt confident enough to loosen the reins. As part of Gray's reigning Indy 500 Champion duties, he was obligated to take a whirlwind tour of Europe's Greatest Hits, including London, Rome, and Paris. And when he'd asked me to go with him...*well, how was a girl supposed to turn that down?* Grayson hadn't been the only one working, though. Genevieve had been good for more than a spread in *Bridal Bliss*. A reputable photojournalist, she had contacts throughout the industry, and with a gentle nudge from Emma, had landed me a stringer position at *Travel Bug* for their Winter Wonderland edition. I'd been snapping pictures left and right from Edinburgh to Zurich, and at the end of the day, I'd found myself with a portfolio Ansel Adams would have been proud of.

With one last wistful glance at the Parisian landscape, now coated in a whimsical pink as the sun stained the frosted canvas, I soundlessly opened the balcony door and slid in, closing it quickly so as not to wake the occupant of our king-sized bed with a draft of icy air. I silently removed my robe and slid back into bed, my naked body sliding between the high thread-count Egyptian cotton sheets. With a gentle heave of the mattress, I rolled onto my side, admiring Grayson in quiet rapture. Dark stubble shadowed his cheeks, and I recalled the prickle of it against my skin in the midst of our intimacy. I wanted so badly to reach out and trace the strong line of his jaw but didn't for fear of waking him.

I loved to watch him sleep. It was only in stillness that I could fully appreciate how handsome he was. He laid on his stomach, sandwiching his pillow between his arms and his head, his face tilted toward me. My eyes ran over his naked body, marveling at its exquisite design. The slope of his shoulders flowed down to the snowy white plains of his lower back. His deltoid muscles rippled underneath his soft skin, speckled with the lightest of freckles. They had been more pronounced in the summer months, but as winter progressed, they were fading back into milky porcelain. My lover stirred, cuddling into his pillow but not waking, and I continued my silent evaluation. Two small dimples stood out at the base of his spine, and while I couldn't see the individual vertebrae, the smooth expanse of flesh formed a shallow concavity there. This created a remarkable sense of symmetry in his body that baffled me. Nothing in nature was supposed to be perfectly symmetrical, but he came pretty damn close.

Taking in the view, the oddest sense of déjà vu hit me. I saw a similar scene in my mind's eye. Grayson's serene face was deep in sleep, but his hair was slightly shorter, and a smudge of deep red lipstick was smeared across his left cheek. The sheets on the bed weren't the crisp white linen of the Shangri-La, but the delicate lavender microfiber sheets I had picked out with care at Bed Bath & Beyond. My lacy rose-patterned bra was hanging tenuously from the post of the headboard, having been tossed aside in a moment of passion. Grayson's neatly pressed shirt, similarly discarded, was a rumpled mess at the foot of the bed.

I blinked, and I was back in our suite in Paris, the sunrise staining the room in tones of gold. Most of my lost memories gripped me in unconsciousness as nightmares when my mind was vulnerable, but this moment of clarity was more of a caress, gentle as the rise of the tide in an inlet leading out to sea. I rolled over onto my back and closed my eyes, testing the limits of this small bit of grace. All at once, I could recall the feel of Grayson's breath on my cheek as he leaned past me to select a deep, emerald green dress from the throngs of my closet. I could hear the hitch of surprise in his breathing when I pulled a box of condoms out of the bedside table. I could recall the large brown eyes, pupils wide, shining with a tenderness that belied the firm grip he had on my backside as he took me.

My eyelids fluttered back open, and I stared up at the ceiling, my heart pounding. The crown molding was blurred with tears of joy and relief. For months now, I'd felt like I was letting Grayson down by forgetting such a vital piece of our relationship. Granted, I'd had no control of the situation. I hadn't willingly let the memory slip, but it felt like a betrayal of our bond all the same.

"What's wrong?" Grayson's voice, raspy with sleep, murmured close to my ear. He pulled himself up onto his elbow, his pectoral muscles flexing under his weight, and reached out to gently brush the tears from my cheeks.

I sniffled and smiled. "Nothing…" I voiced earnestly with a laugh. "I was just thinking it's a shame I only got to wear that rose lingerie once…you seemed to like it." I laughed again and palmed the rest of the moisture from my eyes.

His eyes widened in shock, and he searched mine briefly, deep wrinkles of confusion mingled with hope appearing on his forehead. "You…remember?" His voice was a rough whisper, strained by deep feeling.

New tears popped into my eyes, and I nodded, barely

beginning the affirmative motion before his lips pressed into mine with a force that, under different circumstances, could have been misconstrued as violent. His body pressed into mine, hard and strong under my touch, his arms so tight around me I thought my ribs would crack from the force. The laughter of relief and joy bubbled out of him in a contagious manner that soon had me giggling in return.

After several moments, we lay in the bed no more than a foot apart, gazing at each other, exhausted by the exertion of uncontainable happiness, our palms rubbing sensuously against each other. "I thought last night was the happiest I'd ever been, but…" His words trailed off as his eyes drank in my disheveled appearance, the afterglow of a satisfying evening written all over my face.

I smiled and shimmied closer to him, rubbing my nose against his in intimate affection. "I know," I whispered back. Struck by inspiration, I sat up and looked down into his curious eyes. "I want to marry you."

His lips quirked in an impish grin. "I thought we established that last night."

I smacked him with the back of my hand playfully and smiled. "No, I mean, I don't want a long engagement. I was thinking about the spring."

"Had a lot of time to think, have you? Did you sleep at all?" He sat up with me, rubbing his hands over his eyes and through his hair before blinking owlishly.

I looped my arms over my knees and tilted my head to look at him, my dark hair sweeping down past my face in a thick curtain of springy curls. "I don't want to waste any more time thinking about the future. I don't need a big fancy wedding, Grayson. I just want to be with you."

He was quiet for a moment taking in what I was saying in reflective silence. "Spring, huh?"

I nodded vigorously, visions of peonies and sweet peas dancing in my head.

He shrugged. "Well, why not? Emma may have a thing or two to say about a *small, intimate ceremony,* but she'll have to get over it, won't she?" He smiled deviously and stretched his long arms up over his head, yawning. With a wink, he ripped the sheets back and padded across the floor to the bathroom, his bare bottom nearly translucent in the pale dawn light.

"You know, I was thinking we could hang around here for a few days before we went home, but um…" I cleared my throat dramatically. "I think we should go somewhere warm, preferably with a nude beach. Your ass is unbearably white."

His disembodied head popped out from behind the door jamb, eyes wide in mock offense. "Excuse me?"

I giggled uncontrollably, and he leaped across the room in two bounds landing on the bed with enough force to nearly send me careening off the mattress and onto the floor. He tore the shelter of the fluffy white duvet off me to reveal my naked goose-pimpled body. "Shall we compare whose ass is paler?" he asked, fingers clutching at my arm as I attempted to remove myself from the bed before he could quench his thirst for bare flesh.

"Don't you dare. Grayson, no. Stop. Stop!" I squealed with childish abandon as his fingers tickled me from nape to navel and back again, leaving me breathless.

How had I ended up here? What was so remarkable about me that I should have such an extraordinary story? But as I stared up at the ceiling of my suite, living a life most people only dream of, I thought, perhaps it wasn't the road behind me that mattered, but the road before *us* that was most exciting.

So, with confidence brought on by the prospect of another beautiful day in Europe next to the man I loved, I pulled the covers back over us, rolled toward the phone, and ordered room service.

You only live once, right?